IMMORTAL HEROES

Gleaned from racial memory and older than the annals of history, the mythical hero is a collective self-image. He is larger than life; he defies fate, courts the gods, and ends his cosmic struggle in immortal triumph or tragedy.

There is always an essence of historical reality in heroic myths. They are the folk expression of a people's purpose and experience. They are the reality—and the dream.

Norma Lorre Goodrich retells these old myths with vital and exciting narrative skill. The modern reader will enter the world of his ancient forebears as he relives the adventures of Horus the Avenger, King Minos, Rustum and Suhrab, Rama, Cassandra, and Aeneas. He will thrill to their heroic exploits, and discover that the qualities of valor and wisdom do not change with time.

NORMA LORRE GOODRICH was born in Vermont and attended the University of Vermont, where she won a scholarship to the University of Grenoble, France. She founded a school in France and taught there for ten years; now she teaches at the Fieldston School in New York. She is the author of *Medieval Myths*, also available in a Mentor edition.

ANCIENT
MYTHS

❃ ❃ ❃ ❃

NORMA LORRE GOODRICH

A MENTOR BOOK

NEW AMERICAN LIBRARY

A DIVISION OF PENGUIN BOOKS USA INC., NEW YORK

PUBLISHED IN CANADA BY
PENGUIN BOOKS CANADA LIMITED, MARKHAM, ONTARIO

Library of Congress Catalog No. 60-16972

 MENTOR TRADEMARK REG. U.S. PAT. OFF. AND FOREIGN COUNTRIES
REGISTERED TRADEMARK–MARCA REGISTRADA
HECHO EN WINNIPEG, CANADA

SIGNET, SIGNET CLASSIC, MENTOR, ONYX, PLUME, MERIDIAN
and NAL BOOKS are published in the United States by New American Library,
a division of Penguin Books USA Inc., 1633 Broadway,
New York, New York 10019, and in Canada by Penguin Books Canada Limited,
2801 John Street, Markham, Ontario L3R 1B4

14   15   16   17   18   19   20   21   22

Printed in Canada

Contents

1.

SUMER, 9

Gilgamesh the Wrestler, 9

2.

EGYPT, 25

Horus the Hawk, the Avenger, 25

3.

CRETE AND GREECE, 41

The House of Crete, 43

King Minos II, 63

Theseus and the Minotaur, 75

4.

TROY, 91

Cassandra, 92

5.

PERSIA AND AFGHANISTAN, 106

The Coming of Rustam, 109

Rustam and Kai-Kaus, 129

Rustam and Suhrab, 148

6.

INDIA, 170

Rama and the Monkeys, 173

7.

ROME, 197

The Wanderings of Aeneas, 200

The War in Italy, 231

INDEX, 252

Illustrations

Gilgamesh the Wrestler, 18
Europa and the Bull, 56
Theseus and the Minotaur, 83
The Finding of Zal, 116
The Entrance to the Underworld, 232

Supplementary Charts

Egyptian Religion, 26
Heroes of Crete and Greece, 44
Dynasties of Persia, 110
Comparative Divinities, 200

Maps

Egypt—3000 B.C., 24
Crete (3500 B.C.—1450 B.C.), 42
Cretan Thalassocracy, 62
The Wanderings of Aeneas, 198
Italy in the Time of Aeneas, 230

I

Sumer: Gilgamesh the Wrestler

INTRODUCTION

THE EPIC of Gilgamesh, of which the following story is a composite, was written in Sumerian cuneiform. This language was studied as a classic until Christian times although the Sumerian peoples themselves, conquered by the Semites, had begun to disappear by 2000 B.C. The reader will doubtless recognize in Gilgamesh the prototype of the semilegendary Oriental ruler of antiquity. Many versions of this story have been found, particularly in the library of the Assyrian King Ashurbanipal at Nineveh. Translations of cuneiform tablets are still going on.

European scholars, particularly M. François Thureau-Dangin, were trying to decipher cuneiform in the early 1800's, and great credit must also be given to Sir Henry Rawlinson's translation of the Behistun inscription around 1850. Noted American Sumerologists are Arno Poebel (1881–1958), Thorkild Jacobsen of the Oriental Institute of the University of Chicago, and Samuel Noah Kramer of the University of Pennsylvania.

Descriptions of Gilgamesh, Enkidu, and Huwawa come from archaeological photographs belonging to the Musée du Louvre in Paris.

GILGAMESH THE WRESTLER

IN THE BEGINNING was our mother Nammu, the great goddess whose waters were all the universe. As time went by this goddess, lonely in her limitless vastness, bore two children in human form, first a son named An who stretched across the arc from pole to pole, and whom we call "heaven." Her second child was a female whose name was Ki, and her we call "earth." After their birth An and Ki were first united in the shape of a mountain towering high above the clouds, in cosmic space. From their union was born the great deity of the air Enlil, who in his fatherly desire to create separated the earth from her brother heaven. Then Enlil the

9

air god carried Ki away into the privacy of the clouds and from her fashioned all the animals of the earth, all the plants on mountain, river valley, and desert, and finally man.

From his splendid temple in Nippur, Enlil ruled the world with lifted eyes that shone far over to the east where rushed the muddy waters of the Tigris flowing southward from the desolate hills of Assur, and far to the west where the lordly Euphrates, broad and slow, brought its life-giving waters through the plains of ancient Sumer to the sea. On a white throne in a pure place sat Enlil, like a great mountain, tracing with his fingers the lands and the seas, sending sunshine over the plains and spring thaws from the hills over barren deserts, looking upon his creation and wishing it plenty and prosperity. In his omnipotent majesty Enlil appointed a god of wisdom whose name was Enki and whose main task was to superintend above all places the great land of Sumer through which gold and silver were to flow in ships to the temple of Enlil at Nippur.

Great were the deeds of Enki and many were his gifts to man. Like a good teacher Enki yoked oxen to the plow and in due season showed man how to make grain sprout like jewels in the sunlit fields. From the hills he drove ewes with their lambs and built pens for them. The great fishes of the river he persuaded to lay eggs among the river reeds to nourish the people of Sumer. When the barley bent double under its weight, Enki built granaries and filled them with the grains of the fields and all the fruits of the gardens, with peaches, mulberries, pomegranates, bananas, and apricots. From the clay of the rivers he molded square bricks, and taught the black-haired craftsmen how to construct walls and even lofty cities, tier on tier and adorned with precious cedarwood and lapis lazuli. Around each of the lovely cities of Sumer, Enki built dikes which could be opened during the dry season so that the tender wheat would not burn in the hot sun of noon. Above the luxuriant gardens the waving fronds of tamarisks and date palms he had planted whispered in the south wind. Far in the distance gleamed the blue tile walls and lofty ziggurats of the wealthy city-ports of Sumer.

From Nippur in the center between the two rivers the land of Sumer, or Shinar as it is called in the Bible, extended southward toward the blue waters of the Persian Gulf and the delta region. The powerful city of Lagash, which at its height might have had a population of 36,000, was ruled by a tall, thin king called Ur-Nammu. He was later deified. The city of Ur, where Abraham once lived, covered 150 acres and had a population of 24,000. Its great ziggurat

10

boasted brick columns "overlaid with copper and mother of pearl." At Kish and Eridu were raised massive brick platforms as much as 700 yards square, upon which were built huge temples to the gods. These cities were often at war, striving for supremacy over their tropical valley, the ancient meeting place between Egypt and Asia Minor to the west and India and the Orient to the east. Greatest even among these cities was Uruk, which lay on the east bank of the Euphrates a hundred miles from the sea, between Ur and Eridu on the southeast and Nippur and Lagash on the north. It was such a lovely city that it could have been the Garden of Eden. Its memory was venerated for centuries, well beyond the golden age of the Babylonian Empire, because of the deeds of its great king, Gilgamesh.

Gilgamesh was a king and the descendant of a king. He was born in the royal palace at Uruk to a mother, Ninmah, who "knew all knowledge" and in whom he could confide all secrets. He grew to be strong and powerful, a huge, courageous king, a great hunter of lions and wild bulls, a peerless wrestler, and a dauntless leader in war. His legs were powerful like cedar pillars in the palace courtyard; with his left arm he could hold a struggling lion and in his right a mighty bronze war club. The fierceness of his face could drive terror into his enemies, even into the Agga of Kish, whose siege of Uruk did not last five days.

Dressed on ordinary days in a short-sleeved garment that fell without folds to his knees, his wrists encircled in heavy golden identical bracelets, and with two pet monkeys on his shoulders, the lord Gilgamesh strode daily among his warriors, inciting them to wrestling bouts. His hair was heavy, black, and curly, and dressed in thick rolls of curls from the crown of his head to his forehead, but falling around his nape like a sleek helmet. His black eyes were prominent and thick-lidded under arched brows, his nose large and aquiline, his lips curved and sensuous. He wore his curly beard carefully arranged in twelve long ringlets that ended in a straight row of little curls about the level of his armpits. On days of high ceremony, such as those of the spring corn festival, his long cloak attached to a round headdress made him appear as tall as a god, as high as a mountain, as dazzling as sunlight on the enameled walls of Uruk. Then, indeed, was he called "He who discovers all," and again in worship "Our Lord who saw all." Two-thirds of Gilgamesh was god. The remaining third, however, was man.

With those parts of him that were mortal Gilgamesh loved women. In this desire he was unquenchable, for no one woman could long satisfy his lust. As he rode through the streets of Uruk he would snatch maidens from their father's homes and even wives shopping in the market place or carrying water from the canals. In vain the council protested the rape of their daughters. In his majesty Gilgamesh neither heard their protestations nor heeded their supplications. Even young brides he snatched from their bridegrooms' arms and carried screaming away over his shoulder. Not in all the city, nor even in all the plain of Sumer, was there a man who dared challenge the king to battle or defy him in open combat. So he continued to swagger through the streets, hunt lions in the plains, and steal maidens, especially the slender, almond-eyed daughters of the great nobles, whose perfumed ringlets captured his roving eye.

Finally, in desperation the council of elders of the city made sacrifices in the temple of Aruru, the great mother goddess, patroness of Uruk, beseeching her, "Make another man to match him. Create another mortal who will lay his proud power in the dust, for lo! we can endure his tyranny no longer." Aruru was pleased with their rich gifts and listened to their story sympathetically.

After they had prostrated themselves before her altar, weeping and moaning, the mother goddess, taking pity on the parents of Uruk, slowly descended from her golden couch, descended the winding stairs of the ziggurat, and walked deep in thought across the plain until she came to the riverbank. There, parting the willows and thick reeds, she bent down with the tips of her golden sandals in the dark, wet clay of the river and began to gather it in her hands. Slowly and patiently, reciting a prayer to the god An, who was so holy he had never left his band of stars to walk across the earth, she began to shape a man in his image. As she worked, the south wind blew on the clay image, fanned it for her until the breath of life began to swell its ribs and flutter under its long, silky eyelashes. In this way Enkidu came to Sumer.

Free as the breeze and happy as a young colt in a green pasture, he bounded away from the riverbank and out into the wide desert. Aruru had fashioned him with the hoofs and thighs and long tail of a bull, but from the waist up he was a man, naked and healthy as a wild animal. His hair grew long and luxuriant and his body hardened with the wild grace of his friends the gazelles. His strength was that of An, of his army of bright stars marching upon the paths of heaven. With a sure instinct he protected the wild beasts of the plains, as their patron saving them from the pits of the hunter and directing their flight to desert fastnesses. In time the reputation of his daring and swiftness of foot was

12

the subject of much admiration in Uruk. Even Gilgamesh was piqued in his pride and touched in his sense of his superiority until he finally hit upon a plan to capture the long-haired Enkidu.

Into the royal chamber he called his bravest hunter and sent him out to the desert watering hole where Enkidu at sunset usually led his animal bands. With him the hunter took one of the most accomplished of the palace courtesans, dressed in a sheer gown, with silver anklets on her bare legs and long carnelian earrings in her ears. As they stood in the slanting rays of summer sun, she anointed her breasts and arms with perfume and unloosed the fillets from her hair. When the animals began to come down their usual path toward the water, they scented her and fled wild-eyed. Enkidu scented her also, but he could not turn away. As he approached warily, the courtesan loosened her garments so that he could see how beautiful she was. Enkidu circled closer and finally clasped her in his arms.

As he later withdrew from her arms and tried to rejoin his herds, to his astonishment and sorrow his "desert cattle shunned him." Even the gazelles whom he had protected so long ran away at his approach. With his innocence gone, he no longer belonged among them, even as their protector. Sadly he turned back and fell exhausted by the side of the beautiful courtesan. With soft words and flattery she wound herself around his heart, enticing him to return to Uruk with her, extolling the beauty of the city, its comforts, and the delights of the company of men. Hand in hand, with the hunter as their guide, they returned to Uruk. Far from loving Enkidu, however, the woman was thinking only of the jewels the king had promised her if she could induce the wild man to submit to the customs and restraints of life in a big city.

Little by little Enkidu at the hands of the palace women allowed his hair to be cut and his beard trained and coaxed into fashionable ringlets. For the first time he wore a linen shirt and a conical hat. As he learned the rites of civilization —how to behave at a banquet, and how to make ceremonious compliments at court—he gradually lost his wild-man appearance and something of his brute strength. On the other hand he gained in moral and mental stature.

Soon after Enkidu had been captured and had come to live in the city, Gilgamesh had a terrible nightmare which persisted even after he was awake. In his anxiety he turned to his wise mother and told her of this dream.

Dear Mother Ninmah, who knows all knowledge,
I have had a dream, a black dream in the night,

13

> Of an army, stars of An, flying toward me,
> Of a great warrior, a great stranger, who wrestled with me,
> Who conquered me and overbore me!

Gently Ninmah comforted her son the king. She told him that the dream meant that he would indeed wrestle with a stranger but that from this bout he could make not evil but good come.

Soon after this Gilgamesh planned an evening party, a riotous affair during which, as he and his friends roamed through the streets of Uruk, they would enter certain houses of debauchery. Enkidu was a member of this band of gay young men. However, as Gilgamesh was about to enter the evil house, he found Enkidu not only standing before him but actually barring the door. Red with anger, he aimed at Enkidu a great blow on the side of the jaw, which was intended to dash him to the ground. He found his blow parried, however, and the two mighty giants grasped each other by the shoulders, with heads close together and muscles straining, trying each one to throw the other. It was the only time in his life that Gilgamesh, the strongest wrestler in all the world, had ever felt—arm for arm, back for back, thigh for thigh—a strength equal to his own. Surrounded by a breathless throng of courtiers, lit by the flaring red light of torches, the heroes wrestled. Sweat poured from their mighty muscles, but neither one could budge the other. There was no sound in the night but their sharp breathing. Suddenly Gilgamesh released his hold. He threw back his head and laughed. In a twinkling his anger had vanished. As they stood panting and looking each other full in the face, the prediction of Ninmah came true. Something good came out of the struggle, a friendship that was to last all the days of their lives, that no danger could threaten nor no evil diminish.

From that evening Gilgamesh and Enkidu were inseparable. A fine couch of silk and furs was prepared in the palace for Enkidu. When Gilgamesh presided at the council of elders, his friend sat on his left hand. All the kings of the earth paid homage to him also and knelt at his feet and kissed them. As he and the king walked through the streets or floated down the river in their round skin kelec, all the people raised their voices loud in praise, for the old evil habits were gone from their king. Yet in spite of the luxury and opulence of Uruk, or perhaps even because of them, Enkidu was unhappy. From time to time an old longing would come over him, even in the midst of gaiety, for the savage wanderings of his youth when he had roamed strong and free over the desert and even up to the mountains where

14

the rivers were born. One night Enkidu also had a terrifying nightmare.

In the morning, when he heard his friend's dream, Gilgamesh summoned the dream interpreters to study it. In his dream Enkidu had seen a horrible black monster swooping down on him. It buried its long fierce talons into him and carried him off, as an eagle a lamb, into the black Underworld realm of Nergal, king of eternal darkness. There he was forced to stumble among the dead, who lay in great heaps about him. They were like grotesque birds because of their black, feathered garments. In the gloom he could see that their only food was mud. Enkidu covered his face with his hands and trembled as he recalled with a chill of horror that dreadful scene. After long deliberation the wise men of the king agreed that this dream was a very serious matter. They advised him and Enkidu to sacrifice immediately to the sun god Shamash, whose justice could be invoked in cases of extreme urgency.

As servants prepared the sacred oil for the offering, Gilgamesh and Enkidu proceeded, naked as the ritual required, to the House of Judgment. From there Shamash, who riding daily across the earth in his chariot saw all that happened in the world and even into the future, dispensed justice. As the holy oil was poured in generous libation into the basin, the temple priests studied its pattern. Finally the god spoke through them, telling the king that he must go away, must leave Uruk. While Gilgamesh and Enkidu listened, they made more offerings, a pot of honey and a lapis lazuli jar of sweet butter. Again the god spoke to Gilgamesh, telling him that he must journey indeed even to the Cedar Mountain, which the loathsome monster Huwawa guarded. Once there, he must kill the monster, fell seven cedar trees, and deliver all the land from evil.

No sooner had Gilgamesh and Enkidu left the temple than the king began to shout orders right and left. He called upon the cleverest craftsmen of the city to forge for them magnificent weapons of bronze. On every side he met tears and lamentations, for his subjects were certain that they would never see him again or bask in the protection of his might. In haste the elders calculated the problem of distance, pointing out that the land of the great cedars lay 20,000 hours of travel away, that it would take the heroes two and a half years even to reach it. Secondly they argued the dangers of such a long journey all the way northwestward over the seven mountains to the horizon of the world. Gilgamesh would have to travel to the western rim, where Shamash at sunset disappeared into the bowels of the earth.

Undismayed, the king replied that Shamash had ordered this task himself, and that he had therefore a double responsibility toward them, not only as the instigator but also as the personal deity of travelers.

It was Ninmah, the king's mother, however, who grieved the most deeply. Understanding that her son's determination was not to be shaken, she stepped out on the palace terrace just as the rays of the western sun struck full against it. Dressed in her prayer robes and holding in her uplifted hands a bowl of incense, she prayed to Shamash to protect her child, reminding the god that this battle with Huwawa, guardian of the Cedar Mountain, would be an unequal one since Gilgamesh would be pitted against a horrible monster and not against a man. In her anguish she cried to the god, "Why must it be to my son that you have given a heart that will not slumber?"

Armed with new flashing daggers and war clubs, Gilgamesh and Enkidu set out the next morning on their great adventure. Soon they had left the tropical forests, the buffaloes, and pelicans of the Euphrates delta country, and were striding past the last irrigated plots and out into the rolling yellow plains of the desert. For weeks and weeks they walked through a land that looked as vast as the ocean, guiding their routes always toward the northwest. Under the gorgeous hues of an eastern sky the rolling hills stretched yellow and treeless. Only the hawk and the eagle flew overhead. On certain days black storms would march like succeeding armies along the desert behind them and go crashing into the walls of the Amanus Mountains. It was a desolate land, where they were grateful at night to lie warmly wrapped in their robes, snug in a cairn or against a sheltering boulder. Over all the desert lay a yellowish haze through which the flying clouds cast shadows that stood like gigantic black pillars holding up the sky. Striding through upland pastures of red, blue, and yellow flowers the friends were amused to see that the colors had dyed their own ankles as they brushed against them. At sunset they often turned to look back southward toward their homeland, and watched in awe as the yellow desert slowly turned from lavender to purple.

As they traveled, they discussed the precious cedars they must fell and float down the Euphrates to Uruk, for in the land of Sumer there was neither stone nor timber for building. If Gilgamesh had been alone, he would have dreaded to meet the monster Huwawa, but with Enkidu by his side he did not even fear death or the hideous face of the beast. Every day made them stronger and harder, and more firm

16

in their resolve never to turn back, come what might. Finally they saw over the crest of a hill the magnificent Cedar Mountain. Its dark green trees had been placed in the guard of Huwawa by the god Enlil long before. In delight the two heroes greeted the shade of the scented trees. They quickly followed a path to the very summit, not wanting even to stop and catch their breath. Soon they reached a stockade of seven magic trees, which was the domain of the monster.

Enkidu was suddenly terrified. He begged Gilgamesh to wait until morning so as not to encounter the giant with darkness falling. Gilgamesh would not listen. In a loud voice he cried out to Huwawa, ordering him to come out of his shelter and meet them in battle. Only silence answered his challenge. Huwawa had heard them, but he would not answer. With pounding hearts the heroes listened to the wind in the trees. There was no answer at all from the stockade.

Enkidu then advised Gilgamesh to sacrifice to the gods. The two friends dug a trench in the forest earth and planted the sacrificial seeds they had brought with them. After reciting their prayers Gilgamesh asked their patron Shamash to send Enkidu a dream in the night by which they could either be sure of their victory or prepare for death.

Toward morning Enkidu awoke to find Gilgamesh leaning over him. "It is I who have dreamed," he said. "Or did you awaken me from my slumber? I must have dreamed, for lo! the earth shook, and the heavens rained fire! All around me death fell from the clouds!" Enkidu listened to the dream and reassured Gilgamesh, saying that his dream surely presaged the destruction of Huwawa. Then, as they prepared for battle, Huwawa breathed. Before the tempest of his breath the lofty cedars bowed their heads in obedience all the way down the mountainside. Gilgamesh and Enkidu had hardly time to draw their daggers before the monstrous Huwawa charged toward them, roaring like a tempest, shrieking like all the winds let loose. Gilgamesh caught only one glimpse of that devilish face as it lunged toward him—a horrible, distorted face with yellow, bared teeth and fierce, bloodshot eyes.

Back and forth the battle raged between Gilgamesh and the monster. His dagger was soon red with blood from the gushing wounds he had inflicted. Harder and harder Gilgamesh pressed the monster. His courage and strength welled up in him as he fought. Harder and faster he swung his war club, unmindful of his own danger. Finally the monster fell over backward; and before he could get his footing and rise again, Enkidu rushed over to him and hacked off his head.

17

GILGAMESH THE WRESTLER

The bloody head rolled down the mountainside, bouncing against the trees.

Thus Gilgamesh was free to cut the cedars for the temples of Uruk, and by his courage he delivered the land from evil. The gods of Sumer had abandoned Huwawa and had fought with Gilgamesh and Enkidu.

After the battle the heroes cleansed themselves of blood, put on fresh garments, and made offerings to the gods. Gilgamesh was so handsome in his gold helmet and white tunic that the goddess of love, Ishtar, appeared suddenly before him. While she was congratulating him on his victory, she began to caress his face provocatively and to stroke his shoulders, asking him if he did not begin to love her. Gilgamesh answered her sharply, "What do you do to your loves, Ishtar? When the stallion worships you, do you not put him into the harness and condemn him to pull the heavy war cart? When the shepherds of the hills are charmed by you, do you not transform them into leopards that eat the little lambs? Did you not kill the lovely youth Tammuz, who loved you? Did you not send him to the House of the Dead after the harvest so that every year the snows of winter steal down the river valleys and cover our land with ice?" Thus for the first time was Ishtar spurned by the heroes.

By the time Gilgamesh and Enkidu had felled the cedars and returned to Uruk, the sultry Ishtar had planned a terrible revenge. She had persuaded her father An to send the Bull of Heaven into the city to trample the people, destroy the temples, and slaughter the warriors by the thousands. Gilgamesh and Enkidu rushed into combat. As the king was about to stab the bull, Enkidu seized it by the tail, and summoning all his strength, hurled it against a stone altar. A loud gasp of joy and relief rose from the city residents, who had watched the combat from their walls. Among the temple courtesans lurked Ishtar herself with tears of anger on her face. Quickly Enkidu bent over the dead bull, flayed it, and flung the bloody pelt up into the goddess' face, shouting defiance at her. Laughing over their shoulders, the two friends sauntered to the Euphrates to wash their hands, followed by the acclamations of the people of Uruk. For the second time was Ishtar insulted.

Very soon after this Enkidu became ill, which was certainly due to a curse put upon him by Ishtar. His sickness lasted for twelve days, and at daybreak on the thirteenth day he died in the arms of his friend, who had never left his side. Gilgamesh was frantic with grief. First he tried to call Enkidu back to life by reminding him of their adventures, the wonderful lion hunts they had enjoyed on the plains, their trip to the Cedar Mountain, and their dazzling defeat of the Celestial Bull. Then as the full realization of his loss sank into his soul, he could bear his grief no longer. Like a wild man he rushed out of the palace, fleeing madly from the awful sight of death. Everywhere he wandered, his subjects tried to console the king by holding up to him the memories of his heroism. Gilgamesh could not be comforted, for he realized that as Enkidu was even then in the House of Death, with mud as his only food, so would he be also one day. This terrible thought drove him in his revulsion to leave Uruk just as the yellow spatches of the date palms were bursting into flower, and to roam desolate through the desert, wrestling with the horror of death.

One day in his anguish a possibility occurred to him. There was one man who had received the gift of immortality. Perhaps, if Gilgamesh could find his abode, he would be willing to divulge this secret. Perhaps also Gilgamesh would be able to return to Uruk with it and save the whole race of mankind from their certain death!

This man who had received the secret of immortality was Ut-napishtim, the famous king of Shuruppak. Long before the days of Uruk, Shuruppak had been one of the five royal cities of Mesopotamia. Once the possibility of such a scheme entered his head, Gilgamesh knew no rest. Instead of returning to his home and to his weeping mother, he continued his road straight to the west, traveling as swiftly as he could. With such an inspired goal, how could he fear the dangers of the burning desert? At length, weary and footsore, he reached Mount Mashu, the dazzling western home of the sun god. Blinded at first, for the sunlight was white-hot, he finally made out to his consternation rows and rows of scorpion-men who stood in ranks guarding the entrance to the mountain. His heart sank as he looked at their size. The lower parts of their bodies seemed to rise from the Underworld, while their blazing heads reached high up to the ramparts of the sun god.

At first Gilgamesh could not force his quaking legs to advance, but saying to himself that unless he did confront them, he would also have to taste like Enkidu the bitter clay of death, he finally took a deep breath, walked courageously up to the central scorpion, and bowed low before him. This guardian, apparently recognizing the godly parts of Gilgamesh, pointed toward a gate that swung open, allowing him passage into the dark heart of the mountain. As his eyes became used to the gloom, Gilgamesh managed to follow a wet, cold tunnel that lay ahead of him. Gathering courage as he groped his way forward, he walked so long that he almost lost track of the time. For twice eleven hours he walked without once stopping for rest, and at last in the twelfth twin-hour he saw far ahead of him a shimmering of light.

With a gasp of relief, he stepped out into the sunlight into the garden of the goddess who lived by the shore of the sea. Never even in Uruk had he seen a more beautiful sight. Amid pools and flowers stood the holy tree of the gods, the tree of life, covered with all kinds of delicious, scented fruits. Its branches were not of wood but of lapis lazuli flecked with gold. Under it lay a profusion of precious gems winking and sparkling in emerald light. At the end of the garden was the house of the goddess, and beyond that the blue waters of the sea that no man had crossed, clearer than a mirror, bluer than a sapphire. Dazzled and happy, Gilgamesh stood admiring the peace of the garden, not realizing how he looked after his months of travel. His beard was long and unkempt. His palace garments, which had worn out long before, he had replaced with animal skins. His body was scratched and burned by the sun, his hands bleeding from the jagged walls of the Mashu Mountain tunnel. When the goddess saw him, it is no wonder that she ran screaming into her house and bolted the door.

Gilgamesh had not come this far to be stopped by a frightened woman. Rapping sharply on her door, he ordered her to come out at once and talk with him. The goddess, however, would not open the door. Gilgamesh told her that she must see him or he would burst the locks and break down the door. Apparently she believed him, for she came out and listened. Gilgamesh told her he must find a passage across the sea to the home of Ut-napishtim, but the goddess only laughed. This, she told him, was quite impossible. It was absolutely out of the question, since nobody could find the way except the boatman of Ut-napishtim himself. When Gilgamesh tried to make her understand his sorrow at the death of his beloved comrade, Enkidu, she counseled him in this way: "Go home to Uruk, King, and accept the inevitable with good grace. Think of all the gifts with which the gods have showered you. Be grateful for them. Live in your fine palace. Fight your great wars. Eat and drink merrily. Take a wife and sleep peacefully with her head on your shoulder. This way you will live out your days and accept the bird of death when it flies over you." No matter how she argued, Gilgamesh could not be persuaded. Eventually he had his way and extracted from her directions for reaching Urshanabi, the boatman.

He found him and his boat down by the shore in a little cove. At first Urshanabi shook his head solemnly and affirmed that Gilgamesh would be swallowed by the sea. All around the abode of Ut-napishtim, he said, the sea waters were turbulent and dangerous and full of black crags. This was the precise reason why no mortal had ever succeeded in crossing the ocean. Since Urshanabi with all his tales of danger could not dissuade Gilgamesh either, he finally thought of a way in which the passage might possibly be made. The main thing would be for Gilgamesh not to touch the water, for that meant instant death. He told the king to go back up on the mountain and cut 120 poles, each one 60 cubits (30 yards) in length. In this way Gilgamesh did arrive at the magic abode of King Ut-napishtim, the only mortal thus far who had been given the priceless reward of everlasting life. As the boat of Urshanabi approached each crag rising among the waters of death, Gilgamesh with his superhuman strength pushed the boat away from it. He dropped each contaminated pole into the water as soon as he had used it.

He found King Ut-napishtim sitting in his throne room alongside the queen. When Gilgamesh told him who he was and why he had come, the king only nodded knowingly to the queen and laughed openly at such a foolish mortal. "Shall I tell you how I won immortality?" he asked.

Ut-napishtim then recounted at great length and in great detail the story of a flood that the gods had once sent upon the earth. Weary and travel-worn, Gilgamesh listened to the old tale which he had heard so often at his mother's knee—how the god of wisdom had counseled the building of a great ship, how the king had gathered into it a pair of all the animals and birds of creation, how it had rained for six days and six nights, how Shamash had destroyed all the face of the earth with the flood waters, how on the seventh day the tempest had abated. He went on to tell about sending out a dove, a swallow, and finally a raven that did not return. The boat had finally landed on the mountain of Nizir, where the King Ut-napishtim made sacrifices to the gods. "Thus," he concluded, "have I won eternal life."

"So would I also," replied Gilgamesh, undaunted.

"You would not enjoy it," answered Ut-napishtim wearily. "I wager you would long for sleep. Look here," he said, "I'll wager you could not remain awake for six days and seven nights, as I did!"

Even before he could answer, Gilgamesh had fallen asleep at the very foot of the throne, exhausted by his long travels and the final task of the 120 poles. Ut-napishtim would have been content to let Gilgamesh lie there on the floor until he sank into the sleep of death. In this way would his thoughts have been confirmed. The queen, however, with her woman's heart, was touched. In her pity for the handsome king of Uruk, handsome in a virility and power that shone even through his tattered garments, she urged her husband, as only a wife knows how to do, to grant Gilgamesh his request. They awoke the sleeping king and told him of the flower of youth. It lay at the very bottom of the sea, however, and it would require lungs of iron to swim to such a depth. Gilgamesh was not afraid. He saw that the end of the quest was near, and his sleep had restored his strength.

He ran down to the shore, tied huge boulders to his feet, and dauntlessly plunged down through the clear waters, deeper and deeper past the white ledges of the sea. There in a deep, dark cavern he plucked the thorny plant of eternal youth, wincing as the barbs pricked his fingers. With tortured lungs he struggled with powerful strokes back upward toward the sunlight in the waters of the surface. Strange painted fishes glided past him, curious at the bubbles that arose from his threshing limbs. Once on the surface he loosened the stones from his feet and regained the skiff of Urshanabi. Without a thought of tasting the flower himself, he clutched it in delight. It was the attainment of his life's ambition, a gift to his people such as no king before him had ever had the courage and perseverance to obtain. Refreshed and happy beyond words to tell, he rested in the boat as it made its tortuous passage back to the shores of the goddess.

The long journey home to Uruk was a pleasant one, for Gilgamesh held the flower in his hand and no danger could threaten him. Now and again he smelled its aromatic fragrance. One afternoon, weary and dusty, not many days' journey from home, he reached the shores of a little lake that, unbelievably enough, lay in a desert hollow. The water smelled clean and fresh after his days of travel over a parched land. Having removed his garments, he placed the precious flower securely on a stone right near the water, and plunged in. After his swim he waded ashore just in time to see a snake, which had been attracted by the pungent odor of the plant, disappear with the flower of eternal youth in its mouth. Search as he might, Gilgamesh could never find it again. He sat naked by the little lake and wept.

Brokenhearted, he returned to Uruk, where no welcome could cheer him. "Yes, it is I who have returned," he told his people. "For this have I labored! For this have Enkidu and I toiled! For this have I braved the monster Huwawa! For this have I encountered the Bull of Heaven! For this have I watched my dear friend Enkidu descend to the feathered House of No Return! For this—to have brought eternal life not to my beloved people, but to the race of serpents!"

23

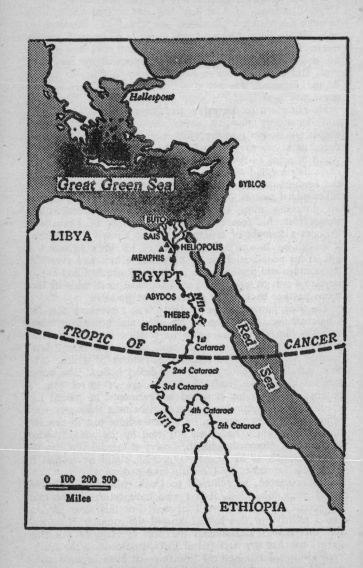

EGYPT—3000 B. C.

2

Egypt: Horus the Hawk, the Avenger

INTRODUCTION

THE FOLLOWING ACCOUNT of the story of Horus, Isis, and Osiris in Egypt is an attempt to incorporate various references to it among the writers of antiquity with recent translations of hieroglyphic texts from Egypt itself. The story of this Triad of Abydos is apparently much older than even the earliest records and may go back as far as 7500 B.C., when, according to a foremost Egyptologist, Sir Flinders Petrie, it is a memory of Asiatic invasion (Seth), repelled by a native king (Osiris).

These three main gods were skillfully incorporated into the Great Ennead, or state religion of Egypt, by the priests of Heliopolis. Aside from a part of the story as told by Plutarch (c. A.D. 46–A.D. 120) and his very modern philosophical analysis of it, apparently no complete text exists in a chronological sequence, as it is presented here. The story was certainly expanded throughout Egyptian history, particularly during the first five or six dynasties when the worship of this Triad was prominent. Therefore we find in the finished story various anachronistic references—to India and to the horse, for example.

All writers about the ancient history of Egypt must acknowledge their debt to the tireless efforts of those scholars who through the long centuries have studied this great civilization which has left behind it monuments of such massive proportions and of such an enduring beauty. Great honors must be paid to the French scholar Jean François Champollion, who deciphered hieroglyphic writing early in the 1800's. Most of us Americans first knew the history of this wonderful land from the inspired writings of James H. Breasted, the especial admirer of the Pharaoh Akhenaton of the Eighteenth Dynasty.

HORUS THE HAWK, THE AVENGER

MOST ANCIENT among the ancient countries of the earth is Egypt. This land was described in antiquity as those portions of the soil of Africa which were flooded once a year for a

THE COSMOGONY OF HELIOPOLIS
OR
THE GREAT ENNEAD

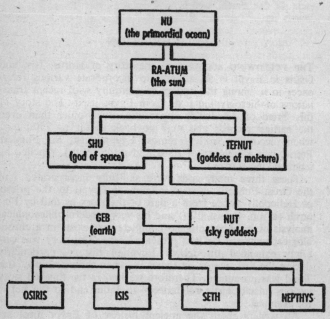

```
                    ┌─────────────────────┐
                    │         NU          │
                    │ (the primordial ocean)│
                    └─────────────────────┘
                              │
                    ┌─────────────────────┐
                    │      RA-ATUM        │
                    │      (the sun)      │
                    └─────────────────────┘
                              │
          ┌───────────────────┴───────────────────┐
   ┌──────────────┐                        ┌──────────────────┐
   │     SHU      │                        │      TEFNUT       │
   │(god of space)│                        │(goddess of moisture)│
   └──────────────┘                        └──────────────────┘
          │                                         │
          └───────────────────┬───────────────────┘
   ┌──────────────┐                        ┌──────────────────┐
   │     GEB      │                        │       NUT         │
   │   (earth)    │                        │  (sky goddess)    │
   └──────────────┘                        └──────────────────┘
          │                                         │
   ┌──────┬───────────────┬──────────────┬──────────────┐
┌────────┐  ┌────────┐      ┌────────┐      ┌──────────┐
│ OSIRIS │  │  ISIS  │      │  SETH  │      │ NEPTHYS  │
└────────┘  └────────┘      └────────┘      └──────────┘
```

THE TRIAD OF ABYDOS

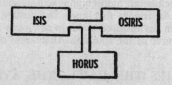

```
   ┌────────┐        ┌────────┐
   │  ISIS  │────────│ OSIRIS │
   └────────┘        └────────┘
            │        │
         ┌────────┐
         │ HORUS  │
         └────────┘
```

∘EGYPTIAN RELIGION

period of a hundred days by the waters of the River Nile, and all those people who drank the waters of that mighty river from Elephantine to the sea were by definition Egyptians. The Nile flows from the left side of the earth—said they—through the country of the Hawk, which we call Upper Egypt, between narrow walls of rock into the right-hand side of the earth, which is Lower Egypt. There the river meets its prehistoric enemy, the Great Green Sea, which once covered all the land. In preparation the Nile divides itself into several streams which force their way through papyrus reeds and marshes into this northernmost triangle or extreme right edge of the earth called the Delta. Speak softly, because as we paddle through the reeds and come out into an open space we may glimpse the baby Horus sitting brown and naked in the middle of a lotus bloom, sucking his chubby finger.

The ancient priests of Egypt were the most learned men in all the world. According to their hieroglyphic calculations time could be divided into units of 360 days, with 5 days left over in each cycle for the birthdays of the gods. Only very intelligent and fearless boys were admitted to a temple school such as the great college at Heliopolis, where they could study the sacred carvings that revealed all the mysteries of the creation. It was in this school that the child Moses is said to have learned the wisdom of the Egyptians. The ordinary people of Egypt knew very little of such lore. They were content to follow the precepts of their own leaders, long since recognized by them as having had powers beyond those of ordinary men, and these had become their gods.

Born on the first of the five epagomenal days, and therefore the greatest of all the gods, was Osiris; the merciful judge of the living and the dead. You could glimpse him in the dark waters of the Nile, his silken black hair flowing with the current. His wife and sister was the lady of heaven, Isis, she of the thousand titles, whose name means chamber of the birth of a god. Her you could see in the golden light of sunrise, clothed in the brilliant green robes of the new day, the lady bountiful who fills your fields with crops and your cradle with a newborn son. Isis herself was born on the fourth day. On the second day was born the elder Horus, a fair god, but one so old his story has been forgotten or else replaced by the baby who later bore a similar name. The third day you must mark on your calendar with three signs of bad luck, for on this day was born Seth, or Typhon, from whom sprang all disharmony and the destructive

27

forces of the earth. On the fifth and last day was born Nepthys, the barren sister of Isis. To her are the dominions of the far lands, the treeless deserts of Libya, and the sterile confines of the seacoasts.

Long before the priests and even before the Pharaohs, the great dark King Osiris ruled in Africa. He was a tall man and slender as all devout Egyptians longed to be so that their bodies might fit as lightly and easily as possible about their immortal soul, or ba. On his head he wore the lofty white crown of Upper Egypt with an ostrich feather on either side of it because these feathers are as light as the truth. A beautiful plaited beard fell from his chin as befitted a great and powerful ruler whose fertility made life swell even in the dry desert. Around his neck and shoulders he wore a white collarlike necklace made of precious gems, ivory, and symbolic beads. Wherever he stepped grew a lily blossom in remembrance of the water lilies in that great lake at the very left edge of the world where Osiris was born and where the righteous who have kept his commandments might hope to find the Isles of the Blessed. His naked body from ankles to wrists was beautifully decorated with crimson painted flowers. Such was Osiris who ruled in Egypt, powerful and black, for black is the color of youth, as white is the color of old heads. To worship him a man must use pure water where the ibis drinks and bring fig leaves so that he may grow potent as the sacred bull, as Osiris.

Osiris had embraced his sister Isis even before they were born, while both were tumbling in their mother's womb. When he had become a man and a king, he married her and took her from among all women as his queen. Together they ruled Egypt, making it a land of music and delight. Gradually Osiris by his teachings and example persuaded the people to put away their former evil habits, especially that of cannibalism, to which his subjects were particularly addicted. He showed them how to cultivate the earth that he made black and fertile each summer with the waters of the Nile. As soon as he saw that the Egyptians had become industrious and skilled husbandmen, he gave them a code of laws by which they could regulate their lives. Then Osiris decided that it was not enough to civilize Egypt, but that he should travel throughout the rest of the world and by the gentle arts of persuasion and music enlighten them also. It may have been during this voyage that the waters of the Nile spread beyond their usual limit of inundation and made fertile even the barren wastelands of the lovely sister of Isis, Nepthys. In any case Nepthys did conceive and give birth to a son, Anubis. Her husband Seth suspected her pregnancy was due to Osiris when he found in Nepthys' bed garlands of such melilot, or sweet clover, flowers as Osiris often wore.

However that may be, Osiris traveled far and wide over the face of the earth, Isis ruled Egypt wisely and well during his absence, and Seth grew more and more evil and jealous. Several times he tried to violate the laws laid down by Osiris and even to change the government, but the watchful Isis always prevented him. One day the return of Osiris was announced through all the land. Seth hastened to invite him to a festive dinner party, and Osiris accepted.

Using promises of great reward, Seth managed to persuade seventy-two of his friends, and also an Ethiopian queen named Aso, who happened to be visiting Egypt at that time, to help him murder the king. After the banquet Seth announced to the company that he had a present to give to one of them. Drawing back a curtain, he showed them proudly a beautiful cedar chest made in the shape of a man and exquisitely adorned with gold and designs. As the assembled guests gasped at the skill of its construction, Seth opened its lid and swore that it should belong only to the man present who fitted it perfectly. One by one the eager guests tried to fit themselves into the box, but they were all too short or too wide for it. Finally Seth called tauntingly to Osiris, "Do you try the precious chest, O King!"

Proudly the tall, slender-hipped Osiris stepped into the casket, lay down with his arms close to his sides, and, of course, he fitted it perfectly—for Seth and his seventy-two accomplices had ordered the box made to his exact dimensions. As soon as Osiris was lying flat on his back, Seth clapped the cover on the chest and began to nail it down. Then he and his treacherous friends poured molten lead all along the joints, thus sealing it hermetically. Within a few minutes they knew Osiris had smothered to death. Then, as previously arranged, they carried the chest to the bank of the Nile and heaved it into the water. As they watched the current catch it and carry it swiftly downstream, the exultant Seth realized that he was the ruler of Egypt. Thus did Osiris die in the twenty-eighth year of his life, on the seventeenth day of the month, just as the moon was beginning to wane.

The news of the king's murder swept swiftly through the land, causing panic and terror in the hearts of the people. The lady Isis was at the time in the city of Coptos. As soon as she heard the dreadful news, she cut off a thick lock of her shining, black hair and put on the long white robe of mourning. Then like a faithful wife she started out along the banks of the river to find the basket and the corpse of her beloved husband. Up and down its banks she wandered weeping and disconsolate, for she could not find it. The longer she searched, the deeper grew her love for Osiris. She hunted especially closely all along the papyrus swamps of the delta, thinking that the casket might have been caught among the reeds.

As she wandered weeping and mourning she asked for news about her dead husband from all the people she met. It grieved her deeply to hear his praises, for this made her loss more unbearable. Messengers told how he had traveled throughout the world with his kinsman Heracles, spreading the science of agriculture, how he had planted grapevines, wheat, and barley in Ethiopia, where he had founded many cities. They told of his great deeds in Arabia and how he had carried the ivy plant even into India, where he had built the great city of Nysa. In this strange country Osiris had delighted in elephant hunts. Messengers reported that after visiting all of Asia he had journeyed westward across the Hellespont and forced those barbarians who lived in southeastern Europe to accept his government.

Isis also learned how her husband had, like the Nile, strayed from his bed and visited Nepthys. Nine months later a son, Anubis, had been born to Nepthys, who in her terror of her husband Seth had exposed the child among the reeds and left him to die. Isis found the baby, so curious with its dog's head and spotted dog's coat. With great love she became a mother to him, and educated him so that Anubis grew up to be the watchdog of the gods of Egypt and, like that wonderful animal, devoted and faithful. For his service Anubis received the gift of human speech and studied medicine and embalming.

One day, weary from her long search and sore from her sobbing, which could be heard all the way from Saïs in Lower Egypt to the holy city of Abydos in the south, Isis sat down on a grassy bank in the delta to watch some little children at play. Now it was common knowledge in Egypt that children will often in their unguarded speech reveal facts of great significance, especially if they are in a holy place or near a goddess. Isis therefore listened intently and questioned them. To her great joy they alone among all the people of Egypt had not only seen the casket float by but were able to assure her that it had passed through the Tanitic mouth of the Nile, a current forever afterward held in horror by all those devoted to Osiris. Thrilled at the thought that her search was near its end, Isis hastened down the river, following its flow through the Great Green Sea until she came to Byblos on the great coast of Syria or Phoenicia.[1] It was here that she found the casket.

[1] Not far from modern Beirut.

The waves had gently washed the casket up on the shores of Syria, where a huge tamarisk tree, thriving and blooming even in the salt spray of the seashore, had lovingly enfolded the box in its trunk. The tough, reddish wood grew tightly around the box, protecting it from moisture and harm. The king of Syria, Melkarth, passing along the beach one day, had marveled at the gigantic tree and ordered it to be cut down and its trunk used as a pillar in his palace.

To this palace Isis went with the sure instinct of a woman searching for the man she loves, and sat down thankfully beside the pillar, stroking its wood lovingly. Before her splashed a lively fountain where the ladies of Queen Ishtar of Syria came every afternoon to bathe. At first Isis would not speak to them but only sat with her cheek against the red wood of the tamarisk pillar. The palace ladies realized that Isis was an Egyptian because of her white linen sheath dress which left her beautiful breasts exposed. They had often seen the ships from Egypt unloading their papyrus in the harbor of Byblos, and they had heard how famed the women of Egypt were for their beauty. Coming closer, they marveled at the way her glossy black hair was braided so that it fell across her bare shoulders in two long plaits. Finally Isis began to talk to them, and as they stepped from the fountain, she showed them how to comb their hair and train its wet curls.

The women had no sooner entered the queen's chamber than Ishtar, so skilled herself in the arts of seduction, smelled the perfume that Isis' hands had stroked upon their bodies and in their hair. When she inquired about it, they told her of the beautiful foreign lady they had seen in the palace courtyard. Ishtar commanded that Isis be brought to her at once. When Isis in her simple white gown was brought before the queen, Ishtar, although not knowing that Isis was a goddess, wanted to keep her near, especially because of the enchanting perfume that surrounded the Egyptian woman like a cloud. She commanded Isis to remain in the palace, where she was to become the nurse to Ishtar's oldest son.

Isis kept her anonymity for some time, remaining in the palace at Byblos to nurse the son of its rulers. Whenever the child was hungry, she let it suck on her divine fingers instead of at her breast. Every evening when the palace courtiers had gone to bed, Isis held the little boy over a flame because in this way she knew how to singe away those parts of him which were mortal only and confer upon this future king the precious gift of eternal life. Then in the dead of night, while the palace slept, Isis would transform herself into a black swallow and fly screaming and chirping around and around the tamarisk pillar, longing to hold her husband in her arms

31

and feel his strong body against her straining breasts. One night Ishtar, awakened by the shrill laments of the swallow, stumbled sleepily into the courtyard just as Isis was holding the baby prince over the flame. Not understanding what the goddess was trying to do, Ishtar screamed; and in that instant the magic spell was broken. Thus Ishtar herself robbed her own son of immortality.

Before the blinded eyes of Ishtar, Isis revealed herself in the full light of her glory as the Lady of the Sunrise, the Queen of the South, the Beautiful, and the Beloved Lady of Abundance. Kneeling at the feet of the great goddess, Ishtar listened to the story of her wanderings, and to the dreadful news of the death of the Nile, Osiris. Gladly she gave the tamarisk pillar to Isis, who with trembling fingers split open its trunk and carefully lifted out the cedar casket containing the body of her lord. Then Isis in veneration gratefully wrapped the tree trunk in pure white linen bands, anointed it with perfumed oil, and caused it to be erected in the temple of Byblos, where ever afterward it was worshiped as the tree that had enclosed a god.

By this time it was morning, and Isis prepared to sail back to Egypt with her husband's body. Very tenderly she placed it in the sun on the open deck, and when the little river that flowed into the sea at Byblos blew chill breezes along its estuary, Isis angrily caused its waters to run dry. Shortly afterward she arrived in the delta of Egypt, where she could easily find a safe hiding place in which to perform the operations that she alone knew. With the help of her sister Nepthys she set about reviving Osiris. From this ceremony comes one of the beautiful hymns to Isis:

Let us praise Isis
Who rules at the beginning of the New Year!
Let us praise her who was a protectress to thee.
What has she not performed!
She has ruled Egypt in dignity and in truth.
She has defended thy rule in thy absence.
She has cut a lock of her hair and has mourned thee.
Her cries of grief have been heard in Abydos.
What has she not performed!
She has sought thee even far over the sea.
She has borne thee home to our land in her arms;
Nor did she rest in her flight,
Not once alight, nor ever rest!
Let us praise Isis who made breath to come from her wings,
Who worked on thy lifeless body with knotted cords,
Who warmed thy body with the warmth of her breast,
Who made air to enter with the beating of her wings,

32

Who made life to flow from thy body up into Isis,
To the chamber of the abode of life.[2]

The news of the restoration of Osiris brought great joy to the people of Egypt, who saw immediately that if their king could be brought back to life after his death, so might they also expect to be. The evil brother Seth, however, haunted the delta region, his red hair flaming and bristling on his head. And there was malice in his heart. Forever afterward the Egyptians abhorred the color red, considering it a manifestation of all the forces of treachery, murder, and jealousy. For this reason in after times the inhabitants of Coptos would not permit within their city the presence of asses because of their reddish coats, and if they found such an animal would hurl him from a cliff. Neither would they allow the use of a trumpet, for this instrument reminded them of the braying of an ass. In these ways and others did they recall how Seth hunted until he found Isis and, mercilessly dragging the goddess after him, shut her up in a dark prison.

This was no fit place for the Lady of Light, and soon by the help and magical powers of the poor, doglike Anubis, whom she had saved from exposure and death, she escaped and fled in great pain to the reeds of the river. There, sitting unattended on a stool, like a plain peasant woman, she labored to deliver her child, the child of her love for Osiris. Straining and moaning, the goddess suffered, but the baby could not be born. Then in her agony two gods appeared and smeared her temples with blood, symbol of life. They brought her amulets also, one of the little beetle which comes to life as the waters of the Nile begin to pour over its banks onto the thirsty desert, and another of the shiny green frog from that African region where rain falls and awakens it from its long sleep in a dry soil. With the help of their incantations the body of Isis burst open and out sprang her beautiful son, flooding the world with his light just as in the darkness before morning the golden sun suddenly appears dazzling and glorious over the eastern rim of a black world. Thus was finally born the son of Osiris, he who was awaited, Horus the hawk, the avenger. His birthday fell on the vernal equinox, just at the very moment when the tender shoots of grain were piercing the black earth of Egypt with their green feathers. He was born as the fruits of the earth are born, by the action of fertilizing water flowing over mother land, and he was born in Lower Egypt among the shrubs and papyri of the delta.

[2] Paraphrased from a hieroglyphic translation into French by the Egyptologist François Chabas (1817–1882).

The peach tree was sacred to Horus because its green leaves were just the shape of his heart and just the size of his little tongue. The baby grew fat on his mother's breast, drinking her milk and gazing up at her adoringly; and so are they represented in statues throughout all of Egypt and even in later millennia in the cultured domains of the Greek and Roman empires.[3]

The climate of the delta was healthful for the little boy, who splashed in the water and playfully hid from his mother under lotus plants. When he was older his father appeared to him often and encouraged him to be strong and manly and to endure pain sturdily. One day Osiris asked him, "What do you think is the most glorious action a man can perform?"

Without hesitation, for like his mother Horus had the gift of fluent speech, the small boy answered, "The most glorious action a man can perform is to avenge the injuries offered to his father and mother." [4]

Much pleased with this first reply, Osiris then asked the child, "What animal do you think is the most useful to a soldier?"

Quickly Horus replied, "I know, a horse!"

At this reply Osiris wondered, because he had expected his son to name that animal in whose constellation the Nile every year begins its inundation. He questioned Horus again, "Why do you prefer a horse to a lion?"

"Because," retorted Horus, "although the lion is really more useful to a warrior in great distress, yet still is the horse more helpful in overtaking and cutting off an escaping enemy host."

As a result of such conversations with his son and their long exercises in the handling and use of the various weapons of war, Osiris felt sure that the boy was ready for the enemy Seth, whom he would one day have to meet in a deadly battle if ever he was to claim his lawful realm in Egypt and rule. However, before this day could arrive, more trials and horrors were reserved for the goddess Isis.

There happened to the gentle goddess the very catastrophe every mother fears and dreads more than anything else in the world. One morning she had left Horus, who was yet a young child, asleep on a mat in the sun and had gone to the city of Buto to buy some provisions for him. Imagine the fear and horror when she hastened home and

[3] See the statuettes in the Metropolitan Museum of Art, New York.

[4] Quoted almost verbatim from Plutarch's treatise *De Iside et Osiride*.

34

found the little boy lying where she had left him, stung to death by a scorpion. The child lay rigid, his body swollen and already growing cold, his lips white with foam, and the mat wet with the tears of fright and pain he had shed. Screaming hoarsely, with the terrible grief only a mother can feel who holds in her arms the lifeless body of her only child, Isis called for help.

From all sides the neighboring farmers came running, and from every little creek in the marsh the fishermen hastened to draw up their nets and paddle furiously to the goddess' side; for these simple people all knew her hiding place and never even at the threat of the torture stick would they have revealed it. From her distant haunts on the barren seacoast the goddess Nepthys also heard her sister's hoarse screams of grief. Swiftly she sped to the scene, pushed through the circle of helpless friends, and counseled her sister wisely, "Call upon the sun god, O Isis! He alone can tell us what to do!"

Together the sister goddesses cried loudly up to the heavens, invoking the aid of the great god Ra; and wonder of wonders, he heard their voices, for Isis was beloved even in the heavens for her devotion, for her loneliness, and for the continuous tribulations she had so dauntlessly undergone. As all the peasants and fisher folk stood with their mouths open in wonder, the sun stopped in its daily course over the cloudless Egyptian sky. For the anguish of Isis the boat of a million years stood still, and slowly from it to earth descended the ibis-headed scribe of the gods, whose name was Thoth.

There are many reasons why the black-and-white ibis was sacred to the inhabitants of ancient Egypt. This bird, which has vanished from the land as have the stories of Isis, Horus, and Osiris, was a tall, slender bird with a long downward-curving bill that waded in the ponds and marshes of the delta. In most ancient times hordes of flying serpents used to swarm into Egypt through a narrow gorge from Arabia just east of the city of Buto. Every spring the ibises would collect and fly up to this gorge, repel the invasion, and devour the serpents. As late as 450 B.C., if one accepts the word of Herodotus, a heap of serpents' bones could still be seen at the entrance to the gorge between two steep mountains. Thoth, who wore the ibis' head, kept the records of the gods. As he listened to Isis's sobbing account, he began to search his memory, for his knowledge was encyclopedic.

Slowly and patiently he repeated to Isis the very secret words that up until then only he had known. Intent on saving her child, the goddess controlled her sobs and memorized the sacred ritual. As she uttered the incantations, the wound on Horus' body opened and the poison oozed out. In a few seconds he caught his breath with a shudder. A gasp of amazement broke from the rapt onlookers. "Horus lives! He lives!" Another name, Mistress of Magic, was added to the many titles of Isis. Slowly and with great dignity the learned Thoth mounted up to heaven and resumed his travels in the Boat of a Million Years. Isis did not forget to transmit these magic words to her temple priests so that from that time onward no little child in Egypt ever had to die from the sting of a scorpion.

By the time Horus approached manhood, Seth had heard of his birth although he either did not believe or did not want to believe that this boy was the son of King Osiris. Certain of his friends, however, did understand that the young boy Isis was raising with such devotion and secrecy somewhere in the delta would one day vanquish the fiery Seth, and rule the Nile so well that the dangers of his flaming red droughts would forever vanish from the land. As Horus continued to grow tall like his father, strong in arm and limb, and skilled in the weapons of war, certain of Seth's accomplices began to desert him and flock to the growing army of Horus. Even a pretty young concubine from the camp of Seth, intrigued no doubt by stories of the shining skin and handsome eyes of the new leader, decided to join him. As she approached his camp, she was pursued by a huge snake. To the increasing renown of Horus and his soldiers, it must be said that far from fearing any such monster, they rushed out and chopped it into pieces. A survival of this encounter remained for centuries in Egypt; a cord was thrown to the ground at the opening of an assembly and then cut up in pieces by the participants.

After her joyful return from Syria, Isis had very carefully hidden the chest containing the body of Osiris so that only she and Nepthys knew where it had been put. The wicked Seth, although he did not believe in the resurrection of the king, was still very anxious to find the chest and the body. During the daylight hours he never ventured in the delta because of Isis' vigilance, but at night he roamed through its trails under the pretense of hunting. When the moon was full, he peered into every cave and hiding place. In this way he finally discovered the chest one night when the goddesses were absent. Drawing his sharp hunting knife, he dragged out the body of Osiris and cut it up into fourteen pieces, throwing each one into the Nile as soon as he had severed it.

Toward morning Isis returned and found the chest empty. In this last and most appalling calamity that befell her on earth the goddess was not alone, for now she had a full-grown son who had been born with the sharp eyes of a hawk and whose role was to be that of the avenger. Although he was not aware of it, the tyrannous rule of the redheaded Seth was soon to draw to a close. Isis swiftly made herself a light boat of papyrus reeds and, leaping into it, started to find the fourteen pieces of the great king's body. As she found each piece, she carried it to her son Horus.

The fierce, man-eating crocodiles of the Nile never touched the goddess or those parts of the king's body she was so tenderly gathering, but allowed her to pass unharmed in her frail craft. Nor did they ever afterward molest any native so long as he remained in a papyrus boat. For this kindness the inhabitants of Egypt even as far south as Thebes venerated the crocodile. In their temples they raised a baby animal and taught him to be tame. They made him earrings of molten stone and sand, put golden bracelets on his forefeet, and when he died embalmed him with the greatest expense and ceremony. This reptile had already earned a reputation for great sagacity even before its charity to Isis, since the female laid her eggs at exactly that place to which the Nile in its flood would rise. The ancients also associated it with their astronomical calculations, for they had observed that the crocodile always laid sixty eggs, which took sixty days to hatch, and that the oldest of their race lived to the age of sixty years.

One by one Isis gathered together the pieces of the body of her lord and carried them to the holy city of Abydos. Horus and Nepthys stood waiting. Because he was a god who had very special and secret knowledge of both black and white magic, Horus assembled together the parts of his father's body. Slowly and tediously he joined bone to bone and flesh to flesh until there appeared before him the very likeness of the great Osiris. After the jawbone had been skillfully placed in the head and the head joined to the trunk of the body, the great king appeared almost ready to receive from his beloved son the breath of life. However, one piece of the body had still not been recovered, the phallus. At the very end of her search Isis learned that it alone of all of the king's body could never be found. It had been eaten by three fishes of the Nile basin, the Lepidotus, the Phagrus, and the Oxyrynchus (*Mormyrus oxyrhynchus,* a species often mummified and used in sculptured decorations). Because of this Isis was obliged to construct models of the genital organs, which were carried by priestesses in all their ensuing ceremonies. In the fourteen days of the waning of the moon the mutilated body was recovered and made whole again. Wherever Isis found a piece of Osiris' body, she caused a magnificent temple to be built to this god, which explains why there were so many of them throughout the land of the Nile. Of these great edifices the principal one was at Abydos itself, where the wealthy and distinguished of Egypt all built their tombs during the earliest dynasties. The inhabitants of Memphis, opposite which the great pyramids were later built, used to assert that their temple contained the body of the king, but they were mistaken.

Having first like a dutiful son cared for the body of his father, Horus then set out in search of Seth. Not only Isis and Nepthys, but Thoth himself was a witness to this monumental struggle. Sharper than the hawk and swifter in his course, the furious Horus pounced down upon the mottled Seth and with his first burst of strength threw him high up in the air, shrieking vengeance on the brother who had twice attacked the person of Osiris, who had usurped the throne, and who had caused the heat and drought to flame far over once fertile valleys and lush crops. As Seth fell to the ground, Horus, black and terrible in his wrath, swooped down upon him again and sent him spinning and reeling over the cliffs of the western hills. For three days and three nights the battle raged. It was observed by Thoth, who had come down from the heavens on purpose to judge it, and fortunate it was that he did so, for his help was soon most urgently required. At the end of the third night the youthful Horus succeeded in mastering Seth. Holding him firmly about the middle of his body, Horus delivered him to his mother Isis. Hurling Seth's ugly red head to the ground, he stood with his foot on it. Triumphantly he bound tight chains around Seth and committed him to his mother's keeping. Then Horus set out to pursue the remnants of Seth's infernal legions.

As soon as Horus had hastened away on his errand, Seth began to wheedle Isis into liberating him. He used strong arguments, reminding her that his warmth was necessary to Egypt. He painted dark pictures for her of the ruin and famine that would befall that fertile land if the Nile waters remained cold. At first Isis turned away from his pleadings. Then he called on her womanly tenderness, showing her the wounds and bruises Horus had inflicted upon him. Finally he appealed to her sisterly love, saying that after all he was her brother and the brother of Osiris, that it was not seemly for one so close in ties of blood to be kept in a dark prison

in chains. At last the goddess felt pity in her heart and released him.

So terrible was the anger of Horus, when upon his return
he found that Seth had been released, that he cut off with
one stroke the crown and queenly head of Isis. It was then
that Thoth asserted his presence of mind and vast store of
learning. Before the goddess could even become aware of
what had happened, he replaced her head and crown with
that of Hathor, the more ancient deity of the female princi-
ple. Thus Isis wore ever afterward the ears and horns of the
cow and appeared in the likenesses of the seven fates, who
supervised childbirth personally.

In the second and even more fierce struggle that followed,
Isis joined her son in a relentless pursuit of Seth. In spite of
her efforts to help Horus, however, Seth managed to catch
him off guard and, reaching upward, tore out his eye, that
part of the body which contained his soul. Then Isis and
Horus renewed their attack, and Horus was able finally to
wrest his eye from Seth's hand. With a final burst of fury
they vanquished Seth and pursued him all the way down the
Red Sea until he disappeared from the land forever. Then
Horus, in ceremonial dress, wearing the feathered headdress
of the hawk, shining and streaming over his shoulders, advanced into the temple of Abydos where he had left the
body of his father. Reverently he approached Osiris and embraced him, thus transferring to that god some of the power
of his double spirit, or ka. In his right hand Horus bore the
eye he had snatched from Seth. Osiris sat on a splendid
throne, bearing the flail and the scepter of royalty. Gently
opening the lips of Osiris, Horus fed him the eye, and Osiris
arose from the dead and lived again! The strength of the eye
flowed through his limbs, and he was a ka-in-harmony.

Then Horus prepared a ladder of many rungs, lacing it well
with leather thongs. Slowly Osiris proceeded from the
temple of Abydos to the gateway of heaven. Wearing wings
and splendid robes, Isis and Nepthys accompanied him on
either side, followed by Thoth, who carried the book of the
gods. Osiris ascended the ladder with the help of Horus,
who pushed him with the tip of one finger. As he arose
higher and higher up the ladder, there came into view on the
eastern brow of the world the lofty mountain of the sunrise,
while on the western side stood the pillared mountain of the
sunset. As the god Osiris ascended, the ladder grew in height
also. Already Osiris could feel the fresh breezes from the four
corners of the earth stir the ostrich feathers in his crown.
The light from the Boat of a Million Years shone radiantly

around him. Then he stepped upon the gleaming crystal floor of heaven itself, which rested on the two mountain peaks.

Even as Osiris was ascending the ladder, there was a great convention of the gods at Heliopolis, where Thoth appeared as an advocate. By the time Osiris had finished mounting into heaven all the evil accusations of Seth were dismissed, Osiris' life was adjudged to have been pure, and Horus was declared his son and heir on earth.

As Osiris advanced over the crystal floor of heaven, the Boat of a Million Years came to a slow halt. Its crew of gods hailed him as the Lord of a Million Years. For ever afterward Osiris ruled the earth, crossing it every day in his solar boat and at night crossing the Milky Way of stars, the Heavenly Nile. His especial realm was that of the dead. Every Egyptian had to pass before him and answer affirmatively to the forty-two commandments in the Book of the Dead. Then his heart was weighed against an ostrich feather, and if it was truly light and free from sin, he could proceed to the Lake of Reeds and the Isles of the Blessed.

Remaining on earth until his time should come to pass before Osiris, the merciful judge of the dead, Horus ruled Egypt and had four sons who lived pure lives in truth and harmony or Maat. Every succeeding Pharaoh of Egypt saw Horus in the graceful flight of the hawks in the southern land and longed for his sed festival when he too would become a Horus. In this ancient land the man who was so unfortunate as to kill a hawk had to submit to the penalty of death. For out of the land of the hawk came the greatest Pharaohs of Egypt: Menes,[5] who first united the land and wore the red and white crowns of Upper and Lower Egypt; Thutmose, who in the great battles of Armageddon and Carchemish conquered the world; and the gentle Akhenaten, whose concept of a universal god stretching out his hand to all of mankind alike, regardless of color or race, was such a failure in Egypt.

[5] Called Men by Herodotus, in 3100 B.C.(?) he founded the city of Memphis.

3

Crete and Greece

The House of Crete

King Minos II

Theseus and the Minotaur

INTRODUCTION

IN THE FOLLOWING three episodes I have attempted to show
by the choice of these interconnected legends—chosen from
the thousands of stories of the Greeks—how the mainland of
Europe was influenced by the older civilization of Crete,
which was in turn deeply affected by Egypt and Phoenicia.
As the stories tell, Crete finally fell to Achaean conquerors,
to the rising cities of Mycenae, Pylos, and Tiryns.

Modern historians, who keep pushing backward into B.C.
times the dates for all these ancient civilizations, now say
that the Minoan thalassocracy in Crete passed through three
periods: (1) 3000–2200 B.C., (2) 2200–1600 B.C., and (3)
1600–1200 B.C. They tell us that Crete was at its peak under
a King Minos in this second or middle period, and also that
Knossos was burned at this time. By 1450 B.C., they say,
Crete had relinquished its supremacy to early Greek tribes.

The interesting point is that these legends about Crete,
once assembled in what would appear to be a chronological
order, bear out the archaeological findings of the twentieth
century in Crete. These stories, which so many Greek and
Roman writers never tired of telling, are more or less true,
and interesting because they reveal history from two points
of view, the Cretan and the Greek. In our own century Sir
Arthur Evans excavated Knossos, found the palace of Minos,
his throne, his theaters, and part of his moldering treasure.
We may turn with renewed admiration to the words of the
poets, particularly to the charming Ovid whose pages were
thumbed so carefully and remembered so well by Shakespeare.

41

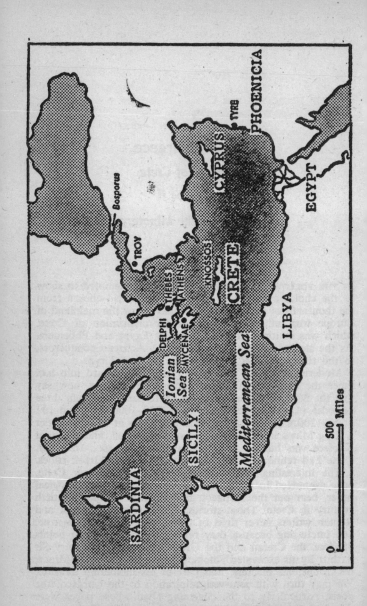

CRETE (3500 B. C.–1450 B. C.)

How unfortunate for us all that Shakespeare did not decide to tell us more of the following stories himself!

THE HOUSE OF CRETE

IN THE BEGINNING was Chaos created, formless and black and vast. Next was fashioned the broad-bosomed Earth, Gaea, upon whose fertile valleys and snowy mountain peaks the deathless gods of Greece have found their dwelling place. Third was created Love, the most beautiful and best-known of all the timeless gods, who alone causes the knees to tremble, the heart to falter, and the wisest plans to be forgotten. Earth bore Uranus, wide and starlit, as a covering mantle for herself, and ever since the sky has veiled her nakedness with floating cloud and wisps of fog. From a union of Earth and Sky were born the twelve Titans; the Cyclops, who had only one eye in the middle of their foreheads; and three monstrous giants, each with a hundred conquering arms and fifty heads. Uranus, recoiling in horror before his unruly progeny, imprisoned them swiftly in the very depths of the earth. Gaea lamented their fate and mourned them with floods of tears.

Then when Uranus refused to release them, especially the Titans, her six sons and daughters, whom she deeply loved, Gaea turned from sulking to a dark scheme of revenge. Beginning with Oceanus because he was the first-born, she asked each one of the Titans to help her tame Uranus, but they were too frightened or too appalled to dare lift up their hands against their sire. Only the last-born of her sons, the crafty Cronus, volunteered. When it grew dark and still, Uranus returned to the bed of Gaea, stretched out his enormous limbs, and fell fast asleep. Cautiously the ambitious Cronus crept from his hiding place and stole forward stealthily, bearing in his outstretched hand the metal sickle that his mother had shaped for him. With a lunge he slashed at the body of Uranus, rendering him incapable of further creation. From the drops of crimson blood sprang the Furies, who throughout all time punish the guilty, pursue them shrieking, and harass them relentlessly. Out of the mutilated pieces that drifted in foam across the summer sea arose, all bathed in sunlight and silver foam, the goddess Aphrodite at Cyprus.[1]

Having thus disposed of his father, Cronus proceeded to free his brother Titans, from whom he continued the creation of the divinities, assigning to each one his especial

[1] Based on Hesiod's *Theogony*.

43

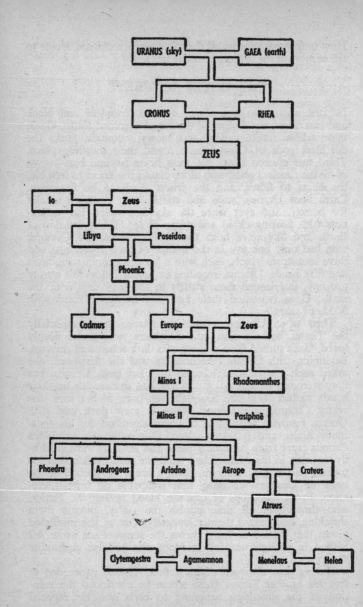

HEROES OF CRETE AND GREECE

domain or province. Cronus knew all this time, however, that the curse of his parent had fallen upon him, for, cautious as he was to veil his face and brandish the sickle, he was doomed forever after. The only way he could escape this punishment would be to remain childless himself. Inevitably, however, he fell into the warm embrace of nature in the person of the great goddess Rhea. Carefully Cronus watched her, and as she was delivered of her children he snatched each one out of her arms and devoured it. Back into the darkness of their father dropped his three daughters, Demeter, Hera, and Hestia, and two sons, Hades and Poseidon. Rhea, the divinity of nature, longed in vain to clasp her children in her arms. In her sorrow and despair, feeling inside her womb the stirring of a new life, she fled to her parents to ask if there were not some way in which she could thwart the evil fears of Cronus and rear a child. After a long reflection Uranus and Gaea hit upon a plan.

As in a dream of beauty Gaea recalled that set like an emerald gem in a sea of blue that is darker than a sapphire, south of the shores of Greece and north of the Nile delta, lay an island fastness. From its little coves and gleaming sandy beaches the hills rise through terraces of oak and olive to snow-covered mountain peaks. What a perfect spot in which to bear a child! When the time drew near for the birth of her son, Rhea, remembering her parent's advice, fled far over the sea to the island of Crete. There in a mountain cave she gave birth to her sixth child, the god Zeus. Behind the entrance to the grotto extended a long chamber, and behind that another one running deep into the mountain among huge stalagmites that stood beside the silent waters of a subterranean lake. Before this hiding place the mountain terraces stretched broad and sloping to the safe interior of the island. Each side of the entrance was guarded by double-edged axes. In such a refuge the newborn child was safe.

Then Rhea returned home to her suspicious husband, and pretending to be delivered of a child, she picked up a huge stone. Wrapping it carefully in the swaddling garments of an infant, she tearfully handed it to Cronus. Unsuspectingly he gulped it down. Thus no search was made for Zeus, and he grew up peacefully in the sunny olive groves of the Cretan mountains.

The king of Crete assigned the care of the baby to two nymphs, Ida and Adrastea. Watchful and gentle, these two maidens bathed the child and fed him milk from a long-haired mountain goat, Amalthea. Placing him in a golden cradle, they dispatched wild pigeons far and wide to bring him honey. Even the lonely eagle from the high crags of

Mount Dicte brought him nectar from the lavender mountain crocus. His nurses made him toys of gold and wreaths of laurel for his head. Around his cradle danced the lithe young warriors of Crete, filing up the mountainsides with their huge shields, singing war songs of courage and defiance, leaping and stamping on the ground in martial unison whenever the baby cried, so that the sound would not reach his ravenous father, Cronus. As the boy Zeus grew older, the young men encouraged him to train with them, to leap and dance, to shoot and hunt, to run tirelessly across the mountain terraces in pursuit of horned goats, and to swim in the warm waters of the clear sea. After Zeus had learned to drive his thundering chariot over the peaks as fast as the eagle and to catch the thunderbolts in his bare hands and hurl them unerringly into the valleys, he dressed himself in the gray fleece of a mountain goat and went to Greece to settle accounts with Cronus.

Aided by the counsels of his crafty grandmother, Zeus forced Cronus to vomit up the five children he had swallowed and also the stone he had mistaken for his last son. Snatching the stone away, Zeus bore it to the high slopes of Parnassus in Greece, where he placed it at the shrine of an oracle. There at Delphi he appointed a priestess, the Pythoness, who sat thenceforth upon a three-legged stool over a steep chasm. Above this gorge rose the Phaedriades, two enormous rocks, that towered to a height of 300 meters and made its approach from the north impossible. Out of this cleft in the earth rolled magic vapors which caused convulsions in those animals or men who dared approach them. From her intoxication the Pythoness at Delphi, chewing incessantly on bay leaves, pronounced the oracular prophecies that rivaled those of Apis, the sacred bull of Memphis, or even those of Zeus Ammon in the Libyan oasis. Thus Zeus was the instrument through whom the ancient curse on Cronus was accomplished. Plunged into the wide-eyed slumber of eternity, Cronus was banished to the far-distant end of the earth, where even now he nods immortally.

Zeus reigned far and wide over land and sea, gathering clouds about him on lofty Olympus, punishing, judging, and receiving homage from gods and men alike. In one of his prolonged travels he wandered far into the western confines of the earth, where in a garden of delight he met the goddess Hera, she of the gentle brown eyes and golden robes. They were married immediately, for it was a case of love at first sight. In honor of their wedding the tree of life was hung with golden apples in the far garden of the Hesperides where first they met.

In spite of her blooming cheeks, in spite even of the children she bore Zeus, it was not a peaceful marriage. Zeus, so strong he could not be budged by the combined forces of all the gods together, greatly feared the jealous rages of Hera when she flew across the earth in her golden chariot, searching for him when he was too long absent. She could excuse his several previous marriages and such children as the nine Muses and the four Seasons that were born to him. What she could not condone was that in time the faithless Zeus began to woo not only nymphs of purely divine birth but also to have affairs with mortal women such as Danaë, whose son was the great hero Perseus.

One sunny day the roving eye of Zeus was caught and charmed by a beautiful maiden named Io, the granddaughter of Oceanus.[2] As Zeus strolled up to her through the green fields along a little river, something warned him that Hera was spying on him. Quickly he changed the maiden into a silky white heifer and shrouded them both with a thick gray cloud. This stratagem only aroused deeper suspicion in his jealous wife. Regal in a golden robe and dazzling in her beauty, Hera suddenly appeared before her nervous husband. Brushing indignantly through the cloud that he had hung over the riverbanks, she strolled up to him, her dangling earrings swinging provocatively against her rosy cheeks. "What a lovely little heifer you have here," she remarked languidly. "I wonder where she came from. I don't recall seeing her in any of the herds around here. Does she belong to anyone in particular?"

"Why no, dear love of my life," Zeus answered, trying very hard to be casual. "I believe she was just born, . . . ah . . . I think she is a new creation, as a matter of fact."

Maliciously the goddess Hera pursued her advantage. "Will you give her to me as a present then, dear husband?"

"My dear lady," stammered Zeus, "I am sure I could not offer you so meager a gift as this animal. Ask me for a cloak of stars. This would really be more appropriate. Perhaps you would like our son Hephaestus to make you a golden throne, down in his workshop under the sea. This would indeed be a present worthy of your golden beauty." With art and cajolement Zeus did his best to turn Hera's thoughts away from the gentle Io, for the god had no intention at all of letting her escape from him. No matter how skillfully he pleaded, Hera, more and more suspicious, would not be diverted.

"Do you mean you refuse to give me this creature?" she finally asked.

[2] Based on Hesiod's *Theogony*.

47

Since he could think of no alternative right at that moment, Zeus had to consent. Reluctantly he handed Io over to his wife. As soon as he had departed, she called Argus and instructed him to watch night and day over the heifer. Now Argus was the perfect watchman, for he had a hundred eyes. While any two of them slept, all the others stayed wide open and vigilant. It was therefore no trouble at all for him to keep ninety-eight sharp eyes on Io, who was still in the shape of a silky young cow. As long as it was daylight, Argus allowed her to roam through the pastures, but every evening he tied her to a tree, and even so he sat nearby. From a distance Zeus watched the disconsolate Io wander up and down along the riverbank. Finally Zeus decided to send the clever Hermes down, for surely he of all gods could outwit Argus.

In the meantime Io herself had at least discovered a way to let her family know what had happened to her. Without letting Argus see what she was doing, she managed to slip closer and closer to the river's edge. Then with one hoof, for the poor girl had no voice with which to call for help, nor any arms to wave with, she managed to trace the letters *I* and *O* on the sand beside the water. Very soon indeed her father, the river god, flowing past toward the sea, saw the letters and realized what had happened. Much as he longed to save her, however, there was nothing he could do.

Then to the delight of Argus the god Hermes appeared in the simple dress of a goatherd, a skin thrown over his shoulder and his pipes in his mouth. After he had prudently called Io away from the river's edge, Argus sat down under a gnarled olive tree and prepared to listen to the concert of Hermes. It was lovely music, indeed, that the god played for him, songs of the birth of Zeus in the hidden groves of Crete and a long tune in praise of country life among pretty white sheep that go jumping over a wall, one at a time, two at a time, three at a time, four at a time. . . . Hermes played more and more softly. Argus began to close his eyes. . . . Hermes played ever so gently, but after a long time he grew sleepy himself. Argus still sat there leaning on the tree and watching with only a few eyes open.

His vigilance presented a real problem, and Hermes was not ready yet to admit defeat. "How would you like me to tell you a story, dear Argus?" he asked.

It is true that by this time the stars were out, and cool breezes were blowing angrily down the river where Io's father rolled and worried in his pebbly bed. Even so, Argus was more than willing to hear a story. Wrapping his goatskin closely around his shoulder, he assured himself that the

48

heifer was securely tied and then settled back contentedly. It was not every evening that a glib stranger offered to entertain an ugly giant like him. Dropping his pipes and waving in their place a magic wand of sleep, Hermes began his tale.

"Once upon a time . . . Are you comfortable, Argus?"

"Oh, yes, very much, thank you, shepherd."

"Once upon a time there was a pretty little nymph whose name I can't quite recall," began Hermes. "Anyway, she was a pretty little thing very much cherished by certain satyrs and queer folk of the forests and streams. She followed in the train of the chaste Artemis, running through the woods with her spotted fawns, playing in the moonlight, and perfectly pure. Then one day the great god Pan came leaping through a forest glade and saw her. Well, you know how amorous Pan becomes. He just fell head over hoofs in love with her. He followed her around, and insinuated he had even mistaken her for that beam of moonlight, the goddess Artemis herself. When he became a little bolder in his advances, the shy nymph shook her curls and ran away from him.

"Pan followed her down the forest paths, calling her sweet names, and trying in every way to woo her. He didn't catch up with her until she had arrived at the banks of a little stream. There she stood leaning far out over the water and calling tearfully to her sisters, the nymphs of the stream. Just as Pan reached out to catch her by the waist, her sisters answered her pleas for help. In a twinkling they had pulled her down to the safety of the river bed.

"Poor Pan found he was clutching in his hands a clump of reeds. In his surprise, and panting from his hot pursuit, he gasped, 'Oooh!' He was so delighted with the musical sounds that came from the reeds that he forgot all about the wretched nymph and began to cut them properly and blow through them again. 'Well, I shall possess your sweetness in one way or another,' he panted. Then he blew a little tune and began to dance. . . . Are you listening, Argus?" Hermes questioned. There against the oak tree lay the giant, sound asleep, with all of his hundred eyes closed at once.

Quickly Hermes drew his knife and killed the giant. Then he rushed over to Io, who stood trembling with fright at the sight of so much blood, and set her free. Next morning, when Hera discovered Argus slain and the heifer gone, she was very angry. Before starting out in pursuit, however, she salvaged the glistening eyes of her faithful Argus and set them all fancifully in the tail of her favorite bird, the peacock, where they may be seen even today.

Even as Io was standing by the water's edge wondering which way to turn, the goddess Hera found her. Immediately she conjured up before the terrified eyes of the maiden a Fury so dreadful, so monstrous to behold that the poor Io, driven mad by the sight, plunged wildly into the sea. Further maddened and tortured by ceaseless bitings and stingings that Hera was causing within her breast as if a million hornets were stinging her to death, she sought refuge in the cool waters of the western sea—which ever since has borne her name, Ionian. No matter where she turned or how furiously she swam, however, the terrible bloody image remained before her eyes, appearing and reappearing just ahead of her. Pitiful and alone, she returned eastward, fighting her way at times through heavy waves up into the sea of Thrace. At length she crossed the Bosporus and began her weary, tormented way southward along the coast line of Asia Minor, past the great cities of Troy, of Byblos and Tyre until she reached the reed bank of the Nile delta. It was that great river that received her, a wanderer over the face of the earth.

Feebly the white heifer struggled with her forefeet to find a firm footing along the slippery banks of the Nile. Raising herself finally upon a grassy plot, she threw back her head, fell to her knees, and gazed up mournfully at the face of heaven. With gentle lowing and with hot tears of anguish, she implored the divinities of high heaven to put an end to her torments.

In the meantime Hera had rejoiced in the sufferings and madness of Io, and had kept a close watch on Zeus so that he dared in no way to alleviate them. When he saw that the maiden had managed to cross the seas and find a willing haven in the black earth of Egypt, he persuaded the vindictive Hera to withdraw her spells. It was, of course, not without difficulty that she consented. Zeus was obliged to promise, to swear even by the black waters of the River Styx, that he would never again woo Io in any way whatsoever. Once the goddess was reassured of this, a transformation occurred in her pitiful victim.

At first Io could not believe her eyes. Suddenly the white hairs that were over her body began to disappear miraculously. Quickly she lifted her hand to her head and found that her horns were growing smaller and soon disappeared. Her eyes returned to their former size and shape. Last of all, the hoofs of the cow were metamorphosed into little toes with pretty pink nails. The only semblance of the heifer which remained in her was its milk-white skin and brown eyes. Very gradually Io tried to stand on her two legs instead of four. For a long time she remained so, standing motionless but erect among the fronded papyrus stems. Most of all she longed to hear her own human voice, but she was afraid to try to speak for fear the goddess Hera had reserved the heifer's lowing as a last punishment for the beauty that had attracted Zeus himself. Eventually Io tried to speak. How happy she was to discover that she could say words just as before! As Io made her way into Memphis, the holy city of Lower Egypt, the inhabitants had no trouble in recognizing her as a manifestation of the beloved Isis, who had worn the horns of Hathor on her head. Io still had other sufferings to undergo, but she was comforted for them all by the love of the Egyptians, by her marriage to the Pharaoh himself, and by her own son, who was later venerated in Memphis as Apis, the sacred bull.

It is not to be supposed, however, that compunction for the trouble he had caused could long deter Zeus from other amorous adventures when an apt occasion arose. One day as he observed the coast of Syria from the heights of Parnassus, his roving eye happened to rest on an exceptionally beautiful blonde. Immediately Zeus moved closer for a better view. He was watching a small island about half a mile off the coast of Phoenicia, which was surrounded by massive walls from which jetties and moles projected into the sea. It was the busy harbor and virtually impregnable fortress of Tyre, a great commercial rival of Sidon and Byblos. It was inhabited by black-bearded Phoenicians, whose robes of many colors were so distasteful to the ancient Egyptians, who wore simple gowns of white linen. The merchants of Tyre had prospered and become wealthy from the sale of linen and woolen materials, which they knew how to dye a brilliant shade of cerise or crimson called "purple" by the ancients. This precious dye was manufactured from a secretion exuded near the head of a little shellfish native to their waters (*Murex brandaris*). When this liquid was spread over wool or linen in the presence of sunlight, it dyed the fabric permanently and became the "royal purple" of the ancient world, to the wearing of which one had to be born.

Determined this time to lay his plans well in advance so as not to be frustrated again by Hera, Zeus asked Aphrodite to prepare the blonde maiden, whose name was Europa, for the great love affair that was to ensue.[3] To this fair princess of Tyre the goddess of love sent a dream during the night as Europa slept soundly on her couch in the royal palace. Just before the rosy-fingered Dawn was ready to mount the eastern skies, Europa dreamed that her homeland

[3] The following account based on Idyl II of Moschus.

51

and beloved Asia were engaged in a terrible war. The whole of her land, the East, rose up wrathful in battle with neighing horses and flashing swords against the whole world of the opposite shores, the West. In her dream she seemed to feel that all of mankind was divided into these two raging camps, the East and the West, which glared at each other through the steady eyes of an old hatred, and then rushed forth to slaughter and utterly destroy the other.

Out of the dust and turmoil of the conflict Europa seemed to see two magnificent women, enemies of old, who faced each other in shining armor and panoply of war. One of them was an Asian woman—or it may have been the mother of Europa, since she hovered about the little princess and sheltered her with naked arms and shield. It was the Western woman, however, who beckoned imperiously to the unresisting maiden. This second person called her loudly with words like, "Come! Hasten to me, Europa!" Out of the fantastic vision her voice came down the wings of the winds and shrieked about the young girl's ears, "Euro . . . pa! Come! Eu . . . ro . . . pa!" Silently and with hesitant feet the princess moved across the spaces of land and sea at this imperious command. "By all the powers above, and by those Fates, daughters of black night, who spin and cut the threads of human lives, you are mine, Europa! The aegis-bearing Zeus has ordained it!"

The sound of her own sharply intaken breath of wonder and surprise awoke the princess from her dream. Shivering, her scalp prickling with little needles of excitement, Europa gazed about the massive walls of her chamber. Quickly she rushed to the window and looked out. To her surprise the world was just the same. On one side of her sailing ships were moving along the blue waters of the port. Above the castle walls the hills and meadows of Phoenicia were gay with the green of spring. In spite of all these familiar scenes, she still could not drive the thoughts of the dream from her mind, so vivid did they seem and so significant. Recalling before her mind's eye the panorama of war and armies, and then remembering the kind face and imperious manner of that bold woman who called her away from her mother, Europa could not help thinking that this dream was a prophecy of what was surely to come true. With a feeling of inner excitement she spent longer than usual at her toilette, choosing with pleasure a beautiful new gown of Tyrian purple which only she as a princess of the royal blood could wear. She dressed her long blonde hair in ringlets and wound the curls over her ears into a coronet

52

at the top of her head. Then when she had recited her morning prayer to Ishtar, she asked the goddess to be watchful over her that day and especially to see that no harm came from the weird, prophetic dream.

When Europa was finally arrayed in her prettiest gown, she summoned her girl friends about her and proposed an outing. With this group of noble young girls she usually spent her days, either in wading along the shores of the sea, in leading dances in the palace rooms or even in the meadows, or in wandering through the hills near her home to gather lilies among the grasses. This morning they set out gaily, walked across the palace lawns and gardens, and climbed the slopes of the hills that slanted gently down toward the sea. Laughing and chatting, they strolled along, each one carrying a May basket on her arm. Every now and then they stopped to catch their breath and listen to the distant sound of the breakers rolling in to the shore and sending little curling fingers of foam to search the black rocks along the beach.

Europa carried a golden basket, an heirloom in her family. It had been made by Hephaestus, the cunning metalworker of the gods. He himself had presented it to Libya on the day of her wedding to Poseidon, whose trident was still revered along the shores of Africa and even among the dwellers of the Nile delta. Libya had bequeathed the beautiful basket to her daughter Telephassa and so to the grandchild Europa. Among the magnificent works of Hephaestus were the dreadful aegis of Zeus, the winged chariot of Helios, the mansions of the gods on Olympus with their massive bronze doors, and the arrows of Hermes and Artemis. It was a basket well worth description, so dazzling was it to the sight, and so artfully fashioned of pure gold.

Against a background of waves Hephaestus had represented the bewildered Io before her transformation into human shape, standing lowing and pawing at the breakers. Two men stood nearby watching to see if the heifer would leap into the water. On the beach stood Zeus himself leaning toward Io and stroking her flanks with his hand, in true loverlike fashion. On the other side of the basket Io was represented in her human loveliness just as she was after her arrival in Egypt. In the background, rolled all in silver, were the seven mouths of the Nile and Zeus represented in gold. On another side stood Hermes piping his sleepy song to the giant Argus, who dozed at his feet. The rest of this wonderful jewel represented the spreading tail of the peacock, bellying out like a sail before the wind and dazzlingly

53

studded with the hundred eyes of Argus. It was in this basket that Europa planned to gather flowers on the May morning after her dream.

The hills of Phoenicia slope gently down toward the island of Tyre. In the spring their pine trees stand dark and fragrant against a pure blue sky. During April and May the hills are a riot of bloom. Europa and her friends had blossoms to choose from of many colors and varieties. There were purple hyacinths and white narcissuses, golden crocuses that thrust their slender cups up from the dark earth, blue violets, and wild lilies. While her friends filled their baskets with flowers of all kinds, Europa chose only the rose, the pride of all the plants of the earth,[4] burying her face in its strange spicy fragrance. Europa was beautiful. Even among her pretty friends she was truly beautiful in her flowing cerise robe with her yellow curls and her golden basket full of roses. It was as if you were to see Aphrodite herself standing in all her radiance among the Graces and outshining them all.

This is the way she looked when Zeus saw her. He was overcome with emotion, for the arrows of the sly imp of Love can pierce the hearts of gods as well as those of men. In a daze he circled around her, numb with joy at the thought of so perfect a beauty. He remembered, however, to divest himself of his immortality so as not to frighten or burn her. He also remembered to disguise himself so well that Hera could never find him. Hastily he transformed himself into a magnificent golden bull that wore in the center of its forehead a star of silver. His horns were slightly curved and thin, like the horned edges of the new moon. His eyes were large and blue, gentle with admiration and sparkling with the thrill and excitement of love.

Although his transformation was swift, he allowed himself to become visible to them gradually so that the virgin maidens of Tyre thought he had been there all the time. With the natural love of the young for animals and their envy of them, the girls ran up to him exclaiming in pleasure and delight. Gently they stroked his satin sides and velvet coat. His breath was like honey or the fragrance of roses; like the smell of summer blowing down green pastures to the sea. With the tips of her fingers Europa touched his lips. It seemed to her that the bull was actually kissing her fingers and nuzzling the palm of her hand. Without any fear whatsoever, she caressed his neck, which was so sleek and soft. Only she could hear the soft noises he was making low in his throat.

As she stood patting him, the bull knelt at her feet and motioned with his head toward his back. Then he looked

4 From Sappho's "Ode on a Rose."

up at Europa questioningly. With a laugh she turned to her friends and said, "Look, dear girls, look at this beast. What do you think he wants us to do? Do you see how he has knelt down before us? Come. Let's take a ride on his back. I am sure he is a gentle creature. Just see his soft eyes. Let's have him give us a ride all around the meadows. You know, if he had a human voice, I would think he was a prince!"

Then the princess, light as a feather, lifted herself up until she was seated on the bull's broad back, her two legs dangling down his left side. As she leaned forward to rest her cheek against his neck, the bull suddenly sprang triumphantly to his feet and with no warning dashed off across the meadow terrace and down the slopes. Europa had hardly time to wave to her friends before she was being carried swiftly across the grass. In vain she tried to turn to call for help. The bull was running too swiftly for her to think of leaping to the ground. When she realized that the beast was heading straight for the seashore, she was certain that she would be drowned in the waves.

But when the bull came to the sea, far from drowning Europa, he glided over the crests of the foamy waves like a swallow. There was really nothing at all to fear. Europa began to like the salt wind on her face and the exhilaration of speed. She saw to her delight that they were no longer unaccompanied. On either side of her, leaping porpoises shot up into the air and dived back under the water only to rise again a few feet farther on. On their backs were the fifty Nereids from the caverns of the sea, riding gaily along beside the princess, only less royally mounted than she. Then, as the southern shore of Cyprus flew by on her right side, she saw to her amazement Poseidon himself with his trident, speeding merrily along before them and leading the way across the depths. Europa began to feel that this was as gay as a wedding day, that these were her bridal attendants. She even heard music and turned in delight to see that the Tritons, blowing on their pearly conch shells, had joined her escort.

Her pleasure was not unmixed, however, because she was not sure it was her wedding they were celebrating. Then too, no matter how hard she strained her eyes to look back, she could no longer see either the islands of Tyre or Cyprus or the headlands of Phoenicia. A little pang of homesickness ran through her heart. With her right hand she clung tightly to the polished horn of the golden bull, and with her left held up her robe so that its embroidered hem would not trail in the water. Before them as they almost flew forward,

55

EUROPA AND THE BULL

Poseidon was leveling out a broad, smooth path right through the sea.

Then it occurred to Europa that the bull might understand her words. Bending down, she began to talk to him. "Dear bull," she said, "where are you taking me? Who are you, wonderful bull?"

The bull answered her in a man's voice.

"Lovely princess of Tyre," he began, "enchanting maiden, do not be afraid. Take heart and be happy, for misfortune shall never touch the hem of your garment! To your eyes I now appear in the guise of a bull, but soon you shall see me as Zeus, the ruler of the heavens. On earth I shall from this day forth come always before you, my beloved, as Zeus Asterius, an earthly king. As a god I may assume any shape I desire."

Europa's heart filled with happiness at the thought that soon she would see her lover drop the guise of a beast and come before her in the royal robes of kingliness.

With a smile she heard him say, "Look far ahead of you, Europa. What do you see there in the distance?"

"I see a cloud," she answered.

"Look again, Europa. Do you not seen an emerald island rising around a lacy ruffle of foam? Those are not clouds you see, but the snow-capped mountains of my beloved Crete, a precious gem in a sapphire sea. For there I was born, hidden by my mother in a cavern deep in the sides of Mount Dicte. Across the steep escarpments of Ida I raced as a boy with the Curetes, warriors of Crete. In my palace at Gortyna shall our marriage be solemnized with all the wreaths and pageants of regal splendor. There shall the high-born maidens lead you, Europa, into my loving arms. Take courage, sweet princess of Asia. This *is* your wedding day. From you shall spring my sons who will rule Crete and the islands of the sea forever afterwards. From you shall rise strong men who will be celebrated in song and story until the end of time."

Phoenix, the king of Tyre, was beside himself with anger when he learned that his lovely daughter had been abducted by the king of Crete. Sternly he commanded her brother Cadmus to set sail at once and never to return to Tyre unless he brought Europa safely home with him. The unfortunate Cadmus, so cruelly exiled from his native land, wandered over the whole world without ever daring to attack the king of Crete. Finally he consulted the oracle at Delphi, who instructed him to found a city, the Boeotian city which he named Thebes. While accomplishing this great project he accidentally killed a dragon sacred to Ares while it was guarding a spring on the slopes of Parnassus. This unfortunate deed, even though Cadmus did penance for it to Ares, brought down upon his head the curse of the formidable god of war. The baleful vengeance of Ares pursued him and his children down through the years until they had all killed each other in the generation after the ill-fated Oedipus. The men of the Tyrian nation in truth walked over Greece with accursed feet; but as Zeus had promised her, the fate of Europa was a happy one.

Three sons were born to Europa and Zeus Asterius—Minos, the oldest, who became King Minos I of Crete; Rhadamanthus; and Sarpedon. Europa was eternally honored in Crete because of her beauty and great virtue; and her name, the "Fair One," was given to the women of the west and to their descendants also. Even the lofty plane tree that witnessed her wedding in southern Crete was revered and repaid by the privilege of keeping its leaves throughout the seasons from that day onward. The Hellotia festivals were celebrated in her honor every year throughout the Mediterranean world.

The most famous of all the sons of Europa was Minos. Profiting from the advantageous situation of Crete at a midpoint between Egypt and Greece and also between Phoenicia and Sicily, he made it the junction of the world, through which later travelers from Greece to Asia Minor would pass in the war party of the friend of Crete, Menelaus, as well as where an even more famous one named Paul would stop on his way from Syria to Italy. Its snowy mountains were a welcome landmark to sailors from all ports as they tossed in the heavy seas of the Mediterranean in winter.

Minos made Crete a great commercial center whose hundred cities were known far and wide for their wealth and luxury. The islanders raised wheat and barley, made *retsina* wine from their vineyards, and spun their flax into linen, which they learned to dye a bright yellow with saffron as well as brilliant hues of red and blue. Their herds of goats and cattle grew sleek and fat on the summer grasses of the mountain slopes and followed like well-bred animals the calls of their piping herders. In every city were thriving industries, for Cretan artisans exported their goods in all directions. They were skilled cabinetmakers, and wood was plentiful. From the lilies and hyacinths that grew wild in the fields specialists distilled perfumes that sold well in every market. The bronzesmiths of Crete made armor and weapons of excellent design, particularly the handy figure-eight shields that covered a man's whole body. They knew how to cut and polish precious gems, and they made signet rings of gold, little charms of silver designed with the image of Rhea, and bars of copper for their business transactions. In every harbor the shipwrights were busy, for Crete under Minos acquired and maintained the mastery of the seas. The greatest of their ports were royal Knossos in the north and Phaestus on the southern shore, which traded principally with Egypt.

Minos attained his celebrated renown, however, for the system of laws he bestowed on his people. These ordinances were later adopted by the Greeks, according to Plato, who greatly admired them. They were so logical and so equitable, in fact, that Plato doubted whether an ordinary mortal could have written them unassisted. Popular opinion explained this by remembering that the king really received them all written out in Minoan script on a tablet which his father Zeus revealed to him in the depths of that Dictean cave where he was born. It was common knowledge that every ninth year King Minos was obliged to retire to the slopes of Mount Dicte where, entering the cave, he sacrificed to Rhea and Zeus, communed with them, and at the end of the ceremonies received a renewal of his mandate of royalty valid for nine more years. After each private discussion with Zeus he inserted new amendments into his legal system.

Although the people of Crete were great builders and their king was immensely wealthy, their cities, unlike most of the others in the ancient world, were completely unfortified. Unlike the Tyrians, who had to live within an *enceinte* of massive black walls that compressed their streets and houses into an island area of less than three square miles, Knossos and Phaestus expanded and built new palaces without fear of enemies, for they controlled the seas. In time they piped water from mountain springs right into the coastal cities through a complicated system of conduits lined with cement. The drainage troughs of Knossos and the sewage systems were unknown in any other area of the world until the time of the Romans. Roads made of stone blocks with shoulders of packed stones and pebbles permitted them to race around from city to city in their chariots.

Fashion and dress were very important in Crete, so much so that they have often been called the Parisians of antiquity. The people were not tall, but they were lithe and athletic. The men wore high linen puttees coming almost up to the knees, and a specially draped short garment or kilt. They wore their hair in long ringlets with a twisted knot at the crown of the head. The ladies of Crete were resplendent in wide ruffled skirts, dainty aprons, bolero jackets, high-heeled shoes, wasp waists, puff sleeves, and naked breasts (in honor of Rhea, the Mother Goddess). They too wore their hair in flowing ringlets. Both men and women had pinched waistlines that emphasized the hips and torso. The men wore wide belts to cinch their waists even more, so that in silhouette they closely resembled the figure-eight shield, one of their prehistoric cult symbols. Bracelets and rings were elaborate and ornate, and often decorated with a fleur-de-lis or a Greek cross.

The black pottery of Crete was one of its principal items of export. Besides pictures of the Mother Goddess, or of religious ceremonies, the artisans used many decorative motifs of the sea. Among lotus and ivy tendrils, they were expert at drawing marine creatures from life, orange coral, the murex from which they extracted the crimson dye, the octopus, and the chambered nautilus, among others. In their palace frescoes they skillfully drew dolphins and olive trees, birds, crocuses, and over and over again the lovely butterflies of the island and their chrysalises—such obvious symbols of death and regeneration. Even the divine Pharaohs of Egypt ordered vases and amphorae from Crete, such fragile objects when compared to the massive pyramids they were building as their tombs.

King Minos devised for his people a prudent and rigorous educational system.[5] The young men were divided into troops led by the father of that young man who was the natural leader and instigator of the group. Every day their parent-leader took them on long marches and exercised them at arms, particularly in the use of the bow and arrow. Since Crete was so hilly, the men preferred light armor and depended in battle upon swiftness of foot and muscular agility. From time to time mock battles between the various youth troops were staged in which heavy blows with iron weapons were borne and inflicted. The disobedient were severely punished, while the outstanding athletes were rewarded with extra portions of food and a higher percentage of wine in their drinking water at table. Meals were taken at public tables, by groups. The boys were trained from childhood to notice neither cold nor heat, to endure pain without speaking, to run long miles over mountainous country, to stand behind their fathers' chairs until invited to join any discussion, and to consider arms the most cherished of all gifts or rewards. They marched with rhythmic steps, interspersed with unison leaps and beatings on their shields, and sang shrill, military songs to the tunes of lyres and pipes.

[5] This account follows that of Strabo.

The main task of Minos was to establish Crete as the un-contested naval power of the time. In this way his thalas-socracy could protect the unfortified cities that extended around the island, all within short distances from the sea. He proceeded to rid the sea of pirates, to subjugate those neighboring lands that were to become his markets for manufactured goods, and to exact a high tribute from them in return for his naval protection. According to plan he con-quered the Cyclades and then the southern shore of Greece, forcing the people of Attica to pay him what Plato called a "cruel tribute."

The rewards of this king after death were even greater than the triumphs of his reign and the fame of his celebrated laws. Both he and his solemn brother Rhadamanthus were appointed by the gods to rule over the dead. Upon the stern, impartial seats of justice they presided as supreme arbiters over the past lives of those who stood trial before them. There was no appeal. The wicked were consigned to black Tartarus, to which certain rivers on the surface of the earth so suddenly and so mysteriously descended. The con-demned had first to pass through a grove of quaking aspens and dark cypresses down to the gates of the Underworld, which were guarded by Cerberus, a huge hound with fifty heads and a bay like the clanging of bronze. Although Cer-berus allowed the guilty to enter the portals of hell, he re-fused their subsequent exit. Then the dead had to be rowed across the black waters of the Acheron by Charon, the ugly old ferryman. The Underworld was nine times encircled by the ink-black waters of the River Styx. If Charon were not paid for their passage, the dead were condemned to wander eternally along the black shores of the rivers. Knowing this, the Greeks always put a coin in the mouth of their dead.

If, on the other hand, the verdict of the great judges Minos and Rhadamanthus was "Innocent," what a marvelous new life was available to the shades who had left the world behind them! Then they were assured an eternity of dreamless bliss, far to the west in the splendid Isles of the Blessed, the per-fumed Elysian Fields of enchantment. In this paradise there was no old age, no hot summers, no snowy winters, no withering, and never any decay. There, crowned with the sweetest flowers of meadow and wood, they reclined in lux-ury under eternally cloudless skies. Soft winds wafted to them the treble songs of birds. Fresh fruits grew just over-head for their delight. There friends and lovers were eternally young, eternally reunited, eternally at peace. On all sides stretched the silver summer sea that languidly lapped the shores of their Atlantis.

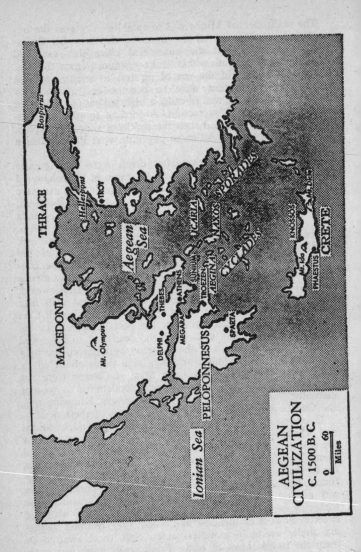

CRETAN THALASSOCRACY

DURING THE THOUSAND or so years that Minoan Crete maintained its supremacy over the Mediterranean Sea there were many kings named Minos, the most heroic of whom is the one referred to as Minos II. During his reign the palace of this king at Knossos was the object of admiration and wonder throughout the world, so much so that its memory was preserved in the words of the poets. This palace, with its maze of passages, was built for Minos by a noble Athenian architect named Daedalus.

It was quite by a strange twist of fortune that Daedalus happened to be in Crete in the first place. This famous craftsman, mechanical engineer, and sculptor had the sort of past he preferred not to have his acquaintances mention. Of course, it is very hard to conceal one's crimes when one is so skillful as to have become famous. However great an architect he was, this Daedalus apparently was only happy when he received high praise, and he had also so doubtful an opinion of his ability and talent that he could not endure competition. Inevitably this strange, brooding nature of his led him into the crime that caused his resultant exile from Athenian territory into Crete, where he had to rely on the protection of Minos.

The old scandal about Daedalus says that one day back home in Athens his sister had brought him a pupil, her twelve-year-old son named Perdix, or Talos. Daedalus proceeded to train him as his apprentice and to let the youngster accompany him wherever he went. Daedalus did not like the boy, and as he grew to know him better, this dislike turned to hatred. Perdix was too precocious. While Daedalus was loftily just beginning to demonstrate a problem, Perdix was already waving his hand in eagerness. What was worse, Perdix usually knew the correct solution. One day while he was walking on the beach with his uncle, the boy stooped over and picked up the white skeleton of a fish. Curiously he turned it over and over in his hands. As soon as they were back in the workshop, Perdix set about copying the backbone of the fish in iron. He had invented the saw. In silence Daedalus brooded, thinking how soon he would be supplanted by such a nephew. Perdix then had the misfortune to invent a pair of compasses.

Almost beside himself with jealous rage, Daedalus profited by the next opportunity that presented itself. One day he pushed Perdix off a tower. For this reason, the murder of a boy related to him by blood, Daedalus had to leave his native land. The goddess of architects, the wise Athena, catching young Perdix in his headlong fall from the tower, transformed him into a partridge. As he walked through the groves of Ida, how often Daedalus must have started at the sudden flushing of a partridge almost under his feet. He must often have watched its whirring flight with the bitter taste of envy still on his tongue.

Despite constant homesickness Daedalus was fairly happy in Knossos because he was busy. King Minos had grandiose ideas, and even more, he was wealthy enough to put them into execution. This Minos was a headstrong, persistent man; and Daedalus came to know better than to thwart his will. Like everyone else around the palace, he heard most of the good stories about his patron. One in particular made the architect rather pity the king's wife, Pasiphaë, the All-Shining.

It seems that once while on a hunting trip Minos had glimpsed the chaste Britomartis running through the forests. Now this maiden was especially sacred to Artemis, herself also a virgin huntress. Even though Minos knew all this, he still thought he could catch the maiden and take her virginity. He continued to steal through the woods in her pursuit, and once he even crept close enough to surprise her. To her horror he declared his intentions, extolling the pleasures of love and accusing her of being the authoress of his sufferings. Britomartis refused him. Then the ardent Minos tried to seize her in his arms, but she managed to slip through his eager fingers. Not the least bit disturbed by her refusal, Minos thought he could in time wear down her resistance. Night and day he continued to pursue her until the poor maiden could hardly find an hour's resting place. Minos stalked her like a deer for nine long months. Finally Britomartis grew frantic. She saw that he was driving her into a corner of the island, and out on a rocky promontory. As she stood panting and trembling on the very brink of the cliff with the sea beating on the base far below her, she saw Minos confidently approaching, the wild smile of victory on his handsome face and his arms outstretched to clasp her. With a long scream the maiden turned and leaped to her death in the sea. Peering over the edge of the promontory, Minos could see her broken body floating in the nets of the fishermen. In honor of her virginity, Artemis herself made the maiden a star in the sky.

This was the Minos upon whom Daedalus depended. The king wished him to remodel the palace and to construct a row of eighteen parallel rooms or magazines in which he could store his wealth. Then he wanted also a stepped theater built in rectangular shape on the northwest corner of the palace. Thousands of blocks of shining white gypsum were cut and polished in preparation, and huge wooden pillars were prepared for a hall of colonnades. In the meantime workmen were digging sewers, laying pipes and drains for sacrificial basins under the altars. Artists from all over Crete were submitting their sketches to Daedalus, for the rooms would be gay with red and blue frescoes. Great care was taken with the throne room for the king.[6] When completed, the palace would occupy a square of more than 150 meters on each side. The most magnificent hall after the central court, which was well over 50 meters long, was to be that of the sacred labrys, or double-edged ax dear to Zeus. News of this hall, or Labyrinth, soon spread to Egypt, where the Pharaoh[7] himself was so interested that he ordered a similar structure to be built.[8] His edifice was called Labyrinth also, but it was a temple. The Egyptians built permanently only for the dead.

Minos on the contrary built for the living. The grandeur and intricacy of his palace are hard to imagine. Try to picture twelve massive courtyards erected parallel to each other.[9] Six of them faced north and the other six south. All together there were three thousand five hundred separate chambers, each leading into the other through colonnaded halls carved with colorful designs and brilliant with frescoes. The roofs and wall which surrounded the whole structure were of gleaming white stone. In this maze of corridors one was soon lost, passing from one room into an arcade, then into a courtyard, and through a forest of pillars into another almost identical room. Minos had several grand staircases leading into lofty halls and courts from story to story up to the flat roofs. The queen and her children each had separate suites provided with windows overlooking the sea to the north. Even the inner rooms on the ground floor were lighted by wells that plunged several floors toward steps that led down many flights to the secret altars of the gods. Down deep in these hollow vaults the sacred bull of Crete, he who in the past centuries had kidnaped the fair Europa and founded the house of Crete, could sometimes be heard to bellow. The earth trembled at that holy roar. Even King Minos, the high priest, would grow yellow with fear and prepare to sacrifice to Zeus deep in the caverns of Mount Dicte.

[6] This can be seen in Crete today.
[7] Amenemhat of the Twelfth Dynasty, perhaps.
[8] Pliny the Elder says it was Daedalus who copied the Egyptians.
[9] Herodotus, Book II.

One morning after a sleepless night full of the sub-terranean rumblings of the huge bull, who seemed to bear the gigantic, labyrinthine palace on his back, King Minos prepared a sacrifice to Poseidon. In his anxiety he began to boast, "Send me a bull, great god of the sea. It is I, Minos, who requests it. I am Minos, the great son of our father Zeus. My voice can command vast fleets to walk like centipedes over the Great Green Sea, swifter than the flight of gulls. I am the master of this kingdom. I can request any gift from the gods, anything that I like. Send me a bull, Poseidon, a monstrous bull from the sea. Here on your altar will I pour forth his blood, and the earth will be calmed."

No sooner had Minos finished his prayer, even while the clouds of blue incense still curled up from the altar before him, than he heard roaring and the pounding of hoofs. His rash prayer had been answered, for there stood a bull such as mortal eyes had never seen before. It was white and magnificent, with polished horns like the new moon, around which curled shiny locks of satin hair. With nervous, impatient hoofs it pawed the earth and snorted. Minos had no desire to cut its sleek throat and offer its blood to Poseidon. What a waste that would be! An ordinary bull would do well enough for the sacrifice, and anyway the rumblings in the earth had long since ceased. Pleased with his decision, Minos ordered the splendid animal to be put in a chamber deep under the palace until it was festival time and the baiting games could begin. What sport this creature would make.

In this way Minos made the error which was to cause Crete such long and terrible sorrow. Poseidon was not deceived. He had sent the bull to Minos for sacrifice, not for sport. The wrath of the sea god was terrible to behold. Instead of going quietly with his captors, the huge bull seemed suddenly to go mad. Snorting and blowing foam from his nostrils, he burst loose from his captors and galloped furiously down the corridor, goring those servants who tried to slip a rope over his horns and around his legs. Screaming, the palace women rushed for shelter from the raging animal. The bull dashed wildly for the grand staircase just as Queen Pasiphaë, who had been alarmed by the shouts, started to descend the stairs.

This was Pasiphaë, mother of the three children of Minos, the lovely sister of Circe, another enchantress. She stood right in the path of the bull, and nobody was near enough to save her. Her ruffled skirt blew in the breezes and her naked white bosom rose and fell quickly in amazement under its diaphanous gauze scarf. Minos and the

66

courtiers awaited the terrible moment, but the anger of Poseidon was more cunning yet than Minos had imagined. Instead of lifting Pasiphaë on his horns and tossing her lovely body in the air, the bull knelt at her feet. In an impulse of love and tenderness Pasiphaë enfolded his neck in her arms. Strolling thus enlaced, and guided by the crafty Daedalus, they passed out of view of the astonished onlookers. The story told by Daedalus spread like wildfire through the palace and out into the town. "The Queen is enamored of a bull!" From time to time in the weeks that followed, herders claimed to have glimpsed the lovers wandering lost in each other far on the slopes of upland pastures.

As if this was not enough, the bull would leave Pasiphaë at night and, blowing fire from his nostrils, lunge wildly through the village, killing the inhabitants and trampling their gardens and cottages. The terror caused by his sudden appearances was so great that people no longer dared sleep. In the palace Minos sat humiliated, listening to his younger daughters crying for their mother. His son Androgeus, who had been reared among the Curetes and who was already a champion athlete, begged to pursue the bull and rid the island of his havoc. Minos dared not allow his son to attempt such a feat. Finally he sent for Heracles, who happened at that time to be in Crete, begging him to include this great service among his twelve labors. The battle that the peerless hero fought with the bull took its place among the annals of the great bouts of the world. In the end Heracles mastered the wild creature and carried him by the sheer strength of his arms all the way across the sea to Greece. Then, with the anger of Poseidon appeased, the pregnant Pasiphaë returned to the palace, where she gave birth to the Minotaur, a creature with the body of a man and the huge horned head of a bull.

Daedalus, steadfast in his admiration of Pasiphaë, was ordered to construct a special room deep in the lowest story of the palace. There the vicious Minotaur was kept, in a place so difficult to find that only its builder and Minos himself had access to it.

Little by little life in Crete returned to normal. The prince, Androgeus, who had not been permitted to pit his strength against the ravaging bull, dreamed of going to Athens. He wanted above all to make a name for himself in some distant land where his father's power would not overshadow him. He was bored with palace life and the chatter of his two young sisters. One summer he finally persuaded his father to let him travel to Athens for the annual festival

67

of Athene, the Panathenaea, at which the greatest athletes competed. There were competitions in discus throwing, track events, jumping, and wrestling. Androgeus had been in training for many years and he looked forward to the opportunity of showing the Greeks how adept he was.

Minos bent every effort to give his son a royal retinue for the trip. Dressed in his finest regalia and accompanied by his friends and trainers, Androgeus departed in the palace yacht. All of Crete awaited in a state of high suspense the outcome of the games. The news brought back to Minos daily was very pleasing. Like any father, he was delighted to learn that Androgeus had captivated the Athenian court by the elegance and refinement of his manners. They heard too how Androgeus had made friends with the nephews of King Aegeus of Athens.

Androgeus won first prize in every one of the athletic events. This was the report he sent back to Crete, and his father was overjoyed. Minos had not realized the physical prowess of his son, overwhelming in comparison with the greatest athletes of Greece. The labyrinthine palace at Knossos was hardly large enough to contain King Minos. Proudly he strutted from court to court, followed by the messengers from Athens. Minos wanted to hear their accounts over and over again. It was the proudest day of his life.

The next arrival from Greece brought Minos the news of his son's death. The king could hardly believe his ears. Sitting down heavily on the nearest bench, he asked the messenger to read the letter to him again.

"To King Minos of Crete from Aegeus. Given by my hand in the city of Athens. We regret to inform you of the tragic death of your son Androgeus. The young prince had charmed us all by his regal bearing and skill in our games, where we awarded him the highest honors. . . . He had left Athens to journey to Thebes in the company of our nephews. Having arrived a little distance, as far as the town of Oenoë, he was set upon by the Bull of Marathon, a huge beast that is still ravaging our outlying districts. We regret that we cannot therefore send you his body . . . receive our expressions of grief . . . tragic end . . . such a regal prince. . . . Aegeus of Athens."

For hours Minos sat alone in his throne room, staring vacantly at the figure-eight shields depicted in fresco on the opposite wall. None of his courtiers dared approach him. High in her penthouse apartment Pasiphaë wept, surrounded by her ladies. Women sobbed in the streets where the Curetes met in silent groups with clenched fists and bitter faces. No one believed the story of any Marathonian Bull. People in Crete remembered how fearful Aegeus had always been of his nephews, how much he had resented their nearness to the throne. Observers from Crete had noted how grudgingly the Athenian king had awarded the prizes, and how closely his uneasy eyes had followed Androgeus and measured his popularity with the masses. What would Minos do, now that he had lost his son and heir? All activity came to a standstill. In quiet lines the sailors waited along the wharves where the great ships of Crete rode at anchor. Even the children stopped their play and listened anxiously, quiet and reflective. The hours dragged by in an ominous silence, while above the shores of Greece the monstrous black clouds of a father's just vengeance gathered.

Suddenly the people heard the death bellow of a great bull and saw a thin wisp of incense rising in the clear air above the palace. The high-priest king was sacrificing. Awed and frightened, they awaited the appearance of their king in his altar robes. When Minos walked stiff-lipped from the palace, his face stern and white, the people of Crete knew how truly great he was. Without wasting a word or a gesture, Minos ordered that the great ships of Crete be provisioned for an immediate departure. "I shall leave tonight," he commanded. "Let everything be made ready in the fleet. We will show King Aegeus what happens to murderers. We will show Aegeus what the wrath of a father can do to Athens."

At port after port the war fleet of Minos called.[10] Through the islands of the Cyclades and into the Aegean he swept majestically, acquainting every land of the loss of his son. Although the kingdoms he visited wished him well, not all of them dared to furnish warriors for him. One afternoon Minos arrived at the island of Aegina in the Saronic Gulf. A crowd of people rushed down to the harbor at the sight of the large fleet, all eager to learn the reason for its coming, all anxious to see the face of such a famous king. Minos was courteously greeted by the sons of King Aeacus, and finally the aged king himself tottered down to the pier.

"Tell us the reason for this visit, for this great honor," said Aeacus.

Sadly Minos answered, "I have come like any father in his grief. The sheeted shade of my son Androgeus, so cruelly murdered by the Athenian king, whose name I cannot mention—for even so much do I loathe him—cries for vengeance. Will you assist me?"

King Aeacus, shaking his head, answered Minos, "You must ask this of me in vain. My city cannot grant you this

10 This account follows that given in Ovid's *Metamorphoses*.

request. We have a very strong alliance with the Greeks. Nonaggression is the very core of our agreement."

Minos left the island of Aegina murmuring to himself under his breath. "This pact you have made with Athens will cost you more than you think, O Aeacus!" No sooner had he put to sea than an Athenian envoy, bearing in his hand the olive branch of friendship, put in to Aegina. There he hastened to give his right hand to the aged king and to his sons, who promised their support to Athens in the forthcoming war. Although Minos knew full well how some of the islands were leaguing with Athens against him, whose family had so many centuries ruled supreme on the sea, he preferred not to dissipate the main thrust of his attack upon such petty powers. Content to measure ahead of time the girth of his enemies, Minos headed straight for Greece, where he began by destroying the coastal cities, one at a time. Minos was not in a hurry.

Then he laid siege to the large city of Megara. The walls of this stronghold were of a very special nature. The god Hermes had aided in their construction. While they were being built, he had laid his lyre upon the stones so that ever afterward they emitted a musical sound when struck. The ruler of this place was an old man named Nisus. Growing from the crown of his head was a long purple lock, which showed plainly among his white hair. This lock ensured the safety of the city, as everyone knew perfectly well. The inhabitants therefore felt quite secure even before the imposing forces of the vengeful king of Crete. The siege had lasted for several weeks already, and the new moon was rising without any decisive engagement. Every day the attackers advanced up to the walls, where they were met by an equal force. Victory herself seemed undecided. Life inside the fortress went on very much the same.

One person among all the people of Megara was particularly interested in the outcome of the struggle. This person was Scylla, the young daughter of King Nisus. Every afternoon she would walk in the sunshine around the walls and play little tunes by throwing pebbles against their stones, just to hear the golden notes of the god's lyre. Then she would lean over the walls and watch the daily battle. Like a good audience, since after all it was not her personal war, this young lady soon came to know the participants each by name. "Who is that warrior, the one on the black horse?" she would ask some passing soldier.

"Oh, that's so-and-so, the Curetes officer from Cydon," he would answer the princess.

"Who's that wearing the red crest on his helmet, the one who looks so fierce?"

"Those are the arms of Phaestus, the great port of southern Crete," an archer would inform her.

With ooh's and ah's Princess Scylla watched the clashing encounters. During the thick of the battle, when the horses reared and snorted and some warrior dealt a brain-splitting blow, she would applaud him and jump up and down in excitement. Readily she changed sides and cheered for whoever was winning that particular engagement. She had never enjoyed herself so much. In vain her attendants prayed her to return to her spinning. In vain they reminded her of the trousseau she was supposed to be embroidering. Scylla shrugged them away impatiently and rushed away to hang over the ramparts, afraid of having missed some deed of heroism.

It was not difficult to find King Minos, even among the brilliant heroes of Crete. He alone rode a pure-white horse, a magnificent stallion with a high curved neck and nervous, prancing legs. He alone wore under his armor a flowing gown of royal purple, the hem and sleeves encrusted with golden threads. He alone wore a helmet of pure gold surmounted with streaming feathers. Rising high in his stirrups, he would draw back his right arm and hurl a slender javelin straight into the breast of a Grecian warrior. With his left hand he would curb the reins tightly enough to bend the proud neck of the stallion. When he took bow and arrow in hand and, pulling the bowstring firmly back to his cheek, let fly the stinging arrow, Scylla would gasp with pleasure and swear he was the perfect image of Hermes. In Scylla's opinion Minos did everything perfectly. If he appeared one day with a golden shield embossed and freshly polished, she would say, "Oh, what a perfect contrast it makes with his helmet." If he galloped to one flank to re-form his battle line, she would shout, "Exactly right, O King. Your line was wavering there. I could see it all from here." Day in and day out, Scylla studied Minos' lineaments and every gesture.

One afternoon when in the heat of battle the king of Crete had pressed the Greeks hard up against their walls and forced King Nisus to re-enter the city, Minos stopped his war horse just under the spot where Scylla was leaning. Breathless and hot, he lifted his heavy helmet from his head to let the cool wind blow on his hair and cheeks. Bending far over the wall, Scylla was able to see his naked face for the first time. "Oh, you are beautiful, Minos of Crete. You are beautiful!" the princess kept whispering to herself. "Oh, you are beautiful. I love you. I love you, King Minos of Crete." Lying

71

flat on the warm wall, her face against the stones, Scylla gazed at him enraptured.

"I wish I were an arrow in the quiver that lies by his hip," she said to herself that night after she was in bed. "How beautiful he is pressing the white horse with his knees! I wish I were the reins of his horse that he encloses in his hand!" Tossing in her soft bed, she indulged in all kinds of fantastic dreams. Perhaps she could throw herself from the tower beside the gate just as he galloped under it. She could see her frail body landing across his saddle. Yes, that was it. He would enfold her in his strong arms and carry her far away over the sea to Crete. If only he would look up and see her! Then he would surely take the city in the storm of his desire and claim her as the spoils of conquest. Maybe he would like it better if she just walked bravely through the gates, her thin dress blowing against her, unmindful of the crashing armor or the hoofs of the rearing horses, straight up to him who was mighty in battle.

Then he would be forced to look at her. He would say, "Oh, my beloved. I have waited for you all my life." At this point Scylla would bury her face in her pillow.

Sometimes in more lucid, daylight moments it would occur to her to wonder what sort of welcome Pasiphaë would make to Minos as he staggered over the threshold carrying a new young wife in his arms. Scylla never particularly cared to dwell on the details. Everyone knew how Pasiphaë had disgraced herself with that Grecian captain named Taurus. Of course, some people were charitable enough to have given the queen the benefit of the doubt. They said—but obviously it was only the gossip of Daedalus—that Pasiphaë had got herself involved with a real bull, and not just a Greek named "Bull." Anyway, she was really a harlot, and Scylla was sure Minos would know how to dispose of her once and for all! Then too it seemed to Scylla that she had heard somewhere that Minos had two daughters, one of them quite a big girl by now. Some gossip had even reported that the older one was quite a beauty, giving promise of a stunning loveliness like that of Aphrodite. Her name began with A too—Ariadne, or something like that. Anxiously Scylla rushed to the mirror to see if she was beautiful. Well, she wasn't really homely. Anyway, Minos would be sure to become infatuated, and that was all that mattered.

The next morning, as Scylla looked longingly out toward the white tents of the Cretan king, she said to herself, "I don't know whether to be happy or sad because of this war. Without the war I should never have seen the hero. No wonder Zeus Asterius carried away Europa, if her children's children were to be as beautiful as this! I am sure Minos will win the war. Great as our warriors are, they cannot compare with him. Now since he is going to win anyway, why should not my love throw open our city gate to him? If I did that, I would be worthy of a hero. If I am going to do it though, I should rather do it sooner than later. What if I hesitated and some young fool shot his lance at Minos? What if he were wounded?" This was a thought Scylla could not bear. Between her and Minos stood only Scylla's father and the precious lock of purple that grew on his head.

As soon as it grew dark, she tiptoed up the winding stairs to her father's chamber and listened at the door. All was still inside. Silently she crept into the room and up to the bed where King Nisus lay sleeping. As quietly as possible she cut the purple lock from his head and stole down the stairs, holding thus the key to the main gate in her hand. On either side of her the sentries lay sleeping. Scylla unlocked the portals and ran unchallenged toward the lofty white tent where Minos was sitting alone.

Panting and disheveled, she finally stood before him, so overcome with emotion she could hardly speak. Before the king could question her, she managed to blurt out, "King Minos, I am Scylla!"

With raised eyebrows the king of Crete looked at her without speaking. "I have unlocked the gates of the city for you, Minos. While my father slept, I stole the key. Here it is. The city is yours. I am not bringing you only a lock of hair but the very life of King Nisus, my father." With a toss of her hand Scylla threw the purple lock across his knees. To her surprise Minos rose, his eyes blazing, and brushed the lock away from him as if it had been a loathsome scorpion.

Scylla continued breathlessly, "I ask for no reward, King Minos. I did it all for love. I only ask you to take me back to Crete as your royal bride."

Minos towered fiercely above her. "To Crete?" he gasped. "I take you to Crete?" With peremptory gestures he waved Scylla out of the tent, where two officers had leaped to attention: "You are the disgrace of the century! You are a monster! What kind of girl betrays her father and her city?" By this time Minos was roaring. "What makes you think I need a woman to fight my wars? May you be swept from the earth! You have betrayed your native land forever. May you be driven from the lands and the seas! There is no room on the face of the earth for traitors. Their punishment is death!"

The following morning Minos entered the fallen city of Megara, where he imposed just laws in accordance with his family tradition and accepted tribute. Then he ordered his men to return to their ships, to weigh the anchors, and to break out the oars. Within a few hours the main force of the Cretans was beating eastward down the coast toward Athens.

Scylla stood long on the shores of Megara watching the Cretan fleet disappear and screaming in terror after them, "What shall I do? Where shall I go? Why do you leave me thus? I cannot return to my father, for I have betrayed him. I cannot go back to the city, for the people will kill me. I closed the gates of the world behind me so that Crete alone might be my home.

"Europa was not your ancestor, Minos! Do you hear me? Your mother was a Caucasian tigress. The story of your birth is false! And so is the tale of Pasiphaë. It is all illusion and dream. Pasiphaë was not bewitched. She preferred a bull to you, Minos!" In despair Scylla leaped into the sea; but as she fell, she was transformed into a sea bird. Since Minos had forbidden her both the land and the sea, she was forever afterward condemned to glide without respite down the draughty winds.

Minos and his fleet arrived safely the same day and laid siege to the city of Athens. Here Minos distinguished himself again for great battles and single combats. While his army sat around the city, well supplied with food from Crete, Athens was ravaged by plague and famine.

At first the city was covered with a heavy darkness. Then within a few days all the animals within its walls—sheep and cattle, dogs and fowl—died from a sudden distemper. Even while their carcasses rotted in the streets and mangers, the citizens were attacked. The first symptom was a burning in the bowels and a difficulty in breathing. The fire was already within them also. Then their tongues grew red and swollen, and their mouths gaped open. The diseased no longer could endure coverings on their beds, but tried to cool themselves by lying on the stones of the roadways. Even the walls and stones grew hot from their fever. The physicians, learned as they were, had no cure for this malady.

Abandoning all hopes therefore of cure, the ill lay as close as possible to the fountains, where they died, sometimes with their corpses rotting in the water itself. People ran wildly from their homes, not knowing the source of their sickness. They died suddenly just as they were about to take the next step, falling on the earth like rotten apples from a moldy tree, or like acorns that the rough winds of autumn scatter and roll over the leaves.

In vain the priests sacrificed to the gods while there was one of them left living or a healthy animal whose blood could be offered in propitiation. Then the elders of the city

74

obtained permission from King Minos to go to the oracle at Delphi. When the Pythoness heard their terrible story, she advised them to submit to the Cretans. She reminded them of the death of Androgeus, of the divine parentage of Minos, and of his heroism. Upon their return they dispatched ambassadors to the Cretan king, begging him for honorable terms of peace.

Minos granted their request, but reminding them of his just and bitter grievance against their King Aegeus, he stipulated that beginning that very year, and every ninth year thereafter, there should be sent to Crete seven youths and seven maidens from among the most comely in the city to compete at the funeral games of Androgeus.

THESEUS AND THE MINOTAUR

KING AEGEUS of Attica lived on after the conquest by Crete, tormented and bewitched by his hideous wife, the witch Medea, whom Jason had abandoned after his quest of the Golden Fleece. Medea had been born on the shores of the Black Sea, a hateful land renowned for its magic. Eighteen years before, Aegeus had loved a gentle maiden named Aethra, whom he had left pregnant in the island of Troezen. Unknown to Aegeus a fine boy had been born to Aethra. His name was Theseus, and he was destined to become one of the most beloved heroes of Greece.

Every year from the age of fifteen Theseus, educated in the tales of his cousin Heracles, had accompanied his mother to the temple of Poseidon. As directed by her he had fought his way through the thickets outside the temple wall and had tried to lift a huge rock that lay half buried at the roots of a plane tree. By the time that he was eighteen he had managed to perform this great feat of strength, which no man before him had been able to do. Under the stone he had found the strong sword of bronze and the pair of golden sandals Aegeus had left there. Knowing Theseus was beloved of the gods who had sent him his superhuman strength, Aethra then told him that he was the son of Aegeus.

Theseus set out for Attica, that fair sunny land that faced south, a land of honey and the olive, with sweet plains and meadows and silver-headed mountains, all engirdled by the blue Aegean Sea. It lay across the straits from his birthplace, behind the blue shores of Aegina. "What would you do, my Theseus, if you were lord of such a land?" his mother asked him sadly, for she knew she would soon lose her son.

"I should become the shepherd over my flocks," the youth

answered, smiling. "I would rid the land of monsters and rule it so well that all my people would mourn my passing."

"Go then to your father," bade Aethra. "You will find him in Athens on the hill of Athena. Give him the sword, and he will welcome you."

The young Theseus set out on foot for his father's palace, taking the long route by the isthmus. In his heart he hoped to do great deeds along the way so that King Aegeus would be proud of him. First he walked into the monstrous spider web of the wicked Periphates, and slew him. Next he encountered Sinis, the robber who waylaid travelers and, tying their bodies to two pine trees, let them rebound and tear the poor victims apart. Him also Theseus slew with his bronze club, at the narrowest part of the isthmus. After this he walked forward to the shores of the Saronic Gulf, where lay the great city of Megara. There he encountered Sciron, who barred the path and forced his prisoners to wash his feet. Theseus killed this giant by kicking him over the cliffs into the sea, where even the carrion-feeding tortoises would not touch his stinking flesh.

After the adventure stories of Theseus and his prowess began to spread through the land, warriors, in imitation of him, cut their hair short so their enemies could not grasp them by it. Theseus continued his long journey, keeping the sea and the strait of Salamis on his right. In the land of Eleusis he met King Cercyon, whose palace court was full of the bones of the men he had killed. Strewing fresh sand on the earth, Cercyon wrestled with Theseus until the stars came out in the heavens. Finally Theseus grasped him by the waist and one wrist and heaved him over his shoulder to the ground. Cercyon died instantly, and Theseus accepted to rule the land. For this feat Theseus purged himself, for he had unwittingly vanquished a member of his own royal family.

As he passed the white peaks of Parnes, Theseus met a pleasant man named Procrustes, who invited him home to dinner. When the hero learned that his sweet-spoken host lured travelers to his palace on the pretense of hospitality only to torture them, Theseus slew him also. Procrustes for years had been trying to fit his guests into a bed. When they were too long for it, he cut off their limbs. When they were too short, as maidens often were, he stretched them until they died. Theseus divided all the wealth of this tyrant among the poor shepherds of the mountain, and then started off again on his journey.

In the early morning he swung along happily down through the mist of the slopes of Parnes, where the oak trees dripped on his head. Underfoot, the pink arbutus bloomed in patches of snow, and the air was perfumed with bay and wild thyme. As he passed through the valleys of Attica, people greeted him warmly, for they knew a god was in him. Finally he saw in reverence the plain of Athens and in the distance the holy hill where Athena dwelled. Breathing prayers, he climbed the sacred stairs of the Acropolis and arrived at the palace of Aegeus. He wondered how his father was, when the land was so ravaged with robbers and giants.

The palace was in a state of confusion. Drunken courtiers lolled at the tables. Sternly Theseus sent a message to the king, who was sitting in his chamber watching the evil eye and murderous hand of Medea. As soon as Aegeus saw the fair hair and stately bearing of Theseus, he loved him at once. Bidding him welcome, they all sat down to dinner—all except Medea, who retired to her chambers. She knew, although Aegeus did not, who the young stranger was. Dressing herself in royal robes and wearing her jewels, Medea prepared a deadly poison mixed in wine. Then, returning to the dining hall, she offered the wine to Theseus.

"Greetings, hero," she said, advancing toward him in all her midnight splendor. "Drink from this golden cup, and you will taste the heady wine of the East."

Theseus looked at her raven hair and especially at her black eyes, which were as dry as the eyes of a serpent. "Do you drink first, Medea," he answered. "Drink or die, Medea," he threatened, lifting his bronze war club.

With a scream of anger Medea dashed the golden goblet to the floor. Wherever the red liquid flowed over the marble, it steamed and bubbled. In the silence that followed, the courtiers heard Medea escaping in her dragon chariot that left a trail of flame in the sky. Thus Medea, who had at an earlier time betrayed her father, burned alive Princess Creüsa of Corinth, and killed her own little children, fled furiously across the eastern sky. Far beyond the two rivers of the land that had once been Sumer she founded a country of Asia, Media. Through the descendants of this land she would one day seek her revenge against Greece.

Then Theseus showed his father the bronze sword and golden sandals he had unearthed from under the stone. Smiling and weeping, Aegeus embraced his son, who had already rid the land of such evil. "This is my son, Theseus, a better man than ever his father was!" he used to say. Relieved in his old age of the heavy responsibility of the throne, Aegeus recounted his troubles to Theseus. He told him of the long siege of Athens and how King Minos had accused him of the murder of Androgeus.

"Who is this King Minos?" cried Theseus. "Let me behold

77

the man who calls my father a liar!" All winter the young hero toiled to put the land in order. First he killed the plotting, drunken courtiers. Next he sought and overcame the Marathonian Bull. When spring came, he noticed how everyone seemed downcast. Although he asked the reason for their sorrow, no person would tell him. To his persistent questions, Aegeus would only reply, "It is hard enough to face sorrow when it comes. Let us not discuss it now."

Later that spring there arrived from King Minos of Crete a splendid herald. In the market place he called, "Hear ye, Citizens! Nine years have elapsed. Have you prepared your tribute for His Majesty of Crete, ruler of the Great Green Sea?"

"What is this dog that dares ask tribute of Attica?" cried Theseus, advancing boldly to the ambassador.

When the herald explained, Theseus listened aghast, for he had not heard of the tribute. In consternation he begged his father to deny the slanderous story of his murder of Androgeus.

Aegeus, turning sadly away, would only reply, "An oath is sacred. The tribute must be sent."

On every hand the people of Athens wept bitterly. They knew the seven youths and maidens would never be heard of again. In horror they pictured what Minos must have made them do. He must have fed them alive to the Minotaur! In their fear and sorrow they had for the moment forgotten Theseus, he who was born to royalty. Before King Aegeus even realized what his son intended, Theseus stepped before the citizens. "Cast lots for the thirteen, if that is your custom. I myself will make the fourteenth!"

At his words King Aegeus groaned in horror. Theseus continued while all the people remained breathless at his courage. "Blood will be answered with blood, fire with fire, and sword with sword. King Minos himself will be broken and the Minotaur also. I swear it. His power began to wane the day that I was born! I, Theseus, have spoken!"

Aegeus opposed strong objections to this sudden vow of his son. In particular he warned him of the Labyrinth from which no stranger could escape, and reminded Theseus that it had been constructed by the devious brain of Daedalus, that accursed renegade. Theseus grew even more determined. After the lots were drawn, he led the unfortunate young people from Athens down to their ship. Its sails were black in token of their country's grief. Theseus encouraged the thirteen youths who were with him by reminding them of his exploits on the way to Attica. When they saw him so confident, they began to believe that he actually would not only kill the Minotaur but that he would rid their homeland of Cretan domination. In parting from his father Theseus promised that upon his return he would hoist a white sail instead of the mournful black one so that King Aegeus, peering out over the sea from the cliffs of Sunium, would know they were all alive and well.

As soon as the Athenians arrived in Crete, at the palace of Minos, the funeral games in honor of Androgeus were begun. Not unwilling to impress the Athenians, who were so soon to die in the bull-grappling games, Minos began the festival with a boxing match in the new theater [11] that Daedalus had built on the northwest side of the palace. Raised stone steps for the spectators faced the opposite end of the rectangular arena. The royalty of Crete had all taken their places when the Athenian youths and maidens entered in single file. Calmly Theseus stood before Minos. The young hero's blond hair shone in the afternoon sun as he remained facing the king of Crete, now ten years past his prime. The little smile on the Athenian's face did not escape Minos. It would be a pleasure to cast this one to the Minotaur, he thought.

Languidly Theseus dropped to a seat in the front row before the king. A herald was proclaiming a champion wrestler named Taurus. The spectators gasped as the great athlete entered.[12] His broad back and chest were swollen with huge muscles of bronze. Huge mounds of iron tissues stood out like boulders under the tanned skin of his shoulders. He was naked except for a loincloth, and a lion's skin which he draped over his shoulder. Massive and leering he stood, his huge legs far apart like the trunks of pine trees.

Even as the herald called for an opponent, a volunteer to meet this champion, Theseus yawned and looked away from the scene in an attitude of perfect boredom. No person rose. No man volunteered. Jeers came from the Cretans, and cries of "Throw him a Greek!" At this taunt two red spots appeared on the cheeks of Theseus, and he rose.

"Do you wish me to fight your champion, Minos?" he asked quietly.

After a nod from Minos, Theseus advanced toward the herald. "Is it a boxing match?" he called over his shoulder. Quickly attendants brought heavy oxskin gloves and bound them on the hands of the two opponents, and strong leather thongs around their arms.

"Kicking is allowed," pronounced the herald. "Do your mightiest with your fists. Remember all your skills."

[11] See Homer, *Iliad*, Book XVIII.
[12] Theocritus, Idyl XXII.

79

Then just as the two were about to start for each other Minos called tauntingly to his man, "Do not kill him, Champion. We have other sports devised for him."

With a furious rush the boxer lunged toward Theseus, his fists flying through the empty air. Lightly the Athenian prince danced to the left and drove his right fist straight home to the other's chin. Then Theseus threw back his head and laughed while his opponent recovered his footing. A second time the huge man rushed forward, head down, hoping by sheer weight to hurl Theseus to the sand. This time Theseus feinted with his right and, having caught the other's glance, landed a left full in his mouth. The monstrous wrestler reeled and spat blood and broken teeth. Then Theseus darted swiftly at the champion and with the heavily weighted glove struck him in the forehead so hard that the skin was ripped from it. But urged on by the shrill cheers of the Cretan spectators, the giant once more rushed toward the slender Greek. This time Theseus rained so many quick blows on his head and pursued him so relentlessly as the other retreated that finally the wrestler sank over backward to the ground and held up his two fists in sign of defeat.

The prize brought Theseus was a garland of lilies. He was about to throw it at the feet of King Minos when, looking toward the royal box, he saw the sweetest of flowers, the princess Ariadne. Looking her straight in the eye, the slow smile still on his lips, Theseus gently dropped the wreath of lilies upon her lap and turned away. Blushing to the roots of her auburn hair, the innocent Ariadne watched the Greek hero until he had sauntered out of the theater. For this she was sent immediately to her chamber and ordered to remain there. Minos had had personal experience with very young maidens. His theory was a practical one: lock them up until they get married. That way you won't have any cities betrayed.

That night while the palace slept, little Ariadne sat at her window looking out toward the shores of Greece.[13] She had been gently reared by Pasiphaë and the palace ladies, who were infatuated with her radiant beauty and soft eyes. She had never been outside the palace walls and had never met a stranger. All her life until then had been games with her sister Phaedra. They had tossed golden balls in the courtyards and sometimes been allowed to watch Daedalus as he modeled his speaking statues. She was so young yet that she had not even thought of love, at least not very seriously. Its torture and happiness had been revealed to her in that instant when the laughing eyes of Theseus had met hers.

[13] From Catullus, "Epithalamium for Peleus and Thetis."

For this reason she sat still and motionless in her chamber, where her father had sent her.

How long she would have continued to sit thus, staring with hopeless eyes out over the dark sea, Ariadne did not know. It was several minutes before she could rouse herself enough to go to her door after she heard the tapping. At the sound of her voice the door was unlocked, and Daedalus entered stealthily.

"Shall I help you, Ariadne?" he asked her. "Do you very much want to see him?"

Silently the little princess nodded. Covering her bright festival dress with a black cloak, Daedalus took her by the hand and led her to the dark, underground chamber where Theseus was imprisoned. There Daedalus left her alone with the Argive hero, while he stood guard outside.

At first Ariadne could not find her tongue. She blushed and hung her head as she felt his eyes move down her body, over her naked breasts and golden girdle. He talked to her softly, praising her long curls shot with gold, her sweet face, the dimple in her chin, her tiny feet. Finally she said that she had come to help him find a way to escape death. Theseus smiled at her childish innocence.

"I am not afraid, Ariadne. I shall not die."

"Oh, but you will," she gasped. "Tomorrow begin the bull-grappling games. Our youths will give a demonstration, and then the Athenians will be thrown into the ring!"

"I have killed giants many times the size of your Cretan bulls," Theseus retorted. "I have crushed their skulls with one blow of my bronze club."

"You don't understand it at all," cried Ariadne with tears in her eyes. "You won't have a club. You will be naked against the bull. Our specially trained youths and maidens let the bull run toward them. They grasp his horns with their hands and vault over his head onto his back. Then they leap toward the youth behind the bull, who catches them with his hands. It is a skill that requires long years of training. If the bull goes mad, our toreadors stab him."

"Very well," replied Theseus. "Then I will wring the bull's neck. How will that be?"

"Even if you escape death," whispered Ariadne between her tears, "you still have to meet the Minotaur."

"Where is he?" questioned Theseus. "Why don't I search him out now and kill him before tomorrow's games?"

Ariadne was just going to tell Theseus how impossible it would be to find his way down through the three thousand five hundred rooms of the palace when Daedalus re-entered the cell. Together he and Theseus worked out a plan,

81

for Daedalus had never forgotten that he also came from the royal Athenian family of Erechtheus, just like Theseus. On a sheet of parchment Daedalus showed his compatriot a plan of the palace and gave him a sword and a long spool of thread to unwind as he went so that by following it he could retrace his steps.

"Will you come with me to Athens, Ariadne?" asked Theseus.

"Oh yes," she answered. "Only you must not hurt my father."

Then Theseus fell at her feet and swore undying love. He told her of the palace at Athens, high on the hill of Athena. He spoke of his aged father, King Aegeus, and how he would love her. He told her how brave she was to end by her marriage the old quarrel between Crete and Attica. He said that through her love the two countries would forevermore live in peace and friendship.

Then, weeping and trembling, Ariadne was led away by Daedalus, who never doubted that Theseus would slay the Minotaur with his sturdy bronze sword, to the Greek ship that had borne the youths to Crete. Afterward Daedalus ran home, gathered his possessions, dressed his boy Icarus, and fled to a secret hiding place he had made on a cliff far from Knossos.

Theseus, sword in hand, ran lightly through the palace, unwinding the skein as he went. Down he sped from one flight to another through corridors dimly lighted with pine torches. To the right he turned through lofty colonnaded halls where the only sound was his breathing and the rapid tread of his sandaled feet. Then he bore left through vaults and arcades and down another flight of dark stone steps. The air grew damp and chill. Once he almost lost his way and had to follow the thread back to a pillared hall. Hurriedly he got his bearings and raced forward and down another flight. Finally he stopped short, for there directly before him stood the awful, deformed brother of Ariadne.

The Minotaur's keen ears had heard the descending steps of Theseus, and he was waiting. His heavy head hung forward on his chest. Huge, protuberant brown eyes, like a bull's, glowered at the hero. Saliva dripped from his open mouth from which long, fanglike teeth protruded. His arms and shoulders were covered with coarse, black hair.

There was a moment before Theseus could recover himself. His first inclination had been to turn in flight, but even at that instant the creature advanced with huge clawlike fingers eager for his throat. Taking careful aim, Theseus slashed him across the left shoulder. The dungeon echoed

THESEUS AND THE MINOTAUR

with the Minotaur's scream of pain, for he had never felt a wound before. Howling and shrieking, he lunged again for Theseus' throat only to be slashed once more. It was a filthy business, for the animal stench in the chamber was almost overpowering. Mastering his revulsion with an almost superhuman effort, Theseus killed the monster with his next thrust, through the heart.

Even before the hideous body of the Minotaur had stopped twitching and writhing on the slippery stones, Theseus had fled upward out of that reeking dungeon. It was not too difficult to follow the thread, but he stopped at every landing long enough to place a smoking pine torch at the base of one of the wooden pillars that held up the ceiling. Panting until his lungs almost burst, he retraced his steps toward the surface, realizing that within a matter of minutes the fumes would give the alarm. His Athenian friends were crouched near the door of their cell. As soon as Theseus opened their prison, they leaped out and helped him set fire to the palace, working their way quickly northward toward the dock. The seven whom Theseus had disguised as maidens stripped off their women's gowns and headed directly for the wharves where the Cretan fleet rode at anchor. Without hesitation—for Theseus had picked them for their knowledge of swimming and rehearsed them well— they plunged into the water and within a few minutes had staved in the bottoms of the wooden galleys.[14]

Within half an hour they had all returned to the Athenian galley, and its thirty muffled oars were dipping into the calm waters of the bay. Before they had cleared the harbor, they began to see smoke and flames rising in long streaks into the black air. When the wind veered, they could even hear faintly the distant cries of the Cretans. Theseus and his friends clapped each other on the back, gulping great draughts of wine, laughing, boasting, and congratulating their great leader. None of them came near Ariadne, who crouched sobbing and weeping on the afterdeck near the helmsman, straining to see once more the shores of her home that she had betrayed, moaning over and over under her breath the names of her mother and father, and seeing for the first time the coarseness and vulgarity of these primitive Greeks into whose ruthless hands she had placed herself.

Back in Knossos, King Minos had been awakened by frightened servants. His palace was in flames. Quickly he gave orders to salvage as much as possible and to move his

[14] From the account of the historian Pherecydes, as quoted by Plutarch.

family to an outer palace. He stood in the central court regardless of his own safety, giving orders and directing rescue operations. It was there that he learned how his fleet had been scuttled. Immediately he realized that the Athenians must have done it. Then he was told that the lower floors had collapsed, but no one had seen the Greeks. Last of all he heard the bitter news that Ariadne was not to be found. Still the palace burned all around him with the thundering roar of falling masonry. It was not until morning that Minos began to reconstruct what had happened. His suspicions were confirmed when he was told that Icarus, the young son of Daedalus, was missing also.

It was Daedalus whom Minos cursed not only for the destruction of the palace, but more especially for having treacherously misled the child Ariadne. Surrounded on every side by death and destruction, knowing that the fast Grecian galley could hide out for months among the numerous isles of the Cyclades, Minos determined first to track Daedalus to earth. His orders were categorical. Any Cretan who knew of Daedalus' whereabouts or assisted him either on land or on sea would be instantly executed. Munificent rewards, on the other hand, awaited his captor or any informant.

Daedalus meanwhile, assisted by his boy Icarus, was hard at work in his hidden atelier. "Let Minos rule the land and the sea," he muttered as he finished his design. "The skies above are henceforth my dominion. Let Minos impose his orders everywhere else. He cannot command the heavens!" [15]

For years this cleverest of inventors had been haunted by the flight of his nephew Perdix. For years he had longed to emulate this feat, not content to build great palaces or life-like statues of men and gods. He had pondered the problem of flight for more than a decade, and had kept a sheaf of notes made from careful observations and calculations of weight and wind. While his son played in the workshop and sometimes hindered his father, as children will, Daedalus constructed from feathers, thread, and wax, two pairs of wings modeled exactly on the wings of eagles, only much larger. When they were finished, he led the little boy out to the edge of the tall cliff where they were hiding, fitted the wings to his little shoulders, and instructed him carefully.

"Icarus, my boy, follow my example and you will fly. Stay well in the middle course, neither too near the sea, which would weigh down your wings with water, nor too high, where the heat of the sun would melt the wax. Especially do not look toward the Great Bear or the flashing

[15] From Ovid, *Metamorphoses.*

sword of Orion. Set your course on me, to the north."
With tears streaming down his face, for the elderly Daedalus
loved his little son dearly, he kissed him good-by and took
to flight from the top of the cliff. Looking back, he saw that
the plucky lad had taken the plunge and was following.

Their wings bore them valiantly to the north and the
Cyclades. Below them they saw Samos, Delos, and Paros, set
like little gems in a glittering sea. Fishermen left their
catches struggling on the lines as they watched the fliers
high overhead. Shepherds on the islands leaned on their
crooks in amazement, believing that they were beholding
gods. In the valleys the plowman stared up in amazement
at these creatures who so upset the laws of nature as to
cleave a passage through the fields of heaven.

Icarus grew weary of following his father. Like any lively
boy, he wanted to sail forth on his own. He began to soar
and dip, pleased to try his wings in his own way. Daedalus
did not know what the boy was doing until he heard his
scream. Turning, he saw the child, frantically waving his
bare arms, plummet down to the sea. The boy had flown
so near the sun that its heat had melted the wax, just as
Daedalus had warned him. In honor of Icarus the waters
where he died were called Icarian, and the island where
Daedalus buried him, near present-day Samos in the Sporades
Islands, was also called Icaria.

Daedalus wandered from country to country in the Mediterranean, with the fleet of King Minos steadily tracking
him. In Egypt he designed a temple to Hephaestus at Memphis. In distant Sardinia he mapped out fortifications for
King Iolaos, the towers of which were named in his memory
Daedaleia. Then he moved to Sicily. From the vapors of
Aetna he made a bath to cure rheumatism. For King Cocalus
he constructed a reservoir, treasuries, and castles. It was
here at last that Minos found him.

As the king of Crete expected, Cocalus shielded his valuable architect and denied any knowledge of him. Minos,
however, relying on the enormous vanity of Daedalus,
showed Cocalus a puzzle that could not be solved. It was a
spiral seashell, and Minos defied any man alive to learn the
secret of its turnings and find a passage through it. Cocalus
took the shell and when he next showed it to Minos there
was a fine thread drawn through it from outer rim to vertex.
Laughing at Minos, Cocalus told him that one of his engineers had tied the thread to an ant which, lured by a drop
of honey, had carried it through the coils of the shell and
discovered the exit. In this way Minos knew Daedalus was in
Sicily, for he alone could so ingeniously have solved this

problem. The Cretan king would have killed him too, except that Minos met his own death there in the palace of Cocalus. Some say a daughter of the king drowned him in his bath.

By noon on the day following their victorious departure from Knossos, Theseus and his band of warriors anchored on the coast of Naxos in the Cyclades. This island, the largest in that archipelago, was a center for the cult of Dionysus. Wading ashore, the Greek heroes proceeded to bathe and sacrifice to the gods for their easy triumph. Theseus carried Ariadne ashore and tried to comfort her, for she had neither slept nor stopped crying since they left Knossos the evening before. Her whole body was racked with dry sobs. Annoyed with her lack of courage, he grudgingly made her a bed beside the beach, where after a little while, lulled by the rhythmic rush of the waves and warmed by the noon-day sun, the little princess fell asleep. Meanwhile the Athenian warriors finished their prayers, took on food and water, and still boasting and laughing, set sail for Athens.

When Ariadne awoke, it was late afternoon. The sun already cast long shadows among the black rocks that lay around her and stretched far out into the foaming sea. At first she could neither remember where she was nor what had happened. Slowly she recalled with a gasp of horror the red tongues of flames as they leaped above her burning homeland. Then she remembered the grinning faces of the Greeks. Looking all around her, she could see no trace of them except for their footprints in the sand. Shading her eyes with her hand, she scanned the horizon. There was no ship in sight. There was not even a black sail silhouetted against the horizon. Frantic, Ariadne began to climb the jagged rocks that projected out into the sea. She cut her hands as she scrambled over them, Ariadne who had never before yesterday even walked outside her carefully tended gardens at Knossos. Stepping in shallow water between two boulders, she cut her feet on the black spines of the sea urchin. Heedless of the blood flowing from the wounds, she clambered on a higher rock and looked again far out over the sea. Great waves came rolling along the deep toward her and tore at her frail garments. Unmindful of them also, Ariadne let them wash her thin robe from her body. She was alone in a world of sea and sky. There was not a person in sight, not a single habitation, only vastness and the surging, white-crested waves of the sea. Then she began to speak to the departed Theseus:

You traitor! So this is the way you have left me,
    Theseus,

Deserted here on this wretched shore where you brought
    me, traitor!
While you go sailing away, completely unmindful.
Yes, scorning the gods you flaunt your broken promise
    to Athens!
Could nothing bend the iron of your cruel decision?
Had you no tenderness in your heart for Ariadne
That its ruthlessness should at last be melted to pity?
Oh! with your once sweet voice you never promised
Me these rocks, nor urged me ever to hope for this fate;
But an honored queen and a lovely wedding you
    pictured
Which the lofty winds have destroyed and completely
    abolished.
    From this day forth let no maiden trust any man's
      swearing,
Nor ever believe that the oaths of a hero are honest
While his crafty brain having schemed ahead how to
    betray her
Will help him swear anything, nor stop him from
    promising everything;
For as soon as the lust of his greedy ambition is sated
His words he will not remember, nor care for his
    swearing![16]

So Ariadne spoke her farewell to Theseus, adding to her
words a curse that he should cause as much sorrow to one
of his family as he had brought to her, and to Crete through
her.

Ariadne stood on the black rock in her naked loveliness
with the setting sun behind her, crowning her long curls in
an aureole of golden light. It is in this position that she is
remembered, for so she stood in her young beauty when
the god Dionysus first saw her. At first he thought she was
Aphrodite rising as at her birth out of the green sea foam.

Dionysus was just returning from a long voyage to the
East, where he had taught the other men of the world the
art of agriculture. His moisture had flowed forth over the
banks of the Nile and made the black earth of Egypt fertile.
He had crossed the Tigris River on a splendid tiger that
Zeus had sent him, and the Euphrates on a cable made of
ivy tendrils and grapevine. He had just come from India,
at the eastern end of the earth, where he had founded the
city of Nysa.[17]

Lifting Ariadne tenderly from her dangerous crag,
Dionysus enfolded her in his gentle arms and carried her

16 Catullus, "Epithalamium for Peleus and Thetis."
17 See Chap. 2, p. 30.

to the shore. Ariadne had never seen a god before, and so she had no idea how much more beautiful they were than mortal men. The god's hair was black and curly, for black is the color of youth as white is the color of old heads. As a boy Dionysus had been enclosed in a chest that had floated over the sea, but now he was a man, tall and handsome, but with the rounded arms and the graceful gestures of a god. His head was crowned with ivy and laurel. In one hand he bore his insignia, the thyrsus or staff crowned with vines. In the other hand he carried a gleaming wine cup from which he made the princess drink until she had forgotten her sorrow. Then she sat across his lap, resting her shoulder on his raised left knee while he stroked her hair with his left hand and wooed her.

The god of the harvest, Dionysus, and the princess Ariadne were married at Naxos, for this was his particular island. Even the great gods and goddesses from Olympus attended the formal wedding. They had three sons and lived happily ever afterward. On her wedding day Dionysus presented Ariadne with a magnificent golden crown, which she always wore as long as she lived. At her death—for her husband could not give her immortality—he threw her crown up into the northern sky, where it may still be seen on a cloudless night as the radiant Corona Borealis.

Theseus and his band of Athenian heroes returned directly home after their short stop at Naxos. With hissing beak their swift galley ploughed the waves while they urged on their oarsmen to greater sweeps with the flashing oars. Theseus could already hear the shouts of the admiring citizens, "Lo! another Heracles!" as they acclaimed him the savior of his people. With shouts of joy the triumphant young men sighted the shores of Greece and the high promontory of Sunium. It was not until he stepped ashore and heard the cries of grief around him that Theseus remembered the white sail. It still lay folded in its chest where his father Aegeus had lovingly placed it. Aegeus, straining his eyes over the blue sea for news of his beloved son, had sighted the black sail over the Athenian galley. Preferring by far a sudden death to the news of the loss of his beloved Theseus, Aegeus threw himself from the cliff of Sunium onto the sharp rocks far below. The gods in this way punished Theseus swiftly for his abandonment and betrayal of the Cretan princess.

Because of his father's suicide Theseus became king of Attica. Using the slogan "Come hither, all you peoples," he persuaded the inhabitants of small outlying towns to move to Athens. In this way he created a powerful state, which he administered well and defended heroically for many years. At the confines of his territories he caused a massive pillar to be erected and carvings to be made on its eastern and western sides to indicate to travelers that they were leaving the Peloponnesus and entering Ionia. Theseus was so respected by his citizens that whenever a great task was to be undertaken by an Athenian, he always remembered this king and affirmed that it could be done perhaps, but "Not without Theseus!"

One of Theseus' greatest exploits was his kidnaping of the Amazonian queen Hippolyta and his subsequent destruction of the fierce hordes of female warriors that, bent on revenge, invaded the kingdom of Attica. This famous fighting queen became his bride after four days, in ceremonies long remembered for their glamor. A later poet has described these nuptials in immortal lines. Theseus says,

> Hippolyta, I woo'd thee with my sword,
> And won thy love doing thee injuries;
> But I will wed thee in another key,
> With pomp, with triumph, and with revelling.[18]

It was indeed a solemn wedding, enlivened with a play about the loves of the Babylonian youth Pyramus and his sweetheart Thisbe.

A son, Hippolytus, was born from the union of Theseus and the queen of the Amazons. At the death of Hippolyta, Theseus married Phaedra, the younger sister of Ariadne. This marriage, however, resulted in great tragedy. Phaedra, far from loving King Theseus, fell passionately in love with the boy Hippolytus. Since this youth had taken vows of chastity, Phaedra's consuming passion caused the death of both of them.

When he was fifty, Theseus began to search for a new bride. Once on a voyage to Sparta he became enamored of a young wisp of a girl whom he saw dancing in the temple of the virginal goddess Artemis. Without reckoning the consequences of his blind passion Theseus kidnaped the girl, who was not even of marriageable age at the time, and hid her with his mother Aethra in the island of Troezen. This young girl had twin brothers, the Dioscuri, who followed Theseus to Athens in an attempt to rescue their sister. Theseus had not realized that this abduction would set off a chain of circumstances that would result in long and bloody wars, and in his own death far from home.

It was not until later years that the huge body of Theseus

18 *Midsummer Night's Dream.*

was carried royally home to Athens and duly buried with great honors in the heart of that city. The ship that had borne him and the youths to Crete was preserved in Athens until 300 B.C. Ceremonies in honor of this greatest hero of Attica were instituted on the eighth day of every month, for it was on the eighth day of the month of Cronus that he had first entered Athens and climbed the holy stairs of the Acropolis in search of his father. The number eight, as the first cube of the first even number and the double of the first square number, aptly indicated the reliable and loyal nature of Theseus, the Immortal Hero.

As the mighty Theseus wandered golden-haired among the immortals in the perfumed Elysian Fields, did he know that the ten-year-old Spartan girl whom he had abducted was becoming, through a chain of violations, one of the most celebrated women the world had ever known, the fateful Helen of Troy?

4

Troy: Cassandra

INTRODUCTION

MANY WRITERS of the ancient world—lyric poets, dramatists, and historians—have mentioned the story of Cassandra. Artists throughout antiquity had rather generally agreed in their representations as to how she looked. One poet, Lycophron, wrote a work in Greek of 1,712 lines recounting her many prophecies in the words of her guardian, some of which you will read in the following pages. As in the case of Ariadne, another favorite heroine, there were widely divergent accounts of the Cassandra story. It was one that apparently held a very special appeal for the ancients.

The historian Plutarch speaks of her tomb, as does Pausanias, who adds that a great hero worship had grown up in Greece around her legend. Vergil, writing from the Roman point of view—since his purpose was to glorify Caesar and the Julian family, who were "Trojans" claiming descent from Aphrodite—mentions Cassandra with great sympathy. Euripides gives her beautiful lines to speak in *The Trojan Women*, and Aeschylus in the climax of *Agamemnon* recounts her death most vividly. Even Cicero in *De Oratore* wittily puts an opponent to rout by retorting "Ajax" when the other styled himself "Cassandra."

The reader will find in the following pages her story as told by the above-named authors, not the more familiar version of the Trojan War as Homer tells it. For a scholarly interpretation of all the classical texts and a detailed study of 123 artists' representations of this princess, the reader may wish to consult the learned dissertation of Dr. Juliette Davreux. This treatise was presented at the University of Liége and published in Paris in 1942.

CASSANDRA

KING PRIAM of Troy was rightfully called the sower of many seeds, for he fathered fifty children. Nineteen of them were born to his royal spouse, Queen Hecuba. Together they lived in a prosperous city, which was encircled by lofty walls and commanded a view over a wide plain watered by the River Scamander. The city of Troy, or Ilion, was on the Asian side of the Hellespont, the strait connecting the Aegean with the waters leading into the Black Sea and its fertile wheat-growing areas.

Priam was proud to trace his ancestry back through seven royal generations to one of the Titans—Iapetus, brother of Cronus. In his family tree he also boasted not only the giant Atlas, but even Zeus himself. Among his allies King Priam could number many lands of Asia—Lycia, Mysia, and Cilicia—and among his friends even the Pharaoh of Egypt.

The royal Priam was not blessed with children alone, but also with great wealth. His forefathers had been accustomed to levy tolls on all vessels that passed through the Hellespont, a practice Priam also continued. By gathering under his protection many of the smaller cities of Asia Minor, he was able successfully to oppose the growing populations of the "barbarian" peoples to the west of his domains, and also to prevent their expansion eastward. Of necessity he kept a watchful eye on the allies and descendants of the kings of Crete and upon their Achaean conquerors. Two of the most powerful lords of the west were the brothers Agamemnon of Mycenae and Menelaus of Sparta, both great-grandsons of the famous King Minos II of Crete. Like them King Priam considered Crete one of the cradles of his race.

The pride and hope of the great Trojan city was its Prince Hector. He was their shield of bronze, the pillar of their palace, sturdy enough to bear upon his shoulders the heaviest of monarchies. Hector had married the white-armed Androm-ache, and to them had been born a strong son, Astyanax. The home of Hector within the city was a place of peace and innocence, because his wife stayed in her own garden, quiet and contented. She only craved the pleasant company of Hector; and when he returned, she greeted him with gen-tle words and obedience. For her dear sake, although the most valiant of the warriors of Troy, Hector was a kind and honorable lord.

Among the many brothers of Hector were other brave men, Deiphobus, Helenus, and Troilus. With only one of her sons did Queen Hecuba have any difficulty, and this was a great sorrow both to her and to King Priam. During one of her pregnancies Queen Hecuba dreamed that the child within her body was a burning brand of fire. Her dream was so strange that the priests of Zelia were consulted. Their verdict was an ominous one. They believed that this unborn child would bring about the ruin of the whole kingdom. They affirmed most categorically that he must be put to death. Although Hecuba and Priam would have liked to raise the baby boy who was born to the queen, they decided in order to fulfil the orders of the temple to expose the child on the slopes of the Trojan Mount Ida.

Fortunately the loss of this one son was compensated in some measure by the births of other children. One of their daughters was Creüsa, who grew up to marry none other than a son of the goddess Aphrodite. This mischievous god-dess had often plagued the ruler of the gods, Zeus, with a de-sire to possess mortal women, and thus had brought down on his head the baleful glances and swift revenge of his wife Hera. Zeus decided to repay Aphrodite by causing her to be faithless to her husband, Hephaestus, in a similar fashion.

Zeus caused Aphrodite to fall passionately in love with a Trojan shepherd who was guarding his flocks on the slopes of Mount Ida near Troy. In order to satisfy her burning desire, Aphrodite went to infinite trouble. She arrayed herself in silken robes, and selected bright jewels for her throat and perfumes for her hair. Then she descended to earth and pre-tended to be aimlessly strolling through the wooded groves. When she had allowed the shepherd to see her naked body, she confessed her passion modestly. He wondered, it is true, how she happened to be accompanied by tame panthers and lions that rubbed against her thighs and rolled like kittens at her feet. Aphrodite invented a plausible story about how she was really the daughter of a minor Phrygian king who was subject to the overlord Priam.

The delighted shepherd led her at once to his humble

couch, where among the bearskin covers she fulfilled Zeus's wish and conceived a son. After the love-making Aphrodite revealed her true character to the shepherd. Awed and terrified, he fell to his knees. He begged her to forgive the indignity, the humiliation he had caused her. Aphrodite forgave him. She even managed to spare him the punishment usually meted out to mortals who had soiled the body of a goddess. He was allowed by her good graces to keep intact his youth, instead of being changed instantly into a senile, doddering old man.

Aphrodite accompanied her rare charity with an admonition. The shepherd was never to reveal at Troy who the mother of his son was. Relenting even more, the goddess, remembering no doubt how ardently this shepherd had caressed her and how pleasantly he had relieved her of her tormenting desire, condescended to tell him a great secret. This son, whom she would bear him, would resemble a god! The poor fellow listened spellbound to this revelation.

"When he is born," she instructed the shepherd, "you are to call him Aeneas." After a thoughtful pause she added, "I think I shall love him very much in memory of our most enjoyable few hours together." The deity turned back over her shoulder and called to the shepherd, who still remained humbly on his knees, "What did you say your name was, boy?"

"Anchises," he answered.

"Very well," smiled Aphrodite. "I shall remember you too one night in the very midst of hell. Good-by, Anchises."

It was this son of Aphrodite, the godly Aeneas, who married one of the princesses of Troy. Another of Priam's daughters was the Chosen One. This was the pure and holy Cassandra.

From her earliest childhood this daughter had set herself apart as a servant of the gods, and her parents had acquiesced in her wishes. This Cassandra had a rather boyish look. She was not tall. Her hair was blonde and very curly, but her eyes were large and black. She had a round face, fair skin, and a slender nose. With quiet, calm steps she went about her duties as a virgin priestess who knew very little about the world and whose thoughts were only on the gods. Both Priam and Hecuba sensed the tranquil strength in this consecrated daughter, and they were very proud of her. Bearing her keys, her forehead bound with the fillets of a priestess, she moved through the shrine of Apollo with gleaming eyes, inspired with the beauty of the world.

The royal baby abandoned by the rulers of Troy upon the slopes of Mount Ida did not die. His hungry cries attracted a she-bear, who nursed him until he grew tall and strong, able

94

to care for himself. He grew up to be a handsome, blond shepherd dressed in leopard skins, and he was happy. Far from the cares of the world, he led an enchanted existence among the docile flocks, and was beloved of the nymph Oenone. Then one day an order from Zeus came to interrupt his carefree life.

The goddess of discord had incited a quarrel between the three great divinities Athena, Hera, and Aphrodite. Zeus had suggested that the handsome shepherd, whose name was Alexander, settle the argument by awarding a golden apple to the most beautiful. Confused by such a difficult choice, and yet preferring quite clearly the gifts of love to those of lands and possessions or wisdom and valor, Alexander chose the goddess Aphrodite. Immediately afterward he set out for Troy, where his parents, forgetting the oracle, welcomed him. Now the goddess of love had so inflamed him with her promise that he should have as his own the most beautiful woman in the world that Alexander did not even cast a backward glance toward his erstwhile love, Oenone. Once established in Troy as a prince of the blood, he set out royally, this perfumed youth, to visit King Menelaus of Sparta.

When ill fortune happens to a family—for, as the oracle of Zelia had predicted, Prince Alexander would bring no good fortune—it never seems to fall singly. As if the very return of this prince had raised an ill storm, evil fortune then blew about the dedicated priestess Cassandra. Her very distinctive charms, her quiet and modest manner, and the singleness of her rapt devotion brought her to the attention of the god Apollo. One day he appeared, splendid and powerful, before her altar. Blinded by the glory of his presence, Cassandra would have fled or fallen before him in adoration. The god's purpose was very different.

"Cassandra, you must yield to me," he commanded.

"I cannot," answered Cassandra. "I have taken vows of chastity. I have sworn to remain a virgin as long as I live. I cannot break such an oath."

"You are to break it for me," answered Apollo. "A god desires you. I wish to possess you now."

"I cannot. I cannot," Cassandra kept moaning, as she twisted her hands in mortification.

"Cassandra, you must lie here now and allow me to embrace you," commanded Apollo, beginning to be impatient at such a whimsical reluctance. "It is a great honor to offer one's virginity to a god. I release you from your vow."

"Oh, no," pleaded the priestess. Clutching her gown across her body, she backed away from the god, who pressed close after her, swollen with passion.

95

"Come, Cassandra," he panted. "You will be rewarded. Well rewarded. Look. I have already given you the gift of prophecy."

Even as he spoke, the trembling Cassandra felt the walls of her head split open with a maze of moving pictures. Swiftly she closed her eyes and held her fingers over them. It was no use. With regularity the awful pictures flicked on and off before her sight. In horror she shook her head and turned it blindly from side to side.

"What do you see, Cassandra?" intruded the voice of Apollo, who hoped to embrace her while her vigilance was relaxed.

Her voice rose to a shriek. "Oh, I see . . . I see my father lying on the ground in a pool of blood, his drawn sword dangling from his lifeless, blue-veined hand. His white beard is stained in blood . . . oh . . . oh," screamed Cassandra. "Do not let me see these horrors!"

"Then will you yield to me?" insisted Apollo.

"No! No!" she answered, sobbing now and raising her hands to her eyes in an effort to erase the flood of pictures. The god abruptly released her rigid, protesting body.

"Then," decided Apollo, "let me give you one kiss before I go." Imperiously he approached her again as she cowered kneeling at the foot of the altar. "Open your lips, Cassandra, and receive one kiss from a god."

Cassandra did as he commanded. She finally opened her lips and closed her eyes. Apollo bent his gleaming face down to hers and instead of kissing her, he blew in her open mouth. "Good for you, stupid girl," he sneered. "You may keep your virginity for a while. Now, you must henceforth prophesy as long as the gods of Troy shall stand on their altars, and almost as long as you shall live, for all I care. You are a prophetess, Cassandra. I have given you this gift as a souvenir."

The god was already taking his leave. Cassandra could see through the bloody images that his radiance was fading, but she could still hear his parting words. "Prophesy, Cassandra. Look every day at your future. Dare to live what you see is going to happen to you. I have given you a second gift, however. Would you like to know what it is? It is this: you will never be believed! That was my second gift. No matter how truly you see into the future, you will never be believed!"

Hopeless and tortured, bloody scenes of battle and sword succeeding one after another before her bursting eyeballs, Cassandra rushed from the temple and into the audience room of the palace. A polite reception was in progress there, for Prince Alexander had found his mortal bride, the most beautiful woman in all the world. He was just then presenting her to his royal parents. King Priam had just extended his right hand to the couple. Queen Hecuba was appraising the bride with critical eyes that rejoiced in her loveliness and in the full lines of her body that would surely make her a warm lover and a tender wife to Alexander.

Cassandra burst in upon this tranquil scene with a piercing wail of despair. It froze their hearts like the sudden icy blast of winter that clarions sleet and driving snow. Transfixed with fear they heard that long shriek curl about their ears and go moaning along the draughty walls of cold stone. The hair stood up on their heads, and their blood turned cold in their bodies. Still Cassandra screamed, another long, vibrating wail of agony. In horror they looked at her torn garments and recoiled. Not even her father could bear the burning, vacant glare of her bright eyes.

"She has gone mad," whispered Priam to himself. "Cassandra, my dear Cassandra, stop!" he moaned.

Her body stiff and rigid, and her face a chalky, distorted mask, Cassandra stole across the marble floor as if she were a tattered wraith treading on air. Her hair fell in damp ringlets over her eyes, but she did not seem to know it. Straight up to the throne she went and, pointing to her brother, Alexander, screamed again in accusation, "Never call him Alexander! This whelp of a she-bear! This soft and perfumed, loathsome lover! He is the breath of murder, the red-hot, scorching breath of destruction and death! He will kill us all! I see our bloody deaths before my eyes! Kill him before it is too late! Kill him! He is a filthy, swollen worm that will send us all into a violent hell! Step on him! Kill him! His name is *Paris*, he-who-is-wed-with-ghastly-death!

"And as for her," she continued, focusing her blazing eyes on the gentle Helen of Sparta, "send her away. Be rid of her! Send home this voluptuous queen, or you will see how the bees will swarm. They will assemble in clouds and swarm leather-shielded over the seas to sting us all to death. Oh, Hector! My beloved Hector!"

Turning to her brother's wife, Andromache, Cassandra knelt at her feet and touched the hem of her garment. The incredulous spectators began to recover their composure and cast pitying glances to the throne where the aged Priam sat flushed and humiliated. "Save Hector, Andromache. You of all women will know how to do it," pleaded Cassandra. Then her head sank to the marble floor, and she appeared to sleep.

At a command from the king two courtiers lifted the limp, fragile body of Cassandra and carried her down to a cell under the palace where her screams would no longer be heard. Everyone in Troy regretted her madness and pitied her, but no one cared to see her again. Within a few weeks she was, in fact, almost forgotten in the press of an emergency. Troy was indeed besieged by an enormous force from Greece and Crete, led by great warriors, Agamemnon, Menelaus, Achilles, Ajax, Idomeneus, Odysseus! Between Troy and the sea they erected a great stockade to protect their fleet; and there on the damp shore, amidst the fogs of summer evenings and the fierce, howling storms of winter, they besieged Ilion for ten long years.

One day the guard whose duty was to sit outside Cassandra's prison requested an audience with King Priam. Although he did not believe her wild dreams, this rough soldier still felt that he must share the responsibility of his knowledge with the king himself, so terrible was it!

"This war drags on, O King," the soldier began, "and still the priestess Cassandra affirms that the Spartan Helen must be returned to her husband, Menelaus. She says Prince Paris has given indeed a just grievance to the kings of the Peloponnesus. She says Prince Paris was a guest in the court of Menelaus. He broke bread with him and ate salt from his table. Then when Menelaus left on a voyage for Crete, Paris persuaded his wife to elope with him to Troy. Thus was a great crime committed. Helen of Sparta brought vast treasure with her. 'She must be returned, and the treasure a hundredfold,' says Cassandra. O King, please hear her prophecies, for I can no longer sleep at night, they so ring in my ears!"

At the words of the guardian, Trojan courtiers had begun to gather around to listen to the prophecies of Cassandra. Somewhat abashed to be speaking before such a large and important assembly, the soldier proceeded, however, to enumerate them.

"Cassandra says that one tragedy above all others shall eat away her heart. She says her brother, our Prince Hector, will die in this war, that he will topple over like a slender pine on the mountainside. Hector will be slain by the swift Achilles, who will hitch the body of our prince to his chariot and drag it through the dust and rocks." Incredulous murmurs came from the palace courtiers.

"When we of Troy ask for its return, Achilles will refuse us; and you, O King, will go a suppliant to the tent of this hero to sue for it. The eagle will make us all pay dear the body of our Hector. He will not render it for pity, but only for gold. With Hector dead from a gaping wound in his throat, his body soiled and desecrated, we shall have lost the pillar of our house. Cassandra says so shall Troy fall!

"She further says Odysseus and Diomedes will enter the city by night and steal the Palladium itself, our holy image of Pallas Athena upon which our lives and safety depend. They will not fear to touch the sacred stone with their polluted hands, even though it fell to us from the very skies themselves. Odysseus will creep into the city disguised as a Greek deserter. He will dare to profane the image, and will send it over the seas to Greece. Cassandra says we have a traitor in our midst, a false woman who will see these furtive thieves, who will recognize the fabled boar's-tusk helmet of Odysseus, and will not reveal their presence to us. This woman is the white dove, Helen of Sparta.

"Now the Princess Cassandra tells another story, which is very wild indeed. She says the Greeks will pretend to leave Troy because they have angered Athena. She says they will construct a mighty horse of fir and oak planks. She says you are not to touch the horse, not to trust it, not to tear down the walls of Troy in order to pull its mighty mass into the city. She says this horse will bring us all to ruin. She says it will be some trick of Menelaus, some stealth of his to enter the city in search of his long-lost wife whom he covets even now. Cassandra says you are not to negotiate with Menelaus or to trust his word, but only the word of Agamemnon.

"Cassandra says our fair city of Troy will fall in the night while its soldiers are sleeping, while we think the Greeks have left for home. Then will come fire and destruction. Then will walls come crashing down over our heads. Then will friend kill friend, for no one will see in the flames and darkness who is Greek and who is Trojan. Then will the bloody Pyrrhus storm our cedar portals with his ax. His father Achilles will be dead by that time. For even the great Achilles will die at Troy.

"It will be good to see Achilles dead, Cassandra says, the valiant Achilles whose mother so feared this war that she concealed him in Scyros dressed up as a virgin. Her love and care will not follow him forever. He will die in the temple of Apollo while bargaining for the hand of Princess Polyxena of Troy. Then will Paris shoot him through the heel with a poisoned arrow; and like a man, not like a hero, will he die while Ajax and Odysseus quarrel over his new armor. Your vengeance will also be swift and cruel, for Troy will haggle over his body with the Greeks.

"Next will die the dainty princess of Troy, Polyxena, not for any sin of hers, not for any quarrel with the Greeks. She will die because she had been promised to Achilles. Cassandra says the Greeks will cluster armor-clad about the altar and pray. Then at a nod from Odysseus will two strong ones lift the maiden high above the altar as you would lift a fawn, hunched forward, its thin neck over the blood basins. Her weak cries of 'Hector! Hector!' will pierce the air in vain, for Hector will lie rotting in his shroud. Her desperate eyes will roam about the temple searching for one kind face among the throng of bearded veterans, war-black, blood-thirsty, foreign warriors. Then will her immolators bind her mouth, for her pitiful cries of pain and fright will have driven the quiet Agamemnon from the temple. So died in her saffron robes his own little daughter when the seas stormed and the winds prevented the Greeks' thousand galleys from setting sail for Troy.

"Agamemnon, king of Mycenae, would have prevented the sacrifice of Polyxena, had he been able, says Cassandra. He will not be able, and so shall perish in agony the frail maiden, Polyxena, at the command of Achilles' ghost. Into the basins will flow her bright, red blood.

"The Greeks will not let Paris live long either—he who should have been put to death at birth, this wretched cause of all our sufferings. He will die too, just as Achilles died, with the sting of a poisoned arrow, with his flesh bloating and putrefying from the jagged wound. Then will Paris remember old friends in his distress. Then will he turn his head away from the gentle dove of Greece when she tiptoes in to measure his minutes with her beautiful, soft eyes.

"Only one person will know the remedy for the envenomed arrows of Heracles, and she will be far away on the slopes of Mount Ida. She will turn deaf ears to Paris' messengers. Only when she sees her faithless lover stretched in rigid death, will Oenone relent and mourn him. Then the nymph in her sorrow will hurl herself from our battlements and die.

"Cassandra says she will return to serve the temple of Athena. She says you will eventually call her up from her dungeon but keep far away from her wild eyes. There will her own story be re-enacted, says Cassandra. This time the lesser Ajax will force his way into the sanctuary, breathing lust all over his stupid, ox's face. Even though Cassandra clutches the feet of the goddess, he will tear at her garments and seize her by the hair. There, in the temple itself, the bearded Ajax will rape Cassandra.

"The goddess, shocked at man's brutality, will avert her eyes from such a horror. Not yet will a Trojan maiden live to be pure and serve the gods! Not yet will a Trojan hero dare to hope while the Greek conquers and burns the city.

"Even Your Majesty, King Priam, you also—Cassandra says—must die in this war. She says the beastly son of Achilles, snakelike in new armor, will tear down the bronze-bound doors of our palace. Like an executioner, Pyrrhus will swing his ax from right to left splitting skulls and mangling bodies. The young prince, Polites, will he send bleeding unto death right in the courtyard shrine where his mother, Hecuba, is crouching. Then, O King, clad in your armor of youth, you will raise a trembling old hand to save your son. You will hurl your feeble spear against the Greek's breastplates. Pyrrhus will laugh at the light blow. He will advance and plunge his steaming sword into your body, up to the hilt into your flesh. . . . How can I bear to hear such horrors?" the soldier cried. "Cassandra says then will our royal ladies be taken prisoner, our Queen Hecuba, Hector's wife Andromache, and herself."

"What of our grandson, Astyanax?" Priam questioned.

"He is also to die, in babyhood, Cassandra says. They will not leave a son of Priam to grow up in whatever corner of Asia he might find a haven, for fear of his eventual revenge. The sly Odysseus will snatch this child from his mother's arms and hurl him down from the walls of our burning citadel. 'Not yet do I see a Trojan hero who will live,' cries Cassandra.

"Andromache will fall to the lot of Pyrrhus. She will follow him gently and without complaint, for she who has known the arms of Hector encircling her in the night will best bear the insults of captivity. Andromache alone will one day remarry a prince of Troy, the courteous Helenus. Together they will make a realm beyond the sea. There, once more secure, Andromache may pray again to the shade of her beloved Hector.

"As for our queen, the lady Hecuba, she will become the slave of Odysseus and be borne by him to Thrace. She will never forgive him for his baseness, particularly for the murder of the child Astyanax. An old, nagging, fearless woman, Hecuba will never cease taunting this Greek, never cease calling him foul names until in desperation and anger, he will lapidate her as one does a mongrel bitch. 'Bitch' he will call her, as he hurls the first stone at her white head.

"May I go on, O King?" the guardian asked. All around him the courtiers of Priam listened with smiles of amusement on their faces at the child's tale he was recounting.

"Go on," King Priam commanded. "What of the Greeks? What kind of story does our daughter make up about them?"

"First Cassandra spoke of Ajax the Locrian, he who will violate her in the temple of Athena. This lesser Ajax will die, she says, but not by his own hand and the sword he had as a present from Hector, as will the great Ajax. This Locrian

101

Ajax will die by drowning in the wild waters of the sea. The goddess Athena will not let them all escape, these impious Greeks. Great winds shall drive this Ajax on the stormy rocks, where he will cling for dear life and boast how beloved he is of those on Olympus. Then will Poseidon split the rock and flood great waves over his head. Then will the sea god choke Ajax with huge throatfuls of sea water.

"Then Athena will send a plague to devastate the Locrians as further retribution for the desecration of Ajax. For the rape of Cassandra, she says, they will be taxed to furnish two maidens per year for the temple of Athena at Troy. The punishment is to last a thousand years.[1] The first maidens will be stoned to death, just like Queen Hecuba, their bodies burned, and their ashes strewn over the sea. As for her punishment to the other Greeks, Athena will disperse them with storms that will rage over their guilty heads for years and years.

"Acamus, son of the Athenian Theseus, will be shipwrecked on the shores of Cyprus. The curse of the gods shall rest above his head until the son of this Acamus is killed in Thrace. Idomeneus too shall drag out his unfortunate life in a strange, new land. This handsome king of Crete shall return to find his island desolate, weed-ridden, its inhabitants decimated by a plague. During his absence at Troy his queen and her daughter will be cruelly murdered.

"Helen of Sparta will return to the Peloponnesus with her doting Menelaus, the curse of thousands upon her lovely head. As a parting gift to Troy she will light torches and lead the Greeks into the palace, where they will fall upon Hector's brother, Prince Deiphobus, as he lies sleeping on his nuptial couch. This prince too will she have added to the list of her conquests after the sudden death of Paris. Menelaus will rush upon the sleeping youth, slit his nostrils, rip off his ears, lacerate his upraised palms, and send him headlong to join the throngs of illustrious dead in the dark Underworld. Menelaus will take his Helen, but they will also be punished with long, sea-tossed voyages along the coasts of Asia and Africa before they ever regain their Spartan court.

" 'Our little war shall be forgot,' Cassandra says. 'It is only one of the many wars fought and to be fought by men of the East against those of the West.

" 'Do you remember the great hero Perseus, he who slew the Gorgon? Far to the east, beyond the double rivers, high on the plateau of Asia, Perseus will father a race of warriors, a band of rulers, whose magnificent King of Kings will laugh before Athens' wooden walls. Their great King Xerxes

[1] Almost until Plutarch's time.

will burn those walls to the ground before he returns to Persia.

" 'Perseus will then provide a champion for the West, who will grow up dreaming of subduing Persia. The world will not soon forget his name. While still young, he will visit his vengeance upon his Persian brother and roll his tide of battle from Macedon to Egypt and even to the land of India. His name will also be Alexander.' "

King Priam sat pensive as these words of prophecy rolled about his ears. Affected in spite of himself, he mournfully asked the guardian, "Is that all? Sees our daughter no hope at all for Troy? Sees she not one of us to live, not one hero to bear our household gods out of the city's burning? Must we all die and our children's unborn children?"

At these questions the soldier shifted from one foot to another and hesitated to answer. Finally he began reluctantly to speak, "Yes, there is one more prophecy. However, I do not understand it at all.

"Cassandra says there is among us, within the walls of our wind-swept citadel, a gentler hero than the world has seen up to now. He is," and here the soldier looked about and lowered his voice, "he is . . . not even the son of a king. He is the son . . . I cannot understand this secret. How could a hero be only the son of . . . He is the son of a shepherd! Yes, that is what Cassandra says. He is the son of a Trojan shepherd, but his mother is Love. His mother is the goddess of Love. His name is Aeneas.

"Now this Aeneas is married to Creüsa, a princess of Troy. It is therefore true that their son Iulus, or Ascanius as he is sometimes called, has the blood of Hector in his veins.

"Cassandra says the night Troy burns, a golden light will come to play around the head of Iulus. This will be a sign from heaven. For that night Aphrodite herself will walk through the city beside them, and they will pass through fire and never feel the flames. That night, in the very midst of hell, the goddess will save Anchises, her son Aeneas, and the grandson Iulus. Not Creüsa. She must stay in Troy to pray for our dead. She will stay to worship the earth goddess, Cybele, whom our ancestors brought with them from Crete.

"Aeneas will carry our household gods safely from Troy. With twenty ships he will wander through the sea until he comes to the land of Hesperia, a fabled country in the portals of the west. His son Iulus will reign in this place of Italy for thirty years. Then for 300 years the lineage of Hector shall be crowned in this western kingdom. After that will be founded from our race a great eternal city. Its name will be

Rome. Mankind by that time shall have reached another Age of Gold.

"This is all Cassandra's dream and all her prophecy."

It was not believed. None of it was believed, for that was the curse of Cassandra. Nonetheless the machines of the gods ground out their irrevocable happenings. Troy fell. The peerless heroes, Achilles and Hector, fought and died. Troy burned and toppled, lofty towers and all. Everything occurred as the prophetess had foretold. Cassandra moved from her temple with the line of prisoners and saw her mother wrapping the tiny broken corpse of Astyanax in bands of linen and laying him to rest on Hector's shield. The sea was red with flames, and the night hideous with wailing. Cassandra moved slowly forward among the women of Troy, down the hill for the last time, across the plain and to the seashore where the loaded galleys from Greece danced, impatient to walk the waves toward home.

Behind her, high on the summit of Mount Ida, flared the bright beacon that would flash its news of victory westward across the Hellespont, to the Lemnian Rock of Hermes, to the heights of Mount Athos, on to a dozen watchful sentinels, and so to the valley that sloped toward the plain of Argos. Here in this valley, surrounded by lofty hills, the wealthy city of Mycenae awaited the return of Agamemnon, its king.

When Cassandra reached the bottom of the hill, she was motioned toward the galley of Agamemnon. This king himself stood by the shore waiting for her. As she approached where he stood tall and somber on the beach, she slowly and deliberately tore from her hair the sacred fillets of the priestess. Untying her keys to the temple from her golden girdle, she dropped them on the wet sand. She neither looked directly at Agamemnon nor spoke to him.

"Is it really you, Cassandra?" he whispered. "My sweet Cassandra. My nightingale." Gently he bent over her bowed head, hoping that she would look up at him. "To me," he murmured, "has fallen the chosen flower of all the beauties of Troy. You shall be met with every gentleness. The gods alone have loved you until now."

The signal fires had done their work well. The news of the fall of Troy had arrived at the golden citadel of Mycenae long before the galley of the king. In her opulent court Queen Clytemnestra welcomed the tidings, for she had waited ten long years for the day that her husband Agamemnon would return.

Hers was not the fate of so many women of Hellas who had to endure the news of their loved one's death and the

104

more awful thought that their bodies lay unburied upon a foreign shore where no loving hands could bathe them and prepare them for their long journey after death. Clytemnestra had not shared her sisters' fortunes. She had not spent ten loveless years awaiting the possible return of her lord. During all this time her hatred of Agamemnon had rankled and festered in her violent heart. She loathed him, even to the sound of his name.

Ten years before, when the gods had prevented the starving Greeks from setting sail for Troy, the warriors, in compliance with the wishes of Artemis, had demanded a human sacrifice. Agamemnon as their king and leader of the expedition had yielded and reluctantly summoned his own young daughter, Iphigenia, under the pretense of marrying her to Achilles. There she had been sacrificed, as Polyxena was later offered to the gods at Troy. Because of the loss of Iphigenia, Clytemnestra had hated Agamemnon.

All this time she and her lover Aegisthus, who was a cousin of the king, had planned a royal welcome. The sharpened ax that Clytemnestra would swing down upon Agamemnon's skull stood ready just inside the bath. The woven, intricate carpets of Tyrian purple, more valuable than gold, were ready to be spread between his chariot and the door. Clytemnestra had, folded and ready also, the swathing robe of royal purple she would throw around him so that, with its folds enveloping his hands and arms, he would never be able to defend himself.

Amidst shouts of welcome the chariot of Agamemnon rolled through the Lion Gate and up to the portal, followed by another splendid one in which stood the princess of Troy, Cassandra. Before her eyes the future was clear and unconfused, only one picture left. Ever since her awakening that morning there had been no more scenes of horror before her eyes, except the last one of her death. Her ears were clear from shrieks and groans. There was no sound at all except the false, welcoming words of the yellow-faced Clytemnestra. As if from far away, Cassandra heard her arguing with her husband. She realized that Agamemnon had finally yielded, that he was allowing his sandals to be removed, that he had agreed to tread upon her crimson carpet royally.

Then Agamemnon, in disregard of protocol, turned to Cassandra's chariot and helped her to descend. Once more she felt the strong, warm touch of his hand. Smiling to his courtiers and friends, Agamemnon entered the portal first, followed by Cassandra.

There was a silent pause while he allowed his wife to

shroud him in the crimson gown. Then the cortege advanced majestically into the central courtyard.

The evil, distorted face of Clytemnestra did not frighten Cassandra, for she had grown used to it in her dreams. In her last moments she concentrated on Hector. At the thought of him whom she would see so soon, her eyes filled with tears.

With yellow teeth bared in her mighty effort to swing the ax powerfully, Clytemnestra brought it down across the head of Agamemnon, who fell heavily to the floor, waving his arms to disengage them. As Clytemnestra's ax struck Cassandra and she fell gratefully, she saw one last thing she had never noticed in her dreams. As she fell dying, Cassandra saw the hand of Agamemnon raised to save her.

5
Persia and Afghanistan:
The Coming of Rustam
Rustam and Kai-Kaus
Rustam and Suhrab

INTRODUCTION

THE EXTENSIVE LEGENDS of Persia were collected by one poet and rewritten by him over a period of more than thirty years. Modern scholars have found from their own research that these stories are faithful retellings of much older material taken from Pahlavi or Middle Persian sources. The poet's name was Firdausi, and he lived from 941 to 1019.

The *Shah Namah,* or *Book of Kings,* of Firdausi covers the history of Persia over a total period of 3,874 years, or from 3223 B.C. to the Mohammedan conquest of Persia in A.D. 651. In the *Shah Namah* we are given the names of the rulers of Persia, whose reigns are divided into four dynasties.

There are several obstacles to the reconciliation of these dynastic lists with the Western beliefs concerning Persia. The greatest difficulty is one of names and the people or places to which the names refer. The territories of Persia varied extensively over its long history from a small area west of the Persian Gulf to the empire of Darius with its twenty satrapies, which included parts of northern Greece and Africa, all of Asia Minor and the Middle East through Afghanistan, and extended into India on the east and China on the north. It would be difficult to say at what time separate dynasties were coruling in these wide domains, and only an extensive knowledge of all the dozens of lost and half-forgotten languages of these many and varied peoples could hope to straighten the tangle of references. Another difficulty is one of geography, particularly for the Westerner.

The ancient Persians looked about them from the central plain of Iran and concluded that the earth was encircled by mountains, a theory similar to that of the Greeks, who decided that it was surrounded by the waters of a stream they called Oceanus. Persia is, indeed, practically surrounded by mountain ranges. The poet Firdausi followed ancient tradition in calling all of them the "Elburz." Modern scholars of Persia, such as Professor James Darmesteter of the Collège de France, have struggled to be more specific.

As far as Persia is concerned, people there have less of a problem. They are not bound by the writings of Herodotus as we are. We speak of their kings by Western names, which were given by the Greeks—Darius, Cyrus, Cambyses, and Xerxes. Persians recognize their own kings by their Persian names, and they regard the *Shah Namah* of Firdausi as verbatim truth.

Occasionally the Western and Eastern views of Persia's history almost coincide. If in the celebrated account of Cyrus the Great, as told by Herodotus, we substitute wherever he says "Media" or "Mede" the Persian word of "Turan" or "Turanian," the two versions are substantially the same. Early Western geographers and Matthew Arnold supposed Turan to have been east of the Caspian Sea, and have talked about battles along the Oxus (Amu Darya) River. Since Firdausi did not commit himself, more recent scholars believe that his Turan referred to the highly contested area in the Caucasus, west of the Caspian Sea.

The Persians performed one of their last great deeds in the ancient world by stopping the eastward expansion of the Roman Empire, and by taking prisoner the Emperor Valerius himself. By A.D. 651 they were conquered by the Arabs, as the *Shah Namah* predicts, and converted to Mohammedanism. Followers of the Persian religion of Zoroaster fled to India, where they live today as the Parsees. Fortunately the

old history of Persia did not die entirely, thanks to the life-
work of the patriotic Firdausi, who was born in the city of
Tus near Meshad in eastern Iran, where some of his story
takes place.

The following chapter is a condensation of Book I and
about half of Book II of the *Shah Namah*. The entire poem
is 60,000 couplets long, an unbelievable feat for one poet.
Four translations have been used:

1.	French	Jules de Mohl	prose	7 vols.	3,500 pp.*
2.	Italian	Italo Pizzi	poetry	8 vols.	4,000 pp.*
3.	English	George and Edmond Warner	poetry	9 vols.	4,500 pp.*
4.	English	Atkinson abridgment	prose	1 vol.	412 pp.

* Approximate figures.

The poem has been partially translated into German, and
other fragmentary translations have been done.

Western readers know the *Shah Namah* from Matthew
Arnold's superb poem "Sohrab and Rustum." Arnold was
accused by a contemporary of having plagiarized Jules de
Mohl's French translation, which was announced to the public by none other than Sainte-Beuve. However, Arnold's
poem was printed in 1853, and the de Mohl translation appeared only in 1876. Arnold's source was Sir John Malcolm's
History of Persia. Arnold said, "For my part, I only regret
that I could not meet with a translation from Firdausi's
poem. . . . I should certainly have made all the use I could
of it."

The modern lover of Persian poetry must give homage
where it is due—to the pioneer work of Jules de Mohl, a
professor at the Collège de France, whose long labors were
interrupted by the Revolution of 1848, so that he died without having finished his translation of the *Livre des rois*. One
of the Warner brothers also died before the work was finished,
but the other brother continued it alone. All of these scholars
were most erudite men; in addition to Persian the Warners
knew Hebrew, Syriac, and Arabic. Of all the translators,
however, the Italian scholar Italo Pizzi, whose version appeared in 1886, is the most unreserved in his love for this
great epic. He says that the poem from its very beginning
gives one the impression of vastness, like that of a starry
sky which unites in its dazzling constellations the infinite
plurality of the world. (*"L'epopea persiana, nel suo insieme,
produce l'impressione dell' incommensurabile, simile alla
vista del cielo stellato, che ruinisce nei suoi fulgidi sistemi di*

stelle l'infinita pluralità dei mondi.") He felt that there is no other country in the world that has such a rich poetic treasure as Persia. (*"Non vi ha forse in tutto il mondo paese più ricco della Persia in leggende eroiche."*)

The American admirer of Persian poetry may remember one of our great scholars, Professor A. V. Williams Jackson, who wrote four splendid books on Persia; who visited Iran in 1903, 1907, 1910, and 1918; who swung on a goat's-hair rope down the side of Mount Behistun to verify the cuneiform translations which Rawlinson had made of Darius the Great's trilingual inscription. Professor Jackson was a Columbia graduate and a professor at that university from 1883 to his death on August 8, 1937. No Westerner ever loved Persia more than did this great scholar. He has also left us in his book *Early Persian Poetry* several translations of the same material the reader will find in the following pages. Professor Jackson's very beautiful poetry is the only one I know that follows the style of Firdausi, rhyming couplets of tetrameter verse with anapaestic feet prevailing.

Firdausi has been compared to Homer, to Chaucer, to Layamon, and to the author of the *Beowulf* epic. While all of these comparisons have some grain of truth, it seems rather that there is no work in the Western world of such length and completeness. Our epics are episodes by comparison.

The government of Iran assures us that even children in the streets of Teheran know whole chapters of the *Shah Namah* by heart. The reader may be interested to know that Columbia University possesses two manuscripts of this work. One, from the sixteenth century, is in book form with a dark red, lacquered cover and a Persian design of roses and lilies. Unbelievably beautiful, it has many full-page illustrations, hand-painted in brilliant colors and with brush strokes so fine that they show every blade of grass and even the hairs in Rustam's eyebrows.

THE COMING OF RUSTAM

BY 2400 B.C. the ancient land of Sumer, the oldest in Mesopotamia, began to be invaded by Semitic warriors whose original homeland may have been Arabia. These fierce invaders, known to us as the Akkadians, swept down over the Tigris and Euphrates valleys under their great King Sargon, as the Amorites under the lawgiver Hammurabi, and as the Assyrians. The Assyrian empire furnished the idea and pattern for later conquests and the organization of conquered nations. According to Western historians, the Assyrian kings

PAISHDADIAN DYNASTY (Ten shahs—2441 years)*

Kauimers	30 years	
Husheng	40 "	
Tahmuras	30 "	
Jemshid (or Yama)	700 "	
Zahhak the Semite	1000 "	
Feridun	500 "	
Minuchir	120 "	(birth of Rustam)
Nauder	7 "	
Zav	5 "	
Garshasp of Balkh	9 "	

KAIANIAN DYNASTY (Ten shahs—732 years)*

Kai-Kobad	100 "	
" Kaus	150 "	
" Khosrau (Cyrus the Great)	60 "	
" Lohrasp of Balkh	120 "	
" Gustasp " "	120 "	(death of Rustam)
" Bahman	99 "	
" Humay (Regent)	32 "	
" Darab	12 "	
" Dara	14 "	
" Sikander	14 "	(Alexander the Great)

ASKANIAN DYNASTY (One shah—200 years)*

Ashgani	200 "

SASANIAN DYNASTY (Twenty-one shahs—501 years)

Shah Namah ends in A.D. 651 with the Arab Conquest.

* These are the totals according to the manuscript which the Warner brothers used.

DYNASTIES OF PERSIA

ruled in unparalleled cruelty and savagery a vast realm that extended from western Egypt across Arabia, through Babylon and eastward toward the Indus River and the great mountain ranges of central Asia. Western historians date their hated conquests and their mass deportations of subject peoples—such as that of the Ten Tribes of the Jews in 721 B.C.—from the fall of Babylon in 910 B.C. to the battle of Carchemish in 612 B.C.

Now, the battle of Carchemish was fought in Syria, a little to the west of the headwaters of the Euphrates, near the Amanus Mountains where Gilgamesh had sought his precious cedars. To this westward spot, close to 300 miles away from the Assyrian capital at Nineveh, near the northern reaches of the Tigris, were the Assyrian wolves driven.

They were defeated by the learned Chaldeans of Babylon, who hired and persuaded Asiatic tribesmen—bigger, more savage, and more warlike, mounted on swifter horses—to hunt down and utterly annihilate the Assyrians. These tribesmen were the Medes and Scythians (Persians and Bactrians) from Iran. From that day onward in history the story of these Asiatic tribesmen has of necessity, and by all rights, also to be heard and considered.

The ancient land of Iran, say the Persians, extended from the Zagros Mountains and the Persian Gulf on the west to the Hindu Kush Mountains and the Indus River on the east. It reached northward on the western shores of the Caspian Sea up to the Caucasus Mountains of what is today the Azerbaidzhan Soviet Socialist Republic. On the eastern shores of the Caspian its borders reached into Turan, or well into the modern province of the Turkmen S.S.R.

This vast tableland of Iran was settled by Asiatic tribesmen whose name was "Aryan," or "noble." They had all come originally from the area of Balkh in the northern province of what is today Afghanistan. From Balkh, this "beautiful city of high flags," successive migrations spread southward from the shores of the Amu Darya (Oxus) River into the Land of the Seven Rivers (the Punjab) and into India.

A second and third wave of peoples moved slowly southwestward across the high plateau of Asia, or Iran. There they may be identified as the Medes, who settled the south shores of the Caspian and built their capital of Ecbatana halfway between the Tigris River and the Elburz Mountains. A second group called Iranians or Persians settled in the area along the Persian Gulf in the land of the Elamites, and their capital was at Susa. The remaining Aryans continued to occupy eastern Iran, or the area around Balkh and Herat, the capital of modern Afghanistan. Leaving aside for the moment those Aryans who invaded India, we find that the three kingdoms of ancient Iran were Media and Persia in the west and Balkh, or Bactria, in the east.

The first king, say the eastern historians, was Yama, who ruled about 3500 B.C. from the city of Balkh. He explained the science of agriculture to his people and the use of metals. With the latter knowledge they forged arms, mounted their horses, and set out to conquer the "eastern and western hemispheres." The horse was one of their great contribu-

111

tions to the Western world. This King Yama is also mentioned in the sacred *Avesta* and in the *Vedas* of India. He founded the Peshdadian Dynasty, which was followed by the Kava or "Wise" Dynasty. The third dynasty of Balkh was called Aspa from its founder Lahra-Aspa, or Lord of Swift Horses. During the reign of the third Aspa king, around 1000 B.C., the great prophet Zarathustra appeared in Balkh.

This prophet converted the King Gusht-Aspa to his way of thinking. Zarathustra said that religion should be a practical way of life, that each man should be able to choose light from darkness, right from wrong, good from evil. He said a man should apply his powers of reasoning directly to the problems of his life and distinguish clearly, by his own powers of thought, the beauty of pure and abstract truth. The thinking of Zarathustra appeared in the five books of the *Avesta*, which were carried into Hind, or India, by the Aryans of Balkh. Fire temples of the Zoroastrian religion were constructed throughout Iran from Kabulistan in the east to Mazinderan on the Caspian Sea.

The second group of Iranians were the Medes. We remember them in Western history for their wise priests or magi. Three of the magi are said to have traveled once, much later, bearing gold, frankincense, and myrrh, to Bethlehem in Judaea. Their journey, which had been foretold by the prophet of Iran, Zoroaster, was made possible by the light of a star which showed them the way to Bethlehem and also guided their homeward journey to northern Iran. The descendants of the Medes worshiped fire and lived in modern times in Kurdistan in the southern Caucasus. It was here that Zeus had chained the fire-bearing Prometheus. It was to this same area also that Jason sailed in search of the Golden Fleece and the Dragon Queen, Medea.

According to the Persians, the third group of Aryan people, who finally became all-powerful in Iran, their first king was Kauimers. He gave them a code of laws and ruled them for thirty years, or from about 3600 B.C. Then came King Husheng, whose reign lasted for forty years. After him ruled a glorious king named Tahumers, who destroyed a great many wicked magi, or evil demons, in Media.

The reign of Jemshid, fourth shah of Iran, lasted for 700 years. In Indian and Afghan tradition he is identified with Yama. This king constructed a *var,* or huge underground palace, in anticipation of the flood that would destroy the earth. Like a bright shepherd he ruled over the seven climatic zones of the earth, and divided all his subjects into four castes, thus making the rulers and warriors distinct from the artisans and peasants. Jemshid built a throne at Persepolis,[1] a platform adorned with forty columns, each sixty feet high. It was upon this platform that the splendid white palaces of his successors could rise proud and gleaming in the southern plain. To this stronghold the King Vishtaspa of Balkh later sent the gold-embossed original copy of the *Avesta;* and here it was burned, along with the palace of Persepolis, in one of Alexander I's drunken orgies.

The rule of Jemshid, so gloriously begun, ended in a darkness that was to last a thousand years. Iran was conquered and Jemshid killed. The conquerors were relatives of the same Semitic warriors from the Tigris-Euphrates valleys to the west of Iran. For a thousand years their awesome king, named Zahhak in eastern tradition, lorded it over the Medes and the Persians. The Assyrians also advanced toward the third kingdom, or Bactria, and besieged the city of Balkh with an army of two million men. Eventually this last stronghold capitulated to them.

The despotic king named Zahhak had come, according to Persian tradition, from Arabia. His capital was in Babylon. From his great palace he ordered tribute from all of Iran, thousands of stallions and tens of thousands of Persian lambs. For a thousand years the heroes of Persia dreamed of unseating this monstrous, three-nosed, triple-skulled, six-eared foreigner. They also thought about liberating and possessing his two wives, who were reputed to be beauties of unequaled charms.

Finally, at the end of the thousand years, a dragon king named Feridun was born in Persia. After good advice, aided by the blacksmith Kava, and escorted by a vast army reinforced with elephants, Feridun conquered Zahhak. Winding him in fetters of lion's hide, he carried the tyrant to Mount Damavand. There in a cave on this more than 19,000-foot mountain he bound him eternally, for eleven millennia to come. He was wise enough not to kill Zahhak, for from his severed body would have crept toads and frogs, and other loathsome creatures. Feridun then proceeded to rule all of Iran for 500 years.

The next shah of Iran was Minuchir, son of Manu, who reigned for 120 years. This ruler gave the southeastern part of his realm—over toward the Indus River, Seistan and Zabulistan—to the command of a great hero named Sam. The hero blessed the shah, wished him a long and prosperous reign, swore to defeat all the enemies of Iran, and left the coronation ceremonies homeward bound for Seistan. His capital lay near a lake into which the Helmand River, which

[1] Near present-day Shiraz.

rises near the Khyber Pass, brings its waters after its 700-mile journey. Sam would have been perfectly happy, for the land was delivered of Assyrian rule, and a good shah was on the ivory throne. One sorrow grieved him deeply. He had no son to follow in his footsteps.

It was with great secret joy that he learned upon his return to Seistan that one of his wives, a lovely beauty with a gentle face like a moon and long, curling ringlets, was expecting a child shortly. Soon after Sam's return a baby was born, but the palace women did not dare to show it to him. It was a very lusty baby with pink cheeks, bright eyes, and strong limbs. But its hair was the color of snow, and so were its eyelashes. For several days the palace women tried to decide what to do.

Finally one of them courageously lifted the beautifully swaddled baby and bore him directly to Sam. "Great warrior, rejoice," she told him. "You have a strong son to follow in your hero's trade. He is a boy fashioned of the whitest silver. Even his hair is silver! Therefore, hero, give thanks to our Maker who willed it thus!"

Sam glanced only once at the child and motioned for him to be taken away. He realized sadly that he would be an object of ridicule throughout Persia with a son whose locks were white with old age. Sternly Sam commanded that the baby Zal be carried to a lonely mountain in India, where rise the loftiest peaks on earth. Here the luckless infant was exposed to die, naked. His father never thought of him again because he knew it must have been the Median demons who had played such a trick on him in order to ruin his otherwise terrifying reputation.

Many years later Sam, perhaps because he was beginning to feel in his bones the first signs of old age, dreamed of Zal, his snowy-haired son. In his dream a caravan laboring northward out of India brought him word that the boy was still alive. When Sam recounted his dream to the magi priests of his palace, they berated him sharply. They told him that even the wild animals of the desert care more for their young than Iranian heroes. They said if Zal had been born to a leopard, that animal would have shielded him from the burning sun and let him nestle close to her at night. The priests advised Sam to spend the rest of his days searching for Zal, if need be. They gave him, however, one word of comfort, saying that the Creator would never let perish from either heat or cold one whom he loved. Sam was sorely ashamed, for looking at his own graying head, he no longer had any such reason to despise a white-haired son.

Calling around him a large band of warriors, Sam galloped away across the Punjab and into India. There on a lofty peak he made out a large bird's nest. It belonged to the simurgh, the fabled bird who nursed her young from breasts like a bat's, while she spread her ruby wings around them to keep them warm. She had taken the baby Zal into her eyrie, had raised him among her young, and had loved him dearly. When Sam shaded his eyes and looked again toward the high black crag, he discerned a handsome youth standing on the rim of the gabled nest. Then the warrior Sam prayed as he had never done in battle, for there was no possible way to scale the rock needle, no way at all.

Fortunately the devoted simurgh, looking down from her unassailable crag, saw the richly dressed paladins of Persia. Saying good-by to her beloved Zal, the kind bird carried him to earth and set him at his father's feet. Zal's eyes were full of tears, for though she had taught him the speech of men, he had never seen a man before. Zal reproached the simurgh for returning him to his father. Then because she loved the boy, the radiant bird plucked out one of her brilliant scarlet feathers. Giving it to Zal, she said, "You will also be my child always. If you ever need me, if you are ever betrayed or in great danger, burn this feather. Then I will fly to your aid at once."

With tears in his eyes Sam thanked the simurgh for having nursed his son with her red milk, and he begged the stalwart Zal to forgive him. Before all the noble paladins of Persia he swore solemnly that he would always treat Zal gently, and that he would allow the boy to rule him in every way that would bring about his son's happiness.

Great was Sam's joy and his heart full to bursting as he saw how the bearded warriors of Iran greeted his son. They walked about Zal marveling at his broad shoulders, his well-developed thighs, his sturdy body. They praised his clear eyes and his hand that seemed so apt to grasp the Indian scimitar. Black silken trousers were brought for him, a gold-brocade tunic, a wide belt, and a dagger. His long, white hair flowing over his shoulders, Zal mounted an Arab steed, and then the whole company set out for Zabul and Seistan.

Before them the drummers kept up an exciting rhythm from their perches on the lead elephants. Clarions sounded. Golden gongs and bells from India shrilled the news far and wide. In his palace at Amul the shah Minuchir heard the glad news and sent a courier posthaste to offer Sam his congratulations. This horseman was followed by a caravan laden with gifts from the shah to Zal—slaves bearing silver platters, loaded high with emeralds and turquoises, Arab

THE FINDING OF ZAL

horses with golden furnishings, rich carpets from Kerman, suits of armor, brocade cloaks with wide golden belts, bows and arrows, and a gleaming signet ring.

Then Sam entrusted all his kingdom to Zal, for the warrior had been commanded by the shah to exterminate a vulture-headed tribe that were robbing and pillaging the shah's domains in Mazinderan, the land of the Medes. Sam left Zal the key to his treasuries and full powers to govern as he pleased during his father's absence. After a sincere exchange of compliments and long farewells, the trumpets sounded, the drums rolled, and Sam set out for war. Zal watched his father's army march out of the city gates until the whole plain beyond was a cloud of dust from their thundering hoofs. Then he sat upon his ivory throne, took counsel with the elders, and ruled Seistan, Hind, and Zabulistan wisely and well. Everyone praised his judgment and respected him so much that they would have sworn his white locks were as black as ebony.

One day Zal decided to travel forth from Seistan and see the vast lands that he was governing. To the north of his capital lay a great city called Kabul. It was a picturesque spot because of the Hindu Kush Mountains that rose to snow-capped peaks behind it. Here reigned a powerful and wealthy potentate named Mihrab who was descended from the hated Assyrian conqueror Zahhak. His domains were not powerful enough to allow him to raise an army against Sam, and so Mihrab contented himself with paying tribute and accepting Sam as his overlord. When news reached Mihrab that the newly found Zal was going to pay him a visit, coming in a lordly procession with minstrels and harpists for the sole purpose of travel and diversion, he ordered his city made festive to receive the youth. Then Mihrab prepared rich gifts—caparisoned thoroughbreds, slave boys, gold coins, spices, and furs—and set out richly dressed to meet Zal's troupe. When Mihrab saw the new prince's cavalcade on the horizon, he and his noble Semitic chiefs dismounted and, leading their horses, advanced on foot toward Zal. Then, kneeling, they kissed the ground and awaited his greeting.

Zal was highly gratified by this proper reception. The youth was in holiday mood. He and Mihrab sat down to a sumptuous feast. Mihrab regaled his guest with dancers and music. The wine cups were kept filled to the brims. Zal discussed his realms learnedly and judiciously, and Mihrab thought to himself, "This is indeed a witty as well as a wise, young ruler. I have apparently nothing to fear from him. Surely his mother was immortal like the phoenix herself."

Flushed with wine and overjoyed to be traveling alone so

117

royally and seeing his rich domains, Zal reflected also upon the grace and manners of his host. "No wonder the Semites ruled Iran so long," he thought. "This Mihrab is a prince. I have never seen a more handsome man. He is tall and as slender as a poplar. His shoulders are broad, his waist narrow, his fingers nervous for the scimitar, and his manners impeccable."

While Zal was inwardly admiring the Semitic Mihrab, one of the noble chieftains at the banquet whispered in Zal's ear, "Noble paladin, this Mihrab had within his palace a beauty such as mortal eyes see once in all a generation of women. This is his daughter, Rudabah! She is descended from the fabled beauties of Zahhak's court. Her portrait hangs in every court from Hind all the way to the China Sea. The lords of Turan sigh as they gaze upon such loveliness. The great master of the easternmost world, the Khan of Chin, dreams of possessing her.

"Her skin is fairer than the palest ivory which gleams in a starlit hall at Persepolis. When you smell the pungent musk, that is the very perfume of her hair. Her ringlets fall to her feet in curls so wide that they would make you an ankle bracelet. Her lips are red as cherries, and her glowing cheeks as pink as the sun-kissed pomegranate. Her slender nose is like burnished silver. She is tall as a teak tree growing in a Chinese garden, and as slender as the cypress. Her silver breasts have in their centers two ruby buds, as rosy as pomegranate seeds. If you were to see her, you would swear you were in paradise where angels sing with nightingales, and all is music and delight."

All night long Zal could not sleep but sat in his golden tent gazing upon the moonlit river and imagining the glowing face of Rudabah. When the first rays of the sun had turned the land of Kabul to crystal, Mihrab came again to pay his respects to his guest. Courteously he asked Zal what he could do to satisfy his desires.

Zal answered that he invited Mihrab and his court to visit him in Seistan. The proud Mihrab replied that this alone he could not grant. "Your father Sam would never allow it," he replied. "Nor would he approve our drinking together until late at night, or your sitting here at Kabul among our Semitic idols." Then since Zal's religion and customs were different from his, Mihrab refrained from praising the Persian lord overmuch.

Zal, on the other hand, quite beside himself with love for the fair Rudabah whom he had not even seen, praised Mihrab and his court so much that the lord of Kabul began to relent and treat the young Zal with less suspicion.

In the palace of Kabul, Queen Sindukht and her daughter nervously awaited Mihrab's return. They hoped all had gone well, for the might of Sam could crush their kingdom like a blade of straw in his left hand. "How is this young lord?" Sindukht questioned anxiously. "Does he resemble some nestling of the mountain peaks? Does he walk like a ruler, or like a fledgling bird?"

"Why, silver lady," replied Mihrab, "he treads the earth like a Persian paladin, with steps so large no other lord except his father could fit his slippers into them. In battle he is as fierce as a crocodile, snapping off heads with one blow of his steely blade. Mounted on his galloping charger, you would say he was a horned dragon. His hands are as encompassing as the branches of the River Nile. He has a lion's heart like a true Persian and the son of a hero, and the shrewdness of an elephant. When he surmounts his turquoise throne and scatters gold on every side of him, you would think him as mighty as the shah. His eye is wise and thoughtful, and on his cheeks the handsome bloom of youth. There is only this one defect in him: his hair is as white as snow."

Mihrab was exceedingly unwise to speak such words before his daughter. The great teachers of the East have often said: "Refrain from describing masculine beauty when women are within earshot. In the heart of every female lurks a living devil. If you only suggest, a woman will search out the way. When desire enters a woman's heart, wisdom flies out the window."

The lovely Rudabah hurried to her chambers completely inflamed with love. She clapped her hands for the five serving girls who had come to her as a gift from the northern province of Turkestan. To them she confided her passion. "I shall not sleep," she cried. "Do you hear me? I cannot eat, I am sure. You must help me out of my distress. I am in love with the lord of our lands, the princely Zal!"

Her damsels were aghast at such folly. They implored her to listen to reason. "Your portrait has been sent even to the great Semitic rulers who dwell in far-off Palestine," they reminded her. "You cannot marry a Persian, a man of another religion and customs, and even more, your father's lord! Think too of your beauty. How could a peerless maiden like yourself wish to wed the nursling of a bird? You have not even seen this lord of Seistan! His hair is as white as that of an aged man! And besides, this Zal could never marry you! What would the warrior Sam say? What would the shah of Persia say? Why, he would bury you in sand, up to your ears!"

Furious with love and anger, Rudabah screamed at them, "What do I care about his face or his hair? I am in love with *him!* No other man shall ever stir my heart as he has done. Do you understand? What I have just said are not light words, but an oath! If I told you that I wanted to eat mud in the dark Underworld, would you offer me roses instead? Perhaps he is neither tall nor dark-haired! He is tall enough for me. He is handsome enough for me. He will give me peace in the burning depths of my passion. Talk not of any other man. The princely Zal alone will bring me peace in my body and peace in my soul!"

Then the maidens of Turkestan took counsel and swore to Rudabah that they would use all their foreign arts of guile and even of magic, and that they would bring Zal to her feet. They urged her to remain hidden in her chambers, to be patient, and to count on them. Above all, they cautioned her not to let her parents guess her secret desire.

Rudabah promised to be discreet. She told them that her love with Zal would be like a lofty tree that dropped precious rubies on the grass instead of petals, as long as she should live.

The slave girls dressed themselves in the five hues of spring and ran toward the rose garden that lay beside the river. On the opposite bank they could see the royal tents of Zal's encampment. Laughing and chattering loud enough so that their shrill voices would carry across the water, they began to gather roses. Slowly they wandered closer and closer to the stream's edge. There on the banks they bent to gather violets. Soon they saw Zal, attracted by their laughing voices, stroll along the opposite bank with his bow and arrows in hand, and attended by a single slave boy. When Zal saw a water bird on their side of the stream, he shot it so that it fell near them. Then he sent his boy across the water to fetch the fowl.

The girls called to the slave boy and began to converse with him. "Tell us," they teased him coyly. "Who is that handsome warrior whose aim is unerring?"

"That is my master, Zal of Persia, a sun for radiance and beauty," he told them.

"Go and tell your master," confided the slave girls, "that if he is the sun in all his radiance, we have within our palace the beauteous moon herself. Surely the sun and the moon should meet on the silken cushions of love."

Zal's heart leaped when he heard their message. Ordering them to await his return, he rushed himself to his tent and had five lengths of golden brocade prepared as gifts for them, and coins and jewels. When the slave boy carried the presents to the girls, he warned them, "My master says if you are faithful, you are like to find jewels often among the roses of his garden."

The slave girls exchanged knowing looks, as if to say that a princely lion of Iran was not so hard to enmesh in their silken coils. Then Zal called the maidens to him and inquired about Rudabah. "Tell me the truth about your mistress," he commanded. "If you lie to me, I shall have you trampled by my elephants!"

The slave girls knelt and kissed the earth at his feet. Then the youngest and prettiest of them spoke to Zal. "Our mistress is the very perfumed breath of spring flowers. She is a rose. She is as beautiful a woman as your father Sam is a matchless man, and almost as tall. She is a whole head taller than yourself. Her face is like a tulip when only one flower is blooming in a garden. She is as sweet as jasmine that blooms in the snow of winter." Then at his further questions they vouched for Rudabah's intelligence and education.

Neither Zal nor Rudabah could wait to see the other. Back and forth all day went the careful messengers, who succeeded in not arousing the suspicions of the palace guards. All the arrangements were finally made. The following morning, just at the first hint of dawn, Zal stole silently to Rudabah's pavilion and called up to her balcony.

The night had been spent in feverish preparation in Rudabah's private chambers. Her whole pavilion had been hung with silken curtains and decorated with the portraits of great kings and heroes. A royal feast had been set out on low tables, and the roasts well marinated in rose water. Dancers and musicians stood ready for her summons. The room was gay with precious vases filled with all the perfumed flowers of the gardens of Kabul. Rich pink and blue carpets covered all the floors with their silky softness. Cushions of brilliant hues and rich fabrics were piled high on Rudabah's couch.

As soon as she heard Zal's voice, the princess of Kabul leaned over her balcony, loosed her scarlet veil, and let her two long ringlets fall down to her feet. Then in soft words she begged him to climb up to her heart.

Zal tossed his lasso up to the parapet, where it caught firmly. Then, hand over hand, he mounted and stood before Rudabah. She had not known that his eyes were blue, the color of lake water at sunrise. Hand in hand the lovers walked into her pavilion, blushing and speechless with joy. It was there that Zal whispered his eternal love to Rudabah. He vowed that neither torture nor death could ever make him unfaithful to her. The passionate Rudabah responded to his

121

love in every detail. She also swore to him undying devotion.

While soft music played and the Indian dancers floated behind the gauze curtains, Zal and Rudabah spent their few moments together. As the first rays of sunlight fell upon their couch, the slave girls announced to them the coming day. Tearfully they parted, cheek from cheek, and hand from hand.

"O sun, could you not wait one minute more?" Rudabah called despairingly. "Please do not leave so soon," she whispered to Zal through her tears. Brushing his own tears from his eyes, Zal retied his lasso to the balustrade and descended. He strode toward his camp as if the strength of a hundred elephants were in his body. Masterful and imperious, he called a meeting in his tent, to which all the magi and wise men of Persia hastened to assemble. Briefly and succinctly he disclosed his situation to them and asserted his firm resolve to marry the lovely Rudabah. After some deliberation the counselors declared themselves unequal to such an affair of state, and they suggested that Zal inform his father at once.

Sam saw the messenger from Zabulistan as the rider approached his mountain camp, having recognized from afar the white horses. When he had read his son's letter, written in the most ardent and yet respectful terms, Sam puzzled greatly. He was not surprised that his son, raised so far from civilization in the weird nest of the simurgh, should fall so violently in love. Shah Minuchir, who hated the Semites most cordially, would naturally be furious. After Sam had slept on the matter—for considering himself bound by the oath he had made to Zal, he could make no hasty decision—he summoned his astrologers and bade them draw up horoscopes of Zal and Rudabah.

All day Sam waited while they prepared their information. Toward evening they approached him, and to his astonishment they were smiling broadly. "Great hero of the golden belt," they cried, "let us announce to you a most glorious event! The blessings of heaven are above our heads in Persia. Let your son Zal be wedded to Rudabah!"

"What have you found, O wise men?" Sam asked eagerly.

"We have seen the sign of an elephant, mighty Paladin. The land of Iran never saw his like. From your son Zal and the lady Rudabah there will be born a hero who shall carve on his ruby signet ring not only the lands of Iran and Hind! To them he shall add the western land of Greece. What is more, he will defeat our enemies from Turan, and drive them howling like jackals into the Turkestan deserts!"

Sam rose joyously and sent a messenger to Zal to say

122

that he was leaving at once for the palace of the shah. Sam said in his letter that although this longed-for marriage had really nothing exceptional in its favor, yet was he bound by oath and would try to arrange something. Sam had a thousand prisoners bound and fettered to take along with him as a present to the shah.

As soon as Zal had received his father's message, he sent an old woman who had been acting as a liaison between him and Rudabah to tell his sweetheart that Sam had hemmed and hawed and finally given his consent. This time the old woman was not so clever, and she was caught by Sindukht with gifts up her sleeves from Rudabah to Zal. Sindukht made her daughter confess that she had a lover. At first Sindukht was very angry and accused Rudabah of throwing herself from a palace into a ditch. Then when she heard that it was Zal of Persia whom she loved, Sindukht grew frantic with despair. She saw before her eyes the clouds of dust the shah would raise around her palace. Even when Rudabah assured her mother that Sam consented to the marriage, Sindukht was not reassured.

Her anger was nothing compared to the fury of Mihrab. He wanted to kill Rudabah immediately. "The shah of Iran does not even like me to mount my horse," he screamed. "Do you think he will let my own daughter rise to a throne in Persia? Look at this wretched child," he yelled. "I wish that I had strangled her at birth." Like a snarling leopard he pointed a shaking finger at Rudabah, who had not come to the audience humbly as her mother had suggested, but stood proudly before her father, dressed in gold brocade and wearing a ruby crown that Zal had smuggled to her.

Sam in the meantime had ridden hard to the palace of the shah, preferring to have their sovereign hear the news from himself directly. Minuchir received him well. All during the feasting the shah listened avidly to Sam's victories up north in Mazinderan. The following morning, however, when Sam broached the question of Zal's marriage, the shah's wrath was terrible to hear. He ordered Sam to horse immediately. His mission was to proceed at once to Kabul. There he was to burn the palace to the ground, to kill Mihrab, his Queen Sindukht, and also Rudabah. The news of the sentence traveled fast. All of Kabul was in an uproar of terror.

Zal also heard of the shah's order. Pale and determined, he rode out to meet his father. On every hand his courtiers advised him, "You have embarrassed your father. Your father is angry. He has reason to be displeased with you. Be humble. Forget Rudabah. She is lost. All is lost!"

Zal answered them all quietly, "What should I fear? Man's only end is dust. Without Rudabah why should I care to live at all?" He greeted his father lovingly, and all the time as they rode side by side toward their palace at Seistan, tears rolled down Zal's cheeks.

In the evening he spoke alone to his father. "What are your quarrels with the Assyrian to me? I am the nursling of an Indian bird, no son of yours. You never rocked me gently in a cradle. You never let me feel my mother's tender arms. You sent me naked to a distant mountain. You deprived me of my childhood, and also of love. It was my Maker who caused my hair to be white. It was no sin of mine. Before the simurgh you promised to help me be happy. Here I stand before you. Do whatever your wrath dictates against me. Only know that whatever you say or do against Kabul, you do and say to me."

Sam's heart was touched. He called the scribes and dictated a long letter to the shah in which he carefully inserted a reference, toward the end, to the effect that it might be better for him and Zal to attack Amul, the shah's palace, rather than the Assyrian Kabul. In the morning he sent Zal himself with the letter, for the shah had never seen the boy. After Zal had spurred out of the palace, desperate with love, Sam sat alone and reflected on how much more difficult it was to be a father than a hero.

In Kabul, Mihrab pondered the harsh exigencies of fate. There was no warrior in his city who would dare to lift a mace to Sam. The only thing that Mihrab could think of to do was to execute Sindukht and Rudabah publicly. Several times he was on the point of putting his daughter to death, and yet he realized that this would be no solution either if what she swore about Zal's love and Sam's consent was actually true. In calmer moments too he savored the sweetness of the revenge if by some chance Rudabah managed to marry this Persian hero. Then would Assyrian blood be close to the throne of Persia, perhaps for a second thousand years.

While Mihrab was debating what course he should best follow, his wife Sindukht, laboring now to save herself and her child from death, proposed another solution. "Why not try buying our lives, my husband?" she inquired.

"Who would dare mention such a solution to Sam?" he retorted impatiently.

"I would dare it," replied Sindukht seriously. As she spoke, she folded her arms gravely across her silver breasts and looked the very picture of courage. "Entrust to me the key to all your hoarded wealth," she demanded.

Mihrab was struck with the daring of her proposition. Without grumbling or even regretting the treasure, he watched her prepare it for Sam. She took 300,000 pieces of gold, 30 horses with silver saddles, 60 slaves bearing golden goblets filled with jewels and rare perfumes, 100 red-haired camels, 100 baggage mules, a jeweled crown suitable for a shah, a gold and inlaid throne as high as a mounted horseman, and 4 Indian elephants loaded with precious carpets and bales of materials. All this she dispatched in haste to the warrior Sam.

Then Sindukht dressed herself in trousers, belted tunic, and helmet like an Iranian warrior. Once she was astride a long-legged stallion you would have thought her a youthful paladin as she spurred her horse as fast as he could gallop along the dusty road to Seistan. She overtook her caravan at the gates of Sam's palace, from which it stretched two miles along the track. Imperiously, Sindukht requested an audience with Sam, who sat bemused upon his ivory throne. Sindukht took off her helmet so that her gleaming black hair set off her face to best advantage. Advancing with the light tread of a pheasant, she kissed the earth at his feet and begged him to accept the treasure.

Sam couldn't imagine who she was or what he was to do. Should he commit himself by accepting? If he refused, then there would be Zal to deal with. Then Zal would reproach him and flop around weeping like the simurgh herself. "Very well, Messenger," he finally acceded. "We accept the treasure in the name of our son Zal." Sindukht's spirits rose, for the old warrior was now committed.

"Your words have made me young again," smiled Sindukht. "Now may I beg of you why you wish to destroy Kabul? It is Mihrab who was to blame for letting these children meet in his palace, and he has been weeping blood for his fault these many weeks. Please do not punish the innocent, great warrior."

While she was talking, Sam sat watching her narrowly through half-closed lids and stroking his silken beard. "Tell me, lady, if you are not by some chance the wife of Mihrab herself," he asked.

"If you will first swear never to injure me or my family, I will reveal my identity to you, great paladin," she answered swiftly.

With a half smile on his lips and a twinkling eye, for Sam dearly loved quick wits, he extended his hand to her. Solemnly they shook hands, and Sindukht fell and kissed the floor at his feet gratefully.

"O, paladin of Persia," she continued without daring to

lift her head, "I am the wife of Mihrab and the mother of Rudabah. If you will spare our lives, I swear that we will praise your name forever."

"Never fear, lady," answered Sam. "I admire your courage. I shall uphold the pledge I just made even if it is to cost me my life. You have my word. Zal shall marry this priceless moon, your daughter Rudabah.

"My son has already gone—not gone, but rather flown like a bird to the shah with a letter. The shah will eventually give his consent, I think, just to be rid of Zal, if for nothing else. My son sighs and weeps so that he is forever standing in a puddle of mud caused by his own tears. The shah will be relieved to be rid of such a dismal companion. As for you, lady, you have the kind of spirit that would make you a good grandmother to my grandson."

Sindukht waited deferentially while the old man mused, "I have seen things in my life," he continued. "I have seen the Assyrians fall and the lowly elevated. It will do my old heart good to see this fabled beauty of yours. They say she is a very moon. I have heard that her ringlets are so wide they would make anklets. Of course, she has the blood of the Assyrian dragon in her veins. Even so," he mused, "I long to see the mother of my grandchild."

Then Sindukht answered him warmly, for she could see he had no more hate in his heart for the Assyrian. "If I were to bring such a king as you into Kabul, my daughter's head would reach the skies." The next day Sam granted Sindukht leave to return with her good news to Kabul.

In the meantime Zal had hastened to the court of Persia, where he was well received as befitted the son of the shah's most renowned warrior. The shah had secret horoscopes drawn up regarding the proposed marriage, and having heard the exciting prognostication, had privately decided to give his consent. However, before doing so he subjected the boy Zal to several tests to determine his fitness for marriage and the responsibilities of such a position.

In solemn audience the wise men of Persia asked Zal the following questions:

1. What are the dozen cypresses decorated with thirty boughs?

2. What are the two horses, one crystal and one pitch, that try in vain to overtake each other?

3. What are the thirty attendants of our king, who seem to be twenty-nine but always count off to be thirty?

4. What is the meadow where a fierce reaper cuts ripe and withered grass alike and hears no cry of despair?

5. What are the two trees, one withered and one green,

to which a solitary bird flies? What is the bird that nests on one in the morning and on the other in the evening?

6. What citizens preferred a thornbrake to a highly fortified city, a preference they will regret one day when the earth quakes?

Zal was allowed to think before giving his answers. All the courtiers awaited the results of his examination. Finally he replied:

"The twelve cypresses are the twelve moons, each with thirty days.

"The two horses are day and night, which gallop fast but never overtake each other.

"The thirty attendants of our shah are the phases of the moon, one of which from time to time escapes observation.

"Time is the mower in your field who cuts down the old and the young alike, and respects no plea.

"One tree is the lighter, summer season and the other the darker or wintertime. The bird is the sun which alternates between one and the other.

"The citizens of the swamp are ourselves who live, whether we prefer it or not, in this wayside inn of life. The city we have lost is our life's work, which is more often than not usurped by others. It will do us no good in time of danger to regret our past achievements. All we can hope to keep on earth is our good name. No one of us is born for anything but death. We enter life by one door and leave by another while time counts our every breath."

On the morning following his highly acclaimed examination, Zal presented himself before the shah. He was dressed for the road and requested permission to depart, alleging that he was very anxious to see his father. The shah only congratulated him on his interrogation, smiled, and answered that he had other plans for the day. The shah even expressed his incredulity, suspecting that Zal was not really that impatient to see his father. The whole day was spent in a magnificent tournament where Zal displayed his horsemanship, his skill, his fearlessness, and his respect for the shah. It was only on the following morning that he was allowed to return to his father.

The wedding of Zal and Rudabah took place at her home in Kabul with festivities that lasted four weeks. Mihrab and Sindukht had arrayed Rudabah in all the rest of their golden treasures and placed her on a throne in the pavilion where she had first met Zal. Sam and his son advanced toward the city royally attired. They were met by Mihrab, who dismounted as they approached. When Sam was formally escorted into Rudabah's chamber and saw her at last, he was overcome by her beauty and by his own emotion. Turning to Zal, Sam congratulated him on his choice and said that no princess in Persia had ever been so lovely.

After the long celebration the wedding party returned to Seistan. Rudabah entered her new capital riding in a silk-curtained couch. Almost at once Sam left again for war, and the young couple ruled together from the ivory throne. Very soon the news was carried to Sam that Rudabah was pregnant. The old warrior smiled to himself, for he knew of the wonderful son she would bear. He sent word that he would hasten to Seistan as soon as the child was old enough to be presented.

All was very far from well at Seistan, however. The body of the lovely Rudabah grew larger and larger. The nine months came and went without bringing a child. Sindukht in agony watched her daughter grow thin and weak. Finally Rudabah went into labor, but the child was too large and could not be delivered. Her screams filled the palace. Over her bed Sindukht tore her hair and cut her cheeks. Neither she nor any wise woman had a remedy. Rudabah screamed and pleaded, and grew weaker by the hour.

Then servants were sent to Zal to tell him that his princess was dying. He hastened to her rooms and saw that she was already unconscious. By this time the palace resounded with the wails of her attendants. Zal ordered them to be silent. He cleared the room and asked Sindukht to light a small fire in the censer. When the flames appeared, Zal held the simurgh's feather over them. Within a matter of seconds the great red bird flew into the curtained chamber, dripping pearls about her like droplets of peace. Zal asked the simurgh to save Rudabah, since this mother-bird had promised him one great favor. "Princess Rudabah is worth more than my life to me, dear bird," he explained.

The simurgh gave her counsel. "The birth of your son will be unnatural," she told Zal. "The Creator has not made him like ordinary mortals. He is an elephant for size, and a lion for courage.

"First you must give your lady the strongest wine you have in the palace. Then you must ask an arch-Mage to come to her. He is to carry a blue-steel dagger. While Rudabah sleeps, he must make an incision downward from the side of her waist, turn the child's head toward the cut line, and draw him carefully from her body. Then he must sew up the incision, cover it with the juice of certain herbs I will give you, and bandage her tightly. She will live to hold the child against her breast, after a day and a night of sleep.

"Some fruits do not fall into the world naturally but have to be plucked from the golden bough of life's tree."

With these cryptic words the simurgh flew back to India.

It was some minutes after the baby had been drawn from the mother's open body before Zal could recover from the marvel of it. Then he was astonished at the size and beauty of the child. Finally he collected his wits enough to send a messenger posthaste to notify the warrior Sam.

The newborn child was the wonder of all Persia. He was from head to toes the very image of his grandfather Sam. Everyone thought so, except Mihrab, who privately felt the baby looked just like him. The child was born without a mark or defect on him, tall, broad-shouldered, long-armed, with wide-open eyes and fists flailing the air. It took the milk of twenty nurses to allay his hunger. His mother named him Rustam, which means "I have borne fruit."

By the time Sam was able to leave his war and return to see his grandson, Rustam was walking. He had grown so strong that his parents were able to seat him on a golden throne atop a splendid elephant. Mounted thus royally, the child Rustam rode out of the city gates to meet his grandfather's procession.

Flags flew along either side of the road, over the heads of the army that had been drawn up at attention. Drummers kept up a rhythmic tattoo. Children strewed the route with flowers. Zal and Mihrab on foot escorted the elephant upon which Rustam balanced proudly. They were amazed to see Sam, who was galloping toward them on a magnificent bay stallion, rein in his horse and dismount. The valiant warrior paid his grandson the unparalleled honor of advancing to meet him on foot.

When Sam had strode up to the side of the elephant and looked up into his small grandson's face, he halted. The child returned his gaze without lowering his black eyes or blinking.

Sam spoke his first words to Rustam in a voice choked with emotion. Holding his hand on his heart he said, "Greetings, great Paladin! May you live long and happily and have the heart of a lion."

To the amazement of the spectators, the child Rustam replied in a clear, treble voice, "Greetings, great Paladin! May I draw my courage from my grandfather Sam, a lion among men."

RUSTAM AND KAI-KAUS

(NOTE TO THE READER: The following episodes from the reign of Kai-Kaus may be of interest for several reasons. First of all, there is the reference to an eclipse of the sun during a battle between the Persian and Median armies. Some modern historians have assumed that this refers to the eclipse of the sun which occurred on May 28, 585 B.C., and which according to Herodotus stopped a battle in the sixth year of a war between the Lydians of Asia Minor and the Medes. The famous Greek astronomer and mathematician Thales, who was born in Miletus on the coast of Asia Minor, is supposed to have predicted this eclipse. Other scholars think the *Shah Namah* could refer to another eclipse, such as the one recorded at Nineveh in 736 B.C. The people of Asia were in any case remarkably good observers. Among the astronomers of the ancient world were the Chinese, whose records contain eighty or so eclipses recorded by Confucius, most of which have been verified by modern science.

Most Western historians are surprised by the account of the Persian conquest of Arabia. The geography of this part of the *Shah Namah*, however, comes from the research of Professor Darmesteter.

Most people who read Persian agree that Firdausi rose to his greatest poetic achievement in the part of the poem that treats the reign of Kai-Kaus. The climax of the *Shah Namah*, however, comes during the subsequent reign of Kai-Khosrau, who the Persians *know* is the shah we in the West do not believe is Cyrus the Great.)

AFTER A GLORIOUS REIGN of 120 years, Shah Minuchir, calling before the peacock throne his son Nauder, entrusted the empire to him, saying, "My caravan is ready to depart. We may all tarry here, but not abide. Put not your faith in a world like this one." Then Minuchir closed his eyes and departed, and Nauder ruled in Persia for seven years.

During this reign the warrior Sam died of old age in Zabulistan. A marble tomb was erected in his memory, and all Iran mourned this great and noble paladin. His death was a signal for an invasion by Afrasiab, the son of the Turanian king. Afrasiab marched against Shah Nauder with 400,000 soldiers. In the ensuing battle he slew 50,000 Persians, took Nauder prisoner, and finally executed him. Persia was only saved by the combined efforts of Zal and Mihrab. Zal, however, would not then accept the crown of Iran, which it was a tradition in his family to refuse, and he put in the palace an aged prince named Zav, who ruled for five years.

The next shah was Garshasp of Balkh, who only reigned for nine years, and who died at the moment when Afrasiab was preparing a second invasion. Courtiers from the west of Iran reproached Zal bitterly for not having slain Afrasiab in the preceding war, a deed which would have ended the threat of his ambitious schemes. Zal, who was beginning to suffer from his long years as a champion warrior, asked for his son Rustam to be brought to him.

"My boy," said Zal, "even though you are too young for the horrors of war, yet must I send you on a dangerous mission, for our land is without a ruler. You must journey alone to Mount Elburz, and bring back our new shah, Kai-Kobad."

Rustam answered that he was ready to go out into the world as a warrior. He called for the mace of Sam, which had remained in Zabul as a trophy since the death of that great hero. No other man had been able to wield it. The youthful ruler, however, swung it over his head joyfully. Then he asked what he was to do for a horse, since he had outgrown the fabled stallions of Zabul, whose strong white backs had carried even his grandfather to war. Rustam needed a taller, stronger mount.

Zal ordered all the herds from Seistan and Kabul, where the special white horses were bred, to be driven past Rustam. The young boy singled out several promising two-year-olds, but they were all too weak for him even without his armor. Then he saw a spirited mare with a broad chest and sleek flanks. She was followed by her colt, which was as tall as its dam. However, when Rustam inquired about that particular colt, the herders told him that, unlike ordinary horses, mother and colt were inseparable. Several paladins had tried to lasso him, but the unnatural mare had attacked them with bared teeth and murderous hoofs. This was the kind of spirit Rustam needed in his own horse.

The colt was a three-year-old, a velvety roan with saffron-colored back and hard, black belly. His conformation was flawless—a deep, broad chest and powerful hindquarters. Rustam caught him on the first toss of his lasso and drove the mare away with a loud cry and a cut across her muzzle.

Expertly Rustam slipped a bridle on the colt, mounted him, and gave him his head. By the end of the first lesson the sturdy animal accepted Rustam as his master. He bore his rider easily at any pace, almost effortlessly. The herders were delighted, for man and horse seemed molded together. Rustam called his colt Raksh. From that day onward the two were a team. Everyone in Persia believed that Rustam and Raksh would put the Turanians to rout and defend the country for centuries to come. At night when Rustam slept in his tent on the battlefields of western Iran, his followers would burn wild rue on either side of Raksh so that no tiger from the Tigris reed beds would steal upon him in the darkness. Even to this day in Afghanistan shepherds will proudly show you Raksh's manger, and about a mile to the west of it, marble slabs to which his hind feet are said to have been tethered at night. Raksh was well-paced, soft-mouthed, and clever. He was so sharp-eyed that he could make out an ant's feet on black cloth at night two miles away.

Their first adventure together was to cross the Great Salt Desert of central Iran and notify Kai-Kobad that, as the only living prince of the blood, he had succeeded to the throne and was requested to found a new dynasty. This they accomplished. The reign of Kai-Kobad lasted a hundred years, and it was a glorious one. The next shah of Persia was his son, Kai-Kaus the Astronomer.

This shah was a personable young man who came to the throne of the richest country on earth in a time of peace. Afrasiab had been driven by Rustam back into Turan, and was happy to have escaped with his life. Rustam would certainly have killed Afrasiab when he pulled him from his horse by grasping the Turanian's wide belt, but fortunately for that dark prince the belt broke, and he escaped. It would take Afrasiab many years to recover from the fright he felt when the mighty hand of Rustam grasped at his waist.

In the unparalleled splendor of his sculptured palace at Persepolis, Kai-Kaus ruled Persia with its plains covered with wild almonds and oaks, its sequestered valleys and lofty mountains, its rich villages surrounded by date groves, its magnificent Alpine terraces, and its wheat fields strewn with scarlet poppies. The country was prosperous and contented. With Afrasiab hiding in Turan, with Zal and Rustam ready to come at any sign of danger, Kai-Kaus could look forward to a long and memorable reign.

What prompted him then to listen to that demon from Mazinderan who, disguised as a harpist, presented himself at Jemshid's throne, and asked to sing to the shah? What caused Kai-Kaus to listen to that devilish lay in praise of Mazinderan? What made him seriously believe that the narrow strip of land between the Elburz Mountains and the Caspian Sea was the richest, the largest, the sweetest in all of Asia?

When Zal was summoned to Persepolis in great urgency by the courtiers and warriors, he could not believe his ears! The shah in person was planning to traverse the Elburz Mountains and conquer Mazinderan! In vain Zal expostulated! To deaf ears he pointed out the hazards of this long journey across the plateau of Iran. Zal spoke of the horrid race of white-skinned people, demons rather, who inhabited the caves of these mountains.

To all of Zal's arguments Kai-Kaus opposed his wealth, his powerful army, his thirst for glory, and his desire to hear the nightingales of Mazinderan, which warbled so much more melodiously on a moonlit night than the plain bulbuls of Persia. When Zal saw that the shah was, although young, as pliable as a withered tree, he shook his head sadly, returned to Seistan, and tried to bear with some degree of equanimity the news of the departure northward of the entire Persian host.

Kai-Kaus advanced by slow stages, resting often and admiring the beautiful mountain country. His route lay upward over the three terraces that rise from the Persian Gulf to the 5,000-foot plateau of central Iran. Here the sure-footed white horses mounted single-file steep cliff walls where the rock strata lay upended from some primeval convulsion. Its white and yellow layers showed bright against the treeless plains. At night they camped in some small, green valley bright with glossy orange trees, and Kai-Kaus mused over his wine glass and remembered sometimes to listen for the nightingales.

One morning when his head was clearer, the shah remembered the prime purpose of his expedition. He sent 2,000 warriors ahead of him to plunder Mazinderan. He ordered them to kill every inhabitant without quarter, and to burn every hamlet and town. For one week his champions slaughtered and looted. Then on the eighth day an unheard-of occurrence brought disaster to the Persians. The great White Demon appeared. Zal had warned Kai-Kaus of him, but the shah had not listened. This was a monstrous demon, whose skin was a clammy, white mass; and he protected with very special magic the land and the king of Mazinderan. He had been summoned from his huge cave on Mount Damavand.

All of a sudden the sun began to be swallowed up! A great stillness fell over all the earth, and an increasing blackness. As it grew darker and darker, a huge storm gathered, slowly rolled in its icy winds, tucked them methodically under its belly, and began to suck them up into its huge bellows. Terrified, the Persians listened as the sky inhaled. There was a moment of silence. Then the storm burst. In an explosive onslaught it blew across the flat tableland where the Persians huddled unprotected. Great chunks of ice ripped through their brocade tunics. Hailstones beat upon their armor and stung the horses, which plunged wildly across the plain.

Arrows fell among the warriors from the bows of the white demons. The pack animals trampled madly over the fallen warriors. The earth was in total darkness. Kai-Kaus and his paladins became completely blind. They could not even see the face of the White Demon when it appeared leer-

133

ing and ghostly white at the horizon's edge. They surrendered quietly to his 12,000 demons, who ripped off their jeweled collars and rings, and tore their weapons from their hands. Kai-Kaus had just time enough to whisper to one warrior to dash for safety through the elephants, and to try to reach Seistan alive. Zal must be notified of their fate. Then the shah and his nobles were driven, battered and blind, to a cave where the demons guarded them closely. They were allotted just enough food and water to keep them alive. The White Demon sent word to Kai-Kaus that if the shah reflected—now that he had all the time in the world for thought, and no more treasure to bother his head about—he might come to hear how beautifully the nightingales of Mazinderan sang!

The shah's messenger flew like smoke the 300 miles southwest to Seistan, stopping only long enough for a fresh horse as each one foundered. Zal listened wearily to his breathless account. "The shah says to tell you that he set forth from Jemshid's throne, his army scented and bedecked like a rose garden in spring. Then came a great darkness and a wind that scattered their silken petals over Mazinderan. The shah says he sighs deeply for not having followed your advice, although what has happened to him was demonstrably no fault of his. He says you are to come at once to his rescue."

Zal called Rustam and to him alone confided the dreadful news of the shah's humiliation. By no means must such news reach Turan. "You must go alone to Mazinderan, my son," he said. "Persia has lost its monarch and its army. Go find these demons and their chief, and crush them crown to spine. Beware, however, of the White Demon himself, for he can turn day to night.

"There are two routes into Mazinderan, the long one taken by the shah, which passes across the terraces and into the mountain game country. This road takes fourteen days. There is a shorter way that you can make in seven days. Its issue is through the Elburz by two precipitous passes. The first of these is a mere fissure in the rock wall only the width of a horseman and very dangerous because of icy water that trickles down it constantly. The second pass lies through a black chasm in the mountain, but you must brave its murky depths. Only beware of lions and demons that infest this gloomy waste.

"I shall pray for you night and day," Zal told his tall, young son. "I know the sure hoofs of Raksh will bear you bravely enough. I shall not worry because your fate is in the hands of our Maker, and your fame so well established that you could never be forgotten."

On the first day Rustam covered a two days' journey, sparing neither himself nor Raksh. Toward evening, as he began to feel faint from hunger, he rode over a wild plain where game abounded. With his lasso he snared a wild ass, and lighting a fire with his arrow tip, he roasted the animal and lay down to sleep until morning. Raksh grazed nearby. During the night a lion crept through the tall grass and sprang upon Raksh. The valiant stallion attacked the lion with his sharp hoofs and sank his teeth deep into the lion's back. Rustam awoke to see Raksh grazing tranquilly, and the lion dead in the grass. Then Rustam scolded his horse. "You were very foolish, Raksh, to fight a lion all alone. Why didn't you awaken me? If something happens to you, I shall have this terrible journey to finish on foot, carrying my tiger skin, my helmet, my lasso, my bow, and my sword." Then Rustam gathered dried grass and rubbed Raksh down, saddled him, and continued his journey just as the sun was rising over the eastern horizon.

All day long Rustam and Raksh traveled through the Great Salt Desert, where the heat was intense under a burning sun. Hour after hour they pressed on without a sign of life in a dazzling inferno. Even the birds had been shrivelled into powder. Raksh grew so blinded and stumbled so often that Rustam had to dismount and lead him by the bridle. Slowly they staggered onward with the afternoon sun full in their faces. At last neither man nor horse could advance any further. Rustam's lips were cracked and his tongue swollen and parched. He sank to the hot sand wearily, unable to continue. Then as he lay prostrate and despairing, he saw a fat ram run past them. With his last ounce of strength Rustam rose to his feet, pulling Raksh behind him, and saw that the ram had led them to a desert spring. He let Raksh take a sip or two of water, and then, bone-weary as he was, Rustam washed his suffering horse, and made his coat clean and glossy again. Then he killed another wild ass, roasted it, and lay down to sleep while Raksh grazed and wandered near the water's edge.

During the night a huge dragon, such as those that inhabit the primeval wastes from the beginning of time, dragged its scaly length across the hard sand to see who had passed the salt wastes of the desert unscathed. Raksh saw him come and galloped to Rustam, pawing the earth and neighing in shrill alarm. When Rustam awoke, the dragon had vanished. Rustam scolded Raksh and told him not to disturb his slumber again. No sooner had Rustam fallen asleep, however, than the monster, breathing fire through his nostrils, reappeared. Once more Raksh beat upon the sand and neighed. Again the

135

dragon vanished. This time Rustam was very angry. He threatened to cut off his stallion's head and carry his weapons on foot to Mazinderan.

When the monster appeared for the third time, Raksh tried to lure him away into the desert where he could outrun him easily. The cumbersome beast only lumbered closer to Rustam. Then the frantic Raksh awoke his master. This time Rustam too saw their peril. "Tell me your name, foul creature," he cried. "Then I shall kill you surely."

"No matter my name," roared the dragon. "This is my land. For centuries not even an eagle has dared to fly over it. Tell me your name so I can dispatch you to your death!"

"My name is Rustam. I am the son of Zal and the grandson of Sam Suwar, champion of Persia."

Rustam joined battle with the dragon in a fight so difficult that Raksh had to come to his aid with hoofs and teeth. When Rustam cut off the monster's head, the whole plain was deluged with gushing streams of steaming blood. After this battle Rustam thanked his Creator humbly for having given him such strength and such an intelligent horse. "I am on earth to fight all enemies of man," he mused. "Dragons, demons, raging elephants, burning deserts, and the storm-tossed seas are all alike to me." This was his third adventure.

On the evening of the fourth day Rustam rode down into a fertile, green valley. There to his surprise was a banquet table set with a feast of venison, wine, and crusty loaves of fresh-baked bread. At the sound of a human voice the demons, who had prepared the feast for their mistress, vanished in a twinkling. Rustam lolled on the bench and ate until he could eat no more. Then he picked up a lute from the table and sang a little ballad, just to himself and Raksh, about the rigors and lack of leisure for love in a hero's life. While he sang, the enchanting mistress of the grove joined him. She was dressed in beauty like a starry sky, but Rustam did not trust her. He poured her a glass of wine, and as he handed it to her he mentioned the name of the Creator. Instantly she leaped away, screaming like a hideous hyena. Rustam threw his lasso unerringly and pulled her back to him. Then he saw to his disgust that she had resumed her true shape, that of an ugly, shriveled witch. Drawing his sword, he slew the repulsive hag.

Rustam and Raksh toiled all through the fifth day in the pass of Mount Elburz. Choosing the shortest route, they plunged bravely through underground caverns, guiding themselves by the courses of subterranean rivers. You would have said that the sun itself had been taken prisoner and even the bright stars had been lassoed. Sometimes overhanging cliffs were so precipitous on either hand that you could not even see the sky. Soaked to the skin, they finally found the exit and looked joyfully across cultivated fields that lay below them like a picture puzzle. As soon as they had picked their way down the mountain, Rustam let Raksh have his fill of tender wheat while the hero laid out his tiger-skin cuirass in the sun to dry. Rustam dropped to the warm earth contentedly and savored the fresh air and spring sunshine.

Then as he dozed Rustam was attacked by Ulad, the young ruler of that land. "Who are you, young man, and why do you let your dappled horse eat my wheat?" cried Ulad.

Rustam was angry. Truly there was not a second's peace in a hero's life. "My name is Cloud," he cried, "if a cloud has the steely claws of a lion and if it rains arrows and war clubs." Swinging to right and left of him, Rustam cut off the heads of Ulad's hunters, two at each stroke. "My name is Cloud," he panted, "for if I were to tell you my real name, your blood would freeze in your bodies." He dispersed Ulad's warriors, pursued Ulad, and pulled him over backward from his horse, the lasso tight about his neck. Then Rustam, riding Raksh, drove the frightened prince along the road ahead of him.

"Be merciful for once and spare my life," pleaded Ulad.

"If you will guide me the hundred leagues to the White Demon's cave where the shah of Iran is imprisoned, I will give you as your reward the whole kingdom of Mazinderan," offered Rustam.

"Between us and the Demon's land," warned Ulad, "are such cliffs that not even a gazelle could scale them, and a river so well guarded that no man can cross it. The White Demon is himself as high as a mountain. You could not, even with your powerful arms, reach up to his waist. These demons command twelve hundred elephants of war. Your shah is closely guarded in their huge cavern. You cannot hope to advance beyond the frontiers of Mazinderan."

Ulad's words only made Rustam laugh. "You come along with me, Ulad," he shouted gaily, "and I will show you how to fight demons. Before I finish with them, they will be so dizzy that they won't know their reins from their stirrups."

Rustam and Ulad galloped all that day and all night. On the morning of the sixth day the Persian hero bound Ulad to a tree for safekeeping, for they had arrived at Mazinderan. After a short nap Rustam awoke refreshed, happy to have come so near to the journey's end. Before him lay the camp of the devil Arzhang, who guarded the entrance to Kai-Kaus' prison. Well protected with his tiger-skin cuirass and bronze helmet,

Rustam rode up to the camp at daybreak on his sixth day and shouted for Arzhang.

It was a cry so loud it seemed the mountain trembled. Hoping to catch Rustam by surprise, Arzhang spurred out at full gallop and charged headlong. Raksh sidestepped; and as the devil flew past, Rustam shot out his hand and caught him by the throat. So great was the impact that Arzhang's head was torn from his body. Then with the head still in his hand, Rustam trotted forward a few paces and tossed the bloody trophy full in the enemy camp. Screaming with terror, the demons fled far over the mountain.

Deep in their cave the Persian prisoners heard the demons departing. Early that morning Kai-Kaus had told his companions that he had recognized the shrill whinny of Raksh, but none of his fellow prisoners had believed him. "Our shah is suffering from hallucinations," they said. Imagine their surprise then when Rustam himself strode into their cave! The young hero's eyes were full of tears. He fell at the shah's feet and thanked the Creator that the ruler of Iran was still alive. The shah ordered Rustam, tired as he was, to set out at once for the White Demon's cave that lay overlooking the Caspian.

"Bring back his vitals," commanded Kai-Kaus. "Three drops of its blood will cure our eyes of blindness."

On the seventh day Rustam crossed seven mountains and saw before him the yawning cavern of the White Demon. He waited patiently until the noonday heat became intense and forced the demons to hide their corpselike white skins within their grottoes. In complete silence Rustam walked alone into the central cave, carrying in his hand Sam's heavy mace. It was so dark inside that at first he could see nothing. He strode resolutely forward while his eyes became accustomed to the murky gloom. Then looming directly ahead of him like a mountain with a lion's mane, lay the chief Demon sound asleep. Rustam could have killed him treacherously. Instead, he shouted at him to rise and fight a man.

The Demon lunged at Rustam, hurling a millstone as he came. Rustam thought, "This is surely my last fight. I'm going to die deep under this mountain." At the thought he remembered the shah of Persia, humiliated and blind. After the monster had passed him in the gloom, Rustam saw him silhouetted against the entrance. Quick to seize his opportunity, Rustam hacked off a hand and a foot.

It was the White Demon's turn to despair. "My hope is gone," he thought. "This must be some great hero come to destroy me. What if this is Rustam, that grandson of the champion Sam? Even if I live, I shall be maimed for life."

In his despair the Demon lurched about the cave, groping for the hero and pouring slippery blood all over the walls and rock floor. Sam's mace smashed at his knees and thighs with ruthless accuracy. Viciously Rustam and the Demon tore at each other's flesh and sought a hold.

Then Rustam, using his great strength, pushed his attack to the utmost. Time and again the great war club crashed against the head and vitals of the monster, gouging out great masses of hide and flesh. Even the floor of the cavern shook under the impact of the blows. So murderous was the assault that not even this greatest of demons could long withstand it, and soon he sank to the floor battered and helpless. "If I live through this day," thought Rustam, "I surely must be immortal." Then he threw himself once more upon the monster and plunged his dagger deep into the Demon's heart. He tore out the liver, and without sparing Raksh, rode swiftly back to the cave where he had left Kai-Kaus the day before.

"May your mother be praised, my boy," cried the shah. "May Zabulistan that raised you be praised! May I be praised, for truly I am the most brilliant ruler on the earth to have at my command so worthy a young fellow!" Then he directed Rustam to squeeze the blood from the Demon's liver into their eyes, and so the paladins of Persia were cured of their blindness. Ulad was rewarded with the kingdom of Mazinderan, and the shah returned in triumph into Persia. For some months Kai-Kaus busied himself with building observatories in Babylon and the Tigris area. Loaded with gifts, Rustam returned home to Zabulistan.

Very shortly, however, Kai-Kaus wearied of his palaces in Persia. In royal state he toured his realm from Turan into Chin, thence southward to Baluchistan and to Seistan, where he spent a month feasting with Zal. Then he learned that the Arabs of Hamaveran, or Yemen, were inciting trading nations along the Gulf of Aden to rise up against Persia. The leader in this plot was the crafty king of Hamaveran. Kai-Kaus hastened angrily to Baluchistan, and there on the shores of the Gulf of Oman he had a splendid fleet built. Embarking with his armies, he sailed along the southern shores of Arabia to Berberistan, the land called Punt by the ancient Egyptians. From this point in Africa, with Egypt on his left and the Berbers on his right, Kai-Kaus launched a mighty offensive against Hamaveran.

The war was a great success. Kai-Kaus controlled once more the sea routes between Africa and Asia. The king of Hamaveran sent him tribute and uncounted riches. What then possessed the Persian Kai-Kaus to covet the daughter of Hamaveran's king? Why could he not have burned for a Persian princess? How did he not realize that this union would involve Persia in a series of wars with the western Arab states?

Ambassadors were sent from Kai-Kaus to the wily king in Hamaveran, asking for the hand of his daughter, Sudaba. Nothing could have been more unwelcome. The Yemenite king had only this one child, whom he loved dearly. He could not bear the thought of losing her, of letting her go away across the sea. Nothing but the Persian victory could ever have persuaded him to part with her. Try as he might, there was no way out of the dilemma for the king of Hamaveran, especially as his daughter Sudaba relished the prospect.

"Do not consider this a tragedy," she answered her father. "It will be a joy for me to wed the shah of Persia." When Kai-Kaus saw Sudaba arrive in her golden litter, he was overjoyed at her rosy cheeks and slender waist. He declared himself completely satisfied with the Arab princess. His courtiers were delighted, for they hoped this marriage would steady the shah.

Shortly after the wedding Sudaba's father invited the shah and a few of his chosen heroes to visit Hamaveran, not in war this time, but in peace. He alleged that he was very lonely for his daughter and longed to see her once more. Sudaba tried to warn her royal husband that the invitation was full of guile, that treachery was intended. She pleaded with Kai-Kaus not to venture into Hamaveran at all, and certainly not with a mere handful of warriors. "Who would dare betray the shah of all Persia, Turan, Baluchistan, Chin, Mazinderan, Hindustan, Balkh, and Seistan?" the shah demanded scornfully. "An attempt on my person is inconceivable!"

Ten days later desperate messengers spurred into Zabul to tell Zal and Rustam what had befallen the Lion of Persia. Kai-Kaus had spent a week feasting and being regaled at the royal city of Shaha[2] in Hamaveran. Then when the Persians least expected it, they had been seized, roughly bound, and transported to a snow-covered fortress, where they were guarded by a thousand picked warriors.

"What of Sudaba?" asked Rustam.

"This lady, strangely enough, defied her father's attempts to win her back to his court. She screamed, tore her hair, and with her rosy nails tore deep mourning grooves in her polished cheeks. Then preferring her husband in exile to her father on a throne, she followed Kai-Kaus to tend him in his captivity."

2 Sheba(?).

This time the fate of Persia's shah spread to Turan, where Afrasiab began to assemble his warriors for an invasion of Iran. Rustam after careful deliberation decided he should go first to Africa before some worse harm could befall the shah. Then he would return to face Afrasiab in Iran, for sooner or later he and Afrasiab were destined to meet in mortal combat.

Rustam wrote to the king of Hamaveran and ordered him to liberate Kai-Kaus at once. All he received in reply was a taunting letter saying that there were pits dug and waiting for Persian champions in Yemen, and one big enough even for Rustam. Meanwhile the combined armies of Egypt, Punt, and Arabia prepared to meet the Persians led by Rustam. Another letter was sent secretly to Kai-Kaus so that he would not despair when he heard how massive a force was being assembled against his Iranians. "Do not fear, great ruler," Rustam wrote him. "When I have finished with them, these foemen won't know their heads from their feet."

"Whip them soundly," replied the shah. "They deserve it. I command you to level your lances at your horses' ears. Think not of me. The world was not spread out to be my banquet solely."

The morning of the battle the three monarchs—of Hamaveran, Berberistan, and Egypt—mounted on three superbly caparisoned elephants, paraded before their troops. Their battle line stretched for two miles. It looked as if all the enemies of Persia, entirely clad in iron, had come together that day. The very earth was weary from their weight and the trampling hoofs of their animals. And what with the thousands of pennants—red, yellow, and purple—it seemed as though all the birds of Africa had lent them their plumage.

Rustam drew up the small force of warriors he had brought with him from Hindustan and Seistan. He assigned his right and left wings to two heroes who were his friends, while he reserved the center, which would spearhead the attack, for himself. Heavily armed, his coiled lasso hanging ready on his saddlebow, Rustam rode up and down his line of battle so that the sight of the celebrated Raksh would give his army courage. The dappled stallion, fat and rested from the plains of his native Zabul, pranced before the Persian warriors. Then Rustam harangued his troops, "Today we must keep our eyelashes wide apart, men of Iran! Today we must look steadily over our horses' manes and level our eyes at our spear points! What do we care for a hundred thousand foes? Our shah has been seized by trickery, through no fault of his own! Today we shall free him from

141

his lonely prison, and all Persia shall thank us! As for Hamaveran and its allies, their noses shall breathe dust! Forward! After me!"

The enemy line was pierced at the first onslaught, and Rustam took sixty enemy chiefs prisoner before he reached the king of Syria.[3] This proud monarch he lassoed around the waist and pulled him through the throngs of enemy warriors as if he were playing polo with his head. Spurred on by Rustam's bravery, the Persian lords did great deeds that day. One by one they saw Rustam single out the enemy leaders and cleave a passage toward them with his polo-playing Raksh. When the king of Hamaveran realized that it was his turn to fall, he sent a messenger to Rustam. He offered total surrender, the return of Kai-Kaus and Sudaba, reparations for the trouble the war had caused, a restitution of Persian valuables, and a reinstatement of Persian suzerainty over the ancient trade routes.

The first act of Kai-Kaus when he had resumed command of his Persian subjects after the battle was to dictate a letter to Afrasiab, who had by that time seated himself upon the throne of Persia. "I am surprised at what I hear of you," wrote Kai-Kaus to the Turanian chief. "It cannot be true that you are trying to fill the throne of Iran! You should be satisfied to remain in Turan, a country which is from all reports by far too large for you. Surely you know what happens to the grasping, to the covetous! They stretch out their cat's paws for honey and prick themselves upon the thorns of Persian roses. Before this happens, you should try to save your pelt, dear Afrasiab! Does the puny cat insist upon annoying the Lion of Iran who sits by all rights of excellence and birth upon his ancestor's throne, upon Jemshid's throne?"

Afrasiab's dark face grew black when he read Kai-Kaus' letter. "Tell your monarch without a country not to give me lessons in covetousness," he snarled to the Persian envoy. "If he had not been so covetous himself, he would not have landed in a Yemenite jail. Tell him that I also am descended from Jemshid, and from Feridun the Dragon King. And secondly, I have been protecting Iran during Kai-Kaus' absence. For otherwise the Arabs would have ravaged it themselves. If he is a king, then let him remain in his own country and rule. Let him not go wandering off to the ends of the earth, leaving his realms shah-less. If he is a lion, then let him hasten to meet the Leopard of Turan!"

Afrasiab was as good as his threat. He waited for the Persian forces to re-embark, traverse the sea, and mount to

[3] This is what our poet says!

the central plateau of Iran. The Turanian king had heard that Kai-Kaus was planning to meet him in person. Afrasiab gave orders to seize Kai-Kaus. What Afrasiab did not know was that Rustam had remained among the Iranian warriors and that he was to lead the central charge, as he had done so effectively in Hamaveran. When Afrasiab saw a great hero spearhead the offensive right through his front lines, with thousands of veteran Iranian warriors pressing close behind him, while the two flanks remained powerful enough to drive around the Turanians in an encircling movement, then Afrasiab called his bravest warriors. "That hero is certainly Rustam," he cried. "Is that not the mace of Sam that he is wielding? If you will take that man dead or alive, I will give you each a kingdom. The parasol of royalty will henceforth be borne above your heads, and you shall marry my daughters!"

Even as he spoke the swarthy Afrasiab saw Rustam bearing steadily toward him! He felt his scalp tingle with the old fear that haunted him still at night. A few minutes later he ordered a retreat. Leaving half his troops wounded or dead on the plain, and his treasure in the silken tents, he collected a bodyguard around him and fled at top speed toward Turan. He did not stop until he was well northward of the Caspian. Men saw his face and cringed, for his lips were dour and drawn. Twice had Rustam made his wine of life turn to vinegar.

After this brilliant victory Kai-Kaus gratefully turned all his thoughts to his realm. Efficient and serious, he collected his tributes from Africa and Arabia, and sent garrisons to the conquered lands. In his proper place, dispensing justice from his ivory throne, he made the people of Persia happy. So great was the wealth of Kai-Kaus that men and demons kissed the earth before him and hastened to do his will. Kai-Kaus said that he had had his fill of adventure. "Our shah has grown tranquil in his maturity," his subjects said. "Now he is going to rule us well. Now he will stay at home. Our land will reach the pinnacle of power and dominion."

In a magnificent ceremony Kai-Kaus honored Rustam by conferring upon him the title of Jahani Pahvlan, Champion of the World. Thus the tireless hero was elevated even above the kings who did service at the court of Persia. Rustam heaved a sigh of relief. He was delighted to see the shah so serious about his kingly duties, and he turned Raksh's head toward Seistan gratefully.

To pass the time away Kai-Kaus gave orders for the building of two palaces in the Elburz Mountains, each one ten lassos wide. One was made of silver and the other of gold.

In the bedrock under them he had tremendous stables excavated in imitation of the *var* his great ancestor had built before the flood. Then he erected a pleasure dome entirely out of crystal with a cupola of black onyx imported from Arabia. From Hind he brought rubies and emeralds to decorate its walls. Inside his lofty crystal dome he stationed learned men who were to spend their lives mapping out the stars and planets. Kai-Kaus took a great interest in their complicated calculations. In such pursuits he spent his time and lived in a perpetual spring, moving from one palace to another as the seasons changed.

As wise a ruler as he had become, Kai-Kaus could not be expected, however, to have discovered every demon in all his wide domains. There were still some evil creatures left who met and plotted in the hidden wilds. "One of you must wean this ruler from his kingdom," said an archfiend. "Otherwise the world will become so insufferably pure that demons like ourselves will find no pleasure in it!" One demon volunteered for the difficult task.

Kai-Kaus was returning merrily to his palace from a hunting trip when he was stopped by a pleasant youth who offered him a bouquet of roses and bent to kiss the earth at the feet of the shah's horse. "Great ruler," said the youth, "you have indeed conquered all the civilized lands. You have imposed your sway from sea to sea. I am amazed that you have not thought of leaving the world some lasting memory of your greatness. Why have you not attempted some feat unparalleled in the rolls of history?"

Why did Kai-Kaus listen to that youth? What made him send his learned courtiers away? How was it that he did not recognize a devil in disguise? Eagerly the shah drew the youth into his private chambers and ordered all his attendants to withdraw out of earshot. Then Kai-Kaus, reclining on his silken cushions, let the false words of the demon drive his wisdom out of his brain.

"You have only conquered bits of earth," the demon urged. "Other men have done the like before and will again. Your very grandson will overtop your conquests and build a pontoon bridge from Asia into Europe. Another of your descendants will conquer the whole world. You have yet performed no feat that is unique," insisted the demon.

"Perhaps you are right," nodded Kai-Kaus. "Continue."

"Excuse me for speaking so frankly," apologized the youth. "Has it not occurred to your royalty that earth is not the proper place for one so glorious? You are a gracious shepherd, that is true, a loving shepherd to these nobles, your blatting sheep."

144

"You are right," sighed Kai-Kaus. "I am engirdled with stupidity."

"What have you learned as you have peered through your crystal dome?" pursued the devilish boy. "What is the secret of the sunset? Have you discovered that? Do you not also long to ferret out the eastern sun's abode? Do you not wish to see the Elburz Mountains as they lie encircling the earth?"

"Why, yes," Kai-Kaus replied. "These are studies worthy of my greatness. Certainly I desire to pierce the secrets of the universe."

"Do you not wish also, great Lion of Persia, to unravel the mysteries of day and night? Your proper place is in the skies. Why do you not turn your piercing brain to its elucidation? How can so glorious a monarch as yourself be satisfied with dust? Unless, of course, you really believe the sky is ladderless!"

The demon talked on and on, but the shah was deep in reverie. All night long he thought and thought, more and more wretched when he considered his transitory fame, less and less interested in his palaces and usual delights. Toward morning he sent a servant to the observatory to ask the wise men, "How far is it from Persia to the moon?" They sent their answer back to him, and still he pondered. He no longer gave audience or attended to his royal duties. Day after day he wrestled with his problem. No person dared disturb his meditation.

One morning he reappeared wreathed in smiles. His orders were secret and urgent. Brave men were dispatched to the mountain eyries and ordered to capture eaglets while the mothers were sleeping. The young birds were carefully nurtured on chicken and breast of lamb. Then when they were full-grown, Kai-Kaus had each one tested. The four strongest, so powerful that each one could lift a mountain sheep in its sharp talons, were selected. The shah inspected them, praised their keepers, and kept his own counsels.

In the greatest secrecy the shah had a frame built of special aloe wood imported from Cape Comorin, the southernmost tip of India. On each of its four corners he had affixed one upright spear. Then from each of the spear's points he let a juicy leg of lamb dangle. In the center of the frame his cabinetmakers lashed a golden throne. Without confiding in any of his ministers, the shah dressed himself in a golden tunic and a jeweled crown. Then he settled back comfortably on the gleaming throne, his feet on a silken cushion, and ordered that the four strongest eagles, which had not

145

been fed for twenty-four hours, be tied by their feet to the four corners.

At once the hungry eagles saw the pieces of meat which hung above them, just out of their reach. Flapping their wings powerfully, they flew toward the meat, and in their attempts to reach it bore the shah of Persia lustily through the air. Kai-Kaus looked smugly from his great altitude. He saw with interest the palace fade from view below him. With a wide smile of achievement on his face, he sipped wine from a golden goblet he had thoughtfully requested just before take-off.

Not many hours passed before the palace had forced the secret of the shah's whereabouts from his confidants. Consternation reigned. Horsemen were sent across the land to Rustam, who donned his battle dress, called Raksh from the meadow, and galloped toward the court. A disorder, indeed, had fallen over the land. On every side fierce wolves devoured the lambs! How sad a country is when no shah rules from his ivory throne! Rustam gathered a band of horsemen and scoured the countryside, sure that the eagles could not have flown too far, dinnerless as they were. Drums rolled as the searchers fanned out over the plateau.

The older warriors of Persia were very disgruntled. By twos and threes they cantered up to Rustam and complained. Old Gudarz was particularly angry with the shah for having drawn him out of his retreat on such a wild-goose chase. "You know I have been a confidant of kings," he grumbled to Rustam. "I have been devoted to our shahs of unsleeping renown. But, never in all my long years, have I met any man whatsoever, of either high or low estate, who was so perverse as this present shah, Kai-Kaus. There seems to be no particle of ordinary sense in him. Do you think his heart is as rotten as his brain?" When Rustam did not answer, Gudarz continued, "Now, take this last prank of his! What man in his right mind would do such a thing? Do you suppose his head was put together upside down?"

Other warriors, friends of Zal, bent close to Rustam's ear to say, "Our shah is insane. See how he is carried off his feet by every wanton wind!"

Rustam thought his own thoughts and made no comment. He pressed the searchers hard and urged them to scan every hill and valley carefully, for Kai-Kaus if still alive would be extremely hungry by that time. Toward evening on the second day, as the riders came up on the crest of a mountain spur, they saw sparkling in the rays of the setting sun what looked like a golden object. It was the throne of the shah.

146

They galloped closer, and there was the King of Kings, seated calmly on his chair. He had just finished roasting and eating a wild duck. All in all he looked very well and extremely pleased with himself.

Kai-Kaus was about to greet his heroes graciously when they burst out at him like angry hornets, "You, sir, belong in a madhouse and not in Persepolis," shouted Gudarz as he dismounted stiffly.

"You have vacated your throne without consulting us," cried another. "What do you mean by dragging us all over the country in search of you?"

"We sent our warriors with you to Mazinderan. You made merry with wine cup and song all along the way. Then what happened to you? Rustam alone could have saved you from the White Demon! Do you realize that?"

"What will we answer," cried another wealthy Persian paladin, "when visitors to our land ask us, 'Where is your shah?' Think occasionally of our embarrassment. 'Oh,' we have to answer. 'Ahem! Our shah has just gone on a little junket, just up to count the stars and see the sun and moon.' "

"Why don't you try to serve the Creator?" cried another. "Haven't you ills enough in your land of Persia? Are there not wrongs enough all around you? First put your house in order, before you go meddling with the world of sky!"

All this time Kai-Kaus sat on his golden throne with his head in his hands. Although he gave no sign, they knew he was listening to their tirade. When every paladin had aired his grievance—all except Rustam, who had remained apart without speaking, as befitted a young man—the shah lifted his weary head and answered them, "Your judgment of me is just. You have convinced me." Then the shah called on the Maker, burst into tears, and crept into the litter that had been brought for him. All the way back to Persepolis he only wept and prayed. He spoke to no one otherwise.

Royally accompanied by the surly and red-faced warriors, Kai-Kaus was driven back to his palace. He refused obstinately, however, to mount upon his throne. There were no more banquetings, and no more audiences. For forty days the shah did penance for his latest indiscretion. He would see no one, but sat alone, his head in the dust. At last he reappeared, smiling and forgiven. "The sun is shining on its favorite land," went out the glad news as Kai-Kaus emerged from his retreat and reigned again.

This is the story of Rustam and Kai-Kaus that every man, woman, and child knows very well—in Persia.

RUSTAM AND SUHRAB

RUSTAM AWOKE one morning with a strange feeling of expectancy. He was restless and tense as if something important were about to happen. All day long he wandered about the palace with this sense of inner excitement. He was bored and exhilarated at the same time. His brother Zuara passed him with the words, "Have you seen the foals? Spring is early this year!" Then Rustam realized the cause of his unrest. It was spring. The New Year had indeed come early.

The tender blades of grass had grown up overnight all over the meadows around Zabul, and overhead the birds flew noisily in pairs. Rustam called for Raksh, prepared his weapons, and set out from the palace on a hunting trip. He felt like leaving the comforts of Zabul behind him and just wandering northward across the plains, with no place special to go, and no other purpose than to renew himself by living close to the earth. It felt good not even to hear voices. He loved the warm spring sun on his bare head and the clean smell of mold and soil. It was wonderful to be young and free. Raksh liked it too after a winter in the stables. He kept tossing his head mischievously and bursting into a mad gallop every now and then.

Day after day they meandered toward the open country of the north until they were almost on the Turanian border. At night Rustam would kill a wild ass with his arrows. Then he would collect dried grass and thorns and get a small fire going. After it had caught, he would pile large branches on it, make a spit, and roast his supper. Throughout the evening hours he would sit by the embers, peacefully wrapped in his blanket, and think of his past adventures. He slept soundly at night beneath the stars.

One night a band of Turkman horsemen riding home across the plains came upon Raksh, who had wandered far from his master. Spurring their horses, they skillfully surrounded the stallion and tried to capture him. Raksh defended himself well. He managed to unseat two of them and wound their horses. The Turkman nomads finally managed to lasso the roan stallion, however, and drive him into their city of Samangan. They planned to share the prize money the king would be sure to give them.

When Rustam awoke in the morning and realized that Raksh was gone, he was white with fury. He saw the deep marks in the meadow and Raksh's hoof tracks blended with those of the nomads' ponies. Shouldering his weapons, he set out in pursuit. His heart ached at the thought of Raksh, who would be hours away by that time. He was discouraged at the possibility that he might have to fight a band of mounted Turkman warriors on foot. He blushed at what the gossips at Afrasiab's court would soon be telling about him. "Here is Raksh. Bold Rustam lost him in the chase. Brave Rustam slept his horse away!"

Rustam had only passed the outskirts of the provincial Samangan when mounted horsemen galloped past him to warn their king that a Persian youth, extremely tall and broad-shouldered, and very kingly in his appearance, was approaching. The opinion was general that it might be none other than the famous Rustam. The king of Samangan and his courtiers hastened to put on their crowns. Then they nervously set out on foot to meet the stranger.

"Can it be the rising sun or the heroic Rustam?" the king inquired anxiously. "Who in my country has dared to meet you in a quarrel? We are all your friends here and your devoted servants. We have no love for Afrasiab! Our lands, our possessions, and our heads, most dear to us, are all at your disposal."

"While I was hunting in your meadows, my Raksh, without halter or rein, strayed away from me," replied Rustam. "I have tracked him to your city. If he is found at once, you will have my thanks and the reward due the honest. If by some chance he is not brought to me forthwith, I shall separate several heads from your chieftains' bodies."

"Do not be angry, noble paladin," answered the king of Samangan. "A horse so well known as your priceless Raksh could not remain hidden. Let me proceed with all gentleness to recover him. Meanwhile, honor us with your company at dinner. Fortune has favored us generously since we have this opportunity of receiving you in our midst. Set your mind at rest. Raksh shall be found."

Rustam accepted the invitation. At once messengers were dispatched to convoke the army chiefs and city dignitaries, who hastened to meet the most famous man in Persia, the champion whose very existence kept Afrasiab north of their own borders. The notables of Samangan outdid themselves in an effort to make their small town palace look as festive as possible. Dancers and musicians were hastily assembled. The cooks bustled and shouted in the kitchens. The wine stewards rushed busily about. Until late at night the guests lolled on cushions and begged Rustam to tell them again of his adventures. Old warriors thrilled and shivered as he talked. Young nobles hung on his every word and studied his face and gestures, so that one day they could tell their grandchildren, "The night I had dinner with Rustam, *he* said to *me* . . ."

The guests were still celebrating when Rustam asked to be shown to his chamber. There the king had laid out perfumes and rose water for his bath. Rustam fell on the bed dizzy from the quantities of wine he had drunk. As he drifted into sleep he saw the door open and slave girls approach his couch with lighted tapers. The room was suddenly full of the heavy scent of roses. Rustam looked dazedly up from his pillow to see bending over him the most beautiful girl he had ever seen in his life.

"Are you real? I cannot believe it," he murmured. Then he lifted himself on his elbow and looked at her face as she bent over him. It was like looking into the heart of a rose. Her cheeks were like petals of dark red velvet. Her eyes gleamed in the soft light of the candles. Her dark hair fell like a cloud over her shoulders and ripe breasts, and her lips were as firm and full as a lover's heart!

"Who are you?" Rustam asked her. "Am I awake? Are you real?"

"I love you, Rustam," she murmured, and ran the soft tips of her fingers reverently across his forehead, down his cheeks, and onto his lips.

Rustam tried to shake the clouds of wine from his head. He stared in amazement at her beauty. "Who are you?" he insisted. "What are you doing in my chamber at night?"

"I am Tamineh, daughter of the king," she whispered. "Until tonight no man but my father has ever seen my face. No man in Samangan has ever heard my name. I vowed that no man should ever possess me because I intended to wait all my life for you. Inside my own chambers and high-walled gardens the tales of your renown were brought to me."

"What do you know of me, Tamineh?" Rustam whispered. Gently he pulled her down beside him on the bed, so that as she talked he could linger over the beauty of her eyes and lips, and run his fingers through her soft hair.

"What do I know of you, my beloved?" she whispered, smiling. "I know you are the bravest man who ever walked the earth. You went alone into the White Demon's cave to rescue the glorious shah. I know that in Arabia you defeated three kings and made them bow their insolent heads in the dust before your feet. The stories of your deeds are more wonderful than a romance. I know you wander lonely through the world, living only to defend mankind from danger, able to bear wounds without a cry and cold and hunger without blanching. You are the only man whom I could love. The wary eagle wheels high overhead when you are near. The fiercest lion fears the sting of your lasso. Whole armies fly in terror at the mention of your name.

"I have so longed to touch your beloved face. I have so longed to feel with my fingers, as now, how broad your shoulders are. I have so dreamed of just the sound of your voice. . . . And more than that, I have a present to give you, Rustam."

"What is it that you have to give me, Tamineh?" he murmured.

"Everyone else in all the lands of Iran seeks you, Rustam," she replied. "They all run after you for one great service after another. 'Rid us of demons. Rescue the shah. Brave dangers we could not face. Do not think of yourself. Come at our bidding,' they say."

"Yes, that is true," he encouraged her.

"I know how lonely you must be," said Tamineh. "I want to give you this gift so that you will never be alone again. I want to give you the most valuable gift a woman can offer the man she loves. Hold me in your arms, closely. I want to bear you a son."

Without letting her move from his side, Rustam dispatched the slaves to notify the wise men of the palace and have Tamineh's father brought immediately. When he arrived, sleepy and slightly drunk from the festivities, Rustam made him understand somehow that he wished to marry Tamineh, and never any other. The king of Samangan could hardly believe his ears. There was no request for dowry, no demand for authentication of lineage, no complication, and very little ceremony. In a daze he regained his quarters, leaving the newlyweds alone, and tried to make himself believe by saying it out loud as if he were really convinced, "My daughter is the wife of Rustam. Naturally, *the* Rustam. My Tamineh is wedded to the grandson of Sam Suwar of Zabulistan, Seistan, and Hindustan." The oftener he said it, the less he believed it. How could such an honor fall upon a desert chieftain?

The next few days sped swiftly by, and Rustam's nights were not lonely. He could not caress his bride enough. He delighted in her silken skin, her slender body, and in her wit and intelligence. When news was brought him that Raksh had been recovered, he hardly listened. He answered yes to all questions that were asked him without taking his eyes from the eyes of Tamineh. He realized, however, and so did she, that he could not stay much longer in enemy territory. His rich kingdoms in the south and his aging parents required his presence. Tamineh only watched him with her soft eyes, and never asked him either when he would go or if he could not remain longer. She was content that her life's desire was being fulfilled.

All through his last night in Samangan, Rustam held his bride closely in his arms and comforted her. No one will ever know what words he said. Then in the early morning, when he had saddled Raksh, he bade farewell to her father and praised him highly. Turning to Tamineh, who stood pale and dry-eyed stroking Raksh's muzzle, Rustam gave her his last directions: "Take my amulet, my beloved Tamineh. It is a famous one. If a daughter is born to you, choose a time when the stars are auspicious, and plait it in her hair. If a son is born, let him wear it. Then he will grow powerful and brave. No fear will ever make my son tremble, and no desert sun will ever scorch him."

Rustam drew Tamineh tenderly against him and held her willowy body once more in his arms. Then he mounted Raksh and rode away among the cheering people of Samangan. Tamineh did not weep until he was out of sight.

Although from that day onward caravans bearing gifts of the value of a king's ransom were dispatched regularly by Rustam from Zabulistan into some unknown area of Turan, Zal never asked his son for whom they were intended. No one in Persia ever heard Rustam mention what befell him on his hunting trip in spring.

When nine months had come and gone, Tamineh gave birth to a beautiful son, whom she named Suhrab because of his smiling, sunny nature. In a month the baby was as large as a year-old child. When he was three his chest was so broad and his arms so strong that he played at warrior with much older boys. By the time he was five, no other lad dared pick a quarrel with him. At ten years of age Suhrab seemed fully grown. Then Suhrab went to his mother and asked her why he had no father. "What can I say when people ask me? Was he some shameful person, or some enemy of Turan? Who was my father? My heart breaks to know!"

Tamineh looked at her handsome son, so much taller and stronger than any of the Turkman warriors in her palace. "Your father is alive, Suhrab," she said. "Here are three priceless rubies from Hind and three purses of gold he sent you at your birth."

"What is his name then?" persisted the boy. "Is he the king of Hind?"

"Yes, he is the ruler of all the southern lands, of Hind, Seistan, and Zabulistan. He is the Jahani Pahvlan, Rustam."

At her words Suhrab's eyes filled with tears. He had never

152

dreamed, in the long years of wondering and imagining, that his own father could be the greatest of all men alive, the kingly Rustam.

"Afrasiab must not know of this," warned Tamineh. "If he knew you were Rustam's son, he would have you killed. I do not want Rustam to know either," she continued, "how tall you are or how gallant. If he knew, he would order you to his side. I cannot lose you, dear Suhrab. You are the child of my love. If I lost you, I would have nothing left."

Suhrab did not agree with his mother at all. "You cannot hide such a thing as this," he cried. "Men have only to look at me to know I am not a Turkman. See how tall I am. Men as tall as I am come only from the blood of Rustam and Sam."

Tamineh pleaded as a mother will. Her caution and prudence were lost on Suhrab, whose will had never been curbed by a father's voice. Dazzled with the knowledge of his glorious ancestry, the boy made plans and built his dream castles high into the clouds. By the time he was fourteen, Suhrab had found a suitable horse—a swift roan from the breed of Raksh—had persuaded his grandfather of Samangan to outfit him, and was ready to seek adventure far from home. Tamineh wept in vain. She could not stop him.

Suhrab's plan was this: he would advance with an army into Iran and with Rustam's help defeat the ridiculous puppet, Kai-Kaus, who was so obviously no proper shah in any sense of the word. Rustam alone should be shah of Iran. Then with his father at his side Suhrab would return northward and depose Afrasiab. At this happy event Suhrab would rule Turan, where his mother Tamineh would be the queen and most honored lady. She would emerge from her desert hiding place and become the envy and admiration of all Asia. All Suhrab would need to put his plan into execution would be to fight his way bravely into Iran so that he could at last meet his father.

Afrasiab, well informed of all that took place in his own kingdom, was delighted with such news. He shook his head with glee, seeing at once that with care he could ruin Rustam. "Of course, this is the son of Rustam, who tarried so long at Samangan." Summoning two of his most valiant warriors, men of proven character and weighty experience, Afrasiab discussed the situation with them. "Go with this youth," he instructed Barman and Human. "By no means let him recognize his father. It will all work out admirably. Either Rustam will be slain by this rash youngster and Kai-Kaus defeated, or Rustam will kill Suhrab. Then when Rustam realizes that he has killed his own son, the heart will go out of him—so much so that we will be able to finish him, or Kai-Kaus without his interference. It will be child's play to dispose of Suhrab, should he be the victor. You can dispatch him any night while he is asleep."

Along with Barman and Human, Afrasiab sent a flattering letter to Suhrab that enjoined him to invade Iran with all confidence. He gave the boy 12,000 picked troops, horses, pack animals, gold, and many rich presents. The two Turanian chiefs were overwhelmed with the stature and prowess of Suhrab. They wrote to Afrasiab that this lad on his roan stallion, so similar to Raksh, loomed more formidable to them than Mount Behistun itself. Thus bravely accompanied, Suhrab invaded Iran, burning everything in his path, wheat fields and villages alike.

Then Suhrab with his Tartar army encamped around the White Castle, a famous fortress commanded by a seasoned warrior named Hajir. Shouting insults back and forth, Suhrab and Hajir fought in single combat. Without much difficulty Suhrab struck the Iranian warrior from his horse. Before Hajir could rise from his heavy fall, Suhrab had dismounted, thrown the warrior on his back, and sat heavily on his chest. Hajir managed to twist himself to one side. He begged Suhrab for mercy so piteously that the youth complied. Binding Hajir's hands behind his back, Suhrab sent him to Human as a prisoner and returned to the castle gates just in time to meet a second champion who spurred out of the fortress and charged him.

Suhrab set his Chinese helmet well over his head and leveled his spear. As this new champion charged, he pulled back his bow and sent a stinging arrow toward Suhrab. Then this warrior, displaying superb horsemanship, wheeled and careened so intricately that Suhrab was unable to catch him. When Suhrab finally managed to send his dart against the enemy's waist with an accuracy and force that would have unseated a less expert cavalier, this champion managed to rise again in the saddle and keep his seat. Then instead of returning to combat, the champion galloped furiously across the plain and out of sight of the castle and the Tartar forces. Suhrab followed hot on his heels and jostled the other's horse so as to break its stride. The two rode side by side until Suhrab, leaning over, managed to yank off the enemy's helmet.

To his amazement he saw that his enemy was a young girl whose long curls blew in the wind behind her head. "If their girls can fight like this one," thought Suhrab to himself, "what must their young men be like in Persia?" Then he expertly coiled his lasso and, standing tall in his stirrups, caught the maiden round her waist. Then he reeled her in, her arms pinioned tightly by the rope.

"What are you doing in all this battle gear?" he asked her. "Who are you?"

"I am Gurdafrid," she answered. "My father is an aged warrior in the White Castle. Are you going to kill me, Champion, or shall we make a truce?" As she spoke, the handsome maiden tossed her hair and showed her pearly teeth.

Suhrab blushed before her saucy charm and could not answer. Pertly Gurdafrid spoke for him, "Oh, come, untie your lasso! You're hurting me." Then as the young giant started to obey her, she enmeshed him well with her flirtatious looks. "You'd better let me go, you know," she told him. "Your soldiers would die laughing if they knew you dueled with girls. We surrender, great warrior," she told him. "Our city and all its wealth is yours."

"Do you surrender also?" Suhrab questioned.

"Oh!" laughed Gurdafrid. "You make hard terms, young Lion. I see that!"

"Shall we make a bargain?" Suhrab asked her, looking straight into her eyes. He still made no move to loosen the ropes that cut into her arms.

"I have spoken," she answered, smiling. "The castle and all its treasure is yours. Only let's not stand here all afternoon. You have my word."

Together they rode up to the fortress where her father hastened to unbar the gates. Then quickly Gurdafrid spurred her horse and dashed inside. Before Suhrab's nose the heavy gates swung shut. Soon he saw the maiden's saucy face over the battlements.

"Warrior! You there!" she called down to him. "Why give yourself such trouble? Go home to Turan. You will never catch me!"

"What of your promise?" Suhrab called up to her. His only answer was her mocking laughter. Then Suhrab swore that he would storm her castle and raze its walls to the ground. "The next time it will be my turn to laugh," he warned her. "Wait till I get you helpless and writhing again in my lasso. Then you will see."

"Suhrab, you won't find a person in Iran to help you win your war," she called. "You may live, but not long. Soon the shah will march his armies out against you. Why don't you go home while you still can? You are no Turanian, anyway! What are you doing in their army? We never saw a champion like you among Turkman chiefs. If you wait here, you are sure to be destroyed. We of Persia have a warrior of our own. Against Rustam you cannot hope to stand, even

155

with arms and shoulders as powerful as you have. Rustam is no youngster either, to be fooled by a girl!"

Suhrab wheeled away from the walls and rejoined the troops. First he gave orders that all the fields and hamlets around the White Castle should be mercilessly laid waste. "We will storm the fortress at dawn tomorrow," he announced, and then retired to his tent, for darkness was falling.

Inside the fortress Gurdafrid and her aged father, left alone to command since the capture of Hajir, dictated a letter to Shah Kai-Kaus and selected their swiftest messenger to stand ready to bear it at top speed. After having extolled the shah, his wisdom, courage, and valor, they told him frankly of their plight. "If you so much as stop to breathe, Persia is lost," they dictated to the scribe. "There is no man in Iran who will stand before the Turanian champion who breathes fire at our gates. Hajir, arrayed in his strongest armor, folded like kindling before his burning lance. This champion's name is Suhrab. He is young, surely not more than an adolescent, but he is as tall and as powerful as Mount Damavand. We cannot believe him to be of Turanian stock. Picture rather Sam at the first flush of his career, rather than Rustam.

"It would be foolish to cast any more of our warriors to this living mountain, and so we will steal out of the castle tonight and leave the place to him. The greatness of this Suhrab surpasses our poor powers of expression. Therefore arm yourself in might and hope all is not lost."

At daybreak Suhrab and his warriors battered down the gates and stormed into the White Castle only to find it undefended. The few people left within its walls knelt weeping and implored the Turanians' mercy. From them Suhrab learned how the garrison had crept out under cover of darkness through a secret passage cut in the rock foundation. An extensive search was made for Gurdafrid, but she was not to be found. This Suhrab regretted more than the escape of the forces. He would have liked to have held this impertinent girl in his arms and heard her cry for mercy.

Kai-Kaus read the letter he received from the White Castle aloud to his courtiers. The shah was very pained, particularly at the fact that Gurdafrid and her father gave him no consolation. "What do you advise?" he asked his champions.

"We must certainly send for Rustam," they replied.

The shah then dictated a long letter to Rustam and ordered the great warrior Giv to prepare his horses and stand by to carry it to Zabul. The shah praised Rustam in the highest terms, reminded him of his past services to the crown of

Persia, and explained the present emergency. Kai-Kaus made the point very clear that he personally was very pained, that in fact his heart ached that Turan should have at present inconvenienced his realm. "At whatever moment this letter falls into your hand," he wrote, "whether by day or in the darkest hours of night, if you should tarry long enough to speak, Iran is doomed. If you should be holding a fresh-plucked rose in your fingers, stop not to smell it! Unless you march forth instantly with your well-known green battle standard, Persia is lost, and your shah is lost! Clothe yourself in valor. The situation, from what I hear, is critical."

The shah ordered Giv to leave immediately and to return without stopping. Giv ran from the palace and leaped on his horse. Away he went like smoke and never halted except for a fresh mount all the way to Zabul. Over 300 miles he sped with neither sleep, nor food, nor rest, nor water. It was Zal who heard the cry from the watchtower, "A rider from Iran as swift as the wind!"

Rustam and his attendants met the weary Giv and drew him into their palace. Here Rustam read the shah's letter while servants bathed and fed Giv. At the end of the first line Rustam began to laugh. "This is just like Kai-Kaus," he said between gales of laughter. When he came to the passage about Suhrab, he could not contain his merriment. He slapped his thighs and stomped around the room, pointing out the words to his friends. "This is really too much," he cried. "A warrior like my grandfather Sam Suwar has appeared. But that's not all! Where has this noble lion come from, if you please? He has sprung from the wilds of Turan, from Afrasiab's soil! This is really too much to ask me to swallow!

"Come! Let us go to my father's palace for feasting," shouted Rustam to Giv and his warriors. "Let us tell this story to the honorable Zal and ask his advice in this matter." While a feast was being served, Rustam continued to joke about Kai-Kaus and his false alarms. Once he fell silent as the thought occurred to him to search his mind well about Tamineh and her son.

"It could not be this champion," Rustam decided. "In the first place, my son is still only a child. Not long ago I sent Tamineh rich gifts for him, and she answered that he was not growing very fast, that in fact he still preferred milk to wine. No, it could not be. Secondly, this Turanian champion is a seasoned warrior. In one onslaught he unseated the valiant Hajir and trussed him hands and feet like a fowl for the oven. That was not the work of a boy, not even my own son."

While Rustam reflected, Giv grew more and more anxious. "We must leave," he told Rustam. "The shah expressly told me not to stop."

"Oh, let us not worry," answered Rustam. "The more we hurry in this world, the quicker we get to the end of our lives, which are only dust anyway. Let us relax a day and lift the wine cups to our thirsty lips. Then we will gird ourselves for war. Battles must wait upon heroes, once in a while." Nothing could move Rustam when he made up his mind. Giv settled back on the cushions and, listening to the music, dozed off. Every now and then the voices of Rustam and his friends reveling and singing would intrude on his slumber.

"This Turanian champion will have to wait for me," Giv heard Rustam say. "He won't run away, at least not until he sees my face and might. At the sound of Raksh's hoofbeats the heroes of Iran will rouse from their fear. They will rush on this Tartar themselves, without needing me at all. This matter is nothing to worry about anyway. Who ever heard of comparing a Turkman to my grandfather, Sam? It's almost insulting."

Rustam had intended to start the following morning, but his head was so foggy with wine that he ordered another banquet instead of his horse and armor. For three days he and his warriors feasted and made merry from dawn until the middle of the night. It was only on the morning of the fourth day that Giv could persuade Rustam to depart. "Don't even give this Suhrab a thought," Rustam reasserted. "The shah won't be angry. By this time their Turanian champion will probably have tripped on a pebble and broken his spine!"

Two Persian champions, Tus and Gudarz, met Rustam and Giv a day's journey from the shah's court. They were reassured by the sight of Rustam and began to agree with him that the whole story was a farce. Laughing and joking, as old comrades in arms will do after a long separation, they strode into Kai-Kaus' presence and saluted him. The shah glared at them in silence without acknowledging their obeisance. They saw his face become purple with rage. He burst forth at them like a caged lion, berating Giv for his delay. Then the shah turned to Rustam, "Who does he think he is that he can disobey my express commands? If I had a sword, I'd lop off his head like a rotten orange. Seize him," the shah ordered Tus. "Seize both of them, him and Giv. Hang them alive, at once!"

Tus in wonderment moved to Rustam and took his hand, intending to lead him out of the palace until both he and Kai-Kaus had time to become calmer. Rustam never moved, but stood looking defiantly at Kai-Kaus. "You are not powerful enough to indulge yourself with such a display of temper," Rustam told the shah. "You rule us worse and worse every day. Very soon, indeed, I see you will not be sane enough to govern at all. Since you no longer need my services, you can go and hang your own enemies yourself! Mazinderan, Hamaveran, Zabulistan, and Hindustan obey my sword, not yours! Why take out your wrath on me?"

Rustam struck Tus's hand with such violence that the warrior dropped to the floor. Then he strode from the audience chamber, down the marble steps of the palace, whistled to Raksh, and was gone. His thoughts were very bitter. How could Kai-Kaus presume to punish him? When just a lad Rustam had placed his line upon the throne. Every man in Rustam's family, for generations back, had deferred to tradition, law, and order in refusing for themselves the crown of Iran. Here was an example of the basest, most thoughtless ingratitude. "Let Suhrab invade Iran, for all I care," mused Rustam. "Kai-Kaus can henceforth fight his own wars!"

After Rustam had left, so angry you would have said his skin was cracking, the warriors of Iran conferred anxiously. Then they sent the oldest and most respected among them to the shah. This was Gudarz. Patiently the old man reasoned with the shah, asked him where Rustam's fault was, and how the shah could be so unmindful of past services. "A great ruler like yourself dare not be hasty or rash in his judgments," he told the shah. Then Gudarz reminded Kai-Kaus of the letter from the White Castle, which expressly stated there was no horseman at all in Iran who would avail against Suhrab. "If you do not persuade Rustam to return," added Gudarz, "then we must fly your palace for our lives instead of rallying to you as we ought to do."

Kai-Kaus admitted the logic of his arguments and ordered Gudarz to persuade Rustam to relent. Gudarz with Tus and Giv overtook Rustam on the road. In vain they apologized for Kai-Kaus. In vain they called the shah stupid, rash, impulsive, thoughtless. In vain they described him as sitting in the palace menaced by Turan, so troubled he was chewing on the backs of his hands. Rustam was not moved by their words.

Deferentially the warriors listened with bowed heads while Rustam raged. "What is your shah to me that I should fear him? He is less than the grains of sand that sift through my fingers. What can he offer me, since he has shown his ingratitude? Do I care for his riches? I have crowns and lands of my own. I have eaten his insolence up to my ears! My only master is the Creator. My only end is dust!"

The only way the three warriors could persuade Rustam to

return was to insinuate that his quarrel with the shah would be interpreted—not by his friends, but by others who only knew him by reputation—as cowardice, as fear of this Turanian champion. Because of this Rustam became reconciled with Kai-Kaus and accepted his profuse apologies. "I am like a tree that planted crooked is unable to grow straight. Any sudden emotion, such as this emergency, puts me out of my normal good humor," said the Shah in his excuse. They spent the evening in revelry, and the following morning Kai-Kaus, accompanied by Rustam and an army of a hundred thousand soldiers, set out to meet Suhrab.

The shah's army encamped upon a plain before the castle seized by Suhrab. When Human, the Turanian, looked out over the battlements and saw the Iranian host, which stretched to right and left as far as eye could see, he was frightened. Suhrab on the contrary marked only the brilliant pavilions of the Persian nobles. "This war will be fought by me in single combat," he assured Human. "You have nothing to fear whatsoever." With a shrug of his shoulders the youth rejoined the merrymaking.

After darkness had fallen, Rustam requested leave of Kai-Kaus to enter the Turkman camp. He left his helmet and royal belt and set out covered with a dark cloak to have a look at the Turanian champion. Unobtrusively Rustam stole outside the circle of the feasters and looked upon Suhrab for the first time. Standing in the unlighted area he marveled at the boy. Suhrab was seated on the turquoise throne that Afrasiab had sent him. On its ivory steps knelt fifty slaves with golden armbands who chanted verses in his praise. Suhrab's shoulders and back were so massive they filled the throne from edge to edge. His naked biceps were as large as a camel's thighs. His merry face gleamed in the firelight, and he was handsome, glowing with health and animal spirits.

Then as Rustam watched fascinated, a Turanian warrior who had stepped outside for a moment saw the strange cloaked man, noticed his extraordinary height, and making a passage through the throng, accosted Rustam roughly. Without seeing the man's face, Rustam reacted like lightning, with the instinctive speed of thought and action that is developed over a period of warring years. Rustam chopped the Turanian across the neck with the outside edge of his hand. The blow was so swift and so accurate that the Turkman fell dead on the ground. Rustam had already made his way quietly out of the camp before Suhrab missed his warrior. When he found Zanda Razm dead on the ground, Suhrab was deeply grieved. This was his uncle, Tamineh's brother, who had accompanied his nephew at the mother's request. Zanda

Razm was the only person in Samangan who had seen Rustam years before during his wedding week. Suhrab had counted on his uncle to point out Rustam to him, and to introduce the son to his father. Suhrab ordered his uncle's body to be honorably borne to Samangan, and then the boy returned to his guests. "The treacherous fiend who has stolen into my camp to kill in the darkness shall not spoil our festivities. Tomorrow early I will wield my lasso in revenge."

Rustam returned through the darkness to his own lines. He was accosted by Giv, who was standing sentry. Overjoyed to see Rustam safe and sound, Giv accompanied him to the shah. Kai-Kaus heard from Rustam himself corroboration of the information sent him by Gurdafrid and her father. "This Suhrab is a champion indeed," admitted Rustam. "To begin with, he is as tall as a cypress tree, like my brother and myself, children of our mother Rudabah." Then Rustam told how he had almost been captured by a Turkman warrior.

"What happened?" asked the shah.

"He never returned to the feast," replied Rustam, laconically. Then the champion retired to his tent after instructing the officers that the troops should stand in readiness all through the night.

The following morning, just as the sun flashed full upon the Iranian camp, Suhrab rode out with Hajir, the Iranian whose life he had spared in their battle before the White Castle. Suhrab was stern-faced and intent. He wore his battle gear solemnly—Chinese helmet, Indian sword, and his sixty-coiled lasso upon his saddle horn. From a hill he could survey the brilliantly colored tents of the Iranian nobles. "Hajir," he said, "I spared your life in battle. If you want to be free, not only free but well rewarded, answer my questions truthfully. I want to identify for me the tents of the Persian paladins which we see spread out below us." Hajir swore that he hated lies more than a crooked arrow.

"Do you see over there," asked Suhrab, "a magnificent tent of gold brocade? It is enclosed with many flags and awnings of leopard skin. Beside it are tethered a hundred or so elephants. Before it is a turquoise throne above which beats a purple flag with yellow sun and moon. Whose tent is that?"

"That is the tent of Kai-Kaus, shah of Persia," answered Hajir.

"To the right of the golden tent is a black one. Do you see it? Beside it are chained lions and many troops with golden boots. The banner is black with elephants upon it. Whose enclosure is that?"

"It belongs to Tus, son of a shah named Nauder," replied Hajir. "His standard bears an elephant. I know it well."

"Now," continued Suhrab, "do you see the large red tent? Before it floats another purple pennant with lions rampant. Beside it are many paladins in armor. Whose tent is that?"

"It belongs to Gudarz, a great general. The paladins are his forty sons who came along to war with him," said Hajir promptly.

"Look sharply now," said Suhrab, "for you shall die if you lie to me. There is a massive tent of bright green silk. Before it on a throne sits a paladin so tall that even seated he towers above his throngs of warriors. Behind him are lined Indian elephants all in chain mail. His banner is green with a dragon on it. A golden lion stands upright on the flagpole. Who is that warrior?"

"I do not recognize him," lied Hajir, who knew Rustam's colors very well. He thought it better to lie for fear Suhrab would go charging impetuously down the hill and slay Rustam as he sat on his throne.

"Why do you not know this one?" persisted Suhrab. "Look how wealthy he is. He must be some very famous paladin."

"I think he must be some lord of Chin who joined Iran since I was your prisoner," was all Hajir could think of to say.

Fate had arisen early that morning. Her web was woven tight about them all. Patiently Suhrab went over the Iranian host one by one until Hajir had identified them all. Then he questioned Hajir again about the green tent.

"See the stallion who tosses his mane so restlessly. Is it not Raksh? Is it not Rustam's horse? The coiled lasso reaches almost to the ground. Is it not Rustam?" cried Suhrab.

"No," lied Hajir again. "Rustam remained home in Zabulistan. It is the annual feast of roses there. He would not come to war."

"What kind of tale is that!" Suhrab replied scornfully. "Rustam not go to war? He is the first in every battle line! Kai-Kaus for all his might would never face an enemy without Rustam! The shah, foolish as he is, still remembers what befell him alone in Mazinderan!"

"Rustam did not come," reaffirmed Hajir. "You would recognize him easily enough. He is so much mightier and handsomer than any paladin you have ever seen. Whole empires topple when he lifts his hand." Hajir would say no more. In his heart he despaired, for he gave Rustam no chance at all to vanquish Suhrab. Hajir would not have minded dying then and there, for he considered the war as good as lost.

162

Angry and frustrated, Suhrab dealt Hajir a blow that sent him headfirst from his horse. His heart ached that after all these toils he had not found his father.

It was the Creator who laid out the world. Would you be the one to criticize its workings? He it was who sent their fates to all the warriors of that battlefield. If you will loiter about in this Wayside Inn of Life, you also will see similar tragedies, pain, sorrow, and all kinds of poison!

Suhrab left Hajir on the ground where he had thrown him. Gathering his reins, he spurred his horse down the hill and across the plain to Kai-Kaus' enclosure. Warriors and slaves fled panic-stricken at his approach, and the shah remained hidden in his tent. "Where is this shah of Persia?" Suhrab called sarcastically. "Why does he not ride forth and fight me? One of his brave men stole into my camp last night and slew my faithful uncle, Zanda Razm! Because of this treachery I have sworn a solemn oath: I shall not leave one single Iranian noble alive upon this field! As for the Shah of Shahs, Kai-Kaus, I shall have him strung up alive upon my scaffold!"

The loud cries of Suhrab echoed across the plain, while the Iranian army listened in silence. Huddled inside his tent, the shah sent off a messenger for Rustam. Again Suhrab shouted, "Will no one come to fight me?" When there was no answer, Suhrab, laughing and mocking them, circled the shah's encampment and with his spear uprooted seventy tent pegs so that the whole tent collapsed upon its shivering royalty inside.

Rustam was dressing when he received the shah's frantic message. Calmly and methodically he continued to adjust his leopard-skin doublet, buckle his wide girdle, and loosen his sword in its scabbard. Stepping out of the tent, he smiled to see Giv himself tightening Raksh's cinches. Clapping his old friend on the back, Rustam mounted and gathered up the reins. Before leaving he turned kindly to Giv, who looked up at him with tears flowing down his wrinkled cheeks. "Did you ever see such a shah as this one?" Rustam asked. "He never invites me to banquets, only to war!" Then, laughing and slapping the reins across his stallion's neck, Rustam rode off with the words, "Do not advance unless you hear from me. Obey no other's orders!"

A hundred thousand Iranians watched their champion and his color-bearer canter across the plain up to Suhrab. Even Kai-Kaus mustered enough courage to step out to his throne while all around him the older warriors of Persia shook their heads sadly to see their champion ride so nonchalantly to what must be his death.

163

"Oh! A champion at last!" called Suhrab scornfully. "And an old one at that!"

"Let us withdraw to some quieter spot where we can meet," replied Rustam calmly.

"Hurry up then, old man," called Suhrab, wheeling his mighty roan stallion. "In truth, the field of battle is no place for you. I shall receive no added glory by killing you in plain sight of your troops. You may have been a fine man once, but your powerful limbs are long stiff with age. One cuff, and I will send you to the dust!"

Rustam looked at him and smiled to see so much ardor and impetuosity. "Young man," he answered pleasantly, "I wonder if you have any idea at all of how cold and hard this earth is upon which we stand. Do you perceive the mildness of the summer air and yet desire to leave it? Have you any notion at all of death?

"I may be old by your standards," Rustam continued, "but I have never been beaten. I hope you are paying attention to what I say," he added, for Suhrab was obviously impatient to begin. "I have fought elephants, fierce crocodiles, demons, and armies, but I have never been overpowered. You will know fear if you insist on fighting me. If you survive, then never fear again. The stars above be witness to my words: my heart aches for you, young man, young Suhrab. I do not want to take your life. There is no other champion like you in Turan. I know, because I have fought them all."

Despite his arrogance Suhrab was moved by the words. "Tell me one thing, great warrior of Iran. What is your name and lineage? Are you not Rustam, son of Zal?"

Shaking his head, Rustam answered slowly, "No, I am not Rustam. He is a mightier paladin with crowns and empires. I am only a lowly warrior. You will have many more like me to vanquish before you meet Rustam and the shah. You have a false opinion of your importance. We would not send Rustam to meet a youngster like you."

For Suhrab all the day was spoiled. It was as if a cloud had overcast the sun. He and Rustam withdrew to a small area far from the troops, and there they met in battle. First they fought with javelins until their weapons' points were broken. Then, wheeling their mounts, they closed with Indian scimitars until the sparks flew red above their heads. The struggle was a draw. Then they wielded maces so strong their armor cracked and the mail dropped from their staggering horses. After these onslaughts each one drew aside to rest a moment, Suhrab exhausted, and Rustam in anguish.

How mysterious are the workings of the world! Wild lions, horses, fishes know their young. A newborn foal totters to its dam. Only the race of men feel no strong stirrings of love for their brothers. Only the father does not recognize his child!

Rustam laid his hand across the mane of Raksh and sighed to hear the stallion's labored breathing. Thoughts of old feuds and wounds ran through his mind. "The White Demon in all his insensate fury was nothing compared to this boy," he mused. "Here before armies an unskilled youth has made me long for death!"

Looking up, the champion saw Suhrab on horseback again and stringing his bow. Heavily Rustam mounted, and the battle began afresh. Arrow after arrow they shot, stinging and clanging on each other's armor, but neither was seriously wounded. Then Rustam grabbed Suhrab by the belt, an old trick of his that had succeeded with Afrasiab once. Suhrab gripped his mount with knees of iron, and Rustam could not unseat him. Then Suhrab brought his heavy iron mace down across Rustam's shoulder so hard that the champion winced in spite of himself and let go Suhrab's girdle. The youth yelled in triumph and taunted Rustam, "Champion of Iran, I saw you flinch beneath my mace. Go home, old man. You cannot fight with me! That nag of yours ambles rather like a donkey."

Rustam spurred away, the youth's exultant cries following him. All along the Turanian front line Rustam galloped, lopping off heads in his anger and driving the troops and horses in panic back upon each other. Then there came to his ears the moans and cries from the Iranians. Rustam, realizing he should not have left Kai-Kaus' side, tore off across the plain to his own lines, where Suhrab was plunging like a maddened elephant. "Stop it!" he ordered. "Save your blows for me." Since darkness was falling, they agreed to meet again at dawn.

Suhrab returned to his camp, where Human hastened to help him dismount and anoint his cuts. "How was their champion?" questioned the Turanian chiefs.

"I hold him peerless," answered Suhrab. "He has the heart of a lion truly, but I have won the day, for I killed many Iranian chiefs while all he did was to ravage our front lines. We fight again tomorrow. Come. Let us feast. You may be sure I shall kill him tomorrow."

Rustam was met by his old friend Giv. "How did you fare?" asked Rustam, for he was worried about the shah.

"This Suhrab is a raging lion," answered Giv. "I kept your rule and made him fight our champions one by one. Perhaps in that way will we wear him out."

The shah greeted Rustam warmly and anxiously scanned

his weary face. He courteously made Rustam lean back on the throne itself and rest while he reported what had happened. "We fought all day," said Rustam. "We strove with javelins, arrows, and maces. This Suhrab never felt my blows. I tried to lift him from the saddle, but I could not even rock him from his horse. We fight again tomorrow, but for once I can promise you nothing. I will do what I can for shah and country, but only the Creator can say which of us will prevail." Then Rustam strode stiffly to his own tent, where his brother was waiting. Rustam would let no one else help him. Zuara bit his lips as he cut away the mail and saw how cruelly Rustam had been wounded.

Half through the night Rustam conversed alone with his brother. "I want you to have our troops in readiness by sunrise," Rustam told him. "Bring Raksh around to me and set out my golden boots. If I manage in some way to vanquish Suhrab tomorrow, we will set out for home as soon as you see me return. Therefore have all the baggage ready to depart. If I am vanquished, as seems will be the case, you will command our forces. Do not tarry one second, not even to mourn me or lament, but push on without stopping to Zabulistan.

"Think of our mother first, and bear her first the news. You will know what to say. Tell her my life was good. Say that I remained undefeated until the day of my death. Especially tell her I forbid her to weep or mourn for me. I have been knocking at the door of death each day, ever since I mounted Raksh and sought for battle. No man can live forever. Tell her to think of Jemshid on his Golden Throne, and of Zahhak. Even they left this world as all must do. Comfort her, for a woman does not understand what a man's life is.

"Tell our father Zal I bid him to fight for the shah. Prepare for siege as soon as you reach Zabul." Then Rustam and his brother searched their minds for precedents and discussed old battles in an effort to decide how best to defeat Suhrab the following day.

At sunrise the two champions rode across the shimmering plain toward each other, and Suhrab was smiling. He greeted Rustam cordially as if the two of them had spent the night banqueting together. Rustam listened sternly to the boy's words, "Let us not fight today, you and I," Suhrab suggested. "Let us sit in the warm sun and clear our brows with some ruby wine. I blush to admit it, old man, but I have a strange affection for you. One could almost say there is some link between us. If we were to stretch out here on the grass, I'll wager you would see we are identical in length and breadth. Surely you will tell me you are Rustam. Indeed, you ought, for enemies should always announce their names to each other."

Rustam dryly replied, "As I recall, our appointment today was for the purpose of wrestling. I am too old for tricks, young hero. Do not attempt to beguile me. You cannot disarm me with words."

"You will regret it if I cannot," answered Suhrab shortly.

The warriors tied their chargers to a rock and, huge in their mail, advanced to grapple with each other. Like two fierce lions they wrestled until the sweat and blood poured from their skins and mingled with the dust. All day long they struggled, almost without stopping to breathe. Then, as long shadows fell across the ground, Suhrab gained the advantage. He somehow seized the belt of Rustam with both hands, and yelling with rage and triumph, threw him to the dust. Then Suhrab pounced upon him and drew his dagger to cut off his head. Rustam caught his breath in time, however, and told him, "You cannot kill me yet. We are in Persia and therefore must abide by Persian custom. It is only the second time that you throw a man that you become a Lion. It is only then that you may cut off his head."

His words stopped Suhrab. Wiping the sweat and blood from his mouth, the youth arose, confident now that he could kill Rustam whenever he chose. Fate had not willed that Rustam should die yet. Who knows whether Suhrab also complied through magnanimity? In any case he returned toward his forces and was roundly scolded by Human and his fellow warriors.

"When will you learn not to despise an enemy, no matter how puny he appears to you?" growled Human. "This is the third time you have underestimated a foe. You never should have let the Iranian chieftain go. You say you had him in your power. Why didn't you kill him?"

Suhrab stood crushed before his fury. "Well, never fear," he answered them. "He will return tomorrow, and then will I kill him for you!"

What happened to Rustam when he raised himself from the ground where Suhrab had hurled him is shrouded in mystery. In after years people used to wonder what occurred, and old men who had known Rustam personally told it this way. It seems that when Rustam was a very young man he had suffered greatly because he was different from his friends and fellow warriors. His tremendous height and strength embarrassed him and made him feel ashamed, since he could so effortlessly vanquish any foe. It seemed to him that he was taking undue credit for his victories. In his sorrow he had prayed to have his force diminished. He had wept and prayed to be like ordinary men so that he could walk into a hall

167

without bumping his head, and stride over sand without sinking deep into it. His prayer had been answered, for Rustam's request was honorable.

In after years old men believed that the day Rustam almost met his death at the hand of Suhrab, he arose from the dust and walked alone to the banks of a nearby river. There he unbuckled his armor and plunged into the icy water. As he bathed, he prayed to have his former strength restored. The cool water flowed over his bruised body, and his prayer was granted a second time.

The warrior who met Suhrab on the following morning was a different man. As soon as the two had tied their horses to the same rocks, Suhrab advanced confidently. The moment he felt the hands of Rustam bending his body backward, however, Suhrab became like a helpless toy. Rustam grasped him firmly by the belt and, lifting him high in the air, hurled him to the ground. Then as Suhrab struggled violently beneath him, Rustam without a word drew his dagger and gave his son a mortal wound.

"Ah," groaned Suhrab as the sharp blade pierced his chest. "Ah," he cried again. "It is all my fault and the fault of my fate that bore me up so soon to cast me down so fast. My mother warned me not to go to Persia." Then looking up at Rustam through anguished eyes, Suhrab lashed out at him. "Run and hide yourself, paladin. Transform yourself into some crawling worm and hide beneath the surface of the earth. For were you some slimy fish that lurks among the weeds of a bottomless pool, or an eagle that soars a mile above us, my father would seek you out. When Rustam hears you have slain his only son, he will choke you with his bare hands. You shall die for this day's work!"

Rustam stood above the writhing youth, his dripping dagger in his heavy hand, when those words struck him. Before his eyes the world spun in a huge maelstrom with him at its center, upside down. Blinded and numb, he fell to his knees, and his tears gushed over his face.

"Suhrab," he moaned. "I am Rustam."

"Cut open my mail, and you will see the amulet my mother bade me take you," sobbed the boy. Rustam did as he bade and saw the brilliant gem.

Then he covered his head with dust as the words of his son pierced his very heart. "Why did you not tell me?" wept Suhrab. "I came to you yesterday in love. Why did you not know me for your son?"

Rustam then held the dagger to his throat, but the hand of Suhrab stopped him. "It must have been my fate to die so young," he cried. "What good will it do to kill yourself? Swift as the lightning came I to this world and on the wind's breath

168

shall I glide away. Perchance you will be my father in heaven. It was the wish of fate for me to die. You could do nothing. Therefore live."

With his head in the dust beside his dying son Rustam crouched, and here the Iranian warriors found him. Their joy turned to consternation when they saw that he had rent his garments and covered his head with dust. "I have killed my son," he whispered to the aged Gudarz who knelt beside him. Fast as a prairie fire spread the word through the Persian army.

In honor of Rustam men everywhere rent their garments also and bent their heads to the dust. Even the Turanian chiefs sat in rows along the ground and wept. Then Gudarz remembered the famous elixir of Shah Kai-Kaus, a marvelous medicine that would stanch the blood of any wound. He told Rustam to take courage and hastened to the shah.

Kai-Kaus refused. All he could remember was Suhrab's threat to hang him, and so Suhrab died. All hostilities ceased between the two hosts, and the Turanians began quietly to withdraw. Zuara fashioned a superb litter of gold cloth and on this Suhrab was transported to Zabul. As the cortege entered the home city, all the warriors removed their belts and fastened them to the bier. Their horses' manes and tails were docked, and their hair covered with dust.

Rustam lifted the cloth from his son's face so that Zal and Rudabah could see him. "He is like a tawny lion," all people said, "who has fallen asleep while playing with war." Rustam sent word to Tamineh and to her also Suhrab's stallion. This sorrowing mother did not long survive her son.

Rustam had an intricate tomb constructed in the shape of a horseshoe for his son's body. For months he mourned Suhrab, but eventually he was able to lift his head and bear his suffering with understanding.

I have written *The Book of Kings*, which will remain as a memory of my life in this world. The palaces men build fall into ruin under the rain and the heat of the sun; I have built with these verses a magnificent palace which the storm and rain will not injure; the years will roll over this book, but men everywhere will recite it. . . . I learned how to weave this golden cloth because I discovered long ago the secret of words.

Oh, you who look into the past, how often are you also joyous like me, and how often like me are you full of sorrow. How astonishing is the swift motion of this vaulted sky above all our heads! How often is the soul burdened with still more recent troubles!

One man's lot is all honey and sugar, good health, sheltered life, and high fortunes; the years of another are so filled with grief and toil that his heart breaks in this fleeting world; a third man's life is spent in disappointment —sometimes he wins, but oftener he loses. That is the way fate lifts us up, and the pain caused by the thorns is greater than the pleasure we felt at the color of the rose. . . . If only the sixty nets of the years were like fishnets, then a clever man could find his way out; but we can none of us escape from this sky that revolves at the will of Him who made sun and earth.

Even the great conquerors of Persia struggled painfully in vain, loved combat in vain, and ceased to take pleasure in their wealth; they too departed for another world and left here all the fruits of their labors.

Consider the fate of the greatest Shah of Shahs, Cyrus the Great; examine once more the old, old stories of the world. Learn how even Cyrus did not remain upon the earth, how men by the millions ceased to obey his commands.

That is the law of every man's life; therefore rid your hearts of all anxiety.[4]

ABU'L-KASIM HASAN [5]
Tus, Iran
c. 1000

6

India: Rama and the Monkeys

INTRODUCTION

HISTORIANS AGREE that the history of India is very long. According to *Ancient India*, published in 1911 by S. Krishnaswami Aiyanger, the original home of the Aryans who conquered India was in the Arctic Circle. He believes the Aryans were living there in 7000 B.C., and that changes of climate forced them to move south. Geologists confirm that

[4] From *The Book of Kings*, Vol. IV, Mohl (French) translation.
[5] Called "Firdausi," which means "of Paradise."

the strongest climatic change the world has known in 100,-000 years occurred in this area between 10,000 B.C. and 5000 B.C. A rapid rise in temperature and flash floods would have driven the inhabitants to seek in central Asia conditions similar to those with which they were familiar. Indian scholars think that the *Vedas,* or hymns of the Aryans, had already been composed by 3800 B.C. They base their belief in part on interior astronomical evidence, which is also confirmed by modern science.

In the third millennium B.C. the Aryan tribes were moving through the Khyber Pass into the Punjab. By 1500 B.C. they had settled along the Doab, Ganges, and Jumna River valleys of northern India. Their language, Sanskrit, which is the parent of the major languages of India, corresponds to Latin, the parent of the romance tongues. Sanskrit is believed to be much older than Latin.

The two epics of India were composed in Sanskrit. Many Western historians, such as Pierre Meile (*Histoire de l'Inde,* Paris, 1951), feel that these poems cannot be dated. Indian students, on the contrary, would assign the *Mahabharata* to the years 1500 B.C.-1000 B.C. This long and very spirited epic tells the story of wars fought when the Aryans were contacting the older residents of India, the civilized Dravidians. Prior to the Aryan invasion there existed two extensive kingdoms along the Indus River, one in the area called Sind (Mohenjo-Daro) and a second in the Punjab (Harappa). Some scientists believe they see similarities between these Dravidians and the early Egyptians, and also with the Australoids. The Dravidians are usually referred to as a short, dark-skinned people.

Most Indian students fix the *Ramayana,* the second long epic of India, at around the year 1000 B.C. Romesh Dutt, its best-known translator, concurs. The following chapter will retell the story of Rama, a story that describes those virtues that for millennia have characterized all that is best in Indian men and women. Mr. Dutt points out the striking contrast between the *Ramayana,* which extols faithfulness, piety, and steadfastness, with the Greeks' reverence of beauty and their emphasis upon gaiety and joy. Like the epic of Persia, the *Ramayana* is the work of one man, the poet Valmiki, whom you will meet in the following pages.

Persia was always the link between India and the West in ancient times. According to a Persian historian named Mohammed Kazim Farishta (translated by Lieutenant Colonel Alexander Dow, Dublin, 1792), Shah Feridun ruled Hindustan before 1429 B.C. Then in 1072 a Persian noble named Rustam deposed an Indian prince named Feros-ra, who later died in Bengal, thus ending a dynasty that had reigned for 137 years. Rustam then placed upon the throne a ruler named Suraja because Rustam felt this area was too distant for him to govern it efficiently. It seems quite certain that Cyrus the Great ruled a part of India around 550 B.C.; and according to the Mount Behistun inscriptions so did Darius, from 521–485 B.C. Through Persia the western or Byblos alphabet made its way into India. Persian annals also tell how that great shah of Persia whom we usually refer to as Alexander the Great also crossed the Hindu Kush Mountains into the Punjab in 327 B.C.

Ancient India apparently never returned the compliment by wishing to conquer or possess any part of the Western world. One of their ideas was that their Himalayan peak, which they called Mount Meru, was at the center of the earth. Paradise was at its summit, and similar beliefs exist about Mount Everest today. They pictured the land of India as lying around this mountain, encircled by a sea of salt water. Other lands lay in concentric circles around India, surrounded by other seas—of wine, milk, sugar-cane syrup, and juices.

The Indians knew of a western land they called Rómaka, where it was midnight when it was sunrise at Lanka in Ceylon. To their immediate west were the Párasica (Persians), then the Yávana (Greeks), and the Raúmaca (Romans). Anyone else was a Barbara, an unidentified foreigner. While the Indians for religious reasons were poor geographers, they were great mathematicians, grammarians, philosophers, and poets. They claim Pythagoras learned his mathematics in India.

Mr. William Robertson, historian to His Majesty of Scotland, writes in Edinburgh in 1791 that India was "the original station of man." He adds that in the mild and fertile regions of the east the most useful of the domestic animals, the horse and the camel, were first bred.

Early historians noted how envious the West always was of the riches of the East. India itself is a country that, judging from the vast numbers of histories and the hundreds of travel books written about it, particularly in the nineteenth century, has always attracted the West. The library shelves on Persia are bare by comparison. The following chapter incorporates descriptions from one of the most novel travel books, *L'Inde* by Pierre Loti. This book was written in India at the turn of the century and tells also of Loti's conversion. Unlike the *Shah Namah*, the *Ramayana* does include descriptions of scenery.

One other Indian work is included because it is representative of the most ancient writing of India and also because

172

it contains the thought of our hero's religion, or an answer to a problem that had been plaguing heroes all the way from Gilgamesh. The philosophy or scriptures of Rama come from the *Katha Upanishad*. The sacred *Vedas* of the Aryans were divided into four types of writing: (1) poetic, (2) Brahmanical, (3) philosophical, and (4) ritualistic. The *Upanishads* are the best philosophical thinking of Brahmanism. They are the commentaries of great thinkers whose pupils sat down beside them (*upa*—near; *ni*—down; *sad*—sit).

The Lieutenant Colonel Dow of Dublin, mentioned above, in addition to being a translator from the Persian and a historian, was an early student of Sanskrit. In the middle 1700's he persuaded a learned pandit from the University of Benares to give him lessons in this mysterious language. The colonel's personal conclusion was that Sanskrit had been artificially created by the Brahmans, just as hieroglyphics had been devised in Egypt and restricted to an educated elect. In his preface Colonel Dow has this to say about India: "Though, in an advanced stage of society, the human mind is, in some respects, enlarged, a ruinous kind of self-conceit frequently circumscribes its researches after knowledge. In love with our own times, country and government, we are apt to consider distant ages and nations, as objects unworthy of the page of the Historian."

RAMA AND THE MONKEYS

ONCE UPON A TIME there lived in the fair kingdom of Ayodhya a prince named Rama who was without an equal for comeliness, courage, and learning. His father was a wise old rajah named Dasa-ratha. Prince Rama was beloved of his father and of his father's wives, who had borne Dasaratha three other sons, both handsome and brave—but not so outstanding as Rama.

One day the rajah of the neighboring kingdom to the east sent a challenge out to the civilized lands of northern India to say that he would bestow his oldest daughter on whatever prince could bend a mighty war bow in his palace. Rama traveled to this land of Videha as soon as he heard the pronouncement. Everyone had spoken of the extraordinary beauty and gentleness of this Princess Sita, and people wondered who would win a maiden so lovely. Suitors hastened to the court of her father Janaka, but they soon left it in great humiliation. No matter how strong they were, they could not even lift the bow of the Rajah Janaka, to say nothing of bend it.

173

Rama and his three brothers were ceremoniously received at the eastern court. Rama asked to be shown the marvelous engine that no prince could move. Before the whole court of Videha the monstrous bow was hauled into the audience chamber. It lay on an eight-wheeled chariot pulled by eight hundred men. Everyone gasped as Prince Rama lifted the bow quite easily. He strung it also, and then asking King Janaka's aid and blessing, Rama bent it until it split asunder with a crack like a clap of thunder. In this way did the Sun Prince Rama, descendant of mankind's father Manu, win his sweet-faced bride.

Messengers rode back to Rama's kingdom of Ayodhya to notify the prince's father, Dasa-ratha. Seven days later the elderly rajah himself arrived in Videha for the wedding. He was most courteously welcomed as an enlightened ruler and a devoted student of the holy *Vedas*. After the early morning rites had been scrupulously performed, a high altar was raised, richly adorned, and encircled by Igni, the holy fire. Then slender Prince Rama advanced to the altar, where he took the hands of Princess Sita, who was arrayed in flame-and-golden draperies. Then Rama's three brothers—Lakshman, Bharat, and Satrughna—all sons of Dasa-ratha by two different mothers, advanced and were wedded to Sita's sisters—Urmila, Mandavi, and Sruta-kriti. After each couple had humbly stepped around the altar, the princes led away their resplendent brides through a shower of drifting petals, and all Videha rang with music and acclamation.

A few days later Dasa-ratha's train, returning homeward to Ayodhya, saw their own fair city of Kosala bright and shining like the Himalayan mountain Meru. The people had sprinkled the ways with rose water and swept them clean. Then they had strewn yellow, perfumed jasmine all along the route. The kindly Dasa-ratha smiled down at his subjects as his chariot bore him among them. All in Kosala were healthy and plump, and no one so poor he could not wear gold earrings and bracelets. Men of all occupations were free from the disgraceful passions—servility, egotism, and the lust for gold. All had leisure to study the *Vedas* and mind enough not to question the will of heaven. In Videha hard labor was not done by men, but by ponderous elephants brought down from the Himalayas or captured in the Vindhya Mountains.

Dasa-ratha and his sons were met by the royal wives—first Kausalya, the mother of the oldest prince and heir, Rama; then Kaikeyi, whose brother ruled in a fierce and warlike western land and whose son was the tall and very handsome Bharat; and thirdly by Sumitra, mother of the twin sons, Lakshman and Satrughna. Each one of the royal mothers was greeted affectionately by the princes, who approached and humbly touched their feet. Then the gentle brides were admired and made welcome. Dasa-ratha looked on his royally married sons and decided it would be safe for him to relax somewhat from the exigencies of kingship. Within the next few days he dispatched his second son, Bharat, to see the world and pay a visit of state to his mother's kingdom, that fierce land in the west.

Then the aged rajah of Ayodhya called a formal assembly of all the Brahmans and chieftains of his lands. Addressing them respectfully, he told them of a suggestion. He asked them if they agreed that he had ruled so long he might be allowed to spend his last few months of life prolonged and served by his three young wives. Dasa-ratha appealed to the wise Brahmans for their thoughts in this matter. He said that he desired their sanction for the coronation of his oldest son, Rama. At once the priests and warriors gave him their consent. Even when Dasa-ratha begged them to speak freely, to reveal any misgivings they might have thought it polite to conceal, his council continued to approve his decision.

Rama was notified that he was to be crowned the following morning. This prince had won the trust and affection of the whole kingdom. From childhood he had been unfailing in his religious observances, humble before the Brahmans, eager to memorize the *Vedas,* and in war the world had never seen his equal. Even the lowliest workingman could obtain audience with this tall prince at any time whatsoever. Rama saw to it that there was no unemployment and no beggars in his land. To his father and the queens he had always been unfailing in his devotion, touching the feet of each of his mothers with equal respect and affection. Rama placed virtue and truth above all else, so that people called him the prince of righteousness. As soon as Rama received his father's directions, he retired to fast and pray so that he would be ready for the coronation in the cool hour of sunrise the following day.

The three queens rejoiced also in the news, as much as the city dwellers. From their private apartments and secluded gardens they could hear preparations for the ceremonies. Poles were being driven into the ground along the roads so that lanterns could glow all through the next evening. Golden bells were strung from the elephants' howdahs. A new white umbrella was being sewn for Rama, wide enough to protect his broad shoulders from the sun.

Kaikeyi, the mother of Bharat, she who had come from

the western land, was selecting jewelry to wear on the morrow when her maid Manthara stalked into the room. The choice of jewelry was very important to Kaikeyi, for she was Dasa-ratha's favorite wife. No matter how much the old rajah respected and admired Rama's mother, Kausalya, he could not take his eyes from the bewitching charms of this Kaikeyi.

The old servant Manthara glared at her mistress and sulked. To Kaikeyi's questions she replied sullenly, "What matter?" or "What is there to be festive about?"

"Stop moping this way, Manthara. There is every reason to celebrate. Our dear son Rama will be crowned at sunrise. He is so beloved of us all, and surely he will make an excellent rajah. He will rule well, and Dasa-ratha will have more time for me!"

"I do not rejoice," Manthara replied angrily. "While Bharat is far away, Rama rises to supreme power. Why Rama? Why not Bharat? Why not your son?"

"That is a mere technicality," Kaikeyi assured the old servant. "Rama and Bharat love each other and will share the rule."

"Do not believe it," retorted Manthara. "If you let Rama gain the throne, that will be the end of your son Bharat." Manthara spoke so convincingly that she succeeded in arousing Kaikeyi's fears. Although this queen had never been jealous of Rama before, now she was thoroughly so. Tearing off her jewels and precious gown, she hurried sobbing and angry to the mourning house. Stormily she threw herself on its unswept earthen floor.

In the cool hours of evening Dasa-ratha, perfumed and freshly bathed, strolled to the apartments of his favorite wife only to find them desolate and empty. Her weeping attendants told the bewildered old ruler that Kaikeyi had been seen weeping wildly and running toward the house of anger. He hurried there, thoroughly alarmed, and found his most treasured wife lying disheveled on the floor. Dasa-ratha lifted her to his lap and petted her.

"Now why is my pretty bird weeping?" he cajoled. "Who has ruffled her silken feathers? Tell me at once, and they shall be punished. My darling shall have anything her heart desires!"

"Do you remember how once years ago I nursed you during a long and dangerous illness?" Kaikeyi asked him. "Do you remember how I healed you of two dangerous wounds?"

"Yes, I remember," answered the king. "You are my charming little bird."

"Do you remember that you promised to grant me two requests, anything that I should ask? Do you remember giving me your sacred word?" persisted Kaikeyi.

"Yes, I remember," answered the rajah. "Only you never made your two requests."

"I am ready to make them now," answered Kaikeyi. "That is why I have come to the house of tears. For if you do not grant them, I shall die of grief this night."

"You shall have your requests," smiled the king. "Do you wish more cities? Do you desire gems, or pearls from Ceylon?"

"My first request is that my son Bharat be recalled from his visit, and that he be crowned in the place of Rama. My second request is that Rama be exiled to the most savage jungles for a period of fourteen years!"

The old king's eyes opened wide in horror. He stared at his wife in amazement and could say nothing. He lifted a trembling hand to his head as if to clear it of this terrible thought.

"Will you dare to refuse me?" asked Kaikeyi. "If you do, people everywhere will call you a liar forevermore."

After a long silence Dasa-ratha spoke. "How shall I tell Rama? How shall I admit this shameful disinheritance of my first-born? How can I expose my son to this cruel banishment?" Looking at Kaikeyi as if he saw her for the first time, he asked, "What are you? Are you some serpent I have pampered and nourished in my heart?"

The following morning at dawn Prince Rama approached his father's throne and, joining his hands in greeting, bowed to Dasa-ratha and Kaikeyi who sat beside him. Rama was astonished to see his father's worn face and to notice that he had been weeping. He was grieved to note that the rajah did not even acknowledge his son's reverence. Turning to Kaikeyi, whom Rama had always held as his mother also, the prince begged her to tell him what he could have done to offend, what injury he could have unwittingly performed. Kaikeyi then coldly told Rama that Dasa-ratha was bound by the oath he had made her. Rama replied that he too was bound by any oath of his father, and he asked Kaikeyi to reveal the oath. "Whatever my father desires, I desire it also," swore Rama. "You have my word."

As Kaikeyi revealed her will, Rama bowed his head. Then without speaking he bowed out of the palace and returned directly to his quarters to prepare for his departure. His instructions to Sita were detailed, "I must leave Kosala to wander through the jungles for fourteen years. I know you will uphold my name and honor during this long separation. Respect my father and serve him like a dutiful daughter.

177

Pay every homage to my mother, and equal duty to Kaikeyi. Let no one say that the wife of Rama showed bitterness or revenge. Take your place among the palace ladies with a serene and open face. Serve also my brother Bharat, for he will be especially aggrieved at his mother's baseless fears. Be careful not to speak my praises or let anyone see you grieve for me. Remember that we are not the victims of my father's vow, but his children happy to accomplish his will. Now we must part, my dear Sita."

Rama would have left his wife then and departed from the palace, but Sita held him back. "My father is a rajah also," she reminded him. "He and my mother taught me, Rama, that a woman's place is beside her husband. They did not tell me that my lot was yours only so long as your fate was an easy, perfumed path. They instructed me to follow you all the days of my life, through luxury and through poverty, through carpeted halls and jungle paths. In Videha also we have wise Brahmans whose teachings could not mislead a princess."

Rama described for Sita the horrors of the jungle. "I must spend fourteen years among tall coconut palms which spring up so fast all around me in the warm rains that I shall go for days among them without seeing the sky. My road shall be through hot green tunnels of vine that are so tightly interlaced no ray of sunlight ever pierces them. I shall have to climb up and down over the roots of banyans that writhe and turn like the gnarled trunks of primordial elephants. For company I shall have only the wild creatures of the jungle, snakes, monkeys, and hordes of crying birds. My only lodging will be a hut of palm fronds, my only food the wild fruits and roots, my only clothing a hermit's coat of bark. Parrots and crows and the white-feathered eagle will roost above me at night. You cannot leave our palace, Sita, to wander fourteen years under giant trees where the tiger crouches to drop on your shoulders!"

"How could I fear tigers when Rama is near to protect me? What sun shall I lack when I am warmed by his love? I shall serve you like a true wife. While you are busy, I will collect food. I will carry your tools. At night we will nestle snugly in our palm hut, and the years of banishment will fly. Let me go with you," pleaded Sita.

Rama consented. Then his brother Lakshman fell at Rama's feet and made a similar request. He begged to be allowed to accompany them both to the forest. Rama refused, primarily because he could not think of leaving his mother alone and unserved since Dasa-ratha was so obviously a prisoner to his craving for Kaikeyi. However, Lakshman reminded Rama that first of all his mother, Kausalya, was a wealthy and powerful queen in her own right, that she owned a thousand villages and had many soldiers at her command. Lakshman also spoke to Rama of Bharat. "When our brother returns, you know he will be horrified at what has occurred. You know he will blame his mother Kaikeyi, and all the more revere and honor your mother Kausalya." Lakshman also argued that Rama should not take the gentle Sita into the jungle all alone. "While you are away for any reason," Lakshman urged, "I will be needed to remain beside Sita. It will take the two of us to protect her from rain and dangers!"

Finally Rama consented to both their requests. Then they all three made their preparations for departure. Sita took with her only her best bracelets and bangles, and only her most perfect gold hoops for her ears. She could fold several saris into a very small square. She took no perfume, for the jungle was full of scented flowers. She took no mascara, for Rama would be there to drive away all demons. Rama and Lakshman, however, made lists and sent the palace smiths and armorers scurrying busily to and fro. They required a supply of swords, daggers, scimitars, shields, suits of mail, bows, cords, and bronze-tipped arrows. All this was loaded into the royal car, where the charioteer Sumantra stood flicking his whip proudly.

The three exiles bade farewell to Rama's mother first. This gentle lady wept so bitterly that Rama took her aside and consoled her with scripture. "Reflect upon the spirit of man; it has no body though it dwells in bodies; it is not corruptible though it dwells in the midst of corruption. Meditate upon the permanence of the spirit. Think how vast it is. See how penetrating. It alone is changeless. It alone never dies. Therefore it is not wise to grieve." Queen Kausalya was calmed. She kissed Sita's long braids that were still wet from her morning's devotions and blessed her for knowing her wifely duties. She praised Lakshman for fulfilling his proper service to his elder brother. Then the three passed out of the queen's palace with Sita between them looking like an amber butterfly.

In the chariot where Sumantra waited were piled high gifts from Dasa-ratha for the three of them, more precious fabrics and jewels than Sita could ever wear. Once they were seated, Sumantra cracked his whip, and the horses started forward. The populace was silent at first, for they could see Rama was praying. To his wife and brother he was saying, "Know that you are the lord of your chariot, the master of your body. Know that your Buddhi[1] is the driver who holds

[1] Reason.

179

in check your impulses, which are the reins." Their progress was slow, for on every side people crowded to praise the three of them, and to catch a last glimpse of their prince. As the chariot passed the palace, Rama was heartbroken to see Dasa-ratha, supported by his courtiers, try to totter toward them. Overnight his father had become an aged, almost a helpless man. Rama ordered Sumantra to whip up the horses so that the parting would be swift.

All day they traveled in the heat and dust through masses of people who knelt all along the route. In the evening they arrived at the banks of the Tamasa River, where they bathed. Rama would neither eat nor drink. Finally he and Sita slept a few hours while Sumantra mounted guard. Then during the night they quietly crossed the river so that the citizens of Kosala upon awakening would find them gone and would return to their families and occupations. On the following day they continued their journey southward, crossing the parallel rivers, until they came to the north shore of the holy river of India, the Ganges, Bride of the Sea. Reverently they watched its russet waters flow majestically before them. Before traversing this river, Rama sent their driver Sumantra home to Kosala, for they had reached the southern boundary of Dasa-ratha's land.

After having prayed, they crossed the sacred Ganges. Rama then led the way through open meadows, traveling single-file with Sita and Lakshman after him. When they grew hungry, they roasted a deer; when they were thirsty, they knelt on the ground and drank spring water from their cupped hands. Sita followed Rama bravely and let no word of complaint escape her lips. At night the brothers made her a bed of sweet grasses under the clusters of bloom of the asoka tree, and she slept peacefully while the courteous tree waved its feathery blossoms and kept the starlight from her eyes.

On the fourth day of their travels they arrived at the junction of the Ganges and Jumna Rivers, where the dark blue waters of the Jumna embrace the ruddy ones of its older sister. In this triangle between the two streams lived a celebrated scholar and hermit to whom students flocked from all of civilized India so that they could sit at his feet and hear him lecture on the holy writings of their land. Rama asked this anchorite for hospitality, and it was granted. The scholar invited Rama and his friends to spend their fourteen years of exile with him. He had already learned of their causeless banishment. Rama was overjoyed because he knew that in studying and learning the years would pass most delightfully, but he was afraid to stay too near the hermit for fear that throngs of curious pilgrims would come to visit the royal exiles and so disturb the holy man's meditations. It was arranged that Rama should cross the Jumna and build a small hut for the three of them only twenty or so miles away. During the fourth night the wanderers slept in the peace and holiness of the hermit's hut.

The next morning Rama and Lakshman felled trees on the north bank of the Jumna River and bound them together with creepers to make a strong raft large enough for themselves and for their possessions. Lakshman wove a seat for Sita, and folded beside her all the precious stuffs Dasa-ratha had sent his oldest daughter-in-law. Sita made their craft gay with wreaths of flowers; and as the princes shoved out into the current and plied their bamboo oars, she prayed to the River Jumna for their safe return and decked its dark blue waters with yellow carnations. Pelicans and herons waded along the sand bars of the southern shore. Beyond that lay the pathless wilderness to which they were condemned.

Shouldering their bundles, they turned bravely away from the sunny riverbank and plunged into the dark tangle of jungle. Lakshman walked first, wielding his ax to cut away the matted vines that barred their route, and Rama lifted his fragile wife over the slippery roots of trees that towered high above their heads. They stopped often with Sita to admire strange berries and flowers that gleamed in the dark tunnel of this forest. Toward afternoon their path began to climb steadily toward the slopes of the mountain Chitrakuta. In its foothills they paid a courtesy visit at the hermitage of the greatest poet of India, the saintly Valmiki. Coming out of his simple shelter, this poet greeted them and blessed them. He told the three wanderers that in after ages countless generations of Indians would retrace their travels every year and would hold in high esteem the peak of Chitra-kuta, their refuge. Smiling at the beauty of the lotus-eyed Sita, the poet Valmiki pointed to the garlands she was wearing and told her that in future millennia the women of India would weave wreaths of flowers from this very mountain. They would call them "Sita's Blossoms" in praise of the princess who had braved these wilds for the love of Rama. "I shall write a poem about love, and I shall call it the *Ramayana*," he said. Farther up the mountain, Lakshman and Rama built of forest timbers and palm leaves a shelter where they slept on the sixth night of their banishment.

On this very night in the kingdom of Ayodhya, Dasa-ratha dreamed of his youth, a dream that presaged his death. Calling his two good wives, Kausalya and Sumitra, the rajah told them of his vision. More than a half century before, when Dasa-ratha was the prince of the realm, the sin of pride ate deeply into his heart. Wherever the young prince went, or whatever he did, adulatory courtiers praised him to the skies so that Dasa-ratha forgot the lessons of humility the Brahmans had taught him and became over-confident and boastful. The one achievement of the youthful Dasa-ratha that was considered most extraordinary by the other warriors of his caste was his ability to shoot at a target by sound, even when the animal was not in sight.

One evening as Dasa-ratha hunted among the reeds of a riverbank he heard the gurgling sounds an elephant makes with his trunk when he plays in the water. Silently Dasa-ratha sent his arrow in that direction, as swift and as venomous as the fangs of a cobra. He heard his arrow strike flesh, and then, instead of the trumpeting of an elephant, a long, human wail that sent shivers down his back rose in the still night. Dasa-ratha plunged through the underbrush to see a young man lying pierced by his arrow. It was the young son of two holy hermits who lived nearby. The boy had been filling his pitcher with water for their frugal evening meal.

Piteously the boy begged Dasa-ratha to pull out the burning arrow, and pitifully he asked the prince why he had murdered him. After the boy had died, Dasa-ratha filled the pitcher with water and bore it to the aged parents. At first they mistook the young prince for their own son, but when they understood what a tragedy the young heir to the throne had caused, they cursed him. The aged couple sought death on their son's funeral pyre. Their curse was that years hence —when he also was old and feeble—he should be deprived of his son and die of grief. "Now I feel the agony of their curse," whispered the aged king. Even as Kausalya and Sumitra stroked his blue-veined fingers, Dasa-ratha died, soon after midnight on the sixth day.

When Bharat arrived home, he was distraught with grief, first at the exile of Rama, which had been ordained while he was absent, and secondly at the death of his father. Accompanied by the two widowed queens and throngs of courtiers, Bharat left Kaikeyi weeping in her palace and set out to bring the wanderers home. Joyfully the charioteer Sumantra led the way to the banks of the Ganges. From there on local residents thronged to show Bharat the wanderers' route. The progress of the royal party was slow, for they had long since left the highways. Engineers were obliged to cut roads through brush and jungle so that the heavy chariots would bear Kausalya and Sumitra comfortably. Their grief was acute when they saw Prince Rama clothed in the bark robe of a hermit, his hair in an unkempt tangle on his head. Queen Kausalya sighed to see Sita's soft skin torn by brambles and her face burned by the wind.

Bharat embraced his brother and begged him to return. He described the sad state of Kosala with its old rajah dead and Queen Kaikeyi sunk in self-reproachment. Rama was not swayed in his purpose. Then Bharat asked Rama to listen to the words of a wise philosopher, a Sophist. While the wanderers attended courteously, the Sophist began to speak.

"Your mind is twisted, Rama, with idle words and false teachings. Why must you care now for the oaths of a dead man? Dasa-ratha has gone, and you should now assume the rule in his place. You must be more sensible, dear Prince. Think not of immortality or of a future life after death. There is no such thing. Learn to live for the present, for this day only. Return to Kosala and joy in your wealth and power. Today is what counts, and there are not enough tomorrows. You also will soon be swallowed by the ravenous jaws of death."

After the philosopher had spoken, Rama and Sita replied, both of them, that they would not consent to return. Rama reasoned in this way, "I know the arguments of the learned Sophist are well-intentioned, but I think they are none the less false. If I were to break my father's oath and return to Kosala, I should become only the shadow of a real man, disguised under the cloak of truth. As far as death is concerned, we can all of us free ourselves of that fear. Your counsels, learned philosopher, may indeed help me to own a fair palace here on earth, but what of the mansions of heaven that I should rather be preparing for myself and for my subjects? Therefore let me follow my own studies in my own way. Let me learn to know that which has neither color, taste, touch, sound, nor smell. Let me meditate upon the infinite, that which is ever constant, so that when I have mastered all base passions I may tread upon the other path that leads not to transient pleasures but to permanent wisdom."

Neither the tears of Bharat nor his pleading could move Rama. Instead he counseled his younger brother to return to Kosala and with the aid of the wise Brahmans to rule the country for the fourteen-year period as his father and mother had ordained. Then Bharat, before bidding farewell, asked Rama for the sandals he was wearing. When Rama had unfastened them and handed them to his brother, Bharat said, "These sandals of our Rajah Rama shall I set upon the throne of Ayodhya. They shall rule our land. As for me, I shall wear also a cloak of bark like my brother Rama. Like him shall I dwell in a hermitage outside our city gates until this prince returns. I too shall seek immortality as he does. I too shall strive to know Purusa, that which is not of this world and which shall set me free also."

To the north returned Bharat with the sorrowing queen mothers and their court. To the south went Rama with Sita and Lakshman following. This time Rama wanted to make sure there would be no pursuit. Week after week they traveled steadily through the Vindhya Mountains and into the Deccan. There they visited a very famous hermit named Agastya, who first had journeyed into southern India to study and to teach the doctrines of Brahma. This holy man gave Rama the magnificent bow of the god Vishnu, which could pierce any enemy as straight as the rays of the sun, and it was Rama as an incarnation of the sun's force, Vishnu, that was revered in later ages in the holiest city of India, Benares on the Ganges. Agastya also gave him the quiver of the thunder god Indra, and the shining dart of Brahma, saying that soon Rama would have need of all these weapons. Agastya pitied Sita for her months of footsore travel. He advised Rama to descend along the steep gorges of the Godavari River until he found an especially beautiful forest. There he and Lakshman were to build a permanent home for the tender princess, who although she had never complained was weary and thin from her long weeks of walking. Agastya warned Rama that they were leaving civilization far behind them and were penetrating into an area where savage tribes lived more like monkeys and bears than like men.

It was late autumn before the wanderers arrived on the cliffs of the Godavari River and found, as Agastya had described, a perfect earthly paradise haunted only by the timid deer. Just as the hermit had instructed, the princes located an open meadow where the grasses were pale and dried, for the sun's chariot was far away in the land of snow, Himalaya. Here on this peaceful meadow the princes built a spacious home with earth walls and floor. Tall bamboo trunks held up a lofty thatched roof scented with the drying herbs of summer. The entrance faced the river where the three bathed every morning. Then the brothers made a couch for Sita, woven from the softest grasses of meadow and field, and perfumed with the petals of the last blooms of the summer. As the winds of winter swept down over them, the little princess lay warm and dry inside her shelter. Even the wild ducks flew far overhead. Along the frozen river the last lotus buds dropped and died. Winter blew over the earth, and the three sat about their fire and tried not to think of home.

The forest where they spent the winter so peacefully was sparsely inhabited by fierce bands of uncultured peoples called Rakshas, who could change themselves into any form that they chose. One day an uncouth Raksha maiden of royal blood discovered the travelers' hut. Her burning eyes fell on Rama. She had never seen a prince with such a lotus-pale skin before, so straight and so handsome. Now this Raksha maiden, called Surpa-Nakha, was overcome by love. In her passion she felt herself to be beautiful and able to inspire his love. Surpa-Nakha could not see herself as uncultured and unattractive, nor did she realize that the brothers would mock her.

"Who are you, handsome warrior?" she called to Rama.

The princes looked up from their hut to see this ugly, misshapen woman peering in at their door. Rama answered her calmly by recounting all the story of their adventures. Then he asked her if she were not one of the southern races, a member of the Raksha tribe that possessed special powers of magic.

"I am Surpa-Nakha. I am the princess of Lanka in Ceylon. I hunt in these woods. I am free. I am very powerful. I have magic. My brother is the dread Ravan before whose face all these forests bend. He lives in Lanka in a great palace. I roam wherever I please with only two warriors." Then without invitation the savage woman entered the cabin and, pointing her dirty fingers at Sita, asked, "Who is the aging, white-faced woman you have on the couch?"

"Please show more respect," Rama cautioned her. "This lady is Princess Sita, my honored wife."

"I am much younger and much more passionate," declared Surpa-Nakha. "Get rid of your woman and marry me. I am very pleased with your appearance, Rama, and will consent to have you as my husband. Don't bother killing your Sita. I will enjoy doing it myself. And I will do the same to your brother. Then you and I will be free to roam like ardent newlyweds all through my forests."

"That is a novel proposition," Rama drawled with a quick smile toward Lakshman. "I doubt if you would care to be my second wife, however, and watch me daily pour out my love to Sita. Why don't you propose to my brother here? He's very handsome and quite alone these days. Why don't you ask him to marry you? He would probably jump at such a chance!"

Lakshman was quick to enter the spirit of the game. Bowing humbly to Rama, Lakshman looked the Raksha girl over

185

carefully and told her, "Surpa-Nakha, you are as pale as a parrot in all your croaking charm and as neat of line as a pregnant elephant. Could such beauty wish to be the bride of a slave? For I am Rama's slave and the Lady Sita's slave."

Surpa-Nakha's ruddy face grew mottled with anger. "You dare to mock me?" she screamed. "Prefer your withered Sita, only prefer a corpse!" Furiously she leaped across the hut toward Sita, who huddled pale and trembling on the couch. In that instant Rama leaped between them and stood with open arms to protect his wife. At the same moment Lakshman picked up a dagger and, grasping the Raksha by her matted hair, pulled back her head and sliced off her nose. Then before Surpa-Nakha could defend herself he sliced open each of her ears. While Rama strove to revive Sita, the Raksha fled screaming from the cabin, calling for her warrior escort.

The battle Rama and Lakshman fought with the two demon warriors was long and dreadful. Sita huddled on her couch of grass, hearing their loud cries reverberate through the trees. Once Lakshman hurried back for a fresh sword. The Rakshas kept transforming themselves into rocks and blunting his weapons. Finally Rama and his brother cut them into pieces and sent Surpa-Nakha howling southward to the palace of Ravan in Ceylon. Once there she emphasized the beauty of Sita and made her brother promise to avenge her.

Ravan, the warrior ruler of Ceylon, was not only vengeful by nature, but devious as well. He dispatched a Raksha disguised as a deer to wander through the forests and lure Sita away. Lakshman and Sita saw the deer standing at the river's edge at sunset. His antlers were all of gleaming sapphires and his manners timid and gentle. Instead of following it, Sita pleaded with Lakshman to capture the deer for her. She told him how lonely she often was in the cabin and how she would love to have this creature as her pet. Lakshman was unwilling to attack the deer.

"You have never seen a real deer with so soft a coat or with jewels on its head," said Lakshman in refusal. "It cannot be an ordinary creature. It must be some trick of the Rakshas, for they will never allow their princess to go unrevenged. Rama and I were very wrong to have angered her. Primitive peoples do not react as civilized ones would do. She did not enter into the spirit of our jesting, and we have made powerful enemies. Do not attempt to approach this deer."

All that evening, however, Sita could not forget the beautiful animal. She described it over and over again to her husband, insisting that its possession would make her so happy. She told Rama how she would care for it, and how fast the long days would pass if she only had this dazzling creature by her side. "When our years of exile come to an end," Sita pleaded, "we could take this jeweled deer home to Kosala with us. Think how thrilled all the palace ladies would be to let it feed from their hands. No other princess in India has so lovely and so rare a treasure." Then when Rama did not appear convinced, Sita told him that if it were really so difficult for him to capture the deer alive, he could kill it and dress the hide so that she would have a carpet to take home with her. "Think what a lovely keepsake that would make!" she sighed. "I want to have some token of our wanderings so I will remember this distant forest."

In the morning Rama strung his bow, and before setting out to chase the deer warned Lakshman to remain with Sita during his absence. All through the daylight hours Rama stalked the magical animal, but although he set his snares carefully, the creature evaded capture. The only way Rama could seize him was to pierce him with an arrow. Cautiously he crept up on the deer and drove him toward the clearing at the river's edge. Then as the animal stepped out of the brush, Rama sent his arrow true to the mark. As the deer lay bleeding, it called out in a piercing wail, in perfect imitation of Rama's voice, "Lakshman! Come to me! I have been wounded! Here in this wood I die!"

Sita and Lakshman heard the throbbing call. "Go to him, Lakshman," Sita screamed. "My beloved Rama is hurt!"

"No, I do not believe it," Lakshman replied calmly. "It is some trick of the Raksha to lure me away from your side. Did you notice how the call came magically, from no particular direction? Rama has never been defeated by an enemy. And even if he were, he would not call like a coward upon his younger brother for help!"

"You have dared to call my husband a coward!" accused Sita, turning upon Lakshman in a sudden fury. "You are a wicked man. I never should have thought it of you!"

"Calm yourself, gentle Princess," said Lakshman soothingly. "I have never heard your voice in anger before. Rama bade me remain here with you."

"You want to betray Rama," screamed Sita. "I see it now. You hope he will be killed so you can usurp the throne. That's why you won't go to his aid. Perhaps you think after he is gone that I will be your bride!"

"Your words cut me like whips," replied Lakshman sadly. "I do not see how I can have merited such an evil opinion. I will go. Despite Rama's orders I will do what you request. Nothing but sorrow can come from the words you have just spoken." Then Lakshman shouldered his weapons and went from the hut, sad and troubled.

After he had left, a twilight silence fell upon the forest. The leaves hung motionless from the trees. Over the Godavari's wide expanse not a wavelet rippled. All the forest creatures, sensing the approach of evil, crept into their burrows like witnesses reluctant to behold its stealthy approach. Only Sita sat unaware in the cool evening air, arrayed in beauty like the new moon. Her jet-black hair fell over her shoulders on the flame-colored sari she had draped about her. As she sat and listened, she saw a poor old hermit approach her hut. His hair was matted and tangled. His feet were naked in coarse sandals. His robe was ragged and the color of russet bark. Over his shoulder he carried a staff with a gourd hanging from it.

Sita was glad of his company. She offered him water and a place to sit beside her. Then the hermit expressed his astonishment at finding such loveliness and refinement in a wilderness. "Are you a nymph? My eyes have never glimpsed your equal. Your slender waist was surely meant for some royal arm to clasp. Your delicate ears were surely intended for the jewels of a king. How can you dwell here and alone in such wretchedness?"

Pleased at the hermit's interest, Sita told him how she was worried about her husband. Then the stranger continued in a soft, insinuating voice, "Why remain here, gentle lady, with a prince who can only provide a thatched roof for your lovely head?"

"I am very proud to be Rama's beloved wife," Sita confided. "Why are you dressed in an anchorite's poverty? Surely you have known palaces and thrones also," she said.

"Indeed I have," said the hermit, throwing off his disguise. "I am Ravan, king of Ceylon!"

Sita screamed in vain. Ravan caught her by her long plaits as she tried to run down the forest path, lifting her easily in one arm. Then, smiling down into her face, he told her, "I have just seized the woman of the peerless Rama. She will make a nice addition to my wives. Do not struggle. Ravan will not let you go."

"My husband *will* return. He will kill you for this," panted Sita. "You don't know how brave he is. He is much stronger than you, much taller than you. I love my husband. I will never be your wife. I am the faithful Sita. Men everywhere praise my virtue."

Ravan carried Sita as an eagle carries a writhing snake. With her in his arms he mounted his golden car that was drawn by winged asses, and they rose high in the air and over the treetops. Sita screamed for Rama without ceasing. Then she invoked the forest creatures and even the mountaintops, calling upon them to tell Rama what had happened to her. She remembered to ask Lakshman's pardon even though he could not hear her, for she knew her own distrust and suspicion had caused her fate. The only creature she saw was the vulture king, who flew along beside them. Sita appealed to him to save her, but the courageous vulture was helpless before the lance of Ravan, and he fell wounded to the ground far below. Sita could only hope some woodland creature had witnessed her abduction.

Her hopes were answered when Rama and Lakshman, searching furiously over hill and stream, came upon the dying vulture. He had been king of his kind for 60,000 years, and Rama was very sad to see his huge body racked with pain. Before he died, the vulture told how Sita had been carried through the air by the dread Ravan. The dying bird could not say, however, in what direction they were heading. To this day the vulture's bones, long since hardened into rock, lie bleaching in the sun and rain of southern India.

The next day Rama and his brother met the monkey king Sugriva and his counselor Hanuman. Rama had heard of these dark-skinned races in southern India, but he had never met them before. The monkeys were amazed to hear of the loss of Sita, and Hanuman sent messengers leaping and chattering through the trees in all directions. Within a few hours he was proudly showing the grief-torn Rama various signs of Sita that his envoys had collected. On one mountain peak they found her sari, and among the tall grasses their sharp eyes spied bangles that she had thrown away to mark her route. Rama was very grateful. He asked Sugriva what he could do to return the favor. He suggested that they swear an alliance, the four of them.

Sugriva told Rama how he also happened to be a wanderer in the forest. Some time before, Sugriva's wicked brother, a gigantic beast named Bali, had stolen Sugriva's wife and driven him from the kingdom. Ever since that day Sugriva and Hanuman had been unable to force Bali's city and depose him. Sugriva shivered when he heard Bali's name and confided to Rama that he would never dare face his beastly brother in single combat. Since they were now sworn allies, Rama encouraged Sugriva and assured him that together they would reconquer his land. Sugriva promised that once he disposed of vast wealth and subjects he would send his forces swinging through the trees so that they could dis-

cover the whereabouts of Sita. To seal the bargain and giv[e]
Sugriva cónfidence, Rama shot one of his magic arrows. Be[-]
fore the monkey king could recover from the fierce twang [of]
the bow, the arrow had pierced seven palm trees, passe[d]
through a hill, and returned to drop at Rama's feet. At th[e]
sight of such prowess Sugriva declared himself convinced.

The following morning Sugriva charged Bali's fortres[s]
striking his chest and shrieking defiance. Bali answered hi[m]
from inside the palace as he armed himself; and then th[e]
two, screaming in high-pitched voices, wrestled mightily i[n]
sight of Rama and Lakshman. For a long time Sugriva wa[s]
inspired by Rama's example, but after several hours he bega[n]
to tire. Bali was much heavier than his brother, his nai[ls]
were longer, and his teeth sharper. When Rama saw that h[e]
was about to kill Sugriva, he went to his friend's rescue. Wit[h]
one arrow Rama slew Bali. When Sugriva invited Rama int[o]
his city, the two princes turned sadly away. "My penance i[s]
to live in a forest," Rama reminded his ally. "I may not ac[-]
cept your invitation."

Rama and Lakshman retraced their weary steps toward th[e]
jungle. No search for Sita could be made then because th[e]
rainy season had begun. Gray clouds as huge as mountain[s]
came rolling in from the sea, so thick they looked like soli[d]
masses instead of air and water. Within hours the hard eart[h]
had become a mass of mud through which no travel wa[s]
possible. Rama and his brother would have welcomed th[e]
rain that fell not in drops but in long lines of water fro[m]
the heavens if their hearts had not been sad for this delay. I[n]
silence they plodded through the dripping forests, mad[e]
themselves a shelter, and waited until the rains had stoppe[d]
and Sugriva could fulfill his promise.

Eventually the skies cleared. Eventually the sun shon[e]
forth once more, flooding the forest with radiance. Ram[a]
and Lakshman smiled again and hurried through the burgeon[-]
ing jungle to Sugriva's city. There were the monkey band[s]
assembled, 10,000 strong, whom the king divided into fou[r]
groups. To the first he assigned the regions of the east, ex[-]
horting his warriors to scan carefully the seacoast and even
the mountains of the sea all the way to where the sacred
Ganges and the Brahmaputra transform themselves int[o]
ocean. To his greatest and wisest warrior, Hanuman, he as[-]
signed the southern lands from the Vindhya Mountains
along the dark ravines of the Godavari. "Look carefully,"
warned Sugriva, "for the forests touch the sea. Look all along
the mountains of Mysore and question our people who dwell
by the southern sea. Ask our relatives who live by Cape
Comorin."

The third group were to depart for the western sea, where coconut palms wave their fronds over a heavy jungle that stretches along deep lagoons. "Look carefully through each busy seaport on this endless western sea. Ravan may be hiding in some leafy bower. Swing from tree to tree, and you will find him. Look most closely along the delta of the Indus. He could be lurking there."

To the mountains of the north Sugriva sent the last search party. "Leap over raging torrents," he urged them. "Fear not the wooded slopes of Himalaya. Look around the fringes of the goddess Nanda Devi. Move to the higher peaks of Dhaulagiri. Fear not Mount Meru itself, though the plateau of paradise be at its summit! We shall not fail the noble Rama. Search northward until you come to the vast, treeless regions of Scythia where dwell the horse-faced women!"

It was the crafty Hanuman who ended all their labors. He it was who had the agility to leap across the sea. Hanuman knew no fear. Gathering his strength in his haunches, he stretched out his slender arms and leaped, borne by the ocean breezes, all the way across the Mannar Straits until he touched the green island of Ceylon, the private domains of Ravan, king of the Rakshas. Swinging noiselessly through the trees, Hanuman glimpsed the disfigured Surpa-Nakha surrounded by her slaves. Around her lay the white-pillared palace of Ravan. Its walks were paved with gold, and its staircases made of ocean coral. Then Hanuman noticed in a far corner of the gleaming court a secluded area hidden under the dense foliage of asoka trees whose masses of crimson blossoms dropped in a thick screen. The entire courtyard was guarded by fierce-looking females, dark and threatening. Silently and nimbly Hanuman swung through the lower branches.

Then he saw a silent woman sitting sorrowful and alone. Her hair fell in a heavy braid down her back. She wore the ugly bark cloak of a hermit. As the monkey warrior studied her appearance, he saw that she was wearing a jewel that Rama had described. Around her neck lay the polished tiger's tooth Rama had given her. This lady must be Sita. Hanuman could see by her attitude of mourning and by her ornaments that she must have resisted Ravan's offers of wealth, that she must, indeed, have remained faithful even in her prison to her lord and master. Softly Hanuman called her name, but she did not lift her head. Then he began in his high voice to sing and chatter the story of Rama. He related it from the very beginning and continued through Sugriva's war with Bali, and he told of the armies of monkey warriors and bears who were massing all the thousands of miles from Mount Meru to rescue the faithful Sita.

"It is a dream that I hear," sighed the princess. "It cannot be true that Rama is so near."

Then Hanuman leaped to the ground and, peering up at her with his wrinkled, kindly face and round, brown eyes, urged Sita to hope again. Into her hand he dropped a ruby ring that Rama always wore, as a token to Sita that her husband was alive, that he loved her still, and that he would rest neither night nor day until he had saved her from her ravisher's sight and palace. "Prince Rama tastes neither food nor drink, takes no pleasure in perfumed champac, neither rests nor ceases. Day and evening he longs for Sita. He will overstride this ocean like a rivulet. No Raksha warrior will stand long before Rama in his wrath. There will be such a war when Rama espies the treacherous Ravan that its echo will ring among the Himalaya until the very end of time."

Then Sita took from her forehead that holy jewel which the god of thunder Indra had given her father on the day of her birth. This jewel had been fastened to Sita's hair on her wedding day, and Rama had never seen her without it. "Give this to my husband," she requested Hanuman. "Tell him how I weep."

Hanuman had remained too long talking to the prisoner. Even as he sensed the danger and leaped into the asoka tree, he was attacked by Ravan's guard. Although the monkey warrior defended himself heroically, he was finally captured and brought before Lanka's King Ravan. His execution was ordered, but the king's younger brother, Vibishan, who had always opposed keeping Sita a prisoner, persuaded Ravan not to kill the courageous monkey. "He was an envoy sent by Prince Rama, and his passage should be assured," urged Vibishan. Ravan then ordered a rag soaked in oil to be tied to the monkey's tail and set on fire. Owing to the prayers of Sita, however, the monkey felt no pain. Instead he leaped wildly through Lanka, spreading fire as he went. When he was sure that even the palace had caught on fire, Hanuman jumped back across the strait to the mainland of India and hastened to Rama.

Rama held Sita's jewel in his hand and thought of all the sorrows that had befallen his gentle wife since her wedding day. He also wept. Even so, he questioned Hanuman closely, "Did Sita weep for love of me, or did she weep for loneliness? Has she remained faithful even in a prison?"

In the spacious white-walled city of Lanka, Ravan called a council of war. Sternly he put the problem of Rama's invading army and asked what he should do. His warriors belittled Sugriva with his army of wild and uncivilized legions that crowded together to fight for Sita and her prince. One after another they boasted of their courage, fine weapons, high battlements, and glory in war. Every warrior approved war except for the younger brother Vibishan. "Ravan had no right to capture the lady of Kosala," said Vibishan. "She will one day be a powerful and noble queen. Her reputation is so spotless that I am not surprised even the beasts of the forest pay her homage and offer to avenge her with their untutored skills.

"This Rama from the north is no ordinary man. He is the mortal aspect of the great god Vishnu. Year after year pilgrims travel to the mountain of Chitra-kuta to worship where he and Sita prayed at the beginning of their exile. He is the idol and star to every boy in India. Would you dare oppose the righteous anger of so just a man?"

Then Ravan's other brother, Khumba-Karna, who had nodded through the long meeting, gave his opinion. "I agree," he said ponderously, "that our brother Ravan should not have kidnaped this high-born lady. This is not the first time that he has succumbed to his craving for women. However, the deed is done, and I consider brother must stand by brother, and subject by king." Then Khumba-Karna yawned and stretched his massive legs that projected five feet beyond his chair. "Just send me the northern sapling, the pale lotus-faced hero. He won't get a second shot. Maybe not even a first. Oh, and one more thing: since you have the woman, Ravan, then possess her." Without waiting for their reactions, this giant fell asleep again.

After Khumba-Karna's well-received discourse, the warriors and Ravan condemned Vibishan by word and contemptuous looks, calling him false and cowardly. Ravan scorned his brother in scathing words—"Relatives are all alike! They smile and lull you with honeyed sounds, but in their hearts they hate you. No one takes so much secret pleasure at the misfortunes that befall a man as do his cherished relatives. Like hungry vultures they hover over his death couch, feeding him healing draughts with one hand, and hastening him out of this world with the other. So is my brother, Vibishan. No doubt he thinks to seize the throne. No doubt he hopes to wed my wife. . . . I will not taint my hands with his murder. Therefore, Vibishan-the-Evil, depart from my lands. Join the other cobras that lie in wait to destroy us."

Bravely Vibishan stood his ground, alone in the circle of hostile faces. "You are wrong, Ravan. You are not only

193

wrong but sinful to say such words and harbor such thoughts. I only want to avoid death and bloodshed. Will you not listen reasonably? Will you not redress your wrong? . . . You will not? . . . Then defend yourself without me." Vibishan then left Ceylon's capital and joined the forces of Rama, whose army had arrived at the Strait of Mannar.

How to pass this channel with a host of bear and monkey warriors presented a problem. Rama solved it by shooting his powerful arrows into the ocean's bed and, when he still received no answer, by threatening to dry up the very seas themselves with bolts of lightning. Then the ocean god appeared upon the horizon, completely amenable and open to suggestion. It was agreed that the architect of the gods could be consulted. At his direction Rama's host began to roll boulders into the channel until they had made a splendid causeway, the vestiges of which can still be seen today. Upon this highway the army of Rama passed and surrounded the capital city of Ravan.

The battles commenced as the Rakshas opened their gates and tried to force a passage through the ranks of Rama's army. Wave after wave poured from the city only to fall in heaps before the onslaughts of the monkey warriors, who threw boulders and uprooted trees at them. Then the fierce Ravan mounted his heaven-made chariot and cut a path through the helpless foot soldiers. Chieftains rushed bravely to meet him, but they could do nothing against the thundering of his terrible war engine. Sugriva fell wounded to the ground, and after him the clever Hanuman. Ravan then heard the call of Lakshman inviting him to battle. Furiously the two shot volleys of arrows at each other, and for a long time the Prince Lakshman managed to cleave Ravan's darts in midair before they pierced his body. But the human skill of the Kosala prince was puny compared to the demoniac force of the savage Ravan. Lakshman fell wounded, but Ravan too had felt the sting of arrows. He quit the field and returned to his walls.

On the second day of battle Ravan succeeded in awakening Khumba-Karna, who had once even worsted Indra, the thunder god. Brahma had intervened and decreed that this terrible giant should slumber for six months and then remain awake for only one day. Ravan, however, overcame his brother's sleeping sickness and urged the giant to fight. He cautioned him to swallow the monkey warriors by the thousands as he had done in the past, and this time to chew them well so that they could not crawl out by working their way hand over hand along the hairs inside his ears and nose. Armed in bronze, Khumba lurched through the opened gate.

As Rama's army hurled trees at him, he caught these missiles in open flight and threw them shudderingly back into the ranks of the warriors, mangling them. First the giant sent Hanuman reeling over backward, and one after another all the native chieftains. There was sore need that day for the magic healing medicines from the slopes of Himalaya! Even Sugriva was dashed unconscious to the ground.

It was not these leaders Khumba was seeking. "I have worsted the god Indra!" he shouted. "Send me not these puny mortals! Where is this Rama we have heard so much about?" There Khumba-Karna made his fatal error. Who was he? Who was a giant to think of conquering Rama?

Pushing Lakshman out of his path like a crumb from the table, Khumba strode toward the tall and deadly Rama. He was met by a flaming arrow that singed off his hair. Another followed and another. Rama fitted at last into his bow an arrow of fire, which pierced the giant's armor and severed his head from his body. Disgusted at the jets of steaming blood that discolored the earth, Rama lifted the body and threw it into the sea. The tidal wave that ensued did not exhaust itself but swept over the entire western sea, which is endless.

A more dreadful war lord even than the giant Khumba was the son of Ravan, Indrajit. This fierce prince was not slain by Rama, because he could surround himself in a magic cloud and remain invisible in the midst of the host while he shot swift arrows at his enemies. Once he terrified Rama by conjuring up on the field of combat the very likeness of Sita, and then pretending to kill her before her husband's very eyes. It was Vibishan who saw through this trick. Although he had been converted to Brahmanism and had joined the forces of India, he still remembered all the Rakshas' black arts. He and Lakshman penetrated into the heart of Lanka and, catching up with Indrajit in his visible form, dared him to fight openly. It was Lakshman who killed this black prince.

Ravan in his grief and fury at the loss of his son decided to kill Sita, as Indrajit had done in semblance on the battlefield. Her attendants barely managed to avert the blows and save the sad queen. "It would bring you too much misfortune, O Ravan, to slay this woman," they cried. "Do battle rather, for it is the fourteenth day of the waning moon. You will have great strength today. After your victories return and claim this Sita. We will array her in splendor for you."

Ravan mounted his golden chariot. From every house in the city his warriors hastened. The sky was darkened. Red flashes of Indra pierced the heavy air. Angrily the earth shook at so much destruction, at so much hatred, at so many deaths. Ravan first encountered his brother Vibishan and sought to kill him. The lance he threw was caught in mid-flight by Lakshman, who cleft it in two. Meanwhile Indra himself dispatched his own chariot, drawn by swans, so that Rama could meet Ravan. Using this and the weapons the hermit Agastya had given him, Rama killed Ravan and ended the war.

A mighty funeral pyre was built for Ravan at Rama's orders. On it were placed the body and arms of Ceylon's king. Vibishan, who inherited the kingdom, lighted the funeral fire. Rama and Lakshman then laid aside their weapons and, standing among the warriors and King Sugriva, awaited the arrival of the princess.

Arrayed in a golden robe, her hair parted in the center and brushed smoothly back from her forehead, the gentle Sita was carried in a golden litter through the city and up to the Kosala princes. At Rama's command she had unveiled her face so that all men could see the princess for whom they had fought. Sita stepped down from the litter in a stilled hush. The assembled warriors had never seen such grace and beauty before. Slowly she walked toward her husband. Lakshman knelt to touch her feet.

Rama neither acknowledged her presence nor spoke. In silence also Sita stood before her lord. Rama seemed to be looking over her head. Little by little Sita's cheeks grew red. Her head fell. Then, turning to Lakshman, she asked him to build a funeral pyre for her also. "Since my husband does not receive me, I must die," she said in a broken voice. "The beginning of the world was in fire and the end of each miserable body."

The throng of warriors moved back so that wood could be placed high in the center of the square. With tears running down his face Lakshman placed the last branches, and at a nod from Sita lighted the fire. Then the princess spoke again, "I swear that I have remained faithful to my husband even in the palace of Lanka." Slowly and with great calm of manner Sita stepped through the ring of flames and was swallowed from view in clouds of gray smoke.

A gasp went up from the assembled crowd. "All desire has fallen from Sita, and she has become immortal," the warriors murmured. "Her heart has one hundred and one nerves, and she has chosen the one leading to the head and immortality! So may we all gain immortality if we seek to know our higher self!" All this time Rama remained motionless with folded arms. The sounds of crackling flames and gusts of smoke blew in his face. People moaned and wept, for they knew the world would never again see such beauty, such devotion, such courage in a woman.

Then before their astonished eyes the great god Brahma appeared above the fire. Parting the flames, he lifted the princess in his arms. Not a strand of her hair had been singed. Not a wisp of her gown had been scorched. "She is pure!" cried the warriors. "The ordeal by fire has shown us her virtue." It was Brahma who placed the princess in her husband's grateful arms.

7

Rome
The Wanderings of Aeneas
The War in Italy

INTRODUCTION

THE FOLLOWING CHAPTER is in part a summary and in part a translation of the *Aeneid* of Publius Vergilius Maro.[1] Vergil created for Rome not only a thrilling hero story. The *Aeneid* is also a travel book in which the poet has incorporated those events of great historical significance that he witnessed during his lifetime (70–19 B.C.) with his own ideas as a poet, scholar, and historian. He is dealing with the world of around 1000 B.C. It was a world in turmoil, marked by the decline of the ancient continental civilizations, the fall of the wealthy maritime powers such as Crete, Phoenicia, Ugarit, and Troy, and the rising threat of the Assyrians from the east.

Vergil, from his point of view—Rome at its height under the Augustan principate—can look back 300 years or so to the Punic Wars. He tells us of the founding of Carthage and Rome. He thinks of Aeneas as the father of his country and explains by legend the old hostility between these two nations.

Modern historians such as Gilbert Picard (*Le Monde de Carthage*, Paris, 1956) inform us that by the year 876 B.C. Tyre was forced to pay tribute to the Assyrian King Ashurnasirpal, and that by 814 B.C. they had sent colonists under Dido to found a permanent colony in Africa from which they could protect their shipping routes from their tin

[1] The chapter sections, indicated by Roman numerals, correspond to the twelve books of the original.

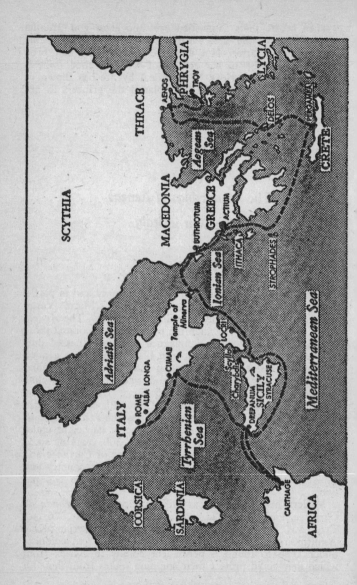

THE WANDERINGS OF AENEAS

port in Spain. Vergil's description of navigation and his geography seem also to be corroborated. M. Picard calculates that the round-trip voyage from Tyre to Tarsis in Spain would have taken three years, at an average distance traveled per day of twenty-five miles. Mariners usually sailed only at night and only between the spring and fall equinoxes. Every winter they beached their ships and raised crops, as Vergil describes. Even the story of Dido, as told by our poet, seems substantially correct, except that Dido may have been sacrificed.

When we come to Vergil's vivid description of the war in Italy, there seems to be less agreement. Our poet accepted, as the reader will see, the classical theory advanced by Herodotus that the Etruscans had gone to Italy from Lydia. In this many modern scholars disagree; Professor Pallottino of the University of Rome supports the theory that the Etruscans were part of the general Indo-European invasion. Vergil departed from classical beliefs in having these famous people fight with Aeneas. Some scholars have suggested that Vergil did this because he wanted them to appear in a sympathetic light, that Vergil believed himself to be of Etruscan origin. In any case, Vergil described the scenes in Italy from actual observation, as Professor Carcopino of the University of Paris has demonstrated.

Vergil through the ages has been and remains a controversial writer. Many people think that in his Fourth Eclogue he announced the birth of Christ. St. Paul is supposed to have visited Vergil's tomb in the Bay of Naples and to have said, *"Quid te fecissem, si te vivum invenissem, maxime poetarum!"* ("How much I would have made of you, had I found you alive, O Greatest of poets!") A practice called *Sors Vergiliana,* consisting of selecting oracular passages from his writings, has been practiced even in our century. Professor Toynbee has quoted Vergil's Fourth Eclogue to demonstrate his idea of history. Professor Carcopino has written a book (1930) to refute the Messianic predictions attributed to him.

Another controversy concerns Vergil's use of the word "Caesar," for the *Aeneid* is not always clear as to which Caesar he had in mind. In any case, as Professor Whitehead says, they were both "men of genius." "That we are seated here, in the clothes we wear, and uttering some of the thoughts we do, is in part thanks, I believe, to Augustus," he says.[2]

Almost countless volumes have been written about this poet through the ages, and he has been widely imitated and ad-

---

2 *Dialogues of Alfred North Whitehead*, ed. by Lucien Price, New American Library, New York, 1956.

mired. He was a man whose love for his country breathes through his poem, a poet who was tolerant of other cultures, and a fine human being who was inspired by country life and the deeds of noble people. Tennyson said of him:

> I salute thee, Mantovano,
> I that loved thee since my day began,
> Wielder of the stateliest measure
> Ever moulded by the lips of man.

COMPARATIVE DIVINITIES

GREEK	SUMER	ROMAN	EGYPTIAN*
Aphrodite	Ishtar	Venus	
Apollo		Apollo	Horus
Ares		Mars	
Artemis		Diana	
Athena		Minerva	
Cronus		Saturn	
Demeter		Ceres	Isis
Dionysus		Bacchus	Osiris
Gaea		Tellus	
Hephaestus		Vulcan	Ptah
Hera		Juno	
Heracles	Melkarth	Hercules	
Hermes	(of Byblos)	Mercury	
Zeus		Jupiter	Amen
		(Jove)	(Ammon)

THE WANDERINGS OF AENEAS

I

I SING OF ARMS and of the man who first from the shores of Troy, driven by fate and the ire of the rancorous Juno, came to the Lavinian shores of Italy. He suffered greatly, this hero, buffeted by winds and stormy seas, uncertain of his route and knowing only that his task was to bear the gods of Troy in his arms, and to found a nation on seven hills in Latium, from which would come the Alban Fathers and the lofty walls of Rome.

* According to Herodotus, who states that almost all of the gods' names originated in Egypt and went from there into Greece. He mentions in his Book II the worship in Egypt of Hercules, Pan, Diana, Minerva, and Mars.

Let the Muse tell this story, let her remind us of why Juno bore this grudge against Troy. Let her say why this great hero, so outstanding in his goodness and unselfish devotion, had to endure so many hardships, had to bow under the vengeance of this goddess, until he could fulfill his destiny.

There was once an ancient city called Carthage, which had been founded by Phoenicians from the trading nation of Tyre. These colonists had built their "new capital" [3] upon the northern coast of Africa, directly opposite Italy and the mouth of the Tiber River. Juno protected their settlement, hoping that it would develop into a maritime power that would in time control the western Mediterranean, as Troy and Tyre had, between the fall of Knossos and the rise of Assyria, dominated the eastern. Juno kept her chariot and her armor in Carthage, so dear was it to her.

The goddess knew that the Trojan Aeneas had escaped from Troy and was even then wandering over the seas to find a home in a new land called Latium. It irked Juno to think that Pallas Athena had destroyed some of her beloved Greeks. It angered her to know that a son of Venus should think of founding a city intended to become a rival of Carthage. Therefore Juno sought Aeolus, the king of the winds, on his floating island, and asked for his help. Aeolus kept the hurricanes and cyclones imprisoned deep in a cave. He had heaped rocks and even mountains over their prison. There he sat on his throne, scepter in hand, holding them down with his weight.

"Help me, Aeolus," pleaded Juno. "These hated Trojans are even now on the sea, driving the bronze beaks of their biremes through the waves. Help me to destroy them, for I wish to keep them out of Italy. If you will annihilate them for me, Aeolus, I will give you fourteen nymphs. One of them is so lovely that you will want her for your wife. I guarantee she will bear you fine sons. Will you help me?"

"Whatever service you ask of me, I will perform for you, fair Queen," answered Aeolus. "You and great Jove have entrusted me with the mastery of these violent winds. I will just let some of them loose. You will see how they will make your Trojans disappear!"

Then Aeolus struck against the hollow mountainside with his spear. At his signal east, south, and sou'wester winds rushed from their dark cavern and swooped like eagles of death huge-winged over the Mediterranean. Gray squalls collected into granite formation, marching over the waves, and rolling darkness and rain under their tread. The winds picked

[3] Qart Hadasht.

up mountains of water and aimed them at the Trojan ships, which quivered like sparrows poised on a thrashing tree-top. The waves grew so gigantic they laid bare between each swell the white rock depths of the Mediterranean.

Aeneas clung to the rail of his plunging ship. The vessel clawed frantically with its oars to climb the steep water walls and then dropped sickeningly into the abyss. Tons of water broke over its prow and crashed along the decks, light-green water flecked with foam. "They were thrice blessed who found their death on the plains of Troy," he thought, wiping the stinging salt spray from his face. "Oh, Hector, why did I not fall beside you?" Even as he called to the helmsman to hold her firm, a blast from the north caught their square sail and blew them broadside to the waves. Down they dropped into the trough of the sea. The waters were strewn with men fighting to stay afloat, clinging to the salvaged wealth of Troy that floated on the waters. Other ships were lifted high by their sterns and scattered on rocks and beaches. Whole shoals of sand were washed up alongside them.

From his home in the depths of the sea Neptune was stirred by this upheaval. Majestically he rose to the horizon's edge and peered over this tumult of waves driven wild by the violent winds of Africa and the frozen north. Neptune sternly called the Zephyr to him and sent him to say to Aeolus that his province was that of wind, but not of water. Neptune ordered Aeolus to recall the winds at once. Then he drove over the green water in his chariot, drawn by prancing, golden-maned horses; and the waters were calmed once more. It was just as when through a crowd of angry, surly people a great hero of famous deed strides confidently. At once the unruly mob grows still and obedient. Then the sea nymphs and Triton hurried to the rescue of the shipwrecked crews, boosted them on board their vessels again, and helped to collect their floating gear. With his trident Neptune himself pried vessels loose from the sandbars and set them bobbing on calm waters again.

As soon as the hurricane had subsided, Aeneas collected the seven remaining ships and led them toward the nearest land, which was the coast of Libya. There they found a sheltered cove with a small island to seaward and two tall cliffs to landward. Its sandy beach was protected on either side by curving rocks. As soon as the battered ships had dropped anchor in shallow water, the sailors leaped ashore through the surf and threw themselves exhausted upon the warm earth. Their clothing was wet and stiff with salt. Achates struck spark from tinder and lighted a small fire in dry leaves. Soon the weary men had gathered resinous kindling and logs so that they were able to dry themselves. Others searched through the stores for dry grain, which they began to pound with stones into meal for their frugal supper.

Aeneas left his men on the beach and climbed the cliffs to the forest. From this high point he looked out over the island and sea hoping to sight some of his Trojan biremes, but the waves to east and west were empty. There was not even a fishing craft in sight. Turning toward the woods, he then had the good fortune to see a herd of deer feeding peacefully under the trees, all in line like a battle formation. It was a perfect target. Aeneas shot seven of the deer, one for each ship, and had them carried down to the beach. Then he broke out jars of wine, for his comrades were discouraged and beaten.

While the stags were roasting, Aeneas tried to encourage his crews. Choking back his own tears and trying to smile, he told his friends, "Now we have indeed seen trouble and dangers! Fresh from the fires of Troy we have been plunged into the stormy depths of the sea. We have passed shoals and dangerous crags. We have lived through a hurricane, at least some of us. Take courage, Trojans, for there are certainly more perils ahead. Someday, I have no doubt, we shall sit about our own hearths again, in new homes that we must strive to build in the land of Latium. We may look back even upon this dreadful day with a kind of fondness." After his words the men ate warm food and sat about their campfires talking of the missing ships and wondering what the land of Italy would be like.

Jupiter, reigning on Olympus at the very vertex of the sky, looked down over the world and the Libyan coast. As he surveyed it, Venus approached and spoke tearfully to him, "Why have you changed your mind? Why did you promise me that my son Aeneas would survive the fall of Troy only to allow him to be battered and driven almost beyond a man's endurance? What crime can my son have committed against you, O ruler of the lands and skies, that all the earth is barred to him, even the distant shores of Italy? Did you not promise me that from the Trojan stock would come a great empire—that men called 'Romans,' born to rule the world, would build an Eternal City? I stood by and watched Troy fall to appease the anger of Juno. All I could do was to lead my son and his boy out of the holocaust. Why are they still being punished?"

Jupiter smiled and softly kissed her pretty lips. "Lady of Cythera, delicate as the sea foam, I have not decreed otherwise. I shall keep my promise. You shall see with your own eyes this city called Rome, and the high-flung walls of Lavinium. When his task is accomplished, you shall bear your great-souled Aeneas, your sublime hero, to the heavens of stars themselves. Your son must live to wage a decisive war in Italy. Shall I show you the hidden scroll of fate?

"Aeneas will vanquish proud warriors and set forth laws and government. His little boy Iulus shall build powerful bastions at Alba Longa. The race of Hector will rule for 300 years until the priestess Ilia [4] gives birth to twins, sons of Mars, Romulus and Remus. Nursed by a she-wolf, Romulus will found the toga'd empire whose great senators shall be called by his name, Romans. I put neither hour nor limit to their dominion; I have given them sway over the earth throughout all time.

"Even Juno, when she sees their reasonable government and their magnanimity, will change her opinion for the better. She too will come to admire the rulers of Rome, draped in their togas of peace or clad in the iron armor of war. She will also love their Caesar named Julius, who will ride in fourfold [5] triumph through Rome, laden with the spoils of the Orient. Greece will fall to Rome, and Egypt. Europe will fall to Rome and bear the imprint of her language and laws. Augustus Caesar will force shut the iron gates of War for the first time in 200 years. Within the Temple of Janus he will bind the clenched fists of Rage with a hundred chains and let him sit there trembling at his bloody jaws."

Jupiter spoke. Then he sent Mercury flying down through the air to Carthage in order to inspire the Tyrian queen who ruled that city with hospitable feelings toward the Trojan wanderers who had just landed on her coast. Thanks to his winged cap and sandals, the messenger of the gods performed his pleasant errand easily. Dido, queen of Carthage, heard from Mercury that by decree of Jove she was to entertain distinguished visitors.

During the night Aeneas worried and made plans. The next morning he had his ships drawn up into a little river and moored along its banks, with branches pulled down over them so that their hiding place could not easily be discovered. Then he and Achates took spears, climbed again up the cliffs, and set out to explore the country. It appeared uninhabited. There were still no signs of the lost ships. As they walked along in the sunshine, they met Aeneas' mother, the goddess Venus, who had disguised herself as a Spartan huntress. The goddess strolled through the trees, her quiver slung over her shoulder, her hair unbound and blowing in the

---

[4] Rhea Silvia.
[5] Gaul, Pontus, Egypt, Africa. September, 46 B.C.

fresh sea air. When she had come up to them, Venus inquired if they had seen her sister.

"We have met no one on the path this morning," Aeneas answered her courteously. "Are you not Apollo's sister, the huntress Diana? Perhaps you would help us. We are lost. If you would tell us what land this is, and who lives here, we will be sure to make many offerings at your temple."

"Oh," replied Venus, "I am not worthy of such honors. I am not Diana. Tyrian maidens often dress in purple, knot their garments above their knees, and go hunting through the woods. However, I can tell you where you are. You are on the coast of Libya, not far from the new seaport city of Carthage, which was built by the Phoenician Dido. Have you heard of her?

"Dido, queen of Carthage, was born in the maritime city of Tyre. Her brother Pygmalion is its king. As a young girl Dido was married to a wealthy Tyrian named Sychaeus. She was a virgin of great beauty. Sychaeus was happy to possess her. Dido returned his love, and they lived in peace. Then one day Sychaeus did not return home. Dido asked her brother, but Pygmalion knew nothing of her husband's whereabouts. The young bride grew sad and longingly searched many days for her husband, with no success. Then one night Sychaeus appeared to Dido in a dream. He said he had been murdered by Pygmalion, who coveted his riches. Since the body had received no funeral, Sychaeus was condemned to wander eternally through the world. He showed his wife the dagger wounds in his breast and told her that he had been stabbed while at the altar, before the penates [6] themselves.

"Fortunately Sychaeus was able to advise his young wife as to a course of action that would save her life and give her full revenge. He told Dido to inform her friends secretly and to collect about her other Phoenicians who were smarting under Pygmalion's tyranny. Dido was a clever woman. She followed her husband's directions, sought friends and found ships that would carry them all safely from the island harbor of Tyre. She dug where Sychaeus had directed and found not only his but also Pygmalion's treasure. All of it was stealthily loaded on biremes, and late one spring night they stole out of the harbor and headed due west. After months of travel they found a perfect site for a harbor and city here on this very coast.

"Then Dido bargained for land upon which to build a city. The native Libyans, fierce and unconquerable tribes, thought to cheat her by giving in exchange for her silver only as much land as could be covered by a bull's hide.

6 Household gods.

Dido was cleverer than they, however. She had the hide cut into strips and was thus able to encompass a fair acreage. On a peninsula in a large bay she built her city, which is still growing rich and active." Then the goddess asked Aeneas who he and his companion were, and why they were lost on the coast of Libya.

"I am Aeneas, whom men call 'good,'" he answered. He told her how he had wandered so long and why, and how he had lost fourteen of his ships. "I am an obscure Trojan driven from both Europe and Asia," he said.

"Whoever you are," replied Venus, "I am sure you are not forgotten by heaven. Do you see those swans that fly over the bay of Carthage? Some will alight in the safe haven of the harbor, and others will follow. So is it with your lost ships; some have already arrived at Dido's city. Others are even now folding their great white wings and gliding inside the breakwater. . . . Follow this path into the city, Aeneas!"

As the goddess walked away from them, her short robe lengthened and fell to her feet. The characteristic perfume of Venus was wafted to their nostrils. She had resumed her divinity. Aeneas started to follow her, but she was already fading from view. "Why do you always trick me with these curious disguises, cruel one?" he murmured. "Why may we never join our right hands together, or speak openly to each other as do mother and son?" His mother had already vanished, happy to know that Aeneas would be well received at Carthage. Through the sunlit air she headed for her birthplace in Cyprus where a hundred flower-decked altars burned incense from Saba[7] to her and where blood sacrifices were never accepted.

Following the path the goddess had indicated, Aeneas and his faithful friend strode to the top of the hill. Below them spread the city of Carthage. As they walked toward it, Aeneas marveled at what a beehive of activity it was. Venus had surrounded her son and Achates in a gray mist so that they could enter the city unseen. They saw work squads paving roads. Other men were hewing stone from the hill for a large theater and carving columns for its stage. All along the way newly arrived Phoenician immigrants were digging trenches around the lots where their homes would be built. Beside the waterfront other groups were dredging the harbor and building piers and docks. It was like watching a hive of bees on a summer morning, whose labors also are divided. The pleasant perfume of thyme and honey was blown by the sirocco through the streets. Aeneas was envious at the sight of so much happy toil. How he wished it

[7] Arabia (Sheba?).

were the high walls of Rome he was seeing grow stone by stone before his eyes!

In the middle of the city was a grove of trees where Dido was having constructed a temple to their patroness, Juno.[8] Here it was that the Tyrians during the first few days of their arrival on the African shore had dug up a horse's skull. Dido had said this was a good omen, for the men of her city would be as fierce and energetic as a fine-blooded horse. Aeneas and Achates walked toward the temple and mounted its broad flight of steps. They felt sure the queen of Carthage would come there for her morning devotions and to dispense justice. Meanwhile they admired the temple, its rows of pillars, and its bronze doors with heavy hinges. Suddenly Aeneas stopped short and grasped his friend by the arm. There upon the temple wall were depicted scenes of the Trojan War; its fame had preceded its heroes!

Holding their breaths in wonder, the Trojans examined the murals. There is the crested Achilles dragging Hector's dead body three times around the walls of Ilium! There is old Priam come with the gold of Troy's treasure to buy back his son's body! There towers Memnon with his Ethiopian armies, hastening to the aid of Troy! There is Rhesus, king of Thrace, another friend of the Trojans, with the white horses he lost to the Greeks! There is the Amazon queen, Penthesilea, lying dead from the lance of Achilles, who afterward regretted having slain one so young and so beautiful. There lies poor young Prince Troilus, no match for Achilles, his spear trailing in the dust. Even in death the youngster still holds the reins of his horses, which are dragging him along beside his empty chariot!

A sound of voices woke them from their memories. A throng of courtiers were approaching the temple, and at their center, moving with smiles and the dignified mien of a queen, came the golden Dido of Carthage. This royal personage took a seat in the temple, where she began to dispense justice, offer sacrifices, and settle the business of the day. Aeneas was about to speak to her when he saw to his amazement three of his Trojan captains, men from the lost ships. While their commander listened, these captains asked Dido for the use of her port and supplies. "We have come not in war but in peace," they said. "Your harbor patrol has refused our men permission to go ashore." Then they explained how they needed to beach their ships and repair them with new timbers. They asked her for materials and explained their plight. "If our leader, the princely Aeneas, were here, he could surely persuade you of our good intentions and establish credit with you.

8 More likely Tanit.

207

"We are bound for a land in the west which the Greeks called Hesperia. Once we arrive there, we plan to construct a city also, great Queen," they said. "Only do not receive us as enemies. We are pious people, not sea robbers, not lawless pirates!"

Dido, looking down at them from her lofty throne, answered graciously, "You must excuse the vigilance of my harbor guards. We are always on the alert for any ships that might even now set out from my brother's kingdom of Tyre. As far as Troy is concerned, we learned long ago her terrible fate. We may live here in the far fringes of the Western world, but Apollo's chariot passes over us also, bringing us news from the east. You may certainly have the full use of my port. Repair your ships at leisure and in entire security. Commandeer whatever supplies you need. Or, if you will, settle here in Carthage. Join forces with me, and I will swear to govern Tyrian and Trojan with equal consideration. I too long to see your famous leader, Aeneas. Scouts in fast ships shall be sent out at once all along the Libyan coast. Perhaps he is not so far away."

At that moment the mist that had shrouded Aeneas and Achates was dispelled. Dido and her courtiers looked at the Trojan chief, to whom Venus had given at birth some of her radiant health and physical beauty. He stood before the Carthaginian queen in an aura as if of sunlight, his fair hair like gold that the artist has inlaid on his ivory statue. Stretching out his hands in welcome to his captains, Aeneas thanked Dido for her hospitality. "How shall I ever repay such generosity?" he asked. "What a wonderful century we live in that has given birth to so magnanimous a queen! How fortunate the parents who reared you! As long as the rivers seek the sea, or the clouds cast shadows over mountain slopes, or stars graze in the pastures of heaven, so long shall men revere your name and honor your reign!"

"Well do I know your Trojan stock, Aeneas. Often have I heard my father tell of the fortunes of Troy. You are the Aeneas whom the goddess Venus bore to the Trojan shepherd Anchises, are you not? I beg of you to be my guest. I who am not unacquainted with grief know how to succor the unfortunate." Dido proclaimed ceremonies of rejoicing to be performed in her temples. Before preceding Aeneas into the palace, she ordered twenty bulls, with swine and sheep, to be sent down to the Trojan ships so that the sailors could feast also.

Aeneas sent Achates back to their vessels to fetch his son Iulus. Since the child's mother had been separated from them during that worse-than-nightmare, the burning of Troy, Aeneas had assumed the double responsibility for his son.

He liked to have Iulus near him as much as possible. Aeneas also asked Achates to bring back gifts for Dido. Fortunately not all their treasure had been ruined by sea water. They still had with them a wool mantle that was stiff with embroidery and gold thread, and a saffron-colored veil bordered with a design of golden acanthus leaves, both of which the Spartan Helen had brought with her to Troy for her licentious marriage. Achates was also to bring the scepter of Priam's eldest daughter, a necklace set with pearls, and a double circlet or crown of gold and gems.

Meanwhile the banquet hall of Dido was being prepared for a dinner. Tables were covered with embroidered cloths and set in the middle of a great hall with silver platters and bowls. The heavy silver was chased and embossed in gold to illustrate famous episodes in the history of Tyre. Counterpanes of royal Tyrian purple were draped over the couches.

Venus was aware of all these preparations. Instead of rejoicing at the honors Dido was heaping upon Aeneas, the goddess was uneasy. She knew the Tyrians by reputation. They traded throughout the seas and were proverbially bilingual in more ways than one. To give a man one's "Tyrian word" or "Punic word" [9] meant as often as not no promise at all. Venus finally called her son, the mischievous Cupid, and explained to him what she wanted him to do. "I will lift Iulus out of the ship and keep him slumbering on a bed of sweet marjoram somewhere in the pine groves of Cyprus, just for tonight. You take his place, and when you draw near the Phoenician woman, pierce her with your subtle arrow. Set her on fire with such a burning flame that she will swoon over Aeneas, and never dream of betraying him."

Cupid gleefully took off his wings as Venus had commanded, and with mischief in his heart solemnly imitated the person and voice of Aeneas' son. He played the part to perfection, making his father very proud of his son's precocity. Dido received the gifts from "Iulus" and could not praise him highly enough. All through the banquet she reclined on her golden couch under a luxurious canopy and drank in the faces of Aeneas and the boy she thought was Iulus. Starved for love after her years of widowhood, Dido feasted as much on their masculine appeal as on the dinner. For the first time in years this young queen forgot her dead husband Sychaeus, and how much she had loved him.

As members of the court joined the banquet, they were invited to lie on sumptuous couches. Fifty maidservants brought bowls of perfumed water for their fingers and held out soft napkins to the guests. Another hundred girls served

[9] *Fides Punica.*

the meats and breads fresh from the ovens. A hundred youths bore goblets and poured into them fragrant ruby wines from the palace cellars. The hum of voices reached the rafters. Everyone admired the boy Iulus, and not even Aeneas suspected there was Cupid in their midst. The saffron veil of the Spartan Helen was lauded as well as the other rare and storied presents Aeneas had made to Dido. Fresh torches were lighted so that the hall at Carthage burned with a cheerful, welcoming light. Even the gilded panels in the ceiling glowed, high up in the raftered roof.

After the tables had been cleared, Dido called for the sacred patera of her ancestors. Into this shallow dish she poured a libation of pure wine. Then she sacrificed to the gods, saying, "O Jupiter, may this day when the Trojan and Tyrian are united together in fellowship be an auspicious one! May it be remembered throughout the generations to come." Then after having invoked Bacchus and the patroness of Carthage, the good Juno, she touched her lips to the bowl and passed it to her guests.

The rest of the evening was spent in conversation and song. A celebrated minstrel named Iopas, who was a Numidian taught by Atlas himself, recited a poem to the accompaniment of his lyre. He told of the stars, the sun's labors, the origins of beast and man, the nature of rain and fire—all songs that Atlas, that first master of astronomy, had composed. All marveled at the skill of the singer and were enthralled by this flowing-haired poet. Dido sighed with longing. She could not bear to dismiss her guests. Again and again she drank deep draughts of love.

"How tall was Achilles?" she kept asking Aeneas. "How were the horses of Diomedes? Tell me again in your words," she begged him. "Speak about Hector again! How I wish I might have seen him! What about Priam? Would you describe again the arms of the Ethiopian Memnon, son of the dawn Aurora? What a shame you were separated from your wife Creüsa during the burning of the city! Tell me again about Hector. Speak of the Greeks and of their tricks. Tell me yourself of your travels, for it has been seven summers now since Troy fell. All this time you have been wandering over lands and through seas. Talk to me of yourself, Aeneas," pleaded the unhappy queen, Dido of Carthage.

II

SILENCE FELL upon the assembled guests. All turned toward the godlike Aeneas, who spoke from his couch, "Unspeakable is the grief you ask me to recall for you, how the

210

Greeks swept over our lofty walls and laid in dust the proudest city of Asia. I was there. I saw it all happen." Aeneas covered his eyes with his hand and bowed his head. After a pause he began again, "Yet, if you wish to hear the death agony of our civilization, if your love for the Trojans urges you to inquire into such an appalling disaster, although my very soul shudders to recall it, I will begin."

Then Aeneas told the whole story of Troy's capture, how through the wiles of Sinon the wooden horse was drawn inside the city's walls despite Cassandra's warning, how Laocoön and his sons were strangled by snakes that rose from the sea, how Priam died at the courtyard shrine, how the victors drew lots for the Trojan women. "It was Hector who saved those of us who are here in your palace tonight, Queen Dido," he continued. "You are wise to ask again for Hector. He was the greatest of us all. I doubt if the world will ever see his like again, a man devoted to his city, unsparing in his toils to the extent that even after death he would not rest for thinking of us.

"There was that time when the first sleep of night, gift of the gods, stole over my aching body—when, behold, in my sleep there seemed to come up to my bed, before my very eyes, Hector himself! But oh, how sad he was! . . ." Aeneas could not go on.

In a rapt silence Dido hung on his words. Murmurs of sympathy rose from the Tyrian nobles. What a terrible story to hear! What could be worse than to see the city your forefathers had built stone upon stone with their bare hands burn and fall in a single night! Dido brushed tears from her eyes at the thought of Andromache's baby, the smiling little Astyanax, torn from his mother's breast and hurled to his death at the foot of the very walls he had been born to rule one day, had the gods willed it.

"Hector!" spoke Aeneas again. "How changed he was from that Hector we knew! His hair was matted with dust and his beard with blood! In his poor body were the gaping wounds of Achilles. His feet were swollen and still bore the marks where the thongs that had attached him to the chariot had cut into his flesh. I spoke to him. . . . He only groaned in reply, at first. At last Hector spoke to me, almost in his old voice, the voice we all in Troy had listened to with such respect and love. 'Go, Aeneas,' he said. 'Go, you who were born of a goddess. Take your household gods, and leave this falling ruin. There is no more hope here, none at all. Believe me, Aeneas, if human hands could have saved these walls, mine would have done so. Take from the temple of Vesta the sacred fire of Troy. Carry it with you into the

211

Western world. There you will place it in another temple to Vesta and find other virgins to guard it. I pass on the torch to you. Take your son and run. My son and I are . . . dead.' The word 'dead' broke from his lips and rang around the hollow rafters long after he had gone. . . ."

Aeneas then told of his combats in the city, how he saw his sister-in-law, Cassandra, with streaming hair and chains upon her wrists, and how he could not deliver her. He also spoke of Helen, whom he had passed crouching at the altar, and how he had longed to slaughter her but was stopped by the goddess Venus from doing so. After having escaped from the city he met his friends on the mountains southeast of Troy. At least he had managed to save his father, Anchises, and his son, Iulus.

III

"THERE ON THE SLOPES of Mount Ida we built ships," Aeneas continued. "All through that spring we toiled. Hard work is the best cure for heartsickness, hard work, and the passage of time. We built ourselves twenty strong biremes with square sails, and at my father's command we shoved off from the shores of Asia forever. Our first thought was to make for the sparsely settled shores of Thrace. We thought of this land because in the olden days, when its King Lycurgus was still alive, Thrace and Troy had known close ties. This was the Lycurgus who was killed by the gods because he resisted the worship of the Thracian Bacchus. There on the indented coast we marked out our walls and built a city which we named Aeneadae.

"One day we prepared to offer a thanksgiving sacrifice to my mother Venus and to the gods who had also favored our enterprise. We had slaughtered a white bullock to Jupiter, as you know is the custom. Then, looking around for some green branches to lay on the altar, I saw not far away a little mound or hill where myrtle and cornel bushes were growing. I strode over the sand and, grasping a small myrtle tree the trunk of which was large enough for arrow shafts, I ripped it from the ground. To my horror its roots dripped huge clots of blackish blood. Shaking with fear now, I pulled at a cornel or dagger-wood bush. The same black omen met my eyes. Clotted blood dripped from its bark and seeped into the sand at my feet. Praying to the local gods of Thrace —for I knew I had to discover the meaning of this omen—I tugged at a third branch.

"Even as I braced my feet and pulled, I heard a voice, coming from the mound beneath me, that made my hair

212

stand up on end. 'Why are you tugging at my grave? Why do you pull out the spears that rise from my mangled body?' cried a hollow voice. 'You are a good man, Aeneas. Why do you desecrate a Trojan grave?'

"Great drops of sweat broke out on my forehead and dripped on my hands. Imagine my horror. I recognized that sound! It was the voice of Polydorus, an old friend and confidant of Priam!

" 'Leave this accursed land of Thrace, Aeneas!' he told me. 'Here I lie struck by the sword of treachery.' At once I understood what had happened to him. Priam, seeing Troy beleaguered, had prepared part of Troy's vast treasure and shipped it secretly in care of Polydorus to his friend, the king of Thrace. Then when the war went badly for us, the Thracians had changed sides. They had rallied to the winning Agamemnon, murdered Polydorus, and confiscated Priam's gold for themselves. What crimes will men not commit when the lust for riches taints their hearts?

"I returned to the beach, where our men surrounded the altar, and told what I had seen and heard. My father, as the oldest of our chiefs, gave his opinion. We all concurred that we must leave that land at once. First we made a funeral for Polydorus. Our women loosed their hair and bore him offerings of warm milk and foaming blood. We made him a high tomb and planted dark cypresses about it so that his shade might finally find repose. Then we packed our goods, hauled our ships down the beach to the sea, and as soon as a fresh south wind sprang up broke out our sails and took to the waves again.

"The wind held strong and steady. Our vessels cut the waves merrily and bore us down the Aegean until we sighted the island of Delos in the center of the Cyclades, birthplace of Apollo. Long ago he had prudently moored this floating island between two others, so that mariners in our modern times have no more trouble making toward it. Here we dropped anchor. We were met at this port by the king-priest Anius, an old friend of my father. He and Anchises discussed our troubles and then led me to the rock shrine of Apollo that stands beside its sacred laurel tree. I prayed to the oracle, asking Apollo to breathe upon us, to fill us with some of his wisdom, to tell us where to go, whom to follow, and how to rebuild another Troy that would withstand the storms of time and the malevolent hands of the land-hungry Greeks.

"Then as my prayer echoed through the sunny air before the shrine, the god answered. While the caldron bubbled, the earth shook, and the sacred laurel whipped in the wind, the voice of Apollo rolled clearly about our ears. 'Return, O

Trojans, to the home of your ancestors!' No more was said. Silence followed the oracle's pronouncement.

"My father gathered around him our chiefs and together we deliberated. The words of Apollo were clear, except . . . where was the birthplace of the Trojan race? My father Anchises searched his memory. Fortunate for us it was that he had obeyed the gods at Troy and consented to join with us! For, you understand, all the learning and records of our city had been burned. We had no wise priests with us to interpret our history. After some thought Anchises said, as he recited over to himself old poems he had heard as a child in Priam's palace, that we must have come from Creta Minoan. 'Surely Crete was the cradle of our civilization. We know its hundred cities ruled the Mediterranean and brought under their sway the blue Aegean. If we wish to go back to the beginnings of time, we must return to Crete. There is also other evidence that should be conclusive. Our great Mother Goddess Cybele, she who is driven in her car by lions, came from Crete. Then too our Trojan mountain was surely named Ida for that high peak of Crete where Jupiter was reared. Our citadel in Troy was also named Pergamum from a town in Crete,' said Anchises.

"Joyously we sacrificed to Apollo, without forgetting white bullocks for the sea god Neptune and a white lamb for the westerly Zephyr. Thanking Anius, we set out for Crete. Three days would see us there, for the journey was not long, only 150 miles. We sailed past Naxos, sacred to Bacchus and his heavenly Queen Ariadne. On the third day our lookout spotted the white mountains of Crete, and soon we were leaping ashore through the clear, warm waters. We found the island deserted.

"Rumor told us that Idomeneus, the descendant of the famous kings Minos of Crete, had returned there after the fall of Troy. He had sworn, for a victorious warrior makes loud boasts, that he would sacrifice the first living thing he met upon the shores of his native land. That creature was his own son, who had been watching for his father's fleet to come bounding over the horizon. Idomeneus slew the boy too, and fled those shores like one pursued. . . ."

More wine was poured in the glasses. Fresh torches were lighted in the banquet hall of Carthage. Queen Dido hung on Aeneas' words while in her childless arms she cuddled the sly imp of Love, thinking that she held the boy Iulus. Everyone listened intently, for it could happen to them. Someday in the future they too like Anchises might have to interpret the dictum of an oracle by recalling the adventures that befell their fellow wanderers from Troy.

214

"There on the silent, deserted shores of Crete, from which our ancestor Teucer had drifted to the headlands of Phrygia, we traced out other walls and built another city, which we called Pergamea after Troy's fortress. The young planned weddings and new houses for themselves. I laid down laws and ordinances by which we could be governed. We pressed oil from ancient olive trees, gathered grapes, and planted crops. . . . Our toil was all in vain. The dog days of July were upon us in all their malevolent heat. In the evening sky Sirius, the Dog Star, directed pestilential winds across Pergamea that withered all our fields and cast a sweatless sickness over our people. The silent hills of Crete, which once had rung to the cymbals of Cybele and the stamping rites of the Curetes, burned in the cloudless heat. My father counseled us to return at once to Delos and beg the priests of Apollo to enlighten us. Perhaps we had not heard correctly what the oracle had commanded.

"Then in my despair, as I lay on my couch that night, I seemed to see our penates—those that I was bearing at the words of Hector—rise before me in a stream of light. Their faces shone illumined. From their kindly images wise words fell upon my troubled ears. 'Troy had more ancestors than one, Aeneas,' they told me. 'Dardanus also was a founder of Troy, he whose brother married Teucer's daughter!' My heart leaped, for in truth I had not remembered before this detail of our storied lore. 'Dardanus came from the portals of the west, from a sunny land the Greeks have always called Hesperia. Teucer, it is true, came from the Dictean shores, but Dardanus came from Italy. Therefore you need not return to Apollo's shrine, for the answer will always be the same. Trust now in your own gods and their inspiration. Do not shirk from new hardships. Your wanderings have only begun!'

"My father Anchises laughed when I told him of our mistake. 'Of course,' he told me. 'We were naturally confused and leaped too suddenly to an obvious conclusion. Now that I reconsider the question,' he continued, 'I remember our priestess, Cassandra. Wasn't she always talking about the west? Wasn't she forever babbling about Hesperia? Not that anyone ever paid any mind to Cassandra's wild words!'

"Once more we set out rollers. Once more we slid our vessels into the surf. Once more we embarked with sacrifices and prayers, for this new voyage was into the unknown. Very soon deep water flowed under our keels. Looking down over the sides, we no longer saw the white reefs of the coast line. The sea became a blue so dark and deep that as one looked down one became dizzy at those bottoms as soundless as the

215

depths of the sky. Our pilot Palinurus, a most skilled mariner, frowned anxiously as he set our course due west, into waters none of us had ever dreamed of daring to sail. The lead vessel plowed bravely forward. Our stomachs tightened as we looked to stern and saw the Cretan Ida drop from view below the eastern wave.

"Our fears were not baseless, as you shall hear. Along about noon Palinurus called me to him and pointed upward. There I saw what he meant. We were riding into a storm. A dark blue cloud enveloped the sea before us. There was no escape. Within a matter of minutes it fell about us. Oily waves rose in huge billows and tossed us eagerly from one crest to another. For three days we rolled, battened down, into the storm, struggling only to keep her prow toward the shifting winds. Palinurus swore he could not tell night from day, and so we drifted over the evil waters of the Ionian Sea. On the morning of the fourth day, however, we sighted land, two islands rising out of the sea. Quickly we broke out the oars, and the men rowed toward them for dear life. Palinurus said we had reached the Strophades, the point of no return. To the westward lay the uncharted depths. We had drifted far northward of our course. Not many miles to the east lay the shores of Greece!

"We thanked the gods that had led us to dry land safely. In the meadows by the shore of these islands we saw herds grazing untended. We killed enough steers for our supper, and setting up couches and tables there in the grass, roasted the animals. We had no sooner begun to eat, however, than the Harpies swooped down upon us. These were huge birds that the sons of the north wind Boreas had driven out of Thrace as far as these wretched islands, the turning place. They had the scaly bodies of lizards, the wings and claws of birds, but the white, famine-pinched faces of girls. Darting down over us, they snatched the meats from our tables and filled the air with their foulness. Their stomachs and tails were smeared with their own filth. Their cries were hideous.

"At my orders we fled to a cave, where we relighted our fires, set up our altars again, and cooked fresh food. All that the Harpies had touched reeked from their droppings. Just as we lifted the meat to our hungry mouths, there they came upon us again. Their fierce claws brushed our shoulders as they trod over the tables and perched squawking on the platters. This time I told our men to prepare their weapons. We lay in wait. As they wheeled down another time, we swung our swords at them. It was no use. Aside from a few filthy

216

feathers that drifted down on our heads, we could not kill them.

"Then their leader, a croaking maiden named Celaeno, perched on a crag over the cave entrance and called to me, 'You Trojan liars, do you want to wage a war on the Harpies? You shall be punished for it as your ancestor was punished when he refused Apollo payment for helping to build the walls of Troy, as he was punished by Hercules, who labored to rescue his daughter. You are not supposed to be here in our islands. Apollo told you where to go, and he told me also. You are bound for Italy. So go there! You have the god's permission and will arrive. Why do you have to come to the Strophades and kill our cattle? Then why try to kill us when we protect our food? My curse is on you! You shall found your great Rome because Apollo is willing, but before you do you shall be as hungry as we are, so hungry you will devour your own tables. Now get out!'

"Anchises bade us loosen the hawsers, unfurl canvas, and fly those ill-omened islands. We begged the Harpies to forgive our intrusion. Fortunately the waves were leveled by this time. The south wind freshened, blowing us easily northward. We were in dangerous waters now. We all prayed that the wind would not drop and leave us drifting upon Greek shores!

"We passed the wooded shores of Zacynthos to port and before long the coasts of Ithaca. You may be sure we thronged to the rails and cursed that land of Ulysses! Then we beached near the promontory of Actium,[10] for winter was upon us. There our young men oiled their bodies and wrestled in honor of Apollo, whose shrine in this place will witness, so I hear, a great battle in future ages. We hauled up our ships and spent the winter overhauling them so that they would be ready for sea at the first breath of the spring equinox. Before leaving Actium I nailed to the gate the bronze shield of that Argive King Abas, a shield sacred to Juno, that we had captured from the Greeks at Troy. I carved these words above it: 'Aeneas dedicates these weapons taken from the victorious descendants of Danaus.'[11]

"Then we embarked and drove along the coast of Epirus until we came to the town of Buthrotum. There we heard an incredible bit of news that gladdened our hearts and quickened our steps as any news from home will do to strangers who wander weary and heartless over stormy seas and

[10] Site of the battle in which Octavian defeated Antony and Cleopatra, 31 B.C.
[11] "Aeneas haec de Danais victoribus arma."
Danaus was an Egyptian king who settled in Greece.

217

along hostile shores. Who do you think was ruling Buthrotum? None other than our old comrade in arms, Prince Helenus of Troy. And who was his wife? The gentle Andromache, she of the white arms, who had fallen to the bloody Pyrrhus. Fate plays strange tricks in this life. Pyrrhus had died, and Andromache had married once more a son of Ilium. Happy at this glad news, I walked along the shores until I came to an altar in a grove of trees. There I saw Andromache herself, who was making her yearly offering to the spirit of Hector. I came upon her unaware. When she looked up from her rites and saw me standing there, a Trojan, from home, in Trojan armor, her body stiffened. She fell almost fainting to the ground.

" 'Can it be you, O goddess-born, whom I see before my eyes?' Then her tragic eyes lighted up. She grasped my arm and cried desperately, 'If you live, Aeneas, then where is Hector?' Realizing her foolishness, she burst into tears.

"My heart broke so at her grief I could hardly stammer out, 'Yes, I live, Andromache. How is it with you, dear sister?'

"I put my arms about her shaking shoulders as she told me of her sorrows, of how cruel fate had been to force her into the bed of a Greek, she who was so in love with Hector; to force her to become pregnant and bear other children, she who could never forget Hector's baby under her heart. As I tried to comfort her, she questioned me about Iulus. 'Does he remember Troy? Does he speak of his own mother, who remained in the burning city? Does he grow up to be honorable and prudent like his Uncle Hector?' We stood there talking by the altar until Helenus came with open arms to greet me. Together the three of us returned to Buthrotum, where they showed me proudly the little Troy that they had built. I rested my hands upon their gate, so like the Scaean gates of home, that Hector had wanted to close against the dogs of war.

"Two days went swiftly by with feasting and talk of home. At last I approached the shrine of Apollo with reverence, asking what omens the winged flight of birds, what auspices were in the stars for us, what counsels he could give us; for I was haunted by the dire prophecy of the Harpy Celaeno. Helenus unbound the fillets from his priest's brow and, leading me bewildered to the temple gates, answered as a seer my request for guidance. 'There would appear no doubt at all but that you will arrive in Italy. However, the omens foretell a long and very perilous crossing. While it is true that the eastern shores of this land lie only across a narrow neck of sea from us, the oracles still predict a long voyage. They tell quite clearly that you cannot settle on the eastern or southern coasts. These are already claimed by colonists from Greece and veterans from the Trojan War who, returning home to Greece, were shipwrecked in Italy. They call their land Magna Graecia.'

"Helenus went on to tell me how I should not try to pass the straits between Italy and Sicily because on the Italian side was the fierce monster Scylla, that barked like a dog and dwelled in a rocky promontory. On the Sicilian side was a whirlpool named Charybdis, which would suck my ships down into the sea's depths. Many more counsels Helenus imparted, particularly about the Cumaean Sibyl and how to profit from her knowledge and vision. Helenus told me that when we sighted, beside a western river, a white sow stretched on the ground and thirty newborn pigs lying at her udders, this would indicate the site of our future city.

"We bade farewell to Helenus and Andromache sadly. They loaded us with gifts, especially fine ones for my honored father, Anchises, he who had been deemed worthy of the goddess Venus' love, and for Iulus presents made by the loom of his aunt. Andromache's tears fell as she clasped my son, for he and Astyanax would be about the same age. Then, after inviting them to come in future years to visit us at 'Rome,' we set off to sea again, our minds stored with their advice and admonitions. When dusk fell, we put in to shore for a rest. At midnight Palinurus awoke us all and announced that he could tell by Orion what course we should make westward. Aurora, the pink-fingered dawn, had hardly started to bathe the eastern sky when we saw clearly before us a low-lying coast.

"It was the faithful Achates with whom the glory rests. 'Italy!' he called. We all rushed forward, and almost with one voice echoed his glad cry, 'Italy! Italy!' My father Anchises wreathed a bowl with flowers, filled it with wine, and prayed to the gods of land and sea to favor us, to let us touch this promised land. We found a harbor sure enough, although it was almost hidden in a curve of shore. Set back from the sea, across a bright, green pasture, was a white marble temple to Pallas Athena.[12] There we intended to pray. On stepping ashore I saw grazing by the temple four beautiful white horses. 'That is a sign of war all right,' said my father. 'However, it could also be an omen of peace, for horses can be yoked to a plow as well as to a war chariot.' We prayed in the temple, for the first time on Italian earth, and remembered to placate Juno, as Helenus had advised us to try to do. Then as quickly as we could, we regained our ships, fortunate to have met no Greek inhabitants of that coast.

[12] Minerva.

"We set sail at once, traveling southward that day across the Gulf of Tarentum, known in the old days to Hercules. From time to time we sighted towns and passed the area settled by the Locrians. Then on our port side we viewed the dread, smoking peak of Aetna. Even as we stared in horror at huge columns of belching fire and smoke that rose from its thundering crater, we were met by a closer danger. At once our ships were caught by some powerful current and drawn forward at a dizzy speed. 'We have come too close to Charybdis!' cried my father. Palinurus urged all hands to the oars. We swung the rudder hard to port. All of our other ships maneuvered likewise as the sea currents tugged at our frail planking. Out of the growing darkness came the ferocious baying of Scylla, somewhere to starboard. We fought for our lives during those twilight minutes as desperate men must fight the sea, black rocks, and darkness. Three times we almost despaired. The elements sought savagely to drag us forward while we struggled to swing to port, away from this swirling chasm.

"By the time we had cleared these dangers, night had descended. The sea was calm. The wind had fallen. Thankful and exhausted, we drifted southward under the fiery shadow of the volcano. On the Cyclops' coast we found a gravel beach where we spent a restless night under the smoke of the burning mountain. Every now and then the earth heaved as the giant Enceladus, who lies buried under Aetna, stirred to ease the pain of his burns or turned over in his sleep. Boulders were cast up to the sky from the lurid crater. The woods where we lay without sleeping were lighted every few minutes by explosions of red and orange fire. The vault of sky above our heads was black. Not a star shone. The night seemed endless.

"We were up and astir long before dawn, anxious to be on our way as soon as there was light enough to guide our course. Suddenly we were aware of eyes watching us. You know how one feels such a presence. Finally we saw a wild man at the edge of the trees. There he hung with hunched shoulders, watching us. He was a Greek. We saw that at once, just as he must have recognized us as Trojans. His garments were tattered, his clothing held together by thorns. His feet were naked; his hair and beard were tangled and matted. With a rush he came across the clearing toward us and fell on his knees.

" 'Take me with you, Trojans. I beg of you to take me with you.' Sobbing, the strange Greek clung to my knees. 'I was your enemy, it is true. I helped to storm your walls. Only do not leave me here on this horrible shore. Cast me into the waves, if you must. Let me at least die by human hands!'

"While we urged him to explain himself, my father Anchises extended his hand to the youth, as a token that he was safely received. Then the fellow mastered his terror enough to tell us his queer story. It seems that he was an Ithacan, a member of Ulysses' crew who had been left behind when the Greeks had escaped from the Cyclops' cave. For three months he had been managing somehow to hide in the woods and escape detection. He told us the horrid story of Polyphemus. This Greek had crouched in the cave and seen the giant, lying on his back, take two Greeks in his huge hands. Beating their bodies on the rock walls to soften them, he had eaten them, gulping them down and biting into their twitching limbs. Then as he lay belching bones and clots of blood, Ulysses' men had thrust a sharpened stake into his eye. They had escaped, all except this one man.

"Even as the Greek finished his sickening tale, we heard a thumping behind us on the mountainside. Turning around in horror, we saw the giant Polyphemus coming down the slopes with his flock of woolly lambs. He leaned upon a pine-tree trunk and felt his way down the mountain by pounding it along the ground before him. Petrified with fear, we watched him wade into the sea water up to his middle. Bending down, he scooped sea water in his cupped hands and washed out the bleeding eye socket. From where we crouched, we could see him grimace and whine with pain. Then in a wild rush of activity we leaped on our ships and bent to the oars.

"Polyphemus heard us. At once he lurched through the surf in our direction, stretching out his huge hands in the hopes that he could catch one of our vessels in his fingers. His roars of anger echoed against the cracked sides of Aetna and brought from their caverns all the race of the Cyclops. As we leaned frantically to the oars, we saw them standing in groups together like clusters of oak trees far away on a hill. We rowed furiously, forgetting even in our panic our close escape of the preceding night, the menace of Charybdis. Fortunately the gods were more mindful than we were. They sent us a brisk north wind that drove us spanking down the coast of Sicily. The Greek we had rescued gave us valuable information. We passed Syracuse, rounded the southern promontory, bore past vast harbors and cities, and arrived finally at Drepanum.

"It was there that I lost my father. It happened suddenly, with no warning. Neither the Harpy nor Helenus had prepared us for the blow. He was the best father a man could ever have. He lightened all my weariness. . . . I hardly know how we got from Drepanum to Carthage, great Queen."

Prince Aeneas finished his story and sat silent.

IV

AFTER THE BANQUET and the story of Aeneas, Dido could not sleep. She knew intuitively that she had heard the words of a man of destiny. She lay all night tossing on her couch, envying him. All at once, in one evening, her own life had lost its significance. Her city now meant little to her, her former pleasures were empty, her life meaningless unless it could be somehow attached to his. She could only dream of Aeneas, of his manly beauty, of his vitality that transcended that of ordinary men, of the glamor that surrounded him. She had not thought of love since the murder of her husband Sychaeus, nor ever thought to feel its burning desire again. Now all she could see before her eyes, whether she opened or closed them, was the face of Aeneas. All she could hear in her ears was the ring of his prophetic words. She believed him, that he *would* lead his people into a promised land that she, Dido, could never share.

At the first light of dawn she summoned her sister Anna, to whom she confided her turmoil. "I know this Aeneas is a god," she confided to Anna. "What magnificent stories he has told me! How has he drained the cup of heroism to its last drops!" Dido went on to explain her predicament. "I love him, Anna." She went on to say that rather than bring shame upon herself, however, she would infinitely prefer to die. "I gave my heart to Sychaeus, and he is dead. Since that tragic day I have thought I was free. I never desired to follow the marriage torches to another wedding bed!"

Anna felt very differently about her sister and Aeneas. "Why must you think, dear sister, of wasting your years in widowhood? Why for the death of Sychaeus must you spend your whole life alone and childless? Surely you have paid enough honors to your husband's shade. Surely you have earned this opportunity for love by having spurned Iarbas, the African king!" Then Anna went on to paint a bleak picture for the queen. She reminded her of how small Carthage was and how vulnerable. She told Dido of the great sandbanks, the Syrtes, that menaced them from the ocean. She reminded her of the fierce Numidians, the Barcaeans, and the Libyan tribes that rode their desert horses through the unknown depths behind Carthage. She spoke also of the danger, how their brother Pygmalion could still at any mo-

222

ment appear with a vast armada at the narrow harbor entrance and force a passage before even the chains could be lowered into place.

"Now on the other hand," Anna reassured, "if this Trojan prince were to fall in love with you, he would want to stay and become our king. You must learn to depend on your allure. Perhaps he has come to us through the powerful graces of Juno. She will help you seduce him. The goddess and you can surely make this son of Venus forget his mother's plans for him. What a glory for Carthage with such a king and queen! This Prince Aeneas has come to us at just the right moment. Look out your chamber window; the storms of winter hold the seas in their icy clutch. He could not leave Carthage in such heavy weather. By the time summer comes, he will never think of leaving you for Italy!"

Comforted and hopeful now, Dido studied her face in the mirror. Carefully dressed, she left the palace and moved in stately procession into the temple. There she sacrificed to Juno, the supervisor of marriage and the personal helper of women, and then to Ceres and Apollo. Royally dressed in Tyrian purple, and more beautiful than any other woman in the city, Dido herself poured a libation on the forehead of a white heifer. Such ceremonies, however, have no power to soothe a woman in love. She roamed in torture through the city's streets just as a deer whose side some shepherd has pierced with his barbed arrow runs to exhaustion over hills and through streams without easing its pain. When she met Aeneas with his Trojan friends and tried to show them her wealth from Sidon and Tyre, her cheeks flushed and her words failed. So day after day she took less interest in her construction projects, failed to order her soldiers out for maneuvers, and neglected to give her captains orders for port clearance. Night after night, perfumed and jeweled, she dined with Aeneas. All she could do was to ask him to tell her again of his adventures. After the guests had left, she sat alone in the deserted banquet hall, miserable and lonely for him who had just left her side.

Juno saw Dido's embarrassment. This goddess sought Venus to complain that Dido, her protégée, should be entrapped by the goddess of love and her bewitching son. Juno proposed an alliance, offering to give Carthage and its peoples to Aeneas as a wedding dowry. Venus saw through this proposition. To her it looked as if Juno were trying to divert Rome's future greatness to African shores. Aeneas' mother astutely objected that it was probably not Jupiter's will that Trojans and Tyrians unite. She added that Juno ought to know her own husband's thoughts better than Venus could ever do.

Juno replied that she would sound out Jupiter on the subject. In the meantime she proposed a plan for uniting Dido and Aeneas. Venus approved, but secretly she laughed.

The following morning, just as Aurora was rising from the eastern sea, a select band of nobles set out from Carthage on a hunting trip. Dido waited at the gate on a slender horse caparisoned with purple and gold. The boy Iulus made his steed prance and cavort; he had received a desert stallion as a present from the queen. Then Aeneas cantered through the gate with the sun about his shoulders and head, just as Apollo looks in spring when he leaves his winter home in Asia and crowned with a golden wreath strides forth to join the dancers at the springtime rites in Delos. The royal party prepared their hunting gear, woven nets and iron-tipped spears. Loosing the hounds, they galloped over the dunes, up steep sand slopes, and into the thick coverts of the Libyan wilderness. Before their compact charge the game fled, wild goats from the rocky ridges of the hills and deer that leaped frantically and bounded through the thickets. Iulus led the way, hoping in his boy's heart that he would come across a fierce boar. He imagined himself struggling alone against the most dangerous creature of the woods and killing it all by himself. He would have tackled a lion single-handed. This boy, who could hardly wait for destiny to give him great deeds to perform, spurred far ahead of the others.

A storm burst upon them without warning. Amid claps of thunder, the rain poured down as if all the heavens had opened wide. Aeneas galloped to Dido's side and, guiding her horse by its bridle, found a shelter for the two of them in a nearby cave. He did not know that Juno had contrived the whole affair, with the tacit acquiescence of Venus.

It was a makeshift wedding, but an impressive one. The lightning acted as marriage torches, the wind as wedding congratulants, and Juno as the matron of honor who led the bride to her marriage bed. Dido wished for no more. She called that her "wedding." In her joy she never heard the wailing of the mountain nymphs who deplored her yielding to such light love, and she a queen!

Rumor saw Dido's surrender. Before the next day she had spread the story with many additions and tasty embellishments through every town in Libya. "Dido has wedded the Trojan Aeneas! Together in sweet love they dally away the winter while their subjects go to rack and ruin. They are both of them heedless of empire and careless of responsibility." This foul-mouthed Rumor, sister of the giant Enceladus, flew like a monstrous bird between heaven and earth every night, spreading gossip, causing friend to fear friend

224

and whole cities to grow alarmed and destroy themselves through hatred engendered by fear and misinformation. Rumor had an eye at the tip of each of her feathers and as many ears. When she swooped over nations, she hissed her lies or half-truths indiscriminately. By day you could see her perched on some city tower, sleepless and avid for careless words, which she hastened to distort into scandal.

Rumor liked this story. She licked her lips as she flew to Dido's rejected suitor. He was Iarbas, not only a ruler of Libya but a son of Jupiter Ammon from the oasis. His father long had ruled and been worshiped in the hundred-gated Thebes in Egypt. Rumor poured out her tale to him, how Dido was sleeping nights in the arms of the perfumed Trojan, how Troy was infamous for the rape of innocent women, how this was another Paris with a Carthaginian Helen. The fierce Libyan king went wild at the thought of Dido in the embrace of another. How dare this Phoenician woman refuse him on the pretext of widowhood, only to fall into the arms of any wandering outcast? Iarbas rushed to an altar—for he had a hundred burning in his desert realm—and cried out in rage to Jupiter Ammon. "Have I not sacrificed faithfully? Have I not fed the gods my choicest rams? Have I not poured libations from my damask couch? See how I am insulted! This woman, to whom for silver I tendered lands so she could build her coastwise station, so she could feed her few miserable followers, has forfeited my tolerance! Will you not punish her?"

Jupiter heard the protests of Iarbas. At once he sent Mercury to ask Aeneas what he was doing in Carthage, whether or not he intended to seek Italian shores, and if he was not concerned over his son's future. Mercury hooked on his ankles his golden wings and flew through the winds to the sandy shores of Libya. On his way the messenger passed close to the giant Atlas, who stood bowed by the weight of heaven, which he balanced on his cloud-covered head. From the pines on the summit heavy snows dropped on his sloping shoulders. From his icy chin glaciers cracked and streams formed. Mercury drifted down through frigid currents until he was poised above the walls of Carthage. To his surprise he saw Aeneas wearing a jasper-studded sword and a Tyrian purple mantle and superintending the construction of ramparts. "Jove wants to know why you are idling away your time, Aeneas! He wonders if you have become so smitten that you neglect your mission! Why do you think you were saved from Troy when Hector was allowed to die? Was it to build the walls of Carthage?" The god only poised above Aeneas' head long enough to speak.

Aeneas was overcome with confusion and guilt. What was he in fact doing so long in Africa? Horrified at what the gods must be thinking about him, he summoned his captains and bade them prepare the fleet at once, but secretly. Aeneas planned to choose the right moment for breaking the news of his departure to Dido. Rumor, of course, forestalled him. She saw the skids being greased. She saw the Trojan sailors stream toward the beach where the ships were being readied. By the time Aeneas re-entered the palace, Dido knew all about his decision.

"What! Did you plan to leave my shores without even telling me?" Dido asked Aeneas. "Did you really think my love would not have warned me of this cruel departure? Have you not loved me at all, or respected the vows we exchanged? Have you not thought once of what will happen to me? Look! It is winter over sea and land. Were Troy still standing, no vessel would reach her coast through such seas! Are you running away from me?

"I beg of you, Aeneas. Do not desert me so cruelly. Do not leave me here to die alone, just because I have loved you. For your sake I foreswore myself. For you I made enemies of the Libyan chiefs who surround me. For you I have lost both honor and reputation among them. You were my guest. I have treated you well, and loved you deeply. If you leave me now, I shall die. Aeneas, if you could only wait until I bore a child, a child of yours to comfort me and give me a reason for struggling against the pain that you cause me. . . ."

"I never intended to leave secretly and without explaining my purpose," replied Aeneas. "Furthermore, nothing I do comes from my own wishes. I was chosen by the gods for the life I lead. The weight of my responsibility, my own and my son's, hangs heavily about my every waking thought. My father's image rises constantly before my eyes. And even now, in broad sunlight, have the gods sent a messenger to me to command my obedience."

Dido pierced him through and through with steady eyes. "Now he wants me to believe the gods have no more urgent business at hand than to send him orders," she said. "You are no son of a goddess. You are as hard as a rock in the Caucasus; your nurse was an Hyrcanian tigress. Did this man ever show pity to me? Did he ever console me? Does he care if I am torn apart by desert chieftains? Let Juno be the judge of what has happened between us! There is no such thing as honor any more. He was starving, shipwrecked, lost, and forlorn—and I welcomed him to my palace! I sought out his lost ships and rescued them! How can I argue with such a

226

man? Go, Aeneas. Seek Italy and your Lavinian shores. I
shall not prevent you. Only I hope someday you have to suffer
as much as I do. Of one thing I am sure, you will never be free
of my curse. From bleak Tartarus where you are consigning
me, I shall follow your fortunes. News of you will seep down
to me in hell, where I am headed." Then Dido called her
servants, who helped her to her chambers. There she threw
herself on the bed and wept.

Aeneas would have liked to remain. He would have liked
to comfort her, but Mercury's command had been too grim.
Instead he returned to the shore to help in the launching of
the fleet. The Trojans hurried about like ants that have
come across a heap of grain which they are efficiently transferring to their tunneled quarters. They form two columns
across the plain, and those that are going push huge kernels
ahead of them or carry them in their mandibles. Others follow
behind as if to urge on the stragglers. So the beach seethed
with hurrying black figures, loading stores, unfurling the
sails, running to their stations. From her high window Dido
watched the piers black with men until she thought her
heart would break. Finally in desperation she sent for her
sister Anna to plead once more with Aeneas, to ask for just a
short delay, a few more days, a last few hours even before he
sailed away forever. "Tell him, dear sister, he has no reason
to leave so suddenly, in this winter weather. I will not injure
him. I never sent a fleet to help the Greeks burn Troy. I never
plotted to march my soldiers through his Scaean gates. I
never violated the grave of his father Anchises. Why does he
treat me with such suspicion? Beg him to stay a little longer.
It is all I ask—no marriage, no contract, no promise—only
that."

Aeneas listened to Anna's pleading. He was moved and sorrowful, but he did not yield. Her entreaties swept over his
bowed head like the gusts of wind that beat against an aged
oak grown on the very crest of an Alpine slope. Though gales
may strew its yellow leaves far into the valley, whip its
limbs, and bend its trunk almost to the ground, the tree will
cling to the depths of the earth, and it will resist their violence. So Aeneas remained rooted to his purpose.

Dido mourned in her palace. People spoke to her, but she
did not hear them. In the temple her sacrifices turned to
black blood. The gods were angry. Dido prepared another
sacrifice. The auspices were so dreadful that she hid them
from sight. It seemed to her that her husband Sychaeus was
calling her from some midnight land, with wails like those of
an owl under a thick, black sky. Wherever she walked, she
was followed by the mocking image of Aeneas. It tracked

her, stalked her, just behind her shoulder, as Orestes was pursued by the Furies for having slain his mother Clytemnestra and avenged the death of his father Agamemnon. In anguish of body and mind the Phoenician queen came to a decision.

Dido called Anna again to tell her that she was going to attempt a desperate remedy. She cautioned Anna to follow her directions meticulously, for she had found a way to cure herself of her love for Aeneas. "This is a ritual I learned from an Ethiopian priestess," Dido confided. "I would not use such magic if I could think of any other solution." She requested Anna to have a funeral pyre built in the courtyard, outside her window. "Take the weapons of Aeneas, and all his clothing that he has left in my room, and place it all at the very top of the mound. Take this bed we slept in too. Put it all on the pyre, everything you can find that has belonged to this Trojan." The pyre was erected and sanctified with special herbs cut in the dark of the moon with bronze sickles. To these were added black milk and a lock from a newborn foal. Three hundred gods were invoked. Altars flamed around. Priests chanted litanies. The charm would be potent indeed, thought the Tyrians. What could their queen not do when she set her mind to magic?

That night, as Dido paced her chamber, Aeneas and his men slept on the decks of their ships. The water casks were filled. All was in readiness for their departure. Silence and black night mantled the earth. Not a sound came from the slumbering city. The gentle waves of the inner port slapped against the wooden hulls of the vessels as they lay moored to the wharves. Suddenly Aeneas sprang to his feet. In sleep he had heard again the voice of Mercury, and seen his intent stare. "Man your stations! Unfurl the sails! Leap to the oars!" he shouted. "There is not a second to lose! We are still in grave danger!" Without waiting for the sleepy men to tumble out, Aeneas jumped to starboard and slashed the twisted ropes that held his fleet to the piers of Carthage. A west wind caught their sails so that when dawn broke and Dido looked out of her window, the Trojan fleet stood well out to sea.

Wildly Dido watched them rise and fall on the ocean swells. Her hatred rose in her throat, and she cursed them and herself. "Why didn't I send out torches last night and burn their ships to bits of charred and blackened refuse? I could have done it. Why didn't I take his beloved Iulus and serve him up to his father in the meats of a banquet? Why didn't I have every last one of their evil, treacherous, lying race put to the sword? I could have done it!

"Today they shall have my answer! I shall make a blood offering to the Tyrian nation, for a nation shall rise beside my bones. May you men of Carthage yet unborn listen well to my story. Trust not the men of 'Rome'! Live to avenge me! May great men of my race in our god Baal rise in their strength and chase the Roman from his Italian shore. From the family of Barca let a conqueror come who can endure all toils, all campaigns, mountain cold, and blindness—but track the Roman down! Let a Hannibal avenge me! From this day forth my people shall hate and loathe the treacherous men of Trojan stock!"

Then Dido and her priests performed holy rites. With one sandal unfastened, garments rent, and blonde hair streaming in disorder over her pale face, Dido officiated as high priestess. She mounted the pyre herself, murmuring strange holy chants. When she had reached the summit, she paused and contemplated the garments of Aeneas that lay at her feet, his shield, and the bed.

"I avenged my husband," Dido thought. "Even an animal could have remained faithful. Why could I, a human being, not have done as much? I built a city, watched it grow beneath my feet, led my people into a new world. The future is theirs. . . . I could have been happy if the Trojans had never contaminated my palace and myself." Dido lifted Aeneas' sword and looked at it lovingly. Without another word she thrust it into her heart.

As soon as the priests grasped what she had done, they shrieked aloud in protest. Frantically Anna mounted the pyre and tried in vain to revive her sister. The sword was well stuck. Three times Dido tried to rise. She opened her eyes and tried to find the sunlight. Moans rose from the courtyard. People despaired to see their queen leaving them. They ran madly about, tearing their garments and their hair. Sunk on the bed of Aeneas, Dido writhed and moaned.

Proserpina was about to mount from the Underworld to liberate the dying queen when Juno took pity on Dido. She quickly dispatched Iris to help her. The goddess of the rainbow arched from the top of heaven to Carthage, in multiple waves of iridescent color. Down this bridge Iris floated in her pink-and-yellow gown. She stooped over the suffering queen and severed the tenuous thread of her life. With a sigh of relief the spirit of Dido darted out into the eastern wind.

ITALY IN THE TIME OF AENEAS

THE WAR IN ITALY

AENEAS AND HIS TROJANS saw from the sea the flames of
Dido's funeral pyre rise into the air above Carthage. "I
have committed a crime against love," thought Aeneas. Although he mourned for Dido, he was still relieved to have
escaped with his ships and to feel once more the roll of the
deck beneath his feet. They crossed the strait between Africa
and Sicily safely and then put in at Drepanum again to celebrate funeral games for Anchises. Prizes were given to the
winners, to men who would shortly found many of the greatest families of Rome. The first contest was a race between
four galleys, the second a foot race, the third a boxing match,
and the fourth event an archery contest. These games were
followed by the Troianus, a demonstration of equestrian skill
led by Iulus. Before the Trojans left Sicily, they sorted out
those people who were tired of travel, or who were too ill
to continue such a life of hardship. King Acestes of Sicily offered these Trojans a home at Drepanum, and Aeneas set out
once more, taking with him into Italy only the most hardy
and adventuresome from among his followers.

ITALY! Almost before the anchors had splashed into the
surf, eager Trojans leaped ashore like youngsters. After so
many years of travel and danger they had reached the western shores of Italy at Cumae, the oldest colony in that unknown west. Here was the abode of the Cumaean Sibyl,
a most renowned prophetess of Apollo. While the men ex-
plored this new coast eagerly, and then settled down to
bringing water and building fires, Aeneas walked to the temple
of Apollo. He paused to look up in wonder at its golden roof.
This edifice had been built and its doors carved many years
before by Daedalus. On the portals of his last masterpiece
this artist had worked two scenes from his homeland—one
showing the death of the Cretan Prince Androgeus and a
second the drawing of lots in Athens for the Minotaur's victims. Daedalus had also represented King Minos' wife
Pasiphaë, and on the last panel Theseus and Ariadne in the
Labyrinth. The sculptor-architect had never finished his work;
he had never been able to master his grief enough to carve
an image of his boy Icarus whose wings had melted into the
Aegean.

**THE ENTRANCE
TO THE UNDERWORLD**

Beside Apollo's temple was the cave of the Cumaean Sibyl with its hundred doors that blew open suddenly and echoed from within its hollow caverns the purposes of the gods. Aeneas prayed and asked the Sibyl to direct him. He remembered not to let her write her prophecies on leaves as she usually did so that the winds within the cave could blow them about and garble or obscure their meaning. By means of the golden bough of Proserpina, to which his mother's doves had directed him in the forest, Aeneas persuaded the Sibyl to accompany him to the Underworld so that he could once more consult with his father. He reminded the oracle that four heroes had dared the journey before him—Orpheus, Pollux, Hercules, and Theseus—and that they had returned safely. The ancient Sibyl finally consented to show Aeneas the way.

The entrance to the Underworld lay through a black, sulphurous cave on the shores of Lake Avernus, an area so poisonous that not even a bird could fly over it and live. Wielding his sword, Aeneas strode resolutely into the yawning tunnels of the earth. What horrors met his eyes as he descended into the blackness! The dead sat about him, those diseased, those senile, those dead in babyhood wailing endlessly for their mothers' breasts. In the shadows he glimpsed King Minos of Crete judging cases before a voiceless jury. A little further on he saw those dead of spurned or unrequited love. Pale and golden in a dark corner, like a slender crescent moon in a midnight sky, he saw, but not at all clearly, the wan silhouette of the Carthaginian Queen Dido.

"Oh, my lost lady, can it be you?" cried Aeneas. "Is it true what I heard about your death? I swear to you, Dido, by all I love above and below the earth, I could stay no longer in Carthage. I really did not know you would take my departure so tragically." Although he begged her to listen further to his explanation, Aeneas could neither make her stay nor heed his words. Like a new moon she looked over him with light about her but no warmth. Despite his pleas her eyes were hard and full of hatred.

Aeneas and the Sibyl also passed the entrance of black Tartarus where the guilty souls were plunged to be scourged, tortured, starved, and judged by the inflexible Rhadamanthus of Crete. Beyond this, in the green pastures of the Elysian Fields, Anchises had been counting the days until he could see his son once more. Here the blessed dwelled throughout a thousand years until their spirits were cleansed with forgetfulness and they again consented to inhabit mortal bodies. While father and son talked together, Anchises let

233

Aeneas glimpse crowds of young men waiting to be born, all the future great men of the empire Aeneas would found. Anchises spoke carefully, advising his son, and encouraging him to be brave, for the perils he had passed were trifles compared to the gigantic trials ahead.

When it was time to say farewell, Aeneas and the Sibyl climbed carefully up to the world, entering it through the gate of false dreams. In the harbor of Cumae his ships still dipped peacefully at anchor where he had left them. The men slept soundly on the decks. No one even heard Aeneas return.

VII

ON THE FOLLOWING DAY the Trojans moved northward along a pleasant coast. At dawn on the second day they spied yellow sand beaches where a swirling river flowed into the sea. Swinging to starboard, they entered the Tiber. They had come to the land of Latium. This was the journey's end.

A hush came over the crews. Silently each ship glided to an anchorage. In the high prow of the lead vessel Aeneas stood with his hand on Iulus' shoulder. "This is Hesperia. This is Italy, my son. This is the land to which the gods instructed me to bring you."

Still under the spell of the momentous day, the crews disembarked upon the soft bright grass of the riverbank. Great chunks of ship's bread were laid on the grass, and the last of their dwindled stores divided on them for the company. Still silent and thoughtful, the weary men ate apples and the crumbs of food. Then they munched on the dried biscuits. Iulus laughed, "Look! We are eating our tables!" Aeneas realized that the words of the Harpy Celaeno had come true. Truly the gods were with them!

He thought otherwise a few days later when fierce Juno herself rushed savagely to the city of Latium to swing open the savage gates of Mars. From her act all Italy burst forth, armed to push Aeneas back into the Tyrrhenian Sea. As far as anyone could remember, there had been twin gates in that place dedicated to the god of war, and overlooked by the two-headed Janus. It was the custom to leave them closed in times of peace and open in days of war. This tradition continued down through the ages even after great Rome had reared her walls beside the Tiber's banks. When the elders voted war, the consul himself, dressed in the striped toga of Romulus, strode to the gates, unbolted their hundred bronze bars, and shouted "War!" as trumpets blared.

This was the land of Latium. Its king was the aged ruler

Latinus, who had one daughter, a lovely girl named Lavinia. Latinus had heard from oracles and even more understood from unusual portents that he should save Lavinia so that she could marry a tall, blond warrior who would one day arrive from over the sea to claim her. Therefore Latinus would not betroth his daughter to a neighboring prince named Turnus. This warlike prince ruled a people called the Rutulians from his capital of Ardea. He was not only eligible, but in love with the girl. Latinus had refused Turnus, however, and welcomed Aeneas' ambassadors eagerly, thinking that this must indeed be the ruler from over the sea to whom the oracles referred. Latinus sent gifts to the Trojans and asked to meet their leader.

Two people in Latium did not agree with King Latinus' policy. One was Lavinia's mother, Queen Amata, and the other was Turnus himself. Encouraged and even enraged by Juno, who saw that it was a question of stopping Aeneas then or never, Queen Amata spread hatred of the Trojans among the women of Latium. They poured from their houses, shrieking and tearing their hair; on the mountain they indulged in bacchanalian orgies, plotted violence, and advocated war. A Fury sent by Juno drove Turnus mad with jealousy of Aeneas. Turnus rushed for his armor, leaped into his chariot, and thundered about the countryside urging neighboring princes to drive Aeneas from his slender foothold at the Tiber's mouth. In order that the farmers and shepherds of the vicinity might clearly see the necessity for war, Juno's Fury contrived to have Iulus and his playfellows kill a deer, not knowing that it was an especial pet of King Latinus' household. When the aged King Latinus hid in his chambers rather than declare war, Juno herself swooped down and opened the bloody gates.

Let the Muse of History remember their names, those long-dead men of Italy who turned their ploughshares into swords, or unclipped their spears from their hearth walls, who fitted old heads to new arrows and answered the call of Turnus. Let Clio not forget either the simple tillers of fields who dropped the goad beside the ox and, picking up two smooth stones from the furrow, loped down the hillsides with no other weapon than those, at the brazen call of war. From mountain pasture, from fertile valley, and from the cold banks of northern rivers an army of men descended to fight Aeneas.

First came the renegade King Mezentius and his more worthy son, down from the shores of Etruria. Close after, crowned in the palm leaves of victory, strode Aventinus, the Italian son of Great Hercules. After him rushed the

235

twins from Tibur. Next came Caeculus, who had founded the town of Praeneste. Along with his simple, barefooted subjects rode the great horseman Messapus, whose father was the sea god Neptune. Also came Clausus from the olive groves of the Sabine Hills, he whose descendants were the Claudian gens of Rome. After Clausus arrived that great loather of Trojans, Halaesus, himself a son of Agamemnon. Next came warriors from Capri, whose shields were of cork, and men from the rich apple orchards of Abella. Virbius came to war also, a descendant of the Athenian Theseus.

Most dauntless of all the enemies of Aeneas was the mighty king of the Rutulians, the suitor of Lavinia, Turnus. He was the chief of all this host, a tall man with a chimera on his helmet that breathed flame in the heat of the battle. Turnus was followed by a band of warriors who despite their valor and arms were dwarfed by their leader. On the bronze shield of Turnus was embossed in gold the story of the Greek maiden Io who had been turned into a heifer. Warriors marveled at the skill of the artist who had depicted in gold the hundred eyes of her guardian Argus, and the despair of her father, the river god Inachus.

Up from the southern lands below the Tiber, Camilla rode proudly to war. This virgin maiden, dear to the huntress Diana, trotted gallantly at the head of her Volscian cavalry. Her hair was bound with golden clips, as was her robe of purple. In fingers unused to spinning and weaving, she bore a quiver such as fierce Lycian warriors had used against the Greeks at Troy. This maiden had been brought up from infancy to be a soldier. Camilla was so fleet of foot that she could run over a field of wheat without ever bending the bearded heads, so swift she could skim over waves without ever denting their undulations. All along her route people ran out of their houses to see Camilla, who would fight with Turnus against the Trojan Aeneas.

Throughout Latium even children lisped the name of Camilla. She was the daughter of an old-time king named Metabus who had ruled in Privernum until he had become so despotic that his subjects drove him from the land. Metabus had just time to grasp in his arms his baby girl, Camilla. Through woods and fields he fled with his pursuers close at his heels. Somehow Metabus managed to elude them. The arrows they shot after him somehow overshot and missed the mark. Hour after hour the despotic Metabus stumbled desperately through ploughed fields and willow thickets until he came to the banks of the Amasenus River. Here he stopped short. The river, swollen with melting snows, swirled wildly before him. There was no way to cross it without wetting the baby, and in any case how could he swim well enough with her in his arms? Then, as he reflected, he heard behind him the cries of his enemies in pursuit.

Praying to Diana, promising her that if she would help him he would devote the baby Camilla to her service, Metabus resolved to attempt a daring feat. He wrapped the baby in layers of cork and bound her to his heavy oak spear, enfolding her with many rows of rope. When he thought that the weight was fixed at the proper place on the spear, he poised it carefully and hurled it, baby and all, across the river. To his great joy he saw them land in the wet turf of the opposite bank. Then Metabus swam to the other shore and pulled the spear from the grass. Eluding all pursuit as well as subsequent offers of hospitality, he raised Camilla to be a warrior and a virgin huntress particularly beloved of Diana. No wonder the residents of Latin towns rushed to their garden gates to see this fabled maiden pass. Many a mother would have liked to have chosen Camilla as a bride for her son, but the maiden was bound by her father's oath and would never consent to marry. Warriors and farmers rushed by the hundreds to fight beside Camilla and Turnus.

VIII

AENEAS HEARD that his offers of peace had not been accepted. He knew that an army was collecting around the standards of Turnus and Camilla. He ordered his men to build a strong camp, but even with that Aeneas wondered how he could ever withstand such an attack as was massing.

One evening while the land and its creatures slept, Aeneas lay thinking. Before his eyes a fog appeared over the Tiber, and the current seemed to cease. The cloud collected in one nucleus, became gray-blue, darker, until there rose through its shifting veils the kindly, white-haired head of the river god. "I am Tiber come to comfort you, Aeneas," he said. "You are not wrong. This *is* the place where the gods of earth and river welcome you. We will proudly bear the weight of your city and of its traffic. Row upstream until you come to the tiny hamlet of Pallanteum. There you will find friends and the site." The god sank back to his sandy bed, but he had stopped the current's flow. Aeneas chose two ships and set out upstream, a passage swiftly cut as through a placid lake.

Shortly he saw on the riverbank a white sow with thirty white piglets, just as the oracle had predicted. Beside it was the small village of Pallanteum. Aeneas was welcomed by its chief Evander and his tall son Pallas. Evander and a few friends had migrated from the mountain-engirdled land of Arcadia in the Peloponnesus, all the way to these hills on the Tiber. Here they lived in poverty and fear, never free from Latin incursions. Evander was delighted to give Aeneas 200 men, first because he would be striking an old enemy, secondly because as a child he had once met Anchises, and thirdly because he wanted his son Pallas to learn warfare from a great master like the Trojan hero.

Evander told Aeneas that there might be in Italy a people who would join with him. They would be a formidable ally. To the north of the Tiber lived a proud Asiatic race called Etruscans. They had come from Lydia in Asia Minor and had always been a warlike people, wealthy and very artistic. These people had been ruled by a cruel king named Mezentius, whom they had driven out of Etruria when he began to chain living men face to face and wrist to wrist with the dead. Mezentius had fled to Turnus' land, where he flaunted his wickedness. The Etruscans in their chariots would have fought Mezentius and Turnus gladly except that one of their venerable seers had told them not to rally to the leadership of any man born in Italy. "Otherwise," said Evander, "I would have offered them my son Pallas. Now you, Prince Aeneas," he continued, "could lead them into battle. Your lineage is fine enough, even for so proud a people as the Etruscans!" As they talked, Evander showed Aeneas his poverty-stricken farms, walked with him through the hedgerows and fields where one day Aeneas would erect a magnificent temple to Venus and a Forum Julium for the citizens of Rome, a place where they could congregate to transact business in the open like the Persians.

It was while Aeneas strolled meditatively along the banks of the Tiber at Pallanteum that his mother was able to bring him gifts as she had promised to do. Appearing before her son, Venus laid against an oak tree the new armor that Vulcan had just completed for him. On the shield the clever smith had stamped the story of Rome. Tears came to the eyes of Aeneas as he saw the fame and exploits of his descendants, whose hopeful young faces he had glimpsed in passing through the Underworld. Reverently he ran his fingers over the shield. Here were Remus and Romulus twisting their heads up to grasp the she-wolf's teats. Here were the Romans seizing Sabine maidens, for they had no women of their own. There were the sacred geese warning Marcus Manlius of the Gauls' approach, the sacred geese that saved the Capitol. Beyond the blond Gauls with their dog collars of gold and Alpine spears you could see two Romans, the

238

wicked conspirator Catiline and the lawgiver Cato insisting that Carthage be destroyed.

On the shield was the fierce battle of Actium, where Augustus Caesar and Agrippa stood for Rome, with Antony backed by the riches of Egypt and the Orient against them. To think that there could be a Roman who would rally the forces of the Red Ocean, the lands of the sunrise, against the might of Rome! A Roman with an Egyptian wife! Beside this horror the monstrous zoomorphic gods of Egypt—a dog-headed Anubis, for example—dared to brandish outlandish weapons in the faces of our great Venus, Minerva, Neptune, and Mars.

On the other hand you could see great Caesar borne in triumph through Rome, followed by the kings he had conquered, chieftains who came from Africa, Spain, Cisalpine and Transalpine Gaul, and even those of the Morini who lived the farthest away, opposite an island Caesar had also subdued, a bleak, windswept place called Britannia. Behind Caesar the Rhine grumbled to feel its first bridge, which he had forced upon it.

Proudly Aeneas lifted the shield, felt it well balanced on his arm, and smiled in pity for Turnus and the warrior maiden Camilla.

IX

WHILE AENEAS WAS ABSENT in the Etruscan cities north of the Tiber, Turnus and his allies from Latium and the land of the Volscians led their army across the plain to the Trojan camp. Aeneas had left orders that in the event that his men were attacked, they should remain behind the walls of their castra, defend their gates from the towers they had built beside them, and on no account venture outside these ramparts. He, Aeneas, would engage in single combat upon his return. His men were obedient. From their walls they watched the enemy host spread out across the plain under a cloud of dust. While the attackers were still a good mile away, twenty or so horsemen broke away from the main body and galloped toward the Trojan camp.

Turnus in all his glory was at their head. The Rutulian king rode a Thracian stallion, a tall black horse with white markings. Turnus was resplendent in shining armor. His gold helmet flashed and sparkled in the sun, and over it rose a stiff red crest, curved and proud like the mane of a war horse. Turnus, holding the reins in his left hand, yanked the stallion's head and forefeet high in the air, and then hurled his spear against the Trojan gate. Then this fierce king called for a champion to come out and fight him. There was no answer from the Trojans inside the camp. Infuriated by this unexpected turn of events, Turnus shouted insults, twitted those inside with the loss of Troy, and galloped his horse around and around the walls, hunting for a way to get inside.

In such a way on a cold winter's night a lean and ravenous wolf circles about a sheepfold. Inside the pens the lambs scent his presence and lie bleating against the warm ewes. So Turnus, starved for blood, panting for murder and the pleasure of the kill, looked for a crack, a hole, an opening in the Trojan wall. With clenched jaws and poised sword Turnus circled, wishing he could reach up to the wall's summit and grab by the throat one of those silent strangers that stood looking down on his fury with level eyes. Meanwhile the allied Latin and Rutulian forces had arrived and were drawn up in silent lines watching Turnus threaten and circle in vain. There was apparently no weak spot in the defenses. Aeneas had designed them well. Racking his brain for some impressive deed to do, Turnus' eyes fell upon the Trojan fleet that lay tied up along the Tiber's bank, protected only by a semicircular earthen wall. Here was at least something to do, thought Turnus. "Make pine torches," he called to his men. "Burn their hated ships! Then we shall be sure to drown them in the sea, those who manage to escape our swords!" Turnus rushed toward the river with the first torch flaming in his hand.

This was the fleet Aeneas had built under the supervision of his father Anchises at Antandros, south of Troy. These were the very planks that had carried him and the Trojans through so many adventures. They were more than ordinary fibers, more than just pieces of wood. The kind Mother Goddess, Cybele, she in whose service the wife of Aeneas had remained at Troy, had given her favorite grove to Aeneas. It was a grove of pine and hardwood trees, oaks and maples, that had long stood drinking the rain and the sunshine on the southern slopes of Ida. These trees the mother of mankind, out of pity, had granted Aeneas. When the goddess had asked Jupiter to protect the ships built from her sacred trees, to save them from storm and disaster, the ruler of Olympus had not agreed to do so. "Aeneas is a man. Like every man he must know all danger, all trials, storm and shipwreck, heartache and disaster. No man can do less!" However, Jupiter did promise Cybele that once the fir and hardwood planks, the beams and masts, had done their task, he would release their spirits from their material form.

Jupiter was just about to take care of this engagement

when he saw Turnus and his bloodthirsty followers swarming over the breastworks toward the little fleet. This was the promised day: the Fates were watching the last few minutes fill up when the curses of Turnus warned Cybele to keep the pine flares away from her sacred vessels. Suddenly a strange cloud of light flushed the faces of the spectators, where crowded on the walls they gasped to see this light travel across the sky from east to west. At the same time they heard the music of the choruses from Mount Ida near Troy. Then a voice to make you shudder cut through the heavens, filling the ears of the Trojans and the Rutulian hosts. "Do not tremble to defend my ships, you Trojans! Arm not yourselves for me! Turnus shall succeed in burning the sea before he lights one of my sacred pines!" With tears in their eyes the strong warriors recognized the accents of the generative force of the earth speaking again. "Go free, you swimmers! Go free as goddesses of the deep! The Great Mother orders it!" As her words blew away like smoke and the bright cloud faded, each brass-beaked ship snapped its cable, lifted its pointed prow, skimmed a few feet over the water, and plunged headfirst under the waves. One after another they glided forward, rose, and plunged like blue porpoises under an ink-blue sea. The Trojans moaned to see them vanish. Turnus stood alone, silhouetted against the blue water, his red crest blowing in the ocean breeze and his lighted torch flaming in his hand. All his followers had crept back and stamped on their torches, guilty and fearful of the wrath of a goddess. Then before their amazed eyes burst rosy and sparkling from the crests of the waves twenty nymphs of the sea. They breasted the swell together, their pink arms flashing as the ships' oars once had done. The fierce soldiers watched them as they bore out to sea.

Only Turnus was unimpressed. All other men were speechless and awed. Even their horses pawed the earth and rolled their eyes uneasily. Even the river god of Tiber lifted an admonishing hand and waved his currents backward upstream lest their force intrude upon the sacraments of Cybele. Only Turnus shouted contemptuously, "Oh, come on, men! These portents are strictly for Trojans. You have seen Jupiter deprive them of their fleet. That saves us the trouble. Isn't that a fact? Follow me, and we'll shove them all into the Tiber as well! We are no Greeks to sit ten years outside a beleaguered Troy! No Vulcan, husband of Venus, had to be cajoled into making armor for me! We don't need a Trojan horse to cover our intent! Here we stand talking while the day is spent. Let food be prepared. Then we'll ring their camp with our campfires and tomorrow let them taste the metal of Italy."

During the night two Trojan youths named Nisus and Euryalus persuaded the chiefs to let them make a dash for it through the Latin troops that sprawled in drunken sleep beside their chariot wheels and dying fires. Iulus urged that the boys be permitted to go, gave them many messages for Aeneas, and promised them rich rewards. The two youngsters, eager for glory, made a wide path of death through the Rutulian soldiers, killing Turnus' favorite augur and many prominent chieftains. They had reached the path that leads up through the trees to Alba when Euryalus stopped to try on a suit of Italian armor and to fit a burnished helmet over his curly head. The glint of metal against a sky brightening with dawn caught the attention of a cavalry column riding down to join Turnus.

Both boys ran through the scrub oak as the horsemen dismounted and fanned out through the bushes after them. Nisus made it! Noiselessly he hoisted himself up over the rocks of Alba where the path to Pallanteum was broad and flat. Euryalus had been caught in the branches because of the plunder he would not or did not let go. Nisus crouched with thumping heart and heard his best friend struggle with his captors. Then Nisus rose and shot two spears that killed two of the Italian cavalrymen. Finally he revealed his whereabouts in the hope that Euryalus would be saved. It was too late, however, and so both were killed in their youth and beauty. Both bent and toppled as does a summer flower uprooted by the cunning, underground plow blade, or as do slender crimson poppies crushed by the overwhelming weight of one summer raindrop.

Their names and their courage are not forgotten. So long as mighty Rome wields her dominion over the lands of the Mediterranean world, so long as the great Capitol rests upon its rock foundation, the names of these brave boys will be remembered. When morning came, the Trojans grieved to see the Italians parade before their walls bearing—with spear shafts for bodies—the bloody heads of Nisus and Euryalus. The black blood had not stopped dripping down before Rumor had swooped with the news into the Trojan camp and set all the women to screaming. Staggering and moaning like an animal in labor, the mother of Euryalus clutched at the walls and stared at her son's vacant white face. Her shrieks and reproaches took all the fight out of the Trojan men, who abandoned the walls and squatted hopelessly in groups of three and four.

They roused themselves, however, when the boy Iulus

walked among them. The Italians had begun their attack. Under heavy, cylindrical shields they moved up to the walls like huge tortoises and began to batter. Others raked the defenders with clouds of arrows as, leaning over the ramparts, they pried at the tortoises with spears and rolled boulders down on the besiegers' heads. Iulus was particularly incensed at the obscenities and boasts of an Italian youngster named Numanus of the Remulus family. "Ha! you Trojans, dressed up in purple and saffron with girlish ribbons on your helmets and sleeves in your tunics. Come out and fight! Come and see what real men are like! We Latins are tough! We bathe our infants in ice-cold mountain streams and train them to hunt, ride, and raze cities for a pastime. You dancing Trojans, either fight or give up!"

Iulus, a golden circlet of royalty on his blond curls, drew back his bow and split the youngster's forehead with his arrow. The archer Apollo saw this feat, and replacing the absent Aeneas, stepped down and told Iulus to stay out of battles until he was a man. Of course, Apollo also praised the boy for his feat. Iulus obeyed, withdrawing to the center of his forces. He remained where the men could still see him, however, and where he could still hear the thud of boulders as they were hurled into the walls by the enemies' catapults.

At one point after a tower had burned and crashed to the ground, the Trojans in the heat of battle forgot and opened one of their gates, pressing hard against the besiegers. By the time one of their chieftains had swung it shut again, Turnus was inside! Like a wolf among lambs he leered at the cowering Trojans and began to lop off their heads. Then a hero, Pandarus, stood up to Turnus. "You are insane, Turnus!" he told him. "We have you now! You are as good as dead!"

Turnus raised his sword and brought it down with such force that he separated Pandarus' head from his shoulders. He smiled sarcastically at his adversaries and said, "Begin, all of you, if you have the courage to oppose me. You can tell old Priam that an Achilles came here too!"

After the swift death of Pandarus, the two Trojans whom Aeneas had appointed as leaders during his absence rallied their forces behind them. Both mature men and brave warriors, they led the Trojans in an encircling movement against Turnus. Well protected by their shields, they pointed a hundred swords eager for his throat. The Trojan Capys was there too, he who would live to found Capua south of Rome. Step by step they forced the Rutulian backward, nor cringed before his feints, until they had driven him to the riverbank. Sweat dripped over his whole body. Turnus could not even breathe. He had retreated right to the night-black water. Before they could come close enough to stab him, however, Turnus leaped into the river, fully clad in armor. Buoyant in the dark water, he floated across to his own men, washed clean of slaughter and ready to begin again.

X

LATE THAT SAME NIGHT Aeneas came sailing down the river with Evander's son Pallas at his side, asking him questions about war and navigation. Aeneas did his best to educate the lad. Behind them came the formidable war fleet of the Etruscan peoples. Even the Muse could not have memory enough to name them all. King Tarchon had sent them from the cities of Clusium and Cosae. The island of Elba, rich in mines, had dispatched 300 warriors, Populonia 600, Pisa 1,000. Men poured from Caere, Minio, Pyrgi, Graviscae swept with malaria, from Liguria, and from proud Mantua on the Tuscan River.[13] In thirty ships the Etruscans swept to the aid of Aeneas, rallied to the standard of this chief from Asia.

Aeneas was holding the rudder of his flagship when he saw the river nymphs encircle him. One of them called Cymodocea told him how she had been changed by Cybele from a ship into a maiden. The nymph held onto the ship's side with her right hand and splashed along with her left. She warned Aeneas of how the Rutulians and Turnus lay in wait for him at the beach, and she spoke of the beleaguered camp. "Prepare for battle!" shouted Aeneas. Ship after ship echoed with the order. As they sailed around the bend of the river, the prince lifted high his new war shield so that it blazed in the sun and flooded his own camp with light. The Trojans, recognizing their leader's sign, sent a fresh shower of arrows toward Turnus.

While the Etruscan King Tarchon maneuvered to drive his ships through the waves and onto the beach—not caring whether or not he split their hulls so long as he gained a beachhead—Aeneas and Achates leaped ashore through the waves. No man could stand before the Trojan Aeneas, no man at all! Aeneas killed them so fast he once had to send Achates back to the ship for fresh weapons. With the prince cutting a passage for them, the Trojans came ashore.

A unit of the Etruscan cavalry led by Pallas met stiff opposition. They would have fled before the attack of young Lausus except that the boy Pallas fired them with his courage

[13] Vergil's birthplace on the Po River.

the way a spark will catch in an autumn field and before you know it send out flames in all directions. Pallas fought like a young lion and so did Lausus on the other side. These two equally matched youths were about to meet when Turnus went to the aid of Lausus. Pallas watched the Rutulian king clear a way through the host in his battle chariot and speed to duel with him. Although Pallas faced him bravely, he was no match for a full-grown man like Turnus. After the second exchange of spears, the boy fell pierced, spurting blood from his mouth. Then Turnus put his heavy left foot on the boy's body and yanked off his wide belt, tugging and pulling at the body as if it were nothing to respect. How foolish those men are who do not curb themselves when they ride on Fortune's crest!

Word of the death of Pallas was brought Aeneas by a runner before foul Rumor could invent more revolting details than those that had actually occurred. The prince grew almost blind with anger. Before his eyes he saw the welcome Evander and Pallas had given him and the Trojans, how they had been the first to offer advice and assistance. In a fury of revenge Aeneas left his own troops and cut a path across the battlefield toward Turnus. The Trojan founding father listened to no pleas for mercy, but killed right and left, and also captured four young men to use as a sacrifice for the offended spirit of Pallas. Aeneas cut his swath straight across the meadow until he had reached his own camp, where Iulus opened the gate and ran out to meet him. Aeneas did not find Turnus because Juno had spirited him away from the field.

Turnus' place was well supplied by the tyrannical King Mezentius, who, driven by the Etruscans, had sought refuge at the Rutulian court. Mezentius was a giant of a man, and his son Lausus was proud of him. Word was brought to Aeneas of the Etruscans that Menzentius was slaying. The prince cut his way toward the center. Mezentius, who saw him coming, sneered and hurled his spear. It missed Aeneas but struck one of his comrades. Then the prince hurled his spear. It pierced Mezentius' groin, but his youngster Lausus rushed to cover his father's escape. Again and again Aeneas tried to persuade Lausus to withdraw, for the prince pitied his youth and the boy's foolish temerity. Lausus would not flee, however; and Aeneas had to kill him, had to pierce his pitiful, thin shield and the woven, gold tunic his mother had made him.

"Poor youngster," said Aeneas to him, bending down to lift Lausus' head from the trampled earth. Then the Trojan prince, oblivious of the weapons Lausus' escort were leveling at him, curtly ordered the enemy to lay the boy upon his shield. "What reward can Aeneas offer such a brave fellow?" he asked while Lausus stared at him with eyes that still understood his words. "I shall not take your armor, son," spoke Aeneas to him softly. "One so brave has every right to keep it. I consign you to the spirits of your fathers. Console yourself that you were not vanquished by a mortal. You fell only before Aeneas."

Meanwhile Mezentius, who lay concealed beside a stream, heard of his son's death. He called for his horse and rushed out at Aeneas. Three times he circled the Trojan prince, who had just finished caring for Lausus' body. Aeneas aimed for his horse and then slew Mezentius, who welcomed death but only begged Aeneas to give him funeral rites. "You know how hated I am by both Trojans and Etruscans," were his last words.

XI

AFTER THIS DAY the Latins asked Aeneas for a twelve-day truce, which he granted. During this time each army erected funeral pyres upon which they burned their dead. Aeneas sent the body of Pallas home on a bier woven of osier and willow, accompanied by all the trophies the youngster had won by his own right, to which were added many other rich presents from Aeneas. While the Trojans mourned and prayed for their dead, great confusion reigned in Latium. King Latinus still wanted to welcome Aeneas as a son-in-law and thereby put an end to the war. Turnus and Queen Amata still hoped to win, however, and redoubled their efforts. Courtiers were of various opinions: many believed the war should be decided by Turnus and Aeneas in single combat. Others wanted to follow King Latinus in his desire to exile Turnus and welcome Aeneas. Still others suggested offering the Trojans a piece of worthless land along the coast, to which they could be safely relegated.

Before any line of policy was reached, Aeneas and his forces were well on the way to Latium. The Latin women, with the girl Lavinia in their midst, rode to the temple of Minerva in their chariots. As they passed through the streets where preparations for combat were being made, Queen Amata and her friends admired Turnus and urged him to bring Aeneas to his knees. Turnus rushed about the palace in a blaze of golden armor. As he finished buckling on his sword and setting his red-plumed helmet on his head, Camilla arrived with her Volscian cavalry. She leaped from her horse at the sight of Turnus. "Remain here to guard the castle," she told him. "I have no fear of Trojans either. I will ride out to meet them." She and Turnus arranged that he would set an ambush for the main body of Trojans led by Aeneas, who had to pass through a mountain defile. Camilla would ride out on the plain and engage the Etruscan cavalry.

Camilla organized her horsemen in a long line facing the Etruscans. At her uplifted arm each warrior drew back his spear, and at her dropped hand spurred forward toward the foe. Darts rained among them like driving snow propelled from all directions by the swirling winds of winter. The riders bore down upon each other in rows like the crests of waves that sweep in from the deep. After the first impact the troops of Camilla reversed their shields behind their backs and fled. Then when the Etruscans were in full gallop behind them, the Volscians turned and let the foe impale themselves upon their long spears. Again it was their turn to wheel and charge down from the castle walls with a roar of fury and neighing of horses like an undertow that dangerously gathers sliding sand and pebbles and attacks the oncoming wave insidiously, from beneath.

Then the two lines closed in single combat, each man marking out his opponent. None could stand long before Camilla, who wielded sword and battle-ax fiercely about her. She rode superbly, with knees alone, guiding her horse to right or left at a touch or change of weight. Her purple gown blew about her shield and left her left breast exposed. Tarchon, the Etruscan king, worked hard among his men to keep them from fleeing headlong before her. Camilla killed one after another of the Etruscan and Phrygian nobles, usually marking those whose raiment would make the richest gifts at the shrine of Diana. No one noticed that she was being stalked by a wily warrior named Arruns, who kept a certain distance from her during the engagement, looking for a chance to pierce her escort. Finally he sent a dart straight to her breast. As Camilla lurched forward, her maiden warriors caught her in their arms. Camilla had just breath enough to send her black news to Turnus before she died.

Turnus recalled his men from their ambush. Ordering them to fall in, he started down the hill and across the plain just a few minutes before Aeneas and the main body of Trojans loped through the pass. As darkness fell, the two columns of Turnus and Aeneas galloped almost neck to neck across the plain toward the city.

TURNUS ARRIVED FIRST and closed the gates behind him. King Latinus, joined this time by Queen Amata, begged Turnus to end the war and forfeit the hand of Lavinia. Instead Turnus sent Aeneas his challenge, saying that he would meet the prince in single combat between the lines of the two armies, at dawn. During the night Turnus inspected his favorite white horses, which would draw his chariot on the morrow. Meanwhile Juno sent Turnus' sister, a maiden who had lost her virginity to Jupiter, down to earth to help Turnus win the combat.

Soon after dawn King Latinus rode out across the plain in a chariot drawn by four horses. He was followed by Turnus behind his white pair. They were met by Aeneas and Iulus, dressed in pure white robes. Before an altar Aeneas sacrificed, prayed, and established the conditions of the combat. "If I lose, I swear that my son Iulus will leave Italy forever and make no claim whatsoever to rule in this western world. If I win, then we Trojans shall build a city called Lavinium in honor of my bride, the princess Lavinia. I swear that I shall not deprive King Latinus of his crown, nor try to impose my power over any peoples who do not wish to live under my sway and protection."

A murmur of admiration rose from the Latin chiefs, who saw that Aeneas was other than the perfumed, curly-haired monster that Turnus had described. Juturna, Turnus' sister, was quick to spread riot among them, however. If only one dart could be shot at this Trojan, there would be a general rush to arms. Only the presence of Aeneas standing high by the altar restrained the men. Somewhere from the crowd of Rutulians beside Turnus came an arrow that wounded Aeneas. As he was helped from the field, the battle began in earnest. Turnus' spirits rose to the skies. Laughing and eager, he leaped into his chariot and, using his sword like a scythe, drove frightened Trojans before him.

It did not take Aeneas and his physicians long to draw the barb from his leg. Immediately he started to buckle on his shin guards. As he settled his helmet and cheek straps he bent over to kiss Iulus. "Learn courage today, my son, and true work. Let others teach you the accidents of fate. Today my right hand will protect you. When you are a man in your turn, repeat over to yourself the tales of the others who have gone before you. Think of your father and your Uncle Hector."

Aeneas mounted and drove into the battle. From a distance Turnus heard him come. He grew pale and trembled as a farmer shudders before the violence he knows is at the center of a black cloud bearing toward his wheat field. Juturna too heard the ominous thunder of the Trojan cyclone. Using her special powers, she hurled her brother's charioteer from his place and, assuming his guise, whipped up the horses so adroitly and guided them so well that Turnus was borne up and down through his cheering men without ever approaching Aeneas. Disdaining to strike the men who flew from him, Aeneas pursued the elusive Turnus in widening circles through the confusion of battle.

Hour after hour Aeneas stalked the Rutulian hero without ever being able to meet him face to face. Then in anger Aeneas summoned his Trojan leaders and told them the time had come to attack the city. "It is no use waiting for Turnus' pleasure," decided Aeneas. "We shall force the city, by arms and by fire, and obtain our treaty from Latinus." At his direction ladders were brought and torches. Battering rams pounded at the gates. The city guard was killed. Queen Amata, seeing that the Trojans had arrived at the palace and supposing that Turnus was dead, hanged herself.

Out on the plain where he wheeled magnificently, Turnus also heard the outcry and saw wisps of black smoke rise from the city's rooftops. Sadly he spoke, "Juturna, I have known for some time that you were my charioteer. You must leave me now. Is it so difficult to die?"

Even as Turnus struggled with himself to make a decision, one of his friends rode up to him. "Turnus," he moaned, for his face had been cut open by an arrow, "how can you desert us now? We are all there in the city trying to stop the Trojan Aeneas, who looms above us like the peaks of the Apennines! How can you still drive about this deserted plain when your friends are dying?"

Still Turnus could not decide. As he looked toward the city he saw one of its towers, a structure he himself had helped to hew and bolt, fall in a crash of burning beams. This decided him finally. He drove toward the walls of the castle. Aeneas heard the word "Turnus" breathed by the crowds, who stopped in their tracks wide-eyed, arms raised, mouths falling open. King Latinus stepped to the wall and watched Turnus approaching the gates and Aeneas striding from the inside through an opening in the ranks. All were hushed to see those two brave men, born in opposite ends of the earth, come up against each other in a battle to the death. The mobs of soldiers drew back. Latins moved over to make room for the Trojans they had been trying to kill the minute before. Women crept from their houses on tiptoe, like heifers that wait to see which young bull will be master of the herd.

And like two bulls they met, Aeneas and Turnus, horn to horn and shield to shield, struggling for footing, swords flashing and then locked to the hilt, forehead to forehead. You would have said Jove held scales where each man balanced evenly the other. Which one is heavier by the added weight of death?

Blow after blow they land until the blood flows from a hundred cuts. Then Turnus lifts his sword in what he hopes will be the final stroke, but Aeneas catches the blow glancing on his shield, and the weapon breaks. For an instant Turnus stares unbelieving at his broken weapon. Then he turns in flight. Aeneas, limping from his wounded knee, follows him close after. As Turnus calls to his men for a sword, Aeneas forbids them to throw him one. Five times they circle the plain inside the ranks of soldiers.

Juno on Olympus saw that her cause was lost. "Let me ask only one favor," she said to Jupiter. "Since the Trojans must win, let the new men of Rome keep the antique courage of the Latin peoples. And let them discard the Trojan tongue, and keep the Latin language for their own."

In passing a gnarled olive tree Aeneas was able to pull out his spear, which he had lodged there before. Turnus countered this weapon by lifting a boundary stone and trying to heave it at Aeneas. Turnus hardly knew what was happening any more. He was like a man who even as he starts to speak feels the paralysis of sleep creep down his tongue. He saw his soldiers in a blurred background, at their center the clear-cut image of Aeneas, stern-faced, deadly. As Turnus shook his head to clear his vision, Aeneas raised the spear and hurled it; for it was the only blow he would have the chance to make. The sharp point pierced the seven layers of Turnus' shield and penetrated his thigh.

A groan came from the Rutulian warriors, who pressed forward as if to come to the aid of Turnus. Their king, however, had already raised his hand to Aeneas. "Spare me," he cried, "for the sake of your father Anchises. Yours is the kingdom. Yours is Lavinia as bride. Only spare me."

Aeneas lowered his sword and gazed at Turnus. Not a sound came from the ranks. Aeneas hesitated. As he thought, he saw displayed across Turnus' shoulder the gilded belt of Pallas. The youngster had been so proud to wear his father's trophy! Turnus had stepped on a dead boy's body to wrench off that belt. "Do you ask me for mercy and wear my young friend's trophy? Turnus, this blow is for Pallas."

Thus Aeneas defeated Turnus, killed him, and built Lavinium not far from the white walls of high Rome.

While I have been singing these deeds, our great Caesar has thundered his war chariots across Europe and up to the deep Euphrates where, a victorious conqueror, he administers justice to willing subject peoples, and has set his feet firmly upon the path to Olympus.

But you and I have finished our journey over the boundless sea;
Now it is time to loose the yokes from the necks of our steaming horses.[14]

[14] Vergil, *Georgics* II and IV.

Index

Abas, King, 217
Abella, 236
Abraham, 10
Acestis, King, 230
Achates, 202, 204, 208, 209
Adrastea, 45
Aeacus, King, 69, 70
Aegeus, King, 68, 69, 75, 76, 77, 78, 82, 89
Aegina, 69, 75
Aegisthus, 105
Aeneas, 94, 103, 199, 202, 203, 204, 205, 206, 207, 208, 209, 211, 212, 213, 222, 223, 224, 225, 226, 227, 228, 229, 231, 233, 235, 236, 237, 238, 239, 240, 242, 243, 244, 245, 246, 247, 248, 249, 250, 251
Aeolus, 202
Aeschylus, 91
Aethra, 75, 76
Aetna, 220, 221
Afghanistan, 107, 131
Afrasiab, 130, 132, 141, 143, 149, 153, 154, 160
Africa, 28, 53, 139, 143, 201, 202, 226, 239
Agamemnon, King of Mycenae, 91, 92, 98, 100, 104, 105, 106, 236
Agastya, 184
Agga of Kish, 11
Agrippa, 239
Aiyanger, S. Krishnaswami, 170
Ajax, 98, 100, 101
Akhenaten, 25, 40
Alba Longa, 204, 242
Alexander, Prince, 95, 97
Alexander the Great, 172
Amalthea, 45
Amata, Queen, 235, 246, 248, 249
Anchises, 103, 212, 213, 214, 215, 219, 220, 233, 240
Androgeus, Prince, 67, 68, 69, 75, 77, 123

Andromache, 93, 97, 101, 211, 218, 219
Anius, 213, 214
Anna, 222, 223, 227, 229
Antandros, 240
Argos, 104
Ariadne, Princess, 72, 80, 81, 82, 85, 87, 88, 89, 90, 91, 214
Armageddon, 40
Arnold, Matthew, 107
Aruru, 12
Arzhang, 137, 138
Ashurbanipal, King, 9
Ashurnasirpal, King, 197
Astyanax, 93, 101, 104
Atlas, 92
Attica, 61, 78, 89
Aventinus, 235
Ayodhya, 173, 174, 175, 181, 184

Bactria, 113
Bali, 189
Balkh, 111, 112, 140
Barca, 229
Barman, 153
Berberistan, 141
Bharat, 174, 175, 176, 177, 182, 183, 184
Brahma, 194, 197
Breasted, James H., 25
Britomartis, 64
Buthrotum, 218
Buto, 34

Cadmus, 57, 58
Caeculus, 236
Caere, 244
Caesar, Augustus, 199, 239
Cambyses, King, 107
Camilla, 236, 237, 247
Carchemish, 110
Carcopino, Professor, 199
Cassandra, 91, 92, 94, 95, 96, 97, 98, 99, 100, 101, 103, 104, 105, 106, 211, 212, 215

252

Catiline, 239
Cato, 239
Catullus, 80, 88
Celaeno, 217
Cerberus, 61
Cercyon, King, 76
Chabas, François, 32
Champollion, Jean François, 25
Chaucer, Geoffrey, 109
Chin, Kahn of, 118, 139, 162
Circe, 66
Clausus, 236
Clusium, 244
Clytemnestra, Queen, 104, 105, 106
Cocalus, King, 86
Coptos, 33
Cosae, 244
Creüsa, 93, 103
Cumae, 231, 234
Cybele, 103, 214, 215, 240, 241
Cydon, 70
Cyrus, King, 107, 130, 170, 172
Cythera, 203

Daedalus, 63, 64, 65, 67, 72, 78, 80, 81, 82, 85, 86, 89
Danaë, 47
Danaus, 217
Dardanus, 215
Darius, King, 107, 109
Darmesteter, Professor, 130
Dasa-ratha, Rajah, 173, 174, 175, 176, 177, 179, 180, 181, 182
Davreux, Dr. Juliette, 92
Deiphobus, Prince, 93, 102
Dhaulagui, 191
Dido, Queen, 199, 205, 206, 207, 208, 209, 210, 211, 214, 223, 224, 225, 226, 227, 228, 229, 233
Diomedes, 99
Doab River, 171
Dow, Alexander, 171, 172
Dutt, Romesh, 171

Ecbatana, 111
Enceladus, 220
Enki, 10
Enkidu, 9, 12, 13, 14, 15, 16, 17, 19, 20, 23

Epirus, 217
Erechtheus, 82
Eridu, 11
Etruria, 235, 238
Europa, 51, 52, 53, 54, 55, 57, 58, 74
Euryalus, 242
Evander, Chief, 237, 238, 244
Evans, Sir Arthur, 41

Farishta, Mohammed Kazim, 171
Feridun, King, 113, 142
Firdausi, 106, 107, 108, 109, 130

Gilgamesh, the wrestler, 9, 11, 13, 14, 15, 16, 17, 18, 19, 20, 21, 22, 23, 110, 173
Giv, 156, 157, 163, 165
Gortyna, 56
Graviscae, 244
Great Ennead, 25
Greüsa, Princess, 77
Gudarz, 146, 147, 158, 159, 162
Gurdafrid, 155, 156, 161
Gusht-Aspa, King, 112

Hajir, 154, 156, 157, 161, 162, 163
Halaesus, 236
Hamaveran, 139, 140, 141, 159
Hammurabi, 11
Hanuman, 189, 190, 191, 192, 194
Hathor, 51
Hector, Prince, 92, 93, 97, 98, 100, 101, 103, 104, 202, 211, 215, 218, 248
Hecuba, Queen, 92, 93, 94, 97, 101, 102
Helen of Troy, 91, 210
Helenus, Prince, 93, 101, 218, 219, 220, 222
Helios, 53
Herodotus, 35, 40, 65, 107, 130, 199
Hesiod, 43, 47
Hestia, 44
Hippolytus, 90
Homer, 79, 92, 109

253

Horus, the Hawk, 25, 26, 27, 34, 35, 36, 37, 38, 39, 40
Human, 154, 160
Huwawa, 15, 16, 17, 19

Iapetus, 92
Iarbas, 225
Icarus, 82, 85, 86, 231
Idomeneus, 98
Ilia, 204
Ilion, 98
Indrajit, 195
Io, 47, 48, 50, 51, 236
Iolaos, King, 86
Iphigenia, 105
Iris, 229
Ishtar, Queen, 18, 19, 31, 32, 53
Isis, 28, 30, 31, 32, 35, 36, 200
Iulus, 103, 204, 209, 234, 243, 248

Jackson, A. V. Williams, 109
Jacobsen, Thorkiled, 9
Janaka, King, 174
Jason, 75, 112
Jemshid, Shah, 112, 113, 116, 142
Juturna, 248

Kai-Kaus, Shah, 129, 132, 133, 134, 138, 139, 140, 141, 142, 143, 144, 145, 146, 147, 153, 156, 157, 158, 159, 160, 161, 163, 164, 169
Kaikeyi, Queen, 174, 175, 176, 177, 178, 182, 183
Kai-Khosrau, Shah, 130
Kai-Kobad, Shah, 131, 132
Kausalya, Queen, 174, 179, 181, 182, 183
Kava, 113
Kerman, 116
Khumba, 194, 195
Khumba-Karna, 193, 194, 195
Ki, 9, 10
Kish, 11
Kramer, Samuel Noah, 9

Lagash, 10
Lahra-Aspa, 112
Lakshman, Prince, 174, 175, 178, 179, 180, 181, 184, 185, 186, 187, 189, 190, 194, 195, 196
Lanka, 185, 192, 195, 196
Laocoön, 211
Latinus, King, 235, 236, 246, 248
Lausus, 245, 246
Lavinia, Princess, 234, 235, 236, 248
Lepidotus, 37
Loti, Pierre, 172

Maat, 40
Malcolm, Sir John, 108
Mandavi, 174
Manthara, 176
Manu, 174
Marcus Manulius, 235
Medea, Queen, 77, 112
Meile, Pierre, 171
Memnon, 210
Menelaus, King of Sparta, 58, 95, 98, 99, 102
Menes, 40
Meshad, 108
Messapus, 236
Metabus, King, 236, 237
Mezentius, King, 235, 238, 245, 246
Mihrab, 117, 118, 119, 124, 127, 129
Minio, 244
Minos II, King, 41, 58, 59, 60, 61, 63, 64, 65, 66, 68, 69, 70, 71, 72, 74, 75, 77, 78, 79, 80, 83, 85, 86, 87, 92, 214, 231
Minuchir, Shah, 113, 122, 130
Mohl, Jules de, 108
Moschus, 51
Mycenae, 41, 100, 104

Nammu, goddess, 9
Nanda Devi, 191
Nander, Shan, 130, 161
Naxos, 87, 89, 214
Nepthys, 28, 30, 35, 36, 37, 39
Nergal, 15
Ninmah, 11, 13, 14, 16
Nisus, King, 70, 71, 73, 242
Numanus, 243

254

Oceanus, 43, 47, 107
Oenoë, 68
Oenone, 95, 100
Ovid, 41, 84

Palinurus, 215, 216, 219
Pallottino, Professor, 199
Pandarus, 243
Paris, Prince, 9, 97, 98, 100, 225
Parnes, 76
Paros, 86
Pasiphaë, Queen, 64, 66, 67, 68, 72, 74, 231
Pausanias, 91
Perdix, 63, 64, 85
Periphates, 76
Petrie, Sir Flinders, 25
Phagrus, 37
Pherecydes, 84
Picard, Gilbert, 197, 199
Pizzi, Italo, 108
Plato, 61
Plutarch, 34, 91, 102
Poebel, Arno, 9
Polites, Prince, 101
Polydorus, 213
Polyphemus, 221
Polyxena, Princess, 99, 100, 105
Praeneste, 236
Priam, King, 92, 93, 94, 97, 98, 101, 103, 209, 210, 211, 213, 214, 243
Price, Lucien, 199
Prosperpina, 233
Ptah, 200
Punt, 141
Purusa, 184
Pylos, 41
Pyrgi, 244
Pyrrhus, 99, 100, 101, 218

Qart Hadasht, 201

Ra, 35
Raksh, 131, 134, 135, 136, 137, 138, 148, 149, 151, 154, 159, 163, 166
Rama, Prince, 173, 174, 175, 176, 177, 178, 179, 180, 181, 183, 185, 186, 187, 189, 190, 191, 194, 195, 196

Ravan, 185, 186, 188, 190, 191, 192, 193, 194, 195, 196
Rawlinson, Sir Henry, 9
Razm, Zanda, 160, 163
Remus, 204, 238
Rhadamanthus, 58, 61, 233
Rhea, 44, 45, 60
Rhea Silvia, 204
Robertson, William, 172
Rómaka, 172
Romulus, 204, 238
Rudabah, Princess, 118, 119, 120, 121, 122, 123, 124, 126, 127, 128, 169
Rustam, 129, 131, 132, 134, 135, 136, 137, 138, 141, 142, 143, 145, 147, 148, 149, 150, 151, 152, 153, 156, 157, 158, 159, 160, 161, 162, 163, 164, 165, 166, 167, 168, 169, 171, 172

Sainte-Beuve, 108
St. Paul, 199
Saïs, 30
Sam, 113, 114, 115, 117, 122, 123, 124, 125, 126, 127, 128, 129, 130, 136, 138, 139, 151, 153, 157, 158
Samangan, King of, 149, 150, 151, 152, 153, 161
Sargon, King, 110
Sarpedon, 58
Satrughna, 174, 175
Sciron, 76
Scylla, Princess, 70, 71, 72, 73, 74, 220
Scyros, 99
Seistan, 113, 117, 119, 128, 133
Seth, 28, 29, 30, 33, 36, 38, 39, 40
Shaha, 140
Shakespeare, William, 41
Shamash, 15-16
Shinar, 10
Shuruppak, 20
Sidon, 51, 223
Sindukt, Queen, 119, 123, 124, 125, 127, 128
Sinis, 76
Sinon, 211
Sita, Princess, 173, 174, 177, 178, 179, 180, 181, 183, 184,

185, 186, 187, 188, 189, 190, 191, 192, 195, 196
Sparta, Helen of, 97, 98, 99
Sruta-kriti, 174
Strabo, 60
Strophades, 216, 217
Sudaba, 140
Sugriva, King, 189, 190, 191, 193, 194, 196
Suhrab, 148, 152, 153, 154, 155, 156, 158, 160, 161, 162, 163, 164, 165, 166, 167, 168, 169
Sumantra, 179, 180
Sumitra, 174, 181, 182
Sunium, 89
Suraja, 172
Surpa-Nakha, 185, 186, 191
Sychaeus, 205, 209, 222
Syrtes, 222

Tamineh, 150, 151, 152, 153, 160
Tammuz, 19
Tarchon, King, 244, 247
Tartarus, 227, 233
Taurus, 72, 79
Telephassa, 53
Tennyson, Alfred Lord, 200
Teucer, 215
Thebes, 56, 68, 225
Theocritus, 79
Theseus, 75, 76, 77, 78, 79, 80, 81, 82, 84, 87, 88, 89, 90, 91, 233, 236
Thrace, 50, 207, 212, 213
Thureau-Daugin, M. François, 9
Thutmose, 40
Tiryns, 41
Triad of Abydon, 25
Troezen, 75
Troilus, 93
Turan, Leopard of, 142
Turnus, 235, 236, 237, 238, 239, 240, 241, 242, 243, 244, 245, 246, 247, 248, 249, 250, 251

Tus, 159, 162

Ugarit, 197
Ulad, 137
University of Chicago, 9
University of Paris, 199
University of Pennsylvania, 9
University of Rome, 99
Ur, 10, 11
Uranus, 42, 43, 44
Urmila, 174
Ur-Nammu, 10
Urshanabi, 22
Uruk, 11, 12, 13, 14, 15, 16, 17, 19, 20, 21, 22
Ut-Napishtim, 21, 22

Valerius, Emperor, 107
Valmiki, 171, 181
Vergil, 91, 197, 199
Vesta, 212
Vibishan, 192, 193, 195
Videha, 173, 174
Vishtaspa, King, 113

Warner, Edmond, 108
Whitehead, Professor, 199

Xerxes, 102

Yama, King, 111, 112
Yemen, 139

Zabul, 131, 140, 141, 148, 156, 166, 169
Zacynthos, 217
Zahhak, King, 113, 117, 118, 166
Zal, 114, 115, 117, 118, 119, 120, 121, 122, 123, 124, 125, 126, 127, 128, 129, 130, 131, 132, 133, 134, 136, 140, 146, 157, 166, 169
Zelia, 93
Zoroaster, 107
Zuara, 148, 166, 169